Anaesthesia
A novel
by
Adrian Horn

Special thanks to:
All those who have helped with this book including librarians and curators, members of 'The Band' past and present and most particularly to Mandy and Isabel for their support and painstaking editing.

PART I

Chapter 1

Monday March 15, 1915

Jan needed a drink. He and Eric got to The Game Cock as Mrs Burton, the landlady, opened the doors at six-thirty pm. A group of regulars had been gathering outside and talking about the war. Jan and Eric followed them in. The dark-green, glass-panelled, double-doors swung open as they pushed inside. Eric got the beers in at the bar while Jan found seats in a favourite corner. He chewed his index finger and thought about the decisions he had to make.

Whilst waiting for Eric and the beer to come he watched the fading evening light throw shadows through the crystal-etched window onto their small, round, beer-stained table. He lit up a Player's Navy Cut and looked downwards. The iron table legs were cast in the barely recognisable shape of Britannia. Cigarette burns cut into the wooden surface and radiated from the edges. He jumped out of his reverie when Eric placed the pint glasses on the table and sat down. Something about Eric had changed. He seemed pleased with himself and the way he walked was more confident. A group of six young soldiers in uniform came in and took up the area to the far end of the bar. They jostled and ribbed each other; the sound of their laughter reached Jan's table.

'They're barely old enough to leave their mother,' Jan said, turning toward the soldiers and shaking his head.

'Well that's me tomorrow,' Eric said, and noisily sucked the head off his pint.

'What was that? I was miles away.'

'Me. I've signed up,' Eric said. Jan stared at him, silent for a moment.

'Are you completely mad?'

'No.'

'What's changed then? You always said you wouldn't go.' Jan picked up his glass then put it down. 'Jesus Christ, you wouldn't get me out there, its absolute bloody carnage.'

'I know; it's just…'

'Yes?'

'It's Frankie.'

'What about Frankie?' Jan asked, as he realised it could only be bad news. He looked down at the table.--

'Killed at Neuve Chapelle.'

'Shit,' he said, softly, not lifting up his head. 'When?'

'Day before yesterday in the morning, that's all we know.'

'Christ.'

'I saw his mother in Brondesbury Road in a terrible state.'

'Of course, she…'

'I stayed with her for at least an hour. I promised her.'

'What? Promised her what?'

'That I'd do what I could to shorten the war…'

'Yes?'

'And join up.'

Jan looked Eric straight in the eyes. He could hardly speak. 'Bloody idiot,' he said at last. 'Signing up won't bring Frankie back.'

'I know that. I'm not stupid.'

'Well you're making a bloody good impression of it.'

'I couldn't help it. I sort of felt…'

'Yes?'

'Obliged.'

Jan shook his head. 'You think it won't happen to you?'

'That's not the point. He was a mate.'

'So?'

'I don't want him to have died in vain.'

'And how exactly,' Jan pressed his index finger on the table, 'does getting yourself blown to pieces help anything or anyone?'

'We've got to stand up to the Boche.'

Jan waved his hand dismissively.

'You couldn't even stand up to Frankie's mum for God's sake.'

'Signing up's the right thing to do, it is for me anyway. We can't let them get away with it. What if they invaded Britain?'

'Well, fight them *then*. Christ Eric.'

'They're a bunch of bloody heathens,' Eric said, with a note of finality. Jan turned his head toward the bar. An old man leaning on the counter sucked on his pipe as he lit it with a match then coughed and spat onto the sawdust on the floor.

'What's that got to do with it? You or me signing up won't change a thing. We don't matter.' Jan downed half his pint and felt better for it.

'Frankie mattered.'

'Yes, he did. And now he's dead. And what for?'

'You don't understand.' Eric was angry and closed his eyelids to calm down.

'You're right. I don't understand.'

'We've got to keep the Germans out,' Eric said, leaning over and almost spitting his words.

'You don't actually think the Germans would come over here do you? They've too much on their plate to invade.'

'Well, I think they would.'

'Read the papers man. They've an Eastern Front to deal with. Anyway, Europe's been at war for hundreds of years. They're always at it.'

'This is different; it's not like any other war. We *have* to win it.'

'Look, I don't hate the Germans or love the Belgians but that doesn't matter. Whatever you or I do won't make a jot of difference. It's all mass hysteria, there's no logic to it.'

Jan bit the nail on his index finger. He pulled it off with his teeth. It ripped the quick and drew blood. He winced slightly, sucked it then put his hand in his pocket. He looked up to the nicotine-stained ceiling and took a deep breath from the tobacco-smoke air.

'For Pete's sakes, Jan, this is different. I'm not doing it for king and bloody country – I'm doing it for Frankie and the rest of them. I don't expect you to understand. Belgium's a peaceful country and we *should* help them because we're a powerful country with responsibilities. It's like with people, you stand up for your friends. That's what I'm doing.'

'Oh, I understand your reasons alright, I just think it's futile, that's all. Countries aren't people. Anyway, *you* couldn't stand up to a high wind.'

'You're full of compliments, Jan. But mark my words, you'll be fighting sooner or later.'

'Bloody won't,' Jan said, draining the rest of his pint and stubbing his Player's out in the ash tray. 'Same again?'

'Go on then. I couldn't change it anyway without deserting, I've signed the paper. So just forget it now and get the drinks.'

Jan made his way to the bar feeling uncomfortable as he squeezed past the young soldiers. Mrs Burton had left her post at the bar to change a barrel in the cellar so Jan leaned on the edge of the counter and looked around. He was looking at some girls from the munitions factory in the corner when Mrs Burton's footsteps clacked up the stone cellar steps and she reappeared behind the bar. She served one of the factory girls first with barley wine then picked up Jan and Eric's pint glasses and pulled the stiff squeaky pump handle several times with her strong right arm before the bitter beer started to flow into and over the glass. Mrs Burton placed the glasses in front of him. Jan handed her six pence. Froth slid down the side of the glasses onto the counter already wet with ale. Jan picked one up in each hand and spilled some beer onto his trouser leg as he carried them back to their table.

'Fancy going up Park Road in a bit and see how we get on? They'll be plenty of skirt there. We'll soon get fixed up,' Eric said.

'You'll be lucky. Anyway, I can't. I've got to be up early. We're rushed off our feet at the office and my father's giving me stick about going out every night.' Jan shook his head, took out two cigarettes and passed one over to Eric.

Eric lit a match. 'You can't get drunk on this stuff anyway.'

Jan looked at his glass. 'They call it *London's Pride* but it isn't. It's watered down.'

'I know and it used to taste so good.'

'The girls in the corner have got the right idea, they're on the barley wine, it's in a bottle and the pub can't tamper with it. It tastes disgusting or I'd have one,' Jan said.

'I know it's really sweet but it's strong and if we pour it into the beer, that'd be alright. I'll get a couple of bottles.'

'You'll need a good drink where you're going.'

'I know, I'm scared shitless. I start training on Monday but it'll be around six months before they send me off, so they say.'

'Steady on man, start at the beginning. Which regiment?'

Eric looked down as he spoke. 'London Regiment, 15th Battalion.'

'I've seen the 15th, everyone has. They're all around London, practically pulling people off the streets. They'll turn anything into a recruiting office. They draw men in like flies to shit.' Jan shook his head. 'They're scraping the barrel now. Have you seen the posters? They're craven. They might as well be honest and use conscription. I don't think they can stoop any lower. Have you seen them? I'd laugh if it weren't so sodding tragic.'

'I know but "needs must". If they don't get the men, we lose the war.'

'Bollocks. Leave Europe to it, that's what I say. Don't expect me to join you.'

Eric went to the bar.

Jan paused, sipped his beer and pulled on his cigarette. Work as a clerk in his father's timber import business was classified as an 'essential industry', so he did have a good excuse. But that wouldn't stop him being accosted in the street. His mother kept pestering him to go off and stay with her family in neutral Sweden, but he didn't want to do that. If people thought he'd deserted Britain he'd never be able to come back. It would be easier to be a conscientious objector but life being the subject of public scorn would be unbearable. His life was here in London. And then there was Lucy. He couldn't go off to Sweden and leave her here. He might never get her back again. She would probably go with him if he wanted her to but it wouldn't be fair on her. How could he ask her to give up her family and friends for him?

Eric came back with the barley wine and poured it into Jan's pint for him. Jan took a good swallow through the foam, put it down and drew in another lungful of smoke. If he drank enough he just might be able to block it all out. 'Mmm.'

'It's quite a good mixture but don't tell too many people or they'll ban it,' Eric said, having tasted his. 'Anyway, there's no way of getting out of it that I can see. You might as well get it over with.' Deep down Jan agreed but he wasn't about to admit it, and he wasn't ready to hand his life over to a bunch of madmen just yet.

'I'm staying out of it,' he said, looking down at his hands and picking at his sore fingernail. Eric was drumming his fingers on the table.

'Can we change the subject?'

'Fine by me.' Jan tapped his finger on the table top sticky with beer.

Eric stubbed out his cigarette in the old saucer put out as an ashtray. 'I'm not trying to persuade you to join up, I don't need to; you're making a good job of that yourself. Look, the war's putting us all on edge and I'm not going to fall out with you over this. I'll save all that for the Germans. Anyway, how's Gladys?'

'Well, you know, she's scared stiff I'll join up and doesn't really believe me when I tell her I won't. Mother's worried about what might happen to her if she goes over to France nursing.'

'Well, I think training to be a nurse is bloody admirable.'

'It is, but she's a trained mezzo-soprano.'

'She's doing her bit though. Have you got another fag?' Eric said looking at his empty packet of ten. Jan handed him one.

'Thanks.' They both lit up. 'She's a lovely girl your Gladys. Sort of girl a man could marry.'

'Steady on Eric, she's my sister. Anyway, what'd she want with you?'

'Don't worry; I won't try it on with her. She wouldn't want me anyway but the way things are going I'm bloody well going to get some before they send me off.'

'Shouldn't be too difficult; what about one of them over there,' Jan said looking over to the factory girls who were laughing and hooting in the corner. 'She's nice, the one just standing up now.'

'Yes, isn't she?' Eric said, jutting his head forward for a better look.

'Christ Eric, don't make it completely bloody obvious.'

'How about we just have another and then I'll go over there and chat her up.'

Jan laughed. 'By the time you find the bottle, she'll be unconscious the way she's going.'

'You're probably right, I wish I could be one of those blokes who can just go up and ask them, bold as brass.'

'And you think you can fight at the front?' Jan turned his eyes to the ceiling. 'Jesus, give me strength.'

'I could really do with a sweetheart, someone to marry and come home to. Someone to send letters to and to dream about.' You don't know how lucky you are having Lucy.'

'Good God, you're not going to be like this all night, are you?' Jan sucked on his cigarette and thought for a moment. 'You're not the only one thinking about marriage. I know a man at Willesden Registry Office, and he says they're working all hours marrying couples before the men get sent off to the front. He says it's the same with the churches.'

'But not me,' Eric said. 'I can't imagine anyone wanting me.'

'They do it for the pension, apparently.'

'That's romantic.'

'I'm only saying what everyone knows. Anyway, love can strike at any time, they say.'

'They say war can help lovers.' Eric looked back over at the girls.

'Bloody hell, Eric. You can be profound at times.' Jan smiled not expecting an answer.

Jan was seeing more of Lucy since she'd been working at the Home Office. Now, at least, they could meet up at lunchtime even if it was just on a park bench. They regularly met on Tuesdays. Jan's father would have let him out of work to see her more or less whenever he wanted; he was so desperate to have him settled with a nice girl. Both his parents were.

'It's frustrating. We can't ever be properly alone together.' Jan moved his head towards Eric's and lowered his voice. 'She wants it just as much as I do, or so she says. But she won't even risk a kiss in public. She's terrified someone who knows her parents will see us.' Jan laughed. 'You know her mother meets her off the train at Uxbridge? Lucy can't even take a later train.'

On most days a letter from Lucy would arrive for Jan at the office. She wrote to him after dinner each night except on Sundays. She said that she longed for him. She said that writing to him was something to do in the evenings. She told him of her dull life at home and that the alternative to writing letters was to knit socks for the troops every night with her mother and sisters. She said she didn't mind that he didn't write back. Jan took her at her word.

As the evening wore on, the factory girls had been getting louder and their language fouler.

'Do you know?' Eric said, pulling Jan's jacket lapel and talking into his ear. 'The longer we sit here, the more attractive those girls look. Are there five or six of them? I can only see four but I think two of them have gone off to the toilet. They keep looking over here. You see the one with the red blouse with white spots? Well, the girl next to her's got a short skirt.'

Jan nodded.

'I saw her legs when she got up,' Eric said.

'Come on, let's go over there before you explode,' Jan said, standing up and brushing cigarette ash off his checked suit trousers.

'Right, let's go for it. Nothing ventured,' Eric said, before swallowing another mouthful of the beer and barley wine mix and wiping the spillage off his chin and moustache with his jacket cuff. He sauntered over to the factory girls with Jan by his side.

'Hello, fancy some company?' Jan said, to help Eric out.

'Piss off you tosser!' said the girl with the red blouse with white dots.

'Go on, sling yer ook,' said another.

'You 'eard her, your sort make me sick,' the pretty girl in the short skirt said. 'My bruvver's fighting and you're here drinkin' every night, I've seen you. Fancy yerself, don't yer'?' Jan recoiled as she spat her words out towards him.

'I've signed up,' Eric said, looking pleased with himself.

'What about im?' the girl in the short skirt asked, looking straight at Jan. 'He's an arse.'

'I'm doing essential war work.'

'My Aunt Fanny,' said the girl in the red blouse. 'I've seen you, you walk about like a bloody poet or sumit.'

The young soldiers who had been steadily drinking at the bar started to sidle over to where the rumpus was. Jan pulled Eric away, back towards their table.

'Come on. We'd best drink up and go before they lynch us.'

'I'm alright, I've signed up.'

'Shut up you sanctimonious pillock,' Jan said, dragging Eric out of the door as the sound of 'and don't come back' resounded from the girls at the far end.

Outside Jan lit up holding his lighter with two hands. 'We've got time for a couple in The Black Lion if we get our skates on. What a bunch of cows. Look at my hands,' he said holding them in the light of the full moon. 'They're shaking like aspens.'

'I'm game, but don't be surprised if it happens again,' Eric said.

'I won't. The whole world's gone completely mad,' Jan said, as they headed down the High Road for The Black Lion.

Chapter 2

March 16 1915

After washing and shaving, Jan put on a white shirt and tucked it in to his grey-flannel suit trousers then attached a clean collar. He took a puff from his cigarette and placed it back in the ash tray on the dressing table. Looking in the mirror he lifted his braces over his shoulders then knotted and straightened the red tie Lucy had given him for his birthday. Downstairs, at the breakfast table, his father, Peter Strang, was ready for work looking similarly smart in a pin-striped suit. He poured hot tea into a china cup from the blue-glazed pot reserved for breakfast.

'One for you?' his father asked.

'Thanks.'

Peter added milk to the tea and handed Jan the cup and saucer.

'You didn't have much to say for yourself when you came in last night.'

Jan looked out of the window into the street. Blue tits were playing in the branches of the cherry trees, nearly ready to blossom, that lined the pavement.

'Don't you know it upsets your mother when you go up to your room without a word?'

Jan sat down at the breakfast table and rubbed his eyes. 'Sorry Father.'

'Out drinking again, I suppose.'

'Just a few, I've got a lot on my mind at the moment.'

His father half-smiled. 'A lot on your mind, well, well. You know there's a war on, don't you?'

Jan leant back in his chair and sighed. 'Can we talk about this later?'

His mother, Eva, came in with three bowls of porridge on a tray.

'Good morning,' she said, placing the cream-grey oats in front of Jan, Peter and one in an empty place on which she sprinkled some sugar and poured on a little milk.

'Mmm, that smells good,' Jan said, breathing in the steam rising from the bowl.

'Don't be silly dear, it doesn't smell of anything. What have you got on at work today?'

'Oh, there's timber coming up from the docks in the morning. I'll be counting it off as the men unload it.'

'That should be interesting.'

He looked at his mother and wondered why, when knowing what he did, she always asked him. But it was nice to be asked and it was easier talking to her than his father. 'It takes forever nowadays, there's no men left with any strength to do the lifting. No doubt I'll take my jacket off and help them. I like a bit of physical work.' Jan looked down to hide his expression.

'Don't be silly dear,' she said. 'You were born with brains. You should leave the heavy work for the men.'

Jan raised his eyes to his mother's. 'I am a man and I can hardly stand there and watch the women work without lending a hand. Anyway, it gives me an appetite and stretches my muscles.'

'You need to sweat off last night's drink,' Peter said.

'Really, Peter.' She shot a glance over to her husband.

Jan ignored him and turned to his mother. 'There's many more women than men there now.'

'That must be difficult.'

'Harry says they can be good workers. You know, they can be just like men at times. You wouldn't believe some of the stories they tell me.'

'And I don't want to hear them.'

Jan reached for the sugar bowl and sprinkled some on his porridge. He poured on some milk and started eating carefully from the edge of his bowl. The door opened from the hall and his sister Gladys came in wearing a white, red and green kimono. Her shoulder-length fair hair was tousled around her head and strands fell down over her face. She sat in front of her porridge.

'Morning Gladys,' they all said.

'Morning,' she replied.

'What are you doing today, dear?' Eva asked.

'Ohh, I don't want to think about it.' Gladys poured herself a cup of tea and after a few spoonfuls of porridge said, 'You know I never saw a man naked before the war, not even in my training.'

Jan looked up.

'Well, not in any sort of detail anyway, and now,' she looked at her mother, 'If there weren't so many bed pans and fetid dressings to get rid of and general skivvying to do, they'd have me washing men's parts all flaming day. Honestly, we never stop.' She leant forward over the table. 'Yesterday we had a case where this man had been shot through a testicle and it had swollen up and -'

'We don't need to know *all* the details dear, not while we're eating,' Eva said, raising her voice.

'Sorry,' Gladys said.

'It must be awful though. I wouldn't want to do it. Not when I was twenty-two. We're very proud of you,' Peter said.

Gladys finished her porridge. 'God I'm ravenous, pass the toast and the butter please.' She looked straight at Jan: 'Don't you sign up.'

Jan was chewing his finger nails. 'Don't worry about that, they won't get me.'

'I couldn't bear it if we lost you as well,' Gladys said.

Eva kissed Gladys on her head and poured tea for herself before sitting down at the table. Gladys lit up a cigarette and blew the smoke into the air above their heads.

Sometimes in the evenings, if they were both in at the same time, Gladys would talk to Jan. He knew his sister better than anyone. He kept her confidence but didn't trust her with his. She just couldn't stop what came out of her mouth. She once told him that she only kept going at the hospital by pretending she was someone better than she was. And Jan knew what she meant. She wasn't what you would call a natural nurse but the war was forcing her into being a good one. When she joined the Whitechapel in 1914 she had no idea that the war would turn out like this; nobody did. After just a year it had taken her youth and innocence and turned her into a confirmed cynic. She told Jan of her fears and anxieties and that she blocked out her horror by throwing herself into the job. As well as the pain of the causalities, she told him of the pain the other girls felt. On most days one of them would get the news that their boyfriend, husband, brother or even father had been blown up or was just missing. She felt their pain and put it at the back of her mind. Her childhood beliefs in Jesus and a good God died as men died before her in hospital beds.

Gladys stubbed out her cigarette hard into the ashtray and swallowed some tea.

'Do you know Eric's just joined up?' Jan said to her.

'No?'

'Oh yes. He starts training on Monday. Last night we were having a few drinks at The Game Cock and this group of factory girls shouted all sorts of abuse at us.'

'You must have been doing something to provoke them.'

'No not at all. It's just they assumed we hadn't joined up so they slagged us off.' Jan shrugged.

'I hope you gave them as good as you got.'

'There was no point arguing. We just slunk off to the Black Lion.'

Eva fidgeted in her seat. 'You should stay away from those sorts of pubs, they're terrible places. And the girls, they're just not your type. You could get into trouble; some of them will do anything when they've had too much to drink.'

'I won't get my head blown off going to the pub though, will I? Anyway, I don't want another woman; I've got Lucy.'

'Ha,' Gladys said.

'She sounds like a lovely girl. When are we going to meet her?' Eva said.

'Soon enough,' Jan said.

'She sounds like a bit if a drip to me,' Gladys said.

Jan ignored her. 'I'll be meeting her today if I get back from the docks in time,' he said, looking towards his mother.

'Good for you,' Eva said.

Jan pushed his porridge bowl away, buttered his toast and spread it with marmalade.

'Come on Jan. The train won't wait,' Peter said.

'Let him eat his toast and drink his tea,' Eva said.

'Five minutes,' Peter said.

Jan and Peter arrived at Strang's Timber Agents on Bishopsgate at around eight thirty. There was plenty of space to walk between the desks and the typewriters click-click-clacked in the background. Through the glass partition of his adjoining office, the coloured stamps on a pile of letters from across the world caught Jan's eye. Jan watched his father sit down in his Windsor chair and sort through the envelopes, putting the invoices and routine letters in a stack for Jan to deal with. His father put a few to one side of his desk to look through himself. Jan suspected they were high-priority orders from the British Expeditionary Force, the BEF. Two secretaries and two clerks, all in their late middle age, worked in a larger, open office and looked busy with typing and paper work. Within the walls of his offices Peter's success was apparent. Britain would always need timber and Peter Strang could supply it. He had made sure the office looked modern by bringing in Swedish desks as well as Remington typewriters from the United States in 1914 before the war started.

On the way into work Peter discussed with Jan ways of speeding up his workers. They didn't seem to understand the urgency of a timber business in war time. There was little Jan could suggest. To dismiss anyone would be counter-productive. Office workers of any description were hard to find and they were lucky to have them, but it didn't always seem like that to Peter. The staff started work at eight a.m. and finished at five p.m. Jan's father believed that they could talk to him about things that concerned them and that he exuded a benign authority. But Jan wasn't so sure and he always knew that he would never be as successful, or command as much respect, as his father.

Mrs Agnoli was the invoice filer, tea lady and general assistant. She had been with them for a month.

'Any chance of a cup of tea?' Jan asked her as she was putting papers into a tall olive-green filing cabinet.

Mrs Agnoli, who had decided to call Jan, 'Mr Jan' and his father 'Mr Strang' to avoid confusion, replied: 'Yes, Mr Jan, of course. I was just giving you and Mr Strang a few minutes to settle in.'

She went away and busied herself in the tiny kitchen where a kettle sat on a small wood-burning stove. Ten minutes or so later she reappeared with two pots of tea, milk jugs and cups.

'Thanks Mrs Agnoli,' Jan said, as she placed the tray on his desk.

'Are you feeling alright, Mr Jan?' she asked. 'You don't look so good this morning.'

'Yes, fine, fine,' he said, feeling dreadful and sucking one of the peppermint humbugs that he kept in his desk drawer.

'How's your lady friend?' she asked, looking right at him with her hands on her wide hips.

'Actually, we don't usually talk about things like that at work. You'll soon get used to our ways. Be careful when you talk to my father. He can be a bit of a stickler about things like that.'

'Oh yes?'

'Yes, try to remember; nothing personal.'

'Oh, don't be embarrassed, I have three sons, I know about these things,' she said, waving a dismissive arm.

'Well, if you must know, I'm seeing her this lunch time.'

'You make her a good woman, Mr Jan, and she'll make you happy. You'll see.'

Jan agreed; Lucy would make him happy. But the world was in turmoil.

'Thank you, Mrs Agnoli. Now I really do need to get down to some work.'

Jan shuffled some papers around whilst, with an all-knowing air, Mrs Agnoli went to deliver Mr Strang's tea. Who needs philosophy when you've got Teresa Agnoli around? Jan thought. He heard the phone ring through the partition, turned his head. His father picked up the receiver.

'Hello? Strang's Timber Agents.' His father paused, listened, drank some tea and stubbed his cigarette out in the clear-glass ashtray. 'Yes, yes, I see Colonel.' He blew the smoke out high into the air. 'I'll do my best but it is very difficult to speed anything up at the moment.'

Jan listened as Peter explained what the Colonel at the other end already knew. The docks were in mayhem with all the men having signed up and the women workers still learning the job. No one could really judge with any accuracy when a ship would dock.

'Yes, yes. I see. Yes, well I'll do everything I can. I'll send my best man down to the docks straightaway. Yes. Yes, of course. Thank you, Colonel.'

He replaced the receiver and Jan felt better already. He would be going down to the docks in a few minutes where he could get some fresh air and, perhaps, a restorative drink at *The Mayflower*.

'Jan, can you come here a moment?' Peter asked, through the partition window. Still holding his cup of tea, Jan got up and went round into his father's office.

'Yes Pa? No need to explain, I overheard. I'll pop off straight away.' Jan picked up Peter's copy of *The Times* from his desk to read on the bus.

'If you get any whiff of when the *Elissa* docks ring me on Harry's phone,' Peter said.

'You know I'm meeting Lucy at twelve thirty though, don't you?'

'This is more important. I've got the whole BEF telling me the war depends on us. If you don't get there on time she'll understand. Now chop, chop.'

Jan enjoyed the contrast to his father's organised office that a trip to the Greenland docks provided. At first appearances, it was complete chaos with no apparent leadership but, in some kind of haphazard way, it worked. Old Harry Burns unofficially ran the place and controlled when the ships were loaded and unloaded. Everything went through him. Jan admired Harry's lackadaisical pragmatism and his way of getting things done, sometimes by circuitous routes. The BEF might have been screaming out for duck boards but the BEF, like everybody else, would have to wait their turn.

Jan skipped down the office steps and out onto Bishopsgate. He got on the horse-drawn omnibus as it was just setting off from the horsebus stop. He grabbed onto the upright pole and jumped up as the vehicle was just moving off. He climbed up the half-spiral staircase to the open upper deck and spread out on a double seat. He watched the scenery and traffic as the bus continued its journey down to the docks via Tower Bridge. It was a clear day. Fresh air blew up the Thames from the North Sea and nearly caught his bowler. He lit up a Player's, inhaled a good lungful, and cleared his lungs with a cough that brought up a gob of phlegm that had been accumulating overnight. An old woman with a headscarf sitting in front of him turned her head round look at him.

'That gas, it's terrible so's I hear,' she said.

'Don't worry, we'll get em back,' Jan said, not wanting to destroy her delusion of him as a gas-wounded hero.

'They're all bastards, them Germans,' she said.

'Yes, they are, aren't they?' Jan said glad that his stop was close.

He got off the horsebus and headed for the *Mayflower* on Rotherhithe Street, only to be greeted by a sign saying *Open at 10.30*. Bloody war, can't even get a drink when you want one, he thought but, on reflection, he knew it was for the best. He was seeing Lucy for lunch and the last thing he needed was for her to think he was tight, not this lunchtime anyway. So, with a bad head and a groggy stomach, he continued to Greenland Dock with noise and hubbub all around. He made a beeline for Harry's cabin.

The clang and clatter of chains and cranes, horses, carts and some motor vehicles soon took Jan's mind off his drink-or-no-drink dilemma. Above all the commotion he could hear angry exchanges coming from groups of old men and young women dockers. Harry Burns was standing outside his wooden-slatted cabin with his arms folded as Jan walked toward him. Two women in overalls and with their hair tied up under dirty headscarves, walked away from him smoking and arguing loudly. They pointed to a crane. Jan wondered if this was the wrong time.

'Alright, Harry?' Jan said smiling.

'Not sose you'd notice,' Harry replied.

'What's up?'

'One of the girls got killed. 'Bout an hour ago.'

'Christ, that's awful. What happened?'

'A crate swung from a crane, cracked her naffin' head. Dead outright she was. Could have been avoided but no one knows what they they're doing anymore. The poor girl left three kids at home and a husband at the front. I can't push 'em too hard to work today, not after this,' he said.

'Jesus Christ. How old was she?'

'Bout firty.'

'I'm so sorry Harry, is there anything I can do?'

'No, nuffin'. Just keep off my back. I've got enough on my plate at the moment without you and your dad giving me a loada grief. Wadaya want anyway?'

'We've had the top brass screaming at us for days.'

'Nuffin' new.'

'I know, but they need the planks from the *ELiza* for the BEF, fast as you can. It can't be that difficult to get them off, can it? I'll help.'

'You can forget it for today or I'll have a riot on my hands. I'll have it done tomorrow first thing.'

'Can we tell the BEF that?'

'Unless another mother gets her head knocked off, you can. The *ELiza* only docked last night. I can't work miracles.'

'I'll have to take some stick when I get back.'

'Tell 'em to talk to me.'

'Don't worry, I will.'

'Sit down, take the weight off your legs, have a cuppa tea.'

Jan sat on a rickety old chair.

'I'm bloddy sick of this naffin' war,' Harry said, by way of invitation for Jan to speak.

'I know. There's no end to it is there? Yes, Harry I'd love a cuppa.'

Harry spooned hot tea out of a copper pan that was bubbling on a brazier made from an oil drum and filled with glowing coals. He poured it into chipped white-and-blue-enamelled mugs. They went into Harry's office. Jan burnt his lips as he sipped the dark-brown tea which Harry had mixed with condensed milk and sugar. It tasted of smoke and was sickly sweet. He couldn't help but pull a face.

'Thanks Harry. Just the job. I'd forgotten how good your tea was,' Jan said.

'Well, you don't have to drink it.'

'Sorry. Look, I wanted to ask you about something else.'

'Well?' Harry leaned forward to hear him better.

'Do you think I should sign up?'

Harry leaned back and looked up to the roof planks. 'Do you wanna?'

'You must be joking, but I don't see how I can avoid it.'

'No, I don't neiver. It's gone too far, the war I mean. You could be the only man under forty left. Don't get me wrong, I don't want see you go off, but what else can you do?'

'I don't know. Cigarette?'

'Fanks.' They lit up from Jan's lighter. 'The way people see it round here is, if you're fit enough to fight and you don't, then you're with them, not us. You get my drift?'

'I know you're right. The war makes no sense to me, but you *are* right; that's how they'll see me. Of course, if I walked with a limp that'd be different,' Jan said, trying to lighten the mood.

'There's some that get out of it that way, but you've got to live with yourself, haven't you?'

Jan nodded repeatedly.

'There's forces in life that we 'ave to go along with whatever we think. I never wanted to marry me wife, but I had to and it's been alright.' He muffled a laugh. 'Well mostly.'

'I think you're psychic Harry.'

'What do you mean by that?'

'I'll tell you another time.'

'You haven't got that girl of yours into trouble 'ave you?'

'No. No, it's not that.' Jan got up and shook Harry's hand. 'Thanks Harry, it's a pretty bloody impossible situation, isn't it?' Jan finished as much of the tea as he could stomach. 'Can I just use your telephone to let them know what's happening?'

'Yes, but it's been on the blink a bit.'

'I'll give it a try anyway,' Jan said, picking up the receiver. 'Hello, hello, can you get me London Wall 2993? Thank you.' Jan drummed his fingers on the table. 'Hello Pa, no go I'm afraid. I know but it's out of my control, a poor girl got killed here earlier and it's just not the time to crack the whip. They're all pretty cut up about it and there could be labour trouble. Have to tread carefully I'm afraid. Harry says he'll start unloading tomorrow first thing so I suppose we've got a date anyway. That's right Pa, we'll have to tread carefully.'

Harry opened the draw of his dirty battered desk and took out a brown envelope and handed it to Jan. 'That's from big Frank,' he said.

Jan opened it and counted out £5 in ten-shilling notes and half-crowns. He handed one of the half-crowns back to Harry and then, as an afterthought, gave him another. 'That's for the girl's family. Thanks for the tea and our chat,' he said shaking Harry's hand. 'I'll try and pop down tomorrow a.m. to see how it's going, if they haven't dragged me off to the front by then. Bye for now.'

'I'll see yer,' Harry called out after him.

Jan hurried off. He couldn't miss his date with Lucy.

Chapter 3

March 16 1915

Lucy waited for Jan outside St James's Park underground station. The street was hectic with horse-drawn carriages and carts. As she looked out into the traffic, one veered suddenly to avoid a motorised delivery van. Women workers and important-looking city gents bustled along the pavements. A newspaper blew by her feet in the strong breeze. She glimpsed the headline: *Britain retakes St Eloi. German attack repelled at Ypres*. But Lucy could only think of her meeting with Jan. Her cheeks were flushed and her heart was beating faster than usual. She hardly noticed the men whose heads turned when they saw her.

Lucy looked younger than twenty-six and dressed in an attempt to appear older. Jan liked the way this had the opposite effect. Her beige winter coat and smart calf-length skirt, designed for the more mature woman, leant her an unintended innocence and coyness. When Jan walked out from the station and saw her in French heels with long brown-plaited hair resting down the back of her coat exposing her small ears, he felt a warm comforting feeling that eased his anxiety. Jan felt as if he'd never been in love before.

Lucy felt him tap her shoulder from behind:

'Ooh, you startled me.'

Standing in front of her and looking straight into her eyes he held both her hands in his. 'You're cold,' he said.

'I know.'

'You do look lovely.'

She laughed. 'Don't be silly, I'm just in my working clobber.'

Lucy felt the skin tingle down her spine and goose bumps come up on her forearms. She hoped some of the girls from the office would pass by and see her with him. Jan was just so good looking: tall, fair-haired and slim. Most men wore moustaches but Jan was clean shaven and knew about style. Today he wore a Burberry top coat and flannel suit with tan brogues, just for work, and a bowler. He always had money in his pocket and his Swedish blood made him positively exotic. The girls would die with envy when they saw him.

Men were such hard work sometimes, Lucy thought. She wasn't sure how long she could ward off Jan's passion and prayed he would ask her to marry him before another girl snatched him away from her. She wanted him the same way as he wanted her and sometimes thought she might explode with anticipation or just give in. If only she could stand up to her parents and spend some time alone with him, then she could really make him hers. After all, there were ways of satisfying him without actually doing it; it was just finding the opportunity and the courage. In the evening, after dinner, as she knitted socks for the war effort with her mother and sisters, they talked about nothing in particular and she would let her fantasies roam. She wanted him to touch her intimately and the frustration was almost too much to for her to bear.

Lucy lightened her step as they made their way past the Ministry of Justice and across Birdcage Walk to the park. They found a bench and, looking over the lake, she rested her head against his shoulder and held onto his arm. The crocuses were out and the sun shone intermittently catching the bright yellow, purple and dusty mustard-yellow stamen of their flowers. Willow leaves swayed in the wind. The daffodils and the trees were in bud. In a few weeks they would open into custard-yellow trumpets shaded by rose-white cherry blossom. Lucy discreetly touched his thigh and kissed his cheek.

'You know I want to, but I can't kiss you on the lips with all these people around. It might get back to my parents. Please be patient, I do love you, you know.'

'I know, I know, but why can't you just tell them to get lost. Other couples do it, nobody minds. There *is* a war on.'

'Oh, you know what mummy and daddy are like, and daddy's been worse recently. If it ever got back to them I'd be toast, It's alright for you. You don't know how lucky you are. Anyway, it's different for men.'

'Surely you can win your parents round?'

'It's such a beastly atmosphere at home. He's always in such a bad mood. No one can do anything right. I wish he'd just go and take a running jump.' She paused. 'Can't we change the subject?' She touched his knee before taking the brown-paper bag out of her handbag and putting it on her lap. She tore it open, started eating and only talked in-between mouthfuls. 'I'm sorry Jan. I've tried to explain. It's just not possible at the moment. Please don't keep going on and making it worse for me than it already is.'

Jan wished he had said nothing. They looked out over the lake as drakes and ducks, pigeons and sparrows, in springtime mood came around their feet looking for crumbs.

'No, no, I'm sorry. I do love you and will wait, it's just...'

'What?'

'Well, it's just…'

'What?'

'Do you think I should sign up?'

Lucy spluttered: 'Absolutely not! What are you trying to do to me, Jan? What good will you be to me blown up into hundreds of pieces or maimed for the rest of your life?'

'Listen to me Lucy, it's not that simple. I don't really have much choice.'

'No Jan. I won't listen to you. Just think how terrible it would be if you died before we could be together.'

'Eric told me last night he'd signed up.'

Lucy covered her face with her hands. 'No. And he was so against it, that's terrible. Why?'

'Our friend Frankie got killed at Neuve Chapelle and Eric promised Frankie's mother he'd get them back.'

'Bloody hell. She must be really distressed but there's no need to get Eric involved. That won't make any difference.'

Jan uncrossed his legs and opened his palms in front of him.

'I know, but it would have happened sooner or later. No one's in charge of their own destiny anymore.'

'Nobody is ever in charge of their destiny.'

'No, of course.'

'Oh Jan, it's all so terrible. Now I've found you. I don't think I could face life without you.'

'I've got to face facts. There's no way out of it. Mind you, Mother wants me to go and live in Sweden with her relatives, but then I'd never be able to come back. Anyway, the war could spread up there and then where would I go?'

'But you don't actually have to. Just lie low; walk with a limp or something.'

'They'll bring in conscription. It's certain the way things are going. I might just as well get it over with.'

'I don't see why. You're doing essential work, aren't you?'

'Yes, but …'

'But nothing, I just won't let you.' Her eyes welled up. 'Change the subject, will you?'

'How can I? We can't pretend the war's not happening.'

'I could go to Sweden with you. Then we could be happy together away from the war.'

'No listen, by the time I've finished my training the war will probably be over.'

'It doesn't look like finishing soon.'

'I'm educated, they'd want me as an officer and that takes a lot more training, maybe a year or even longer. It could all be over by then. The Americans will join us soon and that'll tip the balance.'

'But you think it's senseless and so do I, and I'd see you even less if you were training.'

'I've thought about that too.'

A young man in army uniform approached them.

'Mind if I sit here?' he asked.

'No. No of course not. We'll be moving in a minute,' Jan lied, and Lucy smiled at the soldier.

'Look, I'll have to get back to work soon. Don't do it till we've had a chance to talk about it some more. Promise me Jan. Please promise me,' Lucy whispered so the man couldn't hear.

'Alright but there's something important I want to say.'

'Can't it wait?'

'No.' Jan stood up. He held out his hand. She held it and rose to her feet and they walked along the lakeside.

'Well?'

'You see, it's just that…'

'Yes?'

'If we were married and I was training we could spend my time off together.'

Lucy stopped and, grabbing his arms, turned him round to face her.

'Jan, are you proposing to me?'

'Well, yes, I suppose I am.'

She brushed her hair back with her hand and stamped her foot. 'Don't you think I've had enough shocks for one day?'

'Sorry, I just thought…' Jan could never tell what she was really thinking. She smiled a childlike smile that eased his momentary fear.

'Of course I'll marry you, fathead.' Ignoring the wind that just gusted up and the passers-by that were too occupied with their own business to pay Jan and Lucy any concern, she wrapped her arms around him and he did the same. They squeezed each other tightly. 'Christ, Jan, these are such dreadful times, are you really sure?'

'Of course I am. I love you. I'm tired of the single life.'

'I love you too and I've never wanted to marry anyone else.'

Jan paused in his stride. 'Why didn't you tell me before?'

'I didn't want to frighten you off.'

'Sorry, I haven't even bought a ring.'

'I don't want an engagement ring. You know those things aren't important to me. They're only symbols of possession.'

'You know I've got the money if you want one. I think you should have one if only to show your parents.'

'If I did have one I wouldn't mind if it were the plainest in the shop.' They squeezed hands. 'I'm so happy I could burst but it's a lot to take in at once. My head's spinning.'

'I'd like to see your father's face when you tell him.'

'I'm not going to tell him, you are.'

Jan stood still and tried to hide his worried expression with a smile. 'Are you sure that's wise?'

'Absolutely, that's your job.'

'Well, usually, but after what you've said about him.'

'He'll never agree to it if you don't ask him face-to-face. You have to win him over.'

Jan made a 'phurrr' sound by blowing through his lips. 'He sounds a bit fierce.'

'Yes, I know. But you've got manners.' She smiled back at Jan and pressed his hand in hers. 'He respects that sort of thing; so does my mother.'

'If you say so.'

'I do.'

Jan could see Lucy was working it all out.

'And Claire and Julia can hardly wait to see you.'

'Your sisters are the least of my worries.' Jan lit two cigarettes and handed her one.

'You'll be fine. I'll be close by.'

'I've got it all planned on my side.'

Lucy stopped and looked at him. 'Are you sure, Jan?'

'Oh yes. You can come and live with us in Chichester Road.'

'What about *your* parents; have you asked your mother?'

'Well, not yet.'

'Don't you think you should?'

'Yes, of course but I'm asking you first. Then I'll ask her. She's bound to like you. She's wanted me to get hitched for a long time. They both have. She'd love to have you around.'

'I'm not sure you've thought this through completely.'

Jan smiled. 'Of course I have.'

'What about Gladys?'

'Oh, she won't mind. Anyway, it's none of her business. She's at work so often she'll hardly notice.' He paused to inhale some smoke, his hand slightly trembling as he presented the cigarette to his lips. 'You'll be nearer your work and could get away from your parents at long last.'

Lucy turned her head to blow her smoke out away from the wind. 'Now that would be good. Eva sounds like a real sport.'

'She's got books on fashion, music and art. You'll always have someone intelligent to talk to.'

'That's wonderful. I'd never be bored at home again.'

They resumed their walk round the lake.

'Actually, I'm pretty sure Mummy and Daddy would be glad to get me off their hands.'

'That's good. Isn't it?'

'Yes.'

'That's settled then.'

'Yes, darling, but ask them tonight,' she said, kissing him on the cheek and squeezing his hand.

'I promise.'

'Come on, I'd better get back to work.'

As they walked, a gust of wind caught Jan's bowler and blew it off his head and along the lakeside path. Jan jumped up after it and broke into a gangly run, his jacket and flannels flapping. Lucy giggled. All thoughts of war and of impending doom had momentarily left her. She couldn't think straight at all as they retraced their steps back across Birdcage Walk. Outside the Home Office, Jan kissed her full on the lips and said goodbye. Lucy struggled to let go of his hands. Typists and secretaries returning from their lunch breaks looked at them as they passed. Some of the office girls saw them together. Lucy sensed their envy. She walked up the steps and gave him a final wave from the top before rushing back to her office.

'Come on, tell us all?' Vera asked, as a small group surrounded Lucy at her desk.

'Yes, Lucy, we want to know everything,' another said.

'You kept that quiet, didn't you?' another said.

'He's a looker, isn't he? Does he have any brothers?' Vera asked.

'No, he doesn't have any brothers,' Lucy said. 'Actually, he just asked me to marry him.'

Vera clapped her hands. Beatty the eldest and most world-weary of her colleagues gasped. 'That's wonderful. Let's see the ring?'

'Were going to choose one on Saturday afternoon,' Lucy said.

'Be careful dear. You can't trust the good-looking ones. They can break your heart,' Beatty said.

'Leave her alone,' Vera said.

'I'm only saying. It's the plain stay at home types that's best for marrying,' Beatty said, but Lucy was too excited to let it sink in.

On the train home Jan looked at his father.

'I've asked Lucy to marry me,' he said. He was too tired and lost in his own thoughts, however, to elaborate. He closed his eyes and tried to clear his mind and hoped his headache would leave him.

'Congratulations, I'm very pleased for you and I'm sure your mother would say the same.' Peter Strang could talk incessantly of minor business concerns but present him with something really important and he never knew what to say.

Jan said that he would tell them all at dinner that evening. He thought that, by this method, he would save a lot of added explanations. Now he'd made up his mind he just wanted to get it over with. At the dinner table Eva asked Jan, as she did every night:

'How's your day been?'

'Mixed,' Jan replied. 'A young woman got killed at the docks this morning and we couldn't get the timber we wanted.'

'Oh, how awful,' Eva said.

'I know. It was terrible. With all the deaths since the war you'd think we'd all be used to it by now; but when it's on your own doorstep…'

'You think you will, but you never get over it,' Gladys said.

Jan took a deep breath, counted to three. 'And then I had some good news.'

'Oh good, what was it?' Eva asked.

'I've asked Lucy to marry me.' Jan leaned back from his dinner plate and waited for the response.

'Crikey, what did she say?' Gladys asked, with her mouth full of fried corned beef and boiled potatoes.

'Don't talk with your mouthful, dear,' Eva said.

'She said yes,' Jan said, and let out a short laugh. He felt that at long last he'd been able to say something that pleased both parents. Through innumerable hints, Jan knew that Eva had been hoping for years that he would get married.

'Well that's wonderful darling, I'm so pleased for you.' Nobody said anything else so she looked at Jan. 'She's sounds like a lovely girl.'

'Yes, I know. That's why I asked her.' Jan put a forkful of cabbage in his mouth.

'When are we going to meet her?' Eva asked.

'Whenever we can arrange it.' Jan pulled a face. 'She's got funny parents.'

'What do you mean by "funny"?' Gladys asked

'Strange. I haven't met them yet but they sound protective and pernickety.'

'I'm sure they'll be fine when you get to know them,' Eva said.

'Well done Son, congratulations,' Peter said, as if he hadn't heard the news already.

'Thanks.'

'Are you sure about this? It's easy to rush into things you know.' Peter said.

'Yes, I'm sure. Or I wouldn't have asked her.'

Gladys, who was pouring gravy over her potatoes and mashing it in with her fork, smirked. 'Is she in trouble?'

Jan raised his head and eyes to the ceiling.

'Really Dear, what a terrible thing to say and at such a happy time for Jan,' Eva said.

'Well it wouldn't be the first couple it happened to. One of my friends …'

'Not now Gladys,' Eva said.

'Can we all settle down a bit please?' Peter said. 'Do you know, there were times when we wondered if you'd ever find the right girl?'

'Yes, I know.' Jan hoped this wouldn't go on for too much longer. 'I asked myself the same thing.'

'She sounds like the right sort of girl from what you've told us. Stick with your own class. We were always worried you might get too involved with some of those other girls we've seen,' Peter said.

'I know. Do you remember the one you came home with last Christmas? She had so much rouge on she looked like she was working the streets,' Gladys said.

'Not now Dear,' Eva said looking straight at Gladys.

'You'll be much happier. A man needs stability,' Peter said. 'But have you thought it through?'

'Of course I have. Do you think I'm completely stupid?'

'Yes, we do actually,' Gladys said.

'Bloody hell, Gladys,' Jan said, clanking his knife and fork down on the plate.

'There is a war on and where will you live? What does her father have to say?' Peter asked.

'And her mother; what does she say?' Eva asked.

Jan threw his serviette on the table and crossed his arms. 'I'm not hungry. I need a drink.'

'You should try and eat a bit more,' Eva said.

'I wish I'd never told you now. Look, I've had a long day. Can we save the post mortem for another time?'

'I only thought...' Eva said.

'Can we at least have a glass of wine to celebrate?' Jan asked. 'Anyway, there's something else you should know about.'

'I do have a *Sauterne* I've been saving,' Peter said, and left the room to get it. When he returned, he pulled the cork then placed a glass in front of each of them and poured them all a glass.

Jan felt calmer and more able to tell them the serious news. He was just about to speak when Peter stood up.

'To Jan and Lucy,' he declared, and took the first sip.

Jan drank half his glass. 'It's a bit sweet, isn't it?'

'It's supposed to be,' Gladys said.

Jan looked seriously at his mother and father in turn.

'Will you all please listen to me? I've got something else to say.'

'Okay, Jan, what is it?' Gladys asked.

'Look, I haven't rushed into it, I've thought about it for ages.'

'Yes, and?' Gladys said.

'You see; I'm joining up.'

Jan looked around the table and felt their eyes penetrate him. They were a family who conveyed more through looks and expression than language. He lit a cigarette, sat back and finished his wine. Eva broke the silence:

'But you can't, you just can't. I won't let you!' She looked at Peter across the table. 'Tell him Father, tell him he can't. I just won't have it.'

Jan got up to put his arm around her but she stood up before he could reach her. She collected the dirty plates, rushed into the kitchen. A *clash* and a *clatter* rang out.

'It won't be that bad,' Jan called after her.

'Best to leave her,' Peter said, as Jan got up and followed his mother into the kitchen.

'You could sail away out of danger. My sister said they'd love to have you. No one here needs to know where you've gone. They'll think you've gone to the war,' Eva said to Jan as he joined her by the kitchen sink.

'I know, but,' he mouthed the words slowly, 'I've made up my mind.' Gladys was speaking to Peter in the living room. Jan strained his ears to listen.

'Well, you're a fat lot of good,' Gladys was saying. 'Can't you do something to stop him?'

'He's his own man.'

'Every day I see men back from the front; hundreds of them...'

Her voice faded away and Jan's mother held onto his arm and gave him a pleading look. Gladys raised her voice. 'Calm? Are you joking? I can tell you that there's nothing to be calm about.'

Eva moved to close the kitchen door and Jan stopped her.

'There's no point,' he said. 'Why doesn't anyone here believe me when I say I've made up my mind?'

'... and even if you forget about the wounding, gangrene, amputations, and the gas, half of them have completely "lost it". They're mental wrecks,' Gladys said.

'Will you keep your voice down; you'll upset your mother. Look, he has to play the long game,' Peter said.

'If he does come back, he'll never be the same again; you know what he's like. If he goes out there he can say goodbye to any chance of a decent marriage,' Gladys said.

'You're not listening, Gladys. This is a tactical move. He's playing for time,' Peter said.

Jan wrapped his mother in his arms by the kitchen sink. 'That is what I'm doing. I'll probably never see battle.'

'There's no way out of it, haven't you seen the recruiting stations and the posters and the women handing out white feathers?' Peter said.

'Being an outcast is better than being dead,' Gladys said.

'If he went to your Aunty Elsa in Sweden he'd probably lose Lucy and all his friends.'

'He'll lose them anyway, if he's dead.'

'I can speak for myself,' Jan shouted from the kitchen.

Peter raised his voice and Jan listened harder. 'I was just saying to Gladys that playing for time is probably the best bet.'

'We heard every word,' Jan said, returning to the room. Peter lowered his voice and continued his conversation with Gladys.

'It could be a year or more before he finishes his training and the war might be over by then. It could be over in the meantime, especially if the Americans came in, and they're bound to sooner or later.'

'If you'd seen what I'd seen ...'

'Yes, thank you Gladys, you've already told us what you've seen. Don't you realise you're not helping?'

'It's better to hide the truth, is it?'

'Look, when your mother comes back in here, will you promise to change the subject? It's hard enough for her as it is.'

Gladys made a gesture of folding her arms. 'I promise,' she said.

Peter got up, went into the kitchen and came back with Eva. Jan pulled up a chair next to his mother and held her hand as she blew her nose. I may as well not be here, he thought.

'We've got stewed pears for dessert,' Eva said, motioning to go back to the kitchen. Gladys stood up.

'I'll get them.'

'Thank you, Gladys,' Peter said.

Gladys brought back the bowls on a tray and put them in the middle of the table.

'Thank you,' Jan and Peter said.

Eva looked wounded. She didn't speak or eat.

'It is for the best,' Jan said. 'Signing up, that is.'

'These are nice,' Gladys said. Gladys, Peter and Jan finished eating their pears and custard and Jan wiped his mouth with his serviette.

'Let's change the subject,' Peter said. Nobody said anything.

Jan broke the silence. 'Can we have a proper drink now? I don't know about you lot but I need one.'

'We can't all knock it back whenever we want like you do, you know,' Gladys said. 'I'm back on duty at eight. Matron's a total battle axe. She'd have me executed by firing squad if she thought I was even a little bit tight.'

'Not for me, thank you,' Eva said, her eyes welled up again.

'Eat drink and be merry,' Jan said, and Eva wiped her eyes into her handkerchief. 'I'm sorry, I shouldn't have …'

'So you should be. It's not something to joke about,' Peter said, getting up and going to the drinks cabinet. He brought back a bottle of Johnnie Walker and two glasses for himself and Jan.

'Thanks,' Jan said, as Peter stood by him and poured out two small glasses. 'Look I've made my mind up and that's that.'

'Let's leave the subject for today, shall we?' Peter said.

'Yes, let's,' Jan said. 'By the way do you mind if Lucy comes here and lives with us?' Jan felt their eyes looking at him. 'It's just that I told her she could.'

'Bloody hell, Jan, haven't you sprung enough surprises on us for one day?' Gladys said.

Eva's face brightened. 'Oh, that would be wonderful Dear, we've got plenty of room and …' She scratched her head. 'It would be lovely to have her around.'

'I'll be training for ages,' Jan said, lighting up a cigarette before taking a drink of whiskey, leaving only a drop in his glass.

'Of course she can stay here, we'd love to have her. Can't imagine where you found a nice girl. Not at The Game Cock, that's for sure,' Peter said.

'When I met her she seemed very sensible,' Gladys said.

Jan felt defensive. 'She's a very modern woman actually. She wears some nice clothes.'

Gladys blew smoke across the table in Jan's direction and pulled a face.

Jan ignored her and downed his last drop of whiskey. 'Okay, that's settled then. I'll go and see that old sod of a father of hers one night later in week.' He paused and straightened his back and said in an exaggerated pompous voice: 'Francis T. Green, the Postmaster.'

'And his mother,' Eva added.

Jan wiped his mouth, folded his serviette, rolled it up and put it in the serviette ring.

'I'm off to The Black Lion. I think I'd better give the Game Cock a miss, until I've actually signed on the dotted line.'

'And I need to get to the hospital. I'll walk down the road with you. If I'm late they'll have my guts for garters,' Gladys said.

Jan and Gladys stood up, got their coats from the stand in the hall and turned their collars up.

'Bye Ma, bye Pa,' Gladys called back, wrapping a scarf around her neck with a flourish as they went out into the street heading for Kilburn High Road. She slammed the door behind them.

'Jesus Christ, you wouldn't believe the day I've had,' Jan said.

'Well you should try working at the Whitechapel, that's all I can say,' Gladys said striding down the road into the wind. 'You're a bloody idiot Jan.'

The next day Lucy met Jan for lunch at one of those city tea rooms near St James' Park that filled to bursting around lunchtime. Outside it was warm and the wind had settled. Talking into her ear, to be heard above the noise, Jan told her how pleased his parents were when he told them about the marriage. Lucy tingled with his breath reaching into her ear. Jan knew how to deliver a compliment even in the most unlikely places. Her lips shaped into a smile and her eyes smiled more. Through the steam and cooking smells of the lunch-time rush she wanted Jan to feel her love even if they couldn't be alone. She tried but soon gave up talking above the din about all the things she wanted to do with their lives together after the war. They drank tea and ate a fried egg sandwich each. They held hands under the table and Lucy savoured the moment. She put HP sauce on her egg because she wasn't allowed brown sauce at home. Jan finished his sandwich first and the runny yolk nearly dripped down his tie. As soon as Lucy had finished hers, and dabbed her lips with a hankie, he got up to leave. Outside in the spring air Lucy threaded her arm through his.

'I love the spring,' Jan said.

'So do I,' she said, holding on to him a little tighter.

She glanced at other couples holding hands, linking arms and enjoying the same sunshine, but none of those girls could have felt the magic of romance as she did. Today the sun was shining just for them. She felt fantastic walking down the street with Jan. She wanted to tell everyone that this man was hers.

'I'll talk to Mummy and Daddy tonight and fix it up for you to come round tomorrow night,' she said, before they parted. She was nearly late back for work.

'I suppose it has to be done,' Jan said before kissing her on the cheek. Jan pressed a note in her hand. She walked away and nearly knocked an old man over as she kept turning her head back just to watch the way Jan walked. When he was out of sight she unfolded his note and read: *Love Me on Saturday, Jan* xxx.

'I'm damned if I can see what you see in him,' her father, Francis T. Green, said to her that night after dinner.

Lucy frowned and her mother, Anne, scowled at her husband.

'But you haven't even seen him yet,' Lucy said.

'From what you've said, he seems to care more about his looks than his country,' her father said.

'Really Daddy, please try; just for me. He just cares about his appearance more than most men. He's very presentable; that's all.' She looked at her father like the little girl she had long ceased to be. It always worked better than arguing. She knew how to get around him.

'Well your mother thinks he should shape up given time, so I suppose we should give him a chance. I wish I shared her confidence. Bring him along and we'll see how it goes.'

'Oh, thank you Daddy. You will promise to be nice won't you?'

'Of course I will,' he said, looking a little affronted.

Lucy left the room with adrenaline moving around her system. She prayed it would go well tomorrow and had faith that it would. After all, Jan knew how to behave and would charm her mother even if he didn't completely win over her father. And that was half the battle. If Daddy didn't like him then her mother, with her infinite patience, could bring him round.

She told her parents that she would have an early night, kissed them both on the cheek and went upstairs to lie on her bed and think of Jan for half an hour or so before settling down to sleep. She undressed and put her dirty clothes in the laundry basket and hung her skirt on the back of the chair ready for the morning. Lying on her bed, looking back over the day's events, she heard a soft 'ratatat'. She opened her eyes to see her younger sisters, Claire and Julia, put their heads round her bedroom door. They tiptoed into the bedroom.

'When are we going to see him?' Julia asked.

Lucy sat up and propped her pillow behind her back.

'I'll only tell you if you promise not to stay all night,' she said, patting the bed as an invitation for them to come and sit on it.

Julia, at nineteen, was the youngest of the sisters.

'We promise,' she said, and they both sat down on the edge of Lucy's bed.

'I have to be up for work tomorrow,' Lucy said, 'so I'm going to keep this quick.'

'He asked me to marry him.'

Julia clapped her hands.

'How romantic; I knew he would,' Claire said.

'He asked me in the park. He was terribly nervous.' Lucy went through the events that led up to his proposal. She thought better about telling them that he said he would be joining up, because she still thought she might be able to change his mind. 'I'm going to try and get him over tomorrow night.'

'Brilliant,' said Claire.

'I can hardly wait,' said Julia.

'He sounds gorgeous. Daddy's trying to introduce me to a son of his friend from the church but he's such a bore,' Claire pulled a horrible face. 'I know I'm twenty-four and it's about time I got hitched but I won't step out with him. I couldn't imagine being married to a man like that.'

'I'm sure he'll be very nice when you get to know him,' Lucy said, suppressing a smile.

'He's got spots and greasy hair and he looks about forty,' Julia said.

'I couldn't kiss a man like that. I want someone tall and handsome like your Jan,' Claire said. 'I can't wait to see him and see if he's as good as you say.'

'He's fit, apparently,' Julia said.

'He's also kind and intelligent,' Lucy said.

'And rich,' Claire added.

'Can't we share him?' Julia smiled.

'No, you can't. He's all mine,' Lucy said, pushing Julia on her shoulder.

'He must have some faults,' Claire said.

'Not that I can see,' Lucy said.

'So far,' Claire said.

'Is he a good kisser?' Julia asked.

'What a thing to ask!' Claire said.'

'Well?' said Julia.

'He is actually,' Lucy lowered her voice as if she were sharing the darkest secret. 'He kissed me today in the park and again outside the Home Office. It sent shivers right through me.'

'I want someone like that,' Claire said.

'So do I,' Julia said.

'Well you can't have my Jan,' Lucy said. 'He's all mine.' She made a shooing gesture with her arms. 'Now get out both of you. I've got a long day tomorrow. I need my sleep.'

The sisters left and Lucy, too excited to sleep, could hear them talking and giggling from their room next door. At around eleven-thirty she heard her parents' footsteps mounting the stairs. She listened as they kissed each other good night on the landing before they went to their separate rooms. Lucy was in a heightened state, extra-sensitive to all the sounds inside and outside the house. In her childhood, she imagined there was a kindly presence in her room. Tonight, she had the same feeling and lay awake for what seemed like hours listening to two owls screeching in a call and response, and the sound of distant trains taking troops and materiel to the Channel ports. She would do her best to make sure that Jan didn't get on a troop train.

After work on Friday, Jan and Lucy took the train to her family home in suburban Uxbridge. As the carriage was full they had to stand up. The train swayed and they held onto the handles that hung down from the ceiling like policemen's truncheons. Each time the train braked or lurched forward their bodies pushed together. Jan felt the soft flesh of her breasts press against his chest and smelt rose-petal perfume on her neck. When they reached Acton Town, the train emptied enough for them to sit together. Lucy sat in the corner seat and he squeezed up to her. Lucy blushed as their thighs touched and Jan understood how easily he could trigger her feelings.

At Lucy's house, her mother invited Jan into the hall where a portrait of her father, Francis T. Green, the postmaster, looked down on them from the wall to the side of a central staircase. Her mother wore a green and yellow silk scarf knotted around her throat. It went well with her floral, ankle-length dress and brought colour to her pale face. The house smelt of beeswax and was spotlessly clean and tidy. Floral wallpaper in pastel shades covered the high walls and almost matched the upholstery on the settee and arm chairs and the fitted carpet in the front sitting room. Gentle watercolour landscapes of Scottish glens and highlands framed in ornate gold mouldings argued with the wallpaper. Jan thought the predominantly blue Persian rug seemed out of place; it was of a different character altogether.

Jan was parched and grateful for the cup of tea Mrs Green brought to the side table by his chair. She placed it on a crocheted doily that she said Lucy had made when she was just a slip of a girl. Jan watched Lucy's mother as she went back out of the room. He hoped that Lucy would keep her figure as well as her mother had. She came back with a thin ham sandwich on a rose-painted plate with an embroidered serviette. He shuffled in his seat and hoped he wouldn't have to be a regular visitor.

'Do you mind if I smoke, Mrs Green?' he asked.

'Not at all and you must call me Anne.'

'I'm going to sign up,' Jan told his prospective mother-in-law. She looked shocked.

'I'm so sorry,' she said.

Jan could just make out the sound of Lucy's sisters talking in the hallway. When Lucy's mother opened the door and invited them to join them, he was unsure whether to stand up and introduce himself or to wait until their mother or Lucy initiated the introductions. Introductions were such a palaver. He could have done with something to steady his nerves but was glad now that he'd resisted the temptation to have a drink at the pub across the road from the station.

Lucy's mother, he assumed, was one of those women who notice everything. Lucy introduced Claire and Julia; in turn he held their outstretched hands and, as they smiled and stared into his eyes, he felt hot and his collar stick to his neck.

Lucy always said that her father's bark was worse than his bite. She had told Jan, also, that her parents had made 'discreet enquires' and were aware that Jan's family were respectable, had money and were of the right class. The information though, however welcome, didn't steady his nerves. Her father, about five-foot seven with a thick greying moustache, tweed jacket and tie, came into the sitting room to join them. Jan stood up and his legs shook underneath his loose-fitting trousers. He leaned down and stubbed his cigarette out in the cut-glass ash tray. The two men shook hands; Jan smiled and Lucy's father looked back at him, expressionless.

'At least it's been dry for a few days,' Lucy's mother said.

'Yes, it's been nice hasn't it, Jan?' Lucy said.

'Yes, lovely. A bit windy, though,' Jan said.

'We had a lovely walk in the park yesterday, didn't we Jan?' Lucy said. She stared at Jan for a few seconds.

'Err yes,' said Jan. 'That's one of the reasons I wanted to come round and have a chat with Mr Green.' Again, Jan smiled at his prospective father-in-law. This time he responded with a half-smile and a nod.

'Well, we must go and tidy the kitchen,' Lucy's mother said. Then with more emphasis and looking straight at her daughter. 'Mustn't we Lucy?'

'Yes, we must,' said Lucy.

Jan watched as they walked towards the door and noticed how alike they were in their deportment. Lucy gave him a little wave by wiggling her fingers and left the room with an encouraging smile. She closed the door behind her.

Francis T. leaned his elbow on the white marble ledge over the wide Georgian fireplace.

'We can't light it unless it's bitter,' he said.

'I know, it's the same for all of us,' Jan said, in his best public-school accent.

'We all have to make some sacrifices to win this one,' Francis T. said.

'I agree. It's not a lot to ask.' Jan felt his hand going up to his mouth and checked himself before he chewed his nails. 'To cut down on things, I mean.'

'No. I could do with a decent steak though,' Francis T. said.

Jan didn't know how to respond. He laughed then coughed. 'I have to go down to the docks with my work. We can usually get a few things.'

Francis T showed interest in his expression.

'But not steak I'm afraid.'

'Oh well, never mind. That isn't why you've come here today.'

'Err, well no actually …'

'I can see you making a fine officer,' Francis T. said with the air of an ex-military man who believed he knew what he was talking about. A sudden warmth in his tone gave Jan more confidence. Francis T. motioned with his arm for Jan to sit down.

'Thank you very much, Mr. Green,' Jan said, sitting back in the arm chair.

'I read only this morning that this recent offensive has been very successful: "A model operation" they called it.'

And did you look at the casualties? Jan could have said but didn't. 'So I believe,' he said. He crossed then re-crossed his legs.

'I managed to look at *The Times* this morning. I thought it was encouraging,' Francis T. said, and the two men talked about regiments and how the Post Office Rifles would seem a good regiment for Jan to join. Francis T. offered him a cheroot from a box above the fireplace. Jan accepted with a smile. Before lighting it, he asked to be excused.

He nodded to Claire and Julia as he passed them in the hall on his way to the lavatory. He opened the window in the cubicle and took in five long deep breaths of the cold evening air and tried to steady his nerves.

When he got back he said, 'Lucy is a wonderful girl and I wanted to ask you for her hand in marriage.'

'These are difficult times.'

'I know.'

'You could leave Lucy as a young widow. But I admire you for doing your bit.'

'Thank you.'

'I hope you have sufficient insurance and pension arrangements in place in case the worse came to the worst. You would, of course, heaven forbid it should happen, have an army pension.'

'Oh yes, I can let you see the paperwork if you like.'

'If it's not too much trouble.'

'No trouble at all.'

'Then, all being well, you have my blessing.'

He shook Jan's hand, in a way that only military men did. Jan felt his fingers throb. Francis T. poured them both a brandy from a decanter inside the sideboard. They drank to the occasion and smoked their cheroots. Jan inhaled too deeply and coughed, nearly spilling his drink. He thought his relief must have been obvious but, if it was, Francis T. didn't take any notice.

'Oh, excuse me,' Jan said. Francis T. smiled almost imperceptibly and Jan could see that he might have human characteristics after all.

'Mrs Green and I would very much like to meet your parents sometime soon.'

'Yes, absolutely.' Jan was feeling a little relieved as he sensed their *tête ê tête* coming to a close.

'I'm sure we'll have a lot to talk about.'

'I'll ask my mother to write in the next few days to arrange a meeting,' Jan said.

'Please send our warmest regards.'

'I will. Thank you.'

'That's settled then,' Francis T. said and finished his brandy. He walked to the door and asked Lucy and her mother to come back into the room. Jan saw Lucy's face brighten and a big grin appear as she realised that it had all gone well. She ran up and hugged her father.

'Thank you, Daddy, thank you so much,' she said, and went straight to Jan's side and held his arm.

'Where are you thinking of getting married?' her mother asked both of them.

'Not in a church, that's for sure,' Lucy replied. Her mother looked at her, stunned. 'I don't believe in God, and it's my day not yours,' Lucy said firmly, closing the subject for further debate.

'She has her own mind. You'll find out soon enough,' Francis T. said giving Jan a knowing look.

Jan managed to get a quick pint in at the pub opposite Uxbridge Station. He felt more relaxed as the liquid slid down. He saw the horsebus to Kilburn pull in, drained his glass and ran out to catch it just before it pulled away. He sat on the top and smoked, taking in the cold night air. In Kilburn, he just got to The Black Lion before closing time and ordered two pints and a barley wine. Christ I need this, he said to himself as he sunk the first pint in three successive draughts. He imagined steam coming out of his ears as the pressure from his ordeal escaped.

'I'm going to enlist,' he said to the landlady.

'Well, be sure you come back safe and sound,' she said.

'I'm not off yet, you'll still be seeing me whilst I'm training.' He glimpsed sadness looking back at him from her eyes. 'And I'll have to get married first.'

'That's nice dear,' she said, but was too busy dealing with the rush for last orders to talk for any longer. When they'd finally stopped serving and kicked everyone out Jan walked home getting in at about 10-o'clock. He told Eva, Peter and Gladys all about the pompous Francis T., Anne

Green's fussy housekeeping and Lucy's sisters trying to listen from the hall. They hung on his every word and laughed and nobody mentioned the war. He could hold an audience when he'd had a drink.

Jan ate some bread and cheese with a few pickled onions for a late supper then went up to bed after kissing his mother on the cheek. Lying in bed with his pillow propped up behind his back he smoked and thought about Lucy and the note he gave her. He smiled, wondering how she would take it. He thought about the war and the events of the last few days. Today had felt like the longest day of his life. *How quickly life changes*, he wrote in his diary with a pencil before falling into a deep sleep.

Chapter 4

20 March 1915

On Saturday, Lucy went up to town to meet Jan after he finished work. As she waited for her train she listened to the metallic rattle preceding it coming down the tracks. Her heart pounded. On the platform she took in deep breaths of fresh air to calm herself down. She waited until she got on the train and it pulled away before she lit a cigarette. Ignoring the two young soldiers on the opposite seat who smiled at her, she took out a copy of *Woman's Weekly* from her tan-leather bag, crossed her legs, and flicked through the pages, taking in nothing in particular from the war-time articles on 'mend and make do'. Behind her magazine, she unfolded Jan's note again and read, for the umpteenth time: *Love me on Saturday.* All the way to Liverpool Street she could only think of Jan and making love.

As she left the station and walked into the street a warm and gentle breeze blew the fringe across her eyes. Jan's office, he assured her, was only seven minutes away and her anxiety increased the closer she got.

Outside 55 Bishopsgate she paused and wiped her nose with a hankie that she pulled out from her sleeve. She took in deep breaths. More composed, she walked up the stone steps and opened the wide mahogany door.

Mrs Agnoli must have heard her come in. She walked towards Lucy with open arms. Taking her by surprise she hugged Lucy to her bosom.

'You're a beautiful girl. You'll make him a happy man. I just know you will,' Mrs Agnoli said.

Lucy blushed then saw Jan smiling and walking towards her. He held her hand and guided her into his office as if she were an important client. His hand pushed gently into the small of her back. She would have like to have lingered with the staff for a few more minutes, just to be polite and because she hoped to be seeing more of them.

'I see you've told them all,' she said after Jan had closed the glass-windowed door behind them.

'Yes, I knew you wouldn't mind. Mrs Agnoli has a way of prising information out of unsuspecting people,' Jan said.

Lucy turned to see three heads looking from their desks to Jan's office door. 'Well you'd better introduce me to them properly. If I'm going to be your wife -'

'Come on then. They're all dying to meet you.'

Lucy felt like royalty meeting the public as Jan led her out into the wider office. She shook hands with the two office clerks and met Mrs Agnoli, more formally this time.

At half-past twelve the staff left and Jan locked the main door from inside. They went into Jan's office. For the very first time they were completely alone together with no chance of interruption. The room smelled of pine sap. Lucy told Jan she had to leave the room to go to the toilet. In the cubicle she hoisted her skirt from her ankles to her hips, took her knickers off, folded them once and put them into her bag. She put her foot on the toilet seat, pulled her white silk stockings up tight, adjusted her garters then stroked her legs so the stockings didn't show any creases. She left the cubicle, straightened her skirt, looked at herself in the mirror and brushed the fringe out of her eyes.

Back in Jan's office she sat sideways on the edge of the heavy oak desk. He was on the other side leaning slightly forward in his chair.

'I could be a secretary being interviewed for a job,' she said, looking into Jan's eyes, trying to appear calm and confident. She leant over and took one of Jan's Player's from his cigarette case, then offered him one. Jan flicked his lighter and leaned over the desk, arm stretched. She sucked in the flame, inhaled the smoke lightly then blew it out into the space between them. Jan walked around the desk and stood in front of her. She turned to face him and started to talk about where they might walk in the afternoon, but she couldn't concentrate so gave up talking. Her hand trembled slightly as she stubbed her unfinished cigarette in the ashtray.

She stood up, took his cigarette from his fingers and stubbed it out as well. Then she kissed him full on the lips. Jan pushed forward and she parted her legs a little. He held her head and kissed her neck just below her ear. It sent sensations right down to her toes. Then he ran his hands down her ribs and his thumbs rested underneath her underbodice. He gazed into her eyes and she kissed him more strongly this time. Their lips locked and she stood up. She moved her hands down his back. Jan pushed his hips to her pelvis and she felt his penis press against her stomach.

Jan stroked her breasts through her cotton blouse. She felt tingling sensations going straight through her and could no longer think straight. He started to undo the blouse and fumbled at the first button. Without speaking, one by one, she undid them for him as he watched. He pulled up her bodice to expose her breasts, then touched her nipples with his thumbs, bent his head down and kissed them in turn. His hands moved down to hold her buttocks. Stronger sensations ran through her as he lifted her up so that she was sitting on the edge of the desk. She parted her legs some more and her feet swayed a few inches above the floor. His hips were between her knees and he ran his hands up either side of her thighs to the garters at the top of her stockings. Her excitement was almost unbearable when she saw his expression as he discovered there were no knickers to pull down.

Lucy unbuttoned his braces and let his trousers fall to the floor. Jan pulled his drawers down below his knees. When they fell to his ankles he stepped out of them and she watched his penis sway as he moved his legs. It was the first time she had seen an erect penis. She kicked off her shoes and felt his hands lifting her skirt higher. She took hold of her hem and raised it to her waist. Lucy leaned back on her elbows. Jan pressed his fingers against her sex massaging her gently but firmly. She looked down and watched him, feeling the wetness inside her. The expression on his face was one of total desire. This time when he looked into her eyes, a sensation she had never felt before made her shudder. She felt she could burst.

She looked down as Jan held his penis toward her. She closed her eyes as he gently pushed inside her. She felt a short, sudden pain which she ignored as he moved further inside. Lucy opened her legs wider and rested her heels on the base of his back. He pushed deeper, slowly and rhythmically moving his pelvis. Then fast, then faster. He made a hard thrust a let out a long deep groan. She wondered if he was alright; had he felt some pain? But then he became still and silent leaving his penis inside her limp and lifeless. She didn't understand why he had stopped and felt awkward as he held her in his arms and rested his head on her neck. Should she ask him if he'd finished?

'I have to move,' she said at last. 'My bottom's going numb.'

Jan pulled out. They laughed and she slid down so her feet touched the ground. Her skirt fell back down to her ankles. She held his head and kissed him on the lips.

'I love you,' she said.

'And I love you.'

Lucy and Jan held hands as they walked along Bishopsgate. They looked in the shop windows and in the arcades pointing out to each other the things that they liked. Jan suggested they went down Petticoat Lane to see the market. It was bustling with characters that looked as if they came right out of a Dickens book. The noise of foreign accents mixed with the game Cockney voices.

'Keep your hand on your bag,' Jan said, before Lucy went off by herself to look at the array of fabrics spread out on the stalls. Jan went into The Bell and came back out with a pint of stout that he drank leaning against the wall outside. She was aware of his protective eye watching over her and felt safe as she bartered with the stallholders. She bought two yards of white Aida cloth and some coloured embroidery threads for Claire and Julia to sew in the evenings. The air was heavy with cooking smells and she bought bagels from an overweight Jewess and took them over to Jan. They ate them standing outside the pub and Lucy thought she had never tasted anything so delicious in her life.

'I do love all the banter,' she said. 'But I can hardly understand a word they're saying.'

'Nor can I. I knew you'd like it here. I can get lost in the atmosphere,' he said.

'I know what you mean; it's like a different world. If my sisters could see me now they'd die with envy.'

Jan put his arm around her and gave her a little squeeze.

'For the first time in my life I feel free to do whatever I want,' she said.

They meandered away from the market and up into Liverpool Street. Jan suggested they call into the Great Eastern Hotel. Lucy would have done anything Jan suggested. He found two leather armchairs by the window in the lounge looking out onto the street below. She ordered tea and Jan drank light ale.

'It didn't hurt,' she whispered in his ear. Jan was staring out of the window.

'I'm sorry?'

'When we made love; it didn't hurt,' she kissed him gently on the cheek.

'How do you mean?'

'I was always told it would hurt,' she looked at him and touched his knee, 'but it didn't.'

'That's good.'

She held both his hands, ignoring an old man peeping at them over the top of his paper; then whispered.

'I enjoyed it.'

Jan sucked air through his teeth. 'Good.'

'And I want to do it again.'

'Well there's not a lot of time…'

'Not now, you idiot,' she smiled, wondering why he seemed distant.

'I've been longing for you since we first met,' Jan said, coming back from his thoughts. He lit them both a cigarette. 'I was worried you might not like it.'

'Don't worry darling, I do.' She gazed in his eyes and hoped he knew just how much she loved him. She glanced over to the bar and an overdressed and jewelled woman in her sixties smiled benignly down at them.

'Come on,' Jan said, downing his glass of beer and wiping his mouth on the back of his hand. 'Let's get you a ring.'

Chapter 5

Jan asked Eva to arrange for the families to meet up the following week. The Greens came over to Chichester Road and, after being won over by Eva and Peter's charm, good manners and apparent wealth, felt better about the marriage. A friend of Jan's at the Registry Office tipped him off about a cancellation caused through a prospective groom dying at the battlefront. Jan thought nothing of it except that they were lucky to be fitted in at a time when they would have liked. But Lucy told him that she had a bad feeling and thought there was something not quite right about taking a dead man's wedding slot. Jan thought that it was just groundless superstition and they needed to be pragmatic. So, they set the wedding for Saturday, March the twenty-seventh.

Jan and Lucy knew that both sets of parents were disappointed that it would be held at the Registry Office in Willesden High Road rather than in a proper church but neither of them cared what they thought. It would be their day not their parents.

Eric was Jan's best man.

'You don't have to go through with this if you don't want to,' he said to Jan on the wedding morning when both were feeling numb and a bit drunk from the night before.

'Don't be bloody stupid, of course I do,' Jan said.

'Don't get touchy. It's traditional, I have to ask.'

Jan hated ceremony and was relieved that, because the next couple and the couple after them were waiting outside, the wedding was rushed through in ten minutes. As far as he was concerned it went smoothly. A photographer from Gearing's in The Strand held the traffic up whilst he erected his tripod and took a group picture in the street outside. The main party set off in two cars for the reception back at Chichester Road and others got there by horsebus.

There were thirty-odd guests and the whole of the downstairs was taken up. Jan's aunts, Peter's sisters Karolina and Elina, were in their pearls and dressed respectively in ankle-length violet and yellow, and black and red flowing dresses. They organised and prepared the food and drink, talked in Swedish between themselves and exchanged knowing glances so that they appeared to have their own secret way of communication. They handed round to the guests sardine, corned beef as well as cheese sandwiches on white bread with the crusts cut off and sliced into four triangular pieces. They had arranged slices of cheese and ham and roll-mop herrings with pickled onions and baby pickled cucumbers on several large willow-patterned plates garnished with sprigs of parsley and cucumber slices. The odour of vinegar cut through the smells in the room of cigar smoke, beer and wine. Jan watched Lucy through the corner of his eye. She flared her nostrils as she smelt her food on the plate and the vinegar hit her. She wiped the corners of her eyes with her hankie. She left the herrings and Jan laughed a little as he overheard Elina tell her how good they were for her.

'Would you like mine?' he heard Lucy say.

Jan couldn't have expected any more from his family and felt that the Greens, though unsure, would be impressed by the continental buffet. Peter wanted to pay for the spread as it always made him feel better to foot the bill, a sensitivity he passed on to his son. Francis T., however, wouldn't hear of it. They had arranged beforehand, with Jan as go between, that, as the Strang family had made the preparations, the bills would be sent to Francis T. to settle. The pianist's fee, however, was a matter of contention.

The rain held off that day and, despite news of the German bombardment of Reims, Jan and Eric just about managed to forget the war for a little while. This was despite the pianist's proclivity to play up-to-date jocular and morale-boosting songs.

Eric's speech, though short, was a respite for Jan who sighed in relief when Eric finished without having embarrassed him. Eric, in dramatic style, asked everyone to raise their glasses to the happy couple.

The sound of the pianist singing, 'Mademoiselle from Armentieres, Parley-voo? Mademoiselle from Armentieres, Parley-voo? Mademoiselle from Armentieres, She hasn't been kissed in forty years, Hinky, dinky, parley-voo,' reached Jan's ears, and he looked at Eric and raised his eyes to the ceiling. He let it pass this time because no one was really listening but when he came out with *A Little Bit of Cucumber* Jan left Lucy's side and went over to Eric.

'He thinks he's at the music hall. I can't take much more of this.'

They both went over for a word.

'Can't you play a waltz or two and some ragtime? We're not really in the mood for this,' Eric said.

'Sorry Guvnor. Just thought I'd cheer things up a bit,' the pianist replied.

He started to play a waltz and the front-room floor cleared. Jan took Lucy's hand and started the dancing. When Jan's feet continued moving every time the waltz hesitated, they tripped and stumbled together. Their audience laughed, and when they finished everyone clapped and Jan resigned himself to being the non-dancing type of man. Then more of the guests got up to dance and the children started to play around and enjoy the celebrations as the couple looked on.

Lucy mostly stayed close to Jan as she watched their families and friends chat and circulate. She wanted her sisters, Claire and Julia, to enjoy themselves and to dance and savour the rare freedom of drinking wine and mingling with the guests without being reprimanded by their parents for being impolite, unladylike or just plain silly. She felt pride watching the girls having a great time receiving compliments from the Strang's exotic circle. She knew that her sisters could hardly wait to be married. They had told her as much themselves.

For them it would be to escape their family as much as for anything else, but for Lucy it was for love. Lucy pulled Jan's sleeve to watch a tipsy Eric put his arm around Julia's waist and kiss her neck as they danced the second waltz. Julia giggled and pushed him away. Lucy and Jan laughed.

'That's his confidence shot for another six months,' Jan said.

For Lucy, the whole day had seemed unreal and here, at the reception, she blushed with embarrassment when she watched her uncles and aunts bumbling around. They were morons compared to Jan's bright cosmopolitan group. Seeing her father spend much of the reception puffing himself up and boring people with his tedious anecdotes and grumbles about the modern world increased her sense of being rescued by Jan from her suburban prison. She could see Karolina and Elina swerve to steer clear of her father and avoid his gaze as they handed out sandwiches and pickles and topped up drinks. She wished she had their fashion sense and the courage to wear bright colours, but then she realised that it was *she* who had been transformed, that it was *she* who was wearing a cream and lilac, Nouveaux wedding gown from Liberty's, that it was *she* who was wearing the dress that everyone admired and that it was *she* who was actually married to the tall handsome sophisticate and not them. She was the envy of all the women and girls and she felt wonderful.

How Gladys managed to drink and smoke and stay chatty and keep on her feet for the whole afternoon was beyond Lucy's ken. The only time Gladys toned her stories down was when Eva Lückes, her matron from The Whitechapel Hospital and family friend of the Strang's, came within range. Lucy wondered if she should drink more to make herself more sociable. She knew that she would never be able to keep guests entertained with wild laughter and vivid descriptions of hospital life and the behind-the-scenes goings on of the young nurses and wounded soldiers like

Gladys did. Even if she did drink at every opportunity, she just didn't have the life experience.

But she felt Jan's warm smile and knew that he understood and didn't mind her sheltered upbringing in a humdrum backwater. It was what Jan thought that mattered to her today. Actually, she was relieved that Gladys drew attention away from her and for this she silently thanked her. Lucy was worn out by telling her uneventful life history to the Strangs and their circle. They told her she was fascinating and beautiful but she knew they were just being polite.

She watched her mother enjoying meeting other people for the first time in years without her husband pushing in and dominating the conversation. Lucy's mother was never rid of her responsibilities and Lucy was damned if she would turn out like that.

'Thank God you're nothing like my father,' she whispered in Jan's ear, holding his arm.

Later in the afternoon, Claire, who had clearly drunk too much and was looking distinctly woozy, ran upstairs to the bathroom followed by her mother who quickly came back down red faced and flustered and trying not to show it.

'Claire's in a terrible way. I think it must have been those herrings. Can you come and help?' she asked Lucy.

'I'll come with you but if you think I'm mopping up after Claire on my wedding day you can think again.'

Their eyes met and her mother's flashed angrily. In that instant they both realised that the absolute power she had held over her daughter had left her back at the Registry Office. Lucy knew that now her mother would have to show her more respect.

They went upstairs to the bathroom, saw Claire, and locked the door behind them.

'Ahhurghh, I think I'm going to die,' Claire said, with her head over the toilet bowl and with regurgitated herring and onion clinging on to the ends of her long brown hair.

'Die of embarrassment, more like,' her mother said. 'It's Lucy's day and you have to do this. God help you if your father finds out.'

Lucy and her mother heard a man's footsteps coming up the stairs.

'Oh no I think I'm going to ….,' Claire said and threw up for the second time.

'Shhh, for heaven's sake be quiet,' Lucy whispered. 'You'll completely ruin the day if this gets out.'

'Are you okay there, do you need a hand?' Jan asked through the door.

'We're fine,' Lucy called out. Then, turning to Claire, she said in a hushed voice, 'Whatever will they think of us?'

They heard Jan's footsteps descend the stairs and Lucy felt some relief for her mother and sister that it hadn't been their father: that the immediate danger had passed. Lucy turned to Claire who was now sitting on the toilet seat whimpering with her head in her hands.

'Get up and splash some cold water on your face you stupid trollop and wash the ends of your hair. The place stinks to high heaven and so do you,' Lucy said.

'What were you thinking of drinking all that wine on top of those ghastly pickles?' her mother said.

'I'm sorry, I'm so sorry,' Claire cried.

Their mother got Claire cleaned up as Lucy watched from the edge of the bath.

'Can you use the other one down the landing please?' Lucy called out to Elina, who came along and rattled the door handle no doubt sensing something was wrong. 'I'm fine. I'll be out in a minute,' Lucy said to the closed door. She turned her head back and saw her mother rubbing Clair's back, 'I've saved your bacon today you two and don't you forget it.'

'I'm sorry. I'll be alright now,' Claire said.

Lucy opened the door and, having looked up and down the corridor, declared the coast clear. Claire emerged red-faced, cleaned and purged, followed by her frazzled mother.

When they got downstairs the party was in full swing. The pianist was playing his ragtime numbers. Lucy went straight over to Jan.

'You were in there for ages,' he said. 'Is everything alright?'

'I'll tell you later,' Lucy said. 'You wouldn't believe it.'

'Good-byee, Owld Gal, Good-byee,' the pianist bawled out in his north-London nasal accent.

'It's probably time we were going. Anyway, I can't take much more of this idiot. I'll get Eric to organise the send-off.'

Eric shouted everyone to attention. The guests applauded and jockeyed for position to kiss Lucy and shake Jan's hand as they left for the motor-taxi which was to take them to The Savoy. The pianist played them out with *Aba Daba Honeymoon*.

Jan's hackles seemed to be rising. Lucy held onto his arm.

'Not now darling,' she said in his ear, as he moved back to have another word with the pianist.

Chapter 6

29 March 1915

The Monday morning after their wedding, just as Eric had done before him, Jan signed up for four years in the 15th Battalion, London Regiment, Territorial Force. At home and at work no one wanted him to do it. Harry at the docks, though, didn't believe in bucking the trend. He'd said there was no point in fighting the inevitable and that it was better to fight the German war machine and have done with it. Harry was the wisest man Jan knew and deep down he had to agree with him.

There were so many recruits to process that it took the Army three weeks before they were ready to give him an official Medical Inspection. For Jan, these three weeks were the happiest in his and Lucy's lives so far. They avoided talking about the war and at home things couldn't have gone better.

Jan could tell that his mother took to Lucy straight away. He would overhear snippets of Eva and Lucy's conversations in the evenings as they washed up the dishes after dinner. They talked about fashion, art and music. Eva would tell her about Sweden and her home town of Sundsvall and that one day, when the war was over, they should all go and visit. Lucy told him how liberating it was to talk to his mother about areas of a woman's life that her own mother never talked about and probably never would. One night in bed Lucy, much to Jan's surprise and relief, told him that he didn't need to wear his French letter every time they made love. Eva had taught her to notice the times of the month when she would be safe and for a whole week they made love naturally, just like the first time in his office.

He introduced Lucy to the local pubs. In The Game Cock Lucy said she enjoyed it but couldn't drink more than three barley wines in any evening.

'I'm tired,' she said. 'I have to be on the ball for work in the morning. If I stay any longer, I'll need to wash the smell out of my clothes.'

Most times she would just have the one drink and go back to spend the evening with Eva and Peter. Jan was always home for ten o'clock. Sometimes Gladys joined them in the pub and, when she did, Lucy would stay until they closed at nine-thirty. And when Eric was home from training he would join them in The Game Cock or The Black Lion.

On the day of his medical, Jan thought of running away. It would be easy. He could simply jump on one of the timber ships going back to Sweden. Once there, he could send for Lucy and they could live out their lives there. Though totally feasible, he couldn't bring himself to do it. His destiny was set and irreversible.

He felt sick and had an overwhelming sense of impending doom as he lined up with the other men and stripped, cold and vulnerable, to his drawers. The medical was quick and routine: he was five foot-ten inches and his chest thirty-eight inches with 'girth fully expanded'. His vision was fine and his physical development 'very good'. He was passed as 'fit' for the Territorials as he knew he would be. His hand was trembling so much that he could hardly sign on the dotted line.

'Sorry Sergeant; had a bit of a heavy send off in the pub last night.'

'Don't worry Son, it's normal,' the Sergeant said.

On Tuesday 20 April, Jan, with a thousand others, left at three in the morning by train from Liverpool Street for his army training at Saffron Walden. As they squeezed into the cargo trucks, Jan joined in the chorus of *It's a Long Way to Tipperary* which they sang almost incessantly as the train rocked and bumped them together on the journey. By the time they got to Saffron Waldon he knew the words to the rest of the verses as well as *I'll make a Man of You* and many other songs.

They marched from the Saffron Waldon Station to their Stationary Training Camp, singing the same songs as they went. As the sun rose the wind got up and refreshed Jan's tired face. If it wasn't for the circumstances, he thought it would have been nicer to live here than London. Above the singing and the sound of boots clomping down on the road he could hear the dawn chorus. The hills and fields around the camp looked like a medieval encampment with hundreds of tents and union and regimental flags fluttering in the wind from the top of them. Banks of barely-covered latrines infused the air with a sickly smell.

The Army, unable to accommodate the thousands of new recruits, housed them twelve to a bell-tent, in camp beds. Their feet all pointed to the centre. He thought he'd heard everything when, on the first night, the Sergeant told them all to piss in their boots then tip them out under the tent flap. The Sergeant said it was to soften the leather and make marching easier. Nearly all his group were London men and there were quite a few clerks of Jan's ilk who had worked in offices and had similar occupations to him, so he quickly made some friends. Eric was there somewhere and he would track him down as soon as he could.

On their first full day, they trained for ten hours and Jan, who had always thought that he liked physical exercise, changed his mind. At the end of the day his feet throbbed and were sore with blisters. He ached from his toes up through his ankles, calves and knees to his thighs; his lower back ached the most. The straps of his sixty-pound haversack, that he had to wear for hours on end, cut into his shoulders making deep red marks. Throughout the day he became hot and sweaty, dizzy and faint. Three recruits collapsed in training. At the end of the day he caught the whiff of stale sweat on the other soldiers and understood that he must smell the same.

He looked for Eric that evening and tracked him down in one of the permanent barrack huts. They talked and smoked until just before lights-out at eight-thirty when Jan hurried back to his bell tent, canvas bed and the complaints of tired men. Eric gave him some *Elliman's* Liniment to rub on his legs. It smelt of turps and vinegar and heated up his skin, but what he really wanted was a hot bath. It was the first day that he'd worn a uniform since leaving Southgate College in 1902, when he was sixteen and had vowed never to wear one again.

After a month, Jan, and the men who arrived with him, moved from the bell tents with the canvas beds to dormitories like Eric's. The next batch of recruits took their places in the tents. Cast-iron beds now stretched in rows down the long wooden huts. A few oil lamps made reading easier. Jan kept his clothes and belongings in his trunk that doubled as a bedside table.

Lucy smelt the camp latrines from the train station. The morning mist hadn't lifted by the time she got there so the smell hung in the air. It was midday and five weeks after Jan started his training.

She was worried about Jan; he had so much to put up with. If she were in his place she didn't think she could bear it. He wrote to her every few days and she kept his letters and reread them before she replied to find hints of how she might be able to lift his spirits. Sometimes at night she would cry when she read his attempts to make light of his predicament. She had reread one of his first letters on the train:

My Darling Lucy,

I do hope all is well with you and all at Chichester Road. I'm surviving quite well considering the conditions. Don't forget, I went to boarding school and nothing could surprise me after that. I've seen it all before; most of it anyway.

I do miss my mother's cooking. My stomach's been up and down. They give us congealed stew with watery disintegrated potatoes for our dinner and greasy bacon and bread for breakfast, if we're lucky. We sometimes have an apple after our lunch and, when we do, I keep the core and give it to one of the deserving horses with whom I've made friends. They're teaching me how to ride but I keep falling off. You would really laugh if you saw me. We could do with more food to be honest. I would love some biscuits, and tea that actually tastes like tea.

I'm managing well enough though. Most of the men are cheerful and I get on well with the 'chums' in my tent. I tracked Eric down (he sends his very best) so we get together when time permits. We've swapped books and talk about home and the days when we could go and see a proper football match and have a decent pint. It all seems a lifetime away now. We play football here in the evenings sometimes (tell Father I'm on the right wing). I've learnt loads of new card games.

Eric was quite smitten by Julia at our Reception and has a bit of a crush. He wants to know if she minds if he writes to her.

I miss you all the time but it's worse at night. A few of the men snore badly and there have been some flared tempers. I don't let it worry me but, considering we have to get up at five-thirty, I always feel I could do with a good night's sleep.

Send my love to Mother, Father and Gladys. I can hardly wait to see you on 16th May.

All my love as always,

Jan xxx

She met Jan at the Training Camp gates and they walked to Saffron Waldon. Servicemen were everywhere, their faces grey and tired. The drab khaki uniforms gave the place a dullness that stayed with Lucy after she left. This wasn't the place for a man like Jan; he was sophisticated and needed to keep it hidden. Jan nodded when he recognised someone and they would nod back, and he would salute when he saw an officer even if he didn't know them. They all saluted officers. She felt uncomfortable when the men looked at her with greedy eyes.

'Take no notice,' Jan said. 'You're safe as long as I'm around.'

They drank tea and ate scones at The Regis tearoom in the town centre. 'The pubs are closed on Sunday, I'm sorry to say,' Jan said with a frown, but Lucy was pleased they were shut.

'You don't have to entertain me. I just want us to be close again,' she said, and stroked his calf with her foot under the table. She looked over at another table by a coat stand where a man was picking his nose with his little finger. He stared at it and then chewed it and didn't seem to mind at all that anyone saw him.

'Some of them are pigs,' Jan said with a resigned laugh.

'I brought you these,' she said, and handed him a bag of garibaldi biscuits and a blue, cloth-bound, copy of D. H. Laurence's, *The Rainbow*. 'It's just come out'.

Jan's eyes lit up. He flicked through some pages and looked at the gold lettering on the spine. He snapped it closed and put it in his inside tunic pocket.

'That's wonderful, I'll read it this week and pass it over to Eric.'

Lucy gave him a confident smile. 'I read it myself last week. It should brighten up your evenings.'

Just about all the men brought their visiting sweethearts to The Regis tea room. It was packed and the walls were lined with people waiting for vacated tables. As it was pretty much impossible to talk, they walked down the lanes arm in arm enjoying the spring air. Jan told Lucy that his years of experience of drinking with working men in dockland boozers and back street pubs was training enough for his time with the men here, but she didn't believe him. There was a difference between drinking with men when he could buy them drinks and purchase their friendship, and being with men at close quarters day after day for weeks on end. The lack of sophistication and home comforts was clearly wearing him down, even though he denied it. He told her how, apart from the few friends he'd made, the men teased and mimicked his accent and the way he walked.

'I'm sure they'll offer you a commission soon,' she said.

'It's not as simple as that. I have to do the basic training here first.'

'Well, after that, you can be with men more like you; the kind of men who understand that you need to read a book at night without being interrupted or laughed at.'

'Let's hope so,' he said without conviction.

Lucy wrote to Jan on most evenings after dinner. Eva would write a few lines of her own to put into Lucy's envelope and Lucy wondered why men found it so difficult to write a letter and say how much they missed someone. Jan did make an attempt, she had to give him that, but he was far from being an expert. Lucy told Jan when she was well and if she was ill, when she was happy and when she was sad. She put anything into the letters she thought might interest him and some things that she didn't; just to fill pages. Jan told her that he was amazed at the way she could make the daily events in her life appear interesting. He said that her letters were the highlight of his day.

She wrote about his family and her family, how her work had been; the problems with her supervisors and all the office gossip on which she could elaborate. She read Peter's *Times* and wrote to Jan about politics and the news from the war. Being ever mindful not to irk the camp's incoming letter censor, she packed her letters full of descriptions of nature: of the tree-lined avenues around Kilburn and of Queen's Park; the lake and the trees, flowers and wildlife in St James' Park where they used to meet for lunch. They were talking about draining the lake to make space for a training ground, she told him. She wrote of other people's dogs and cats around Chichester Road and learnt their names.

She never ran out of things to write about and always tried to include some of the hopes and ambitions she had for the two of them. She would suggest names for the children they would have after the war and write about how they would bring them up to be good peace-loving human beings. She talked of her fears for Jan and the other poor men and prayed that Jan would never actually have to fight or to ever kill a man.

One evening in June, Jan sat up on his bed and read her letter that came that day; it smelt of *eau de Cologne*. An extra page sealed with wax and folded neatly inside the main letter and envelope made him smile as he opened it. He loved surprises:

My darling Jan, it's so hot tonight I've come to bed early and am lying under a single sheet wearing nothing at all. I had to write to you here and now because I feel so passionate thinking about you. I could scream with desire. You have been on my mind all day and the feelings won't go away. Now they are increasing and when I touch my skin the feelings get stronger. I wish you were here to love me darling. I can't imagine how I'll get through the night without your touch.

Night-night, dearest Jan.
All my love,
Lucy. XXX

Jan read the letter over and over and couldn't disguise the smile on his face from the men in the dormitory.

'That's cheered you up. Give us a read,' Freddie Brown called out from the bed opposite.

'Bugger off,' Jan snapped, his heart beating from fear that the other men might get their hands on it and make him a laughing stock. It was just like at his old school, so he knew what to do. When the dormitory was empty he would cut a slit in his mattress with a razor blade and hide it in there. He could then read it when he needed excitement along with the others he hoped she'd send. Until that time he wouldn't let his letter leave his person for a second. He undid a button in his tunic and slid it in safely.

The next evening, he shied off when the other men were playing football. He penned his reply alone sitting on top of his bed:

Lucy darling, you are the most thoughtful girl in the world. Your letter really hit the spot. I wish I could write to you in a similar vein but the camp censor could read it and cause me great embarrassment. I have to be so guarded about what I write but please, when you can, send me more like this. It could actually make life here worth living. It excites me terribly.
 All my love,
 Jan xxx

The only time Jan had off was on Sunday afternoons and early evening, so Lucy would come on the train on Sundays, unless they had been cancelled. That summer, when the sun shone, they made love by the river where swallows and martins swooped down to pick flies from just above the water. Jan and Lucy would lie in the fields among the buttercups and purple grasses that covered them in clouds of pollen, and they would walk back to the camp hand in hand with dry grass and tiny spiders in their hair. On the days when it rained they would make love in a wood but if there was drizzle or the rain was light they would cuddle under a blanket in the fields. Neither had known such tenderness and obsession for another.

Jan now realised that he had always been lonely until he had married Lucy. he wanted to touch her constantly. She asked him teasingly if, or when, his passion would fade and he would tell her not to be silly and that he would always love her. Lucy would bring a blanket, some food and a couple of bottles of Worthington, which they would let cool in the river then drink after their lovemaking on the bank with their feet dangling in the water. When the sun hid behind the clouds, they would lie on their backs and look up at the sky and pick out shapes that reminded them of animals and mythical gods. They would laugh and hold hands wishing that these moments could be captured and returned to when times got hard. And in the weeks and months that followed they would remember the love and passion they shared by the river and in those fields.

Jan would take Lucy for a drink to The Cross Keys in Saffron Waldon. The 'Keys' was always busy and stayed open only because a diminished Essex constabulary turned a blind eye to the Sunday Drinking Laws. Lucy drank to keep Jan company, just as she had done back in Kilburn, but she became easily bored after an hour or so. It had always been clear to her that Jan enjoyed the pub. She watched his mood lift after the first few drinks. He would order them beer, pork pies and pickled eggs and onions that, after being washed down with the local ale, would burn in their stomachs and make them burp for the rest of the day. And they would laugh and look at the love in each other's eyes and hold each other as if they could never be parted.

They talked and talked. Lucy shared Jan's views on most things but knew when to keep her own counsel in a crowd. She had always admired the way that Eva and Peter had brought Jan up so that good manners were second nature to him. She would be sure to pass this down to their children after the war. Jan was so polite and calm and pleasant after a few drinks, but when he drank more than four or five he could scare her. On those Sundays at The Keys, Lucy learnt to disentangle him from the arguments that could follow when he took exception to other men's views.

'If you don't agree with them, say nothing,' she, who had twenty-seven years of dealing with an argumentative father, would say.

She had never really experienced mixing with rough men before and was sorry that Jan didn't have the choice. Feeling so uneasy in their company she would rather have gone to one of the farmhouses that sold tea and cakes to the soldiers. She said so but Jan ignored her. She hated the way the men lacked graces of any sort and used filthy language, even without a drink inside them. Lucy hated swearing. She felt for Jan and was sure that if she had to spend every day and night with such crassness she would have something to say as well. But it was the other men's opinions more than their crassness that spurred Jan's reactions in the pub. One Sunday afternoon in The Keys, a drunken soldier came over to their table and called him a 'bleeding cocksucker' who didn't know what a proper fight was. That he couldn't teach a child a lesson, let alone the Germans. She pulled Jan back to his chair firmly by his arm, just as he was about to get up.

'No Jan. Think it through, it's not worth it.'

'But he's asking for it.'

'My poor baby,' she said stroking his hair.

'Stop it. Don't do that,' he said pulling her hand away.

'Sorry.'

'No, no, I'm sorry it's just that…'

'What?'

'Well, it's just that…'

'Yes?'

'You don't understand. I have to stand up for myself. They'll rib me all week if I don't.'

'We don't have to come here every Sunday, do we? We *could* avoid this.'

'But it's the only chance I get for a drink all week.'

At the beginning of August, in Jan's fourth month at Saffron Waldon, Captain Carling called him in to his office in the parlour of the requisitioned farm house. Jan immediately wondered if his collection of letters from Lucy had been rumbled and he was in for a grilling. He knocked on the door.

'Enter.'

Jan walked in, stood to attention and saluted.

'Private Strang reporting, Sir.'

'Stand easy, Strang.'

'Yes, Sir.'

Captain Carling had the look of a gentleman officer. He was one of those white-moustached officers in ill-health who had been brought out of retirement to run the training camps. All the men understood that the old guard had little idea about modern warfare.

'Strang, we think you've made a good job of your time here and have kept your head in some tricky situations.'

'Thank you, Sir.'

'We think you'll make a good officer and I'd like to recommend you to train as a Second Lieutenant.' Captain Carling looked up from his desk and smiled. 'How do you feel about that?'

'I'd welcome it, Sir.'

'Well, I'm pleased to hear it.' Captain Carling stood up from his chair and shook Jan's hand. 'I'm sorry we're all in such a rush. In other circumstances we could have discussed it over a drink.'

'I understand, Sir,' Jan said, returning the smile.

'You'll need to finish your training here, of course.'

'Yes, sir.'

Captain Carling sat down behind his desk. 'If all goes according to plan you'll be transferred to the Inns of Court Officer Training Camp in Berkhampsted in October. They'll teach you how to ride a horse…,' he looked up and grinned; '… a bit better than you can now; field tactics, of course, and ways to command the respect of your men.'

'I'd like that, Sir.'

That night Jan wrote to Lucy:

4th August 1915

My Darling Lucy,

I just had to tell you. I've been to see Captain Carling today. He says they want me to train for a commission when I've finished here in October. It's in Berkhampsted and I'll be able to get home some weekends and you should be able to visit any Sunday.

Isn't it wonderful? I won't be going to war, not for a good while anyway. I'm brimming with pride that they think I can do it. I'll have to ride a horse properly and learn how to gallop into battle. Let's hope it never comes to that.

Eric finishes his training in three weeks and will be off to Flanders. I'll miss him.

I'm so looking forward to seeing you on Sunday and not just for the biscuits.
All my love,
Jan xxx

Chapter 7

Saturday 9 September 1916. Victoria Station.

'If you get hurt,' Lucy said, handing Jan a small, flat tin of morphia pills that she had bought for him from Savory & Moore's. 'Put one of these under your tongue and it'll take the pain away.'

Jan's parents were looking the other way.

'I don't think you're supposed to have them so keep them hidden,' Lucy said, and smiled at him, but they both knew each other too well to be fooled by smiles on a day like this.

'I'll only use them if I have to,' he said, knowing that he'd use them sooner than that. There was a slight tremor in his voice that was the result not of fear of the front line but of last night's farewell drinking session with his chums at The Game Cock, where he drank so much light ale, barley wine and whiskey that he didn't remember getting home. Lucy said she watched him fall through the front door when he came back and helped him to bed. Jan thought she had every right to give him hell today and was expecting some reprimand but she didn't even mention it and, because she didn't, he felt more guilt. With cold fingers she placed into his hand a small strange wood-carved figure about an inch long.

'Take this with you for good luck,' she said.

'What is it?' Jan asked.

'It's called a touchwood and you touch it when you want –'

'Good luck,' Peter, who had just sidled up next to them, said.

'Exactly,' Lucy said.

'I'll need to touch it all the time in that case,' Jan said, as he put his arms around her and kissed her on her head. 'I love you,' he said into her ear.

'And I love you,' she whispered back.

A loud hoot sounded from the straining steam engine. It pierced Jan's ears. A great cloud of steam hissed as it rose from the funnel at the front of the locomotive. Eva and Peter stood on the platform next to Lucy, both waiting their turn to wish him farewell.

'Do be careful,' his mother said as Jan bent down to kiss her on the cheek.

'I'll be fine and back home for Christmas,' he said, wrapping his arms around her. She looked up to him and kissed him then turned the other way hiding her face.

'She'll be fine soon. Don't worry,' Peter said, and slipped him a half bottle of whiskey when Eva's back was turned. 'Don't tell your mother,' he said in Jan's ear.

Jan quickly put it in his trench-coat inside-pocket.

'Good luck Son.' Peter shook Jan's hand warmly.

'Thanks, I'll need it.' Jan turned back to Lucy and squeezed her to him for one last time. Showing no emotion he turned his back on the three of them and climbed up into the train.

It was a dank and drizzly day. The weather matched his mood. He felt sick to the depths of his stomach. Last night's booze was wearing off and indigestion burned and bubbled up his oesophagus. Waving at Lucy and his parents from the window he saw hundreds of men squeezing into the carriages heading for Southampton and the troop ship to Le Havre. Some soldiers didn't appear to have loved ones to see them off. Others, apparently unable to face farewells, boarded the train without looking back.

The noise on the platform resounded around the station and into the carriages: Boots clattered on stone as soldiers ran down the stone slabs. Doors banged and shouts from on and off the train created a cacophony in Jan's head. Windows crashed down and a thousand men or more tried to hang their heads out for a last wave, look or blown kiss. They all pretended cheerfulness amid the morning mist, steam and the confusion of hurried goodbyes. It was the ones who waved them off that cried, not the men. As the train slowly pulled out from the platform, a deafening noise of cheers and yells erupted but when the train picked up momentum and left the station, the cheers rang hollow and petered off. The smiles left the men's faces and near silence descended. Then there was only the clackety-clack of the carriage wheels left to echo round Jan's head.

He made his way down the corridor to his officer's compartment. Two fresh-faced officers were already settling down.

'Is this seat taken?' Jan asked, smiling at them as he sat down and the train picked up speed.

'I see you're with the Rifles,' one of them said.

'Oh yes, that's right,' Jan replied. 'Sorry, I was miles away.'

'Not far to come then?' the other asked.

'No, not too far. What about you?'

'Oh, we came down from Lancaster overnight; with the King's Own. Phew what a trip that was,' he said, wiping his brow and winking at his friend.

His friend smiled. 'We polished off a bottle of scotch; wish we hadn't now. I could have done with the sleep to be honest.'

'Well, my name's Strang, Jan Strang.' Jan offered his hand. They had a couple of day's growth on their chins and it looked like fluff. Surely they were too young to be officers.

'And I'm Harry Lewis and this is Ernie Illingworth,' Harry said, and they all shook hands and chatted.

The conversation petered out and Jan reached into his pocket for the half-bottle of whiskey his father had given him. As he felt his hand on the stopper, he changed his mind. A hair of the dog would have settled his queasiness and he could pass it over to the boys who would probably have felt better for it, but he was an officer and had to keep up appearances. He had to remember that. He would be leading his first platoon when they got to Southampton.

'I had a heavy night myself. It's all coming back to me now, I'm afraid,' Jan said looking at Harry and Ernie as they all shared a laugh. Then the wooden carriage door slid open and another five officers of various builds and ages came in.

'Morning chaps, budge up,' a fifty-year-old from Wales with a handle-bar moustache said.

'Morning,' they all replied as they shuffled up and put their bags on the overhead criss-crossed net-luggage rack. The introductions started all over again. After about fifteen minutes the conversations died down and they all settled down to read papers and stare out of the window; to be left with their private thoughts.

Jan unwrapped the brown paper around the cheese and chutney sandwich that Lucy had made for him before they left. He ate it and felt a little better. He wiped his fingers and his mouth on his clean, freshly-ironed handkerchief. He crossed his legs, picked up *The Times*, turned to the 'Roll of Honour' and scanned the figures: 142 Casualties to Officers', 70 Australian Losses and 4,890 Losses in the Ranks. After checking that no one he knew had been killed or wounded he turned the page.

'There's some good news here,' he said out loud. 'It says: "The broad feature of the situation upon all fronts is that the enemy have been reduced to the defensive. The longer the enemy dash their heads against Verdun the better for the Allies."'

'That looks promising,' the fifty-year-old Welshman said, and they all agreed.

Jan shuddered, put the paper down and wished he hadn't said anything. He hated drawing attention to himself.

The compartment rattled and the train wheels followed a familiar oscillation. He tapped his fingers on the arm rest; he'd heard the rhythm before the war in one of the Piccadilly clubs before he and Lucy got married. He put his paper down and asked if anyone else wanted to read it, then folded it in half and passed it to the Welshman. Jan's thoughts turned to Lucy. He missed her already and knew that he would never be able to talk to anyone the way he could with her. Lucy understood him as nobody else ever would or could. If he managed by some miracle to survive they would build such a wonderful life together.

Jan looked out of the window and watched the scenery fly past. The whole world was in some kind of irreversible bloody delusion. There was no sign of the war ending either. It was a bloody stalemate. He might end up mad like some of the men he saw on the street and in the pubs and, if he did, he hoped Lucy could still love him.

Bored of countryside seen through mist and drizzle and droplets forced northwards on the window, Jan cast a glance at Harry and Ernie. They were too young to die but then so were they all. He turned his gaze to a thirty-something officer opposite him. Most likely he had a wife and children. Then he looked at the next officer and the one after that. And he went, in turn, through all of them and imagined what their lives were like and who they had left behind.

'Mind if I open the window?' he asked.

'No, not at all; please do,' they mumbled, and Jan leaned up and slid the top window open allowing the stale air and tobacco smoke to be replaced by fresh damp air. He coughed and looked out at what might be one of his last views of England then lit a cigarette and offered them round. As the train drew up to Southampton Station, Jan sensed their trepidations.

'The time of reckoning approacheth,' the Welsh officer said. 'Better wait for the men to get off first. We officers don't want to get ruffled in the crush; best to look dignified, eh?' he said making an exaggerated twiddle of his moustache.

On the platform Jan saw a sergeant walking towards him with a baton tucked underneath his arm. His stride had purpose.

'Gud afternoon, gentlemen. I'm looking for Lieutenant Strang,' he said to a group of men nearby.

'That's me,' Jan said.

'Gud afternoon, Sar,' he said saluting. 'I'm a Sergeant Crawford, awaiting odders Saar.'

'Pleased to meet you Crawford. Gather the men and round them up outside the station please Sergeant; I'd like to address them myself to begin with.'

Crawford went off and rounded them up.

'Arteenshun!' he belted out, once he had them standing in four straight lines. 'Men salute,' he ordered. Then he turned to Jan. 'They're all yours, Saar.'

Jan thanked him, breathed in deeply, pulled his shoulders back, exhaled and turned to the men; there must have been fifty of them. His knees shook.

'Now listen to me men. I'm your CO. We'll be seeing a lot of each other in the next weeks and months and we will face challenges that will test us to the limit.'

A man shuffled his feet in the back row; another at the front looked straight into Jan's eyes, fixed on his every word.

'Whatever happens I want you all to never forget that we are the Post Office Rifles and we have a reputation to maintain. We must support each other at all times and strike the fear of God into the enemy.' Jan turned to Crawford and nodded.

'Hip! Hip!' Sergeant Crawford yelled out

'Hooray!' they all responded. 'Hooray!'

Jan felt invigorated now and his head had completely cleared. 'Now I want you all to stand up straight, hold on to your caps and kit bags and march down to the troop ship. Thank you, men.' He turned to Crawford. 'They're all yours Sergeant.'

'Yes Saar! 'Men, by the left quick maarrch…'

Jan's heart beat fast and his back was wet with sweat. That went well, he thought as he marched behind the men to the *Invicta* that would take them over the Channel. Down at the dockside the men's march slowed to a walk as they crossed the gang plank. The ship rocked and knocked against the quay After a couple of hours they steamed off to Le Havre.

'Stormy weather,' Jan said to Sergeant Crawford on deck.

'Yes, Saar.'

Lucy, Eva and Peter waved goodbye to Jan and headed off home on the Kilburn train. Lucy felt queasy in her stomach which she took as an omen. She felt an air of foreboding settle around them in the carriage. Eva was first to break the spell. She turned her head to Lucy.

'How are you feeling now, dear?'

Lucy had been staring at the reflections in the carriage window. 'Actually, I'm not sure, it still hasn't really sunk in; sort of numb I suppose. I never really thought we'd seen enough of each other since his training. But what about you? It must be awful for you seeing Jan go off like that.'

'I pray for him and those other poor men and the horses,' Eva said.

'So do I. It's all we can do,' Lucy said.

Peter reached out and held Eva's hand. 'We have to trust that they know what they're doing; we've really no choice.'

'But they *don't* know what they're doing. That's the problem,' Lucy said.

'I know,' Eva said, as the train pulled into Queens Park.

'Come on, let's get back and light the fire,' Peter said, with Eva holding on to his arm. Lucy wondered if she'd ever hold onto Jan's arm again as they turned into Kilburn Lane and walked in the damp air back to Chichester Road.

Peter helped Eva and Lucy off with their coats and hung them on the hat stand by the front door. Eva started to talk as they went into the living room:

'I'll put the kettle on. It's such mucky weather. I think we're all ready for a cup of tea aren't we? I'll make some sandwiches for lunch, shall I? I've got a lovely piece of cheese and some nice tomatoes.'

Lucy welled with concern as she followed Eva into the kitchen.

'We used to have a lovely girl helping us before the war' said Eva. 'She's making shells in a factory now.'

Eva filled the kettle. Lucy looked and listened, she'd heard the story before. 'I bumped into her the other day, she looked terrible; yellow skin. She's working a twelve-hour day and it's very hard work, she says, very hot and no men for the heavy lifting. Dorothy was always a lovely girl. We just called her Dot. I know her mother - such a nice family,' Eva said, lighting the gas stove with a safety match.

'Shall we just have tea for now and leave the sandwiches for later?' Lucy asked, hoping Eva would relax.

'You're such a good girl Lucy; so thoughtful,' Eva said.

Lucy held her close to her chest and Eva gently rested her head on Lucy's shoulder. They made the tea together and Lucy brought it in on a tray and put it on the side table. Lucy poured out three cups with milk and handed one to Peter. When she sat down, Peter offered her one of his cigarettes. She drew the smoke in and felt it calm her nerves. She sat down, crossed her legs, swept her hair off her face and leant back.

'I don't understand why all this has to be,' Lucy said, addressing neither of them in particular.

Peter looked at her and nodded. Eva looked outside through the window. 'The mist's turning into quite a fog.'

'If we could bottle it up and send it over to the front, the Germans could choke to death on it,' Peter said and then turned to Lucy. 'I really am sorry Jan got into such a state last night. I think he's fallen in with a bad crowd down at the pub. I'm always telling him he should find a nice club if he wants a drink but he doesn't listen to me. He never has.'

'It doesn't matter now,' Lucy said and rested her cigarette in the ashtray beside her. 'I don't know what I'll do if he doesn't come back to me, you hear of such terrible things; so many dead and wounded. London's full of amputees everywhere you look.' She blew her nose into her hankie then pulled on her cigarette. 'All the girls at work have lost someone they know. Everyday there's more bad news.'

'Well, the Americans should be coming in soon and that'll finish off the Germans,' Peter said.

'How do you know?' Lucy snapped. 'They haven't come in so far, why would they now?'

'Well, you see, it's because …'

'Not now, thank you,' Eva said. She sat next to Lucy on the settee. 'Try to be strong, dear.' Eva held Lucy and Lucy put her arm around Eva's shoulders. 'We'll get through this together. Jan's always had the luck of the devil. He'll be home again soon enough. You'll see.'

Jan felt tired now. He found his way to his officer's cabin where he went through more introductions with more fellow officers. A forceful westerly wind threw waves up and the *Invicta* rose and fell. They could hear the crests crashing down on the deck.

'It's a rough sea even for the time of year,' Lieutenant Charlie Baker, who seemed to know what he was talking about, said.

Jan lay back on his bunk. He thought it only polite to reply.

'I know. We don't have far to go though. We'll be over on the other side soon enough.'

'It'll be five or six hours in this weather. Then we may have to wait a while to dock. There's a lot of traffic both ways,' Charlie Baker said.

'Best not to eat anything, till we get over the other side,' said Second Lieutenant Jack Bell.

The storm got worse as the *Invicta* steamed out across the Channel and Jan's stomach churned. He got up from his bunk.

'Just off to get some air,' he said.

'Better to stay where you are,' Charlie Baker said.

'Don't worry about me,' Jan said, closing the cabin door behind him.

The stairs to the top deck were roped off and the doors to the outer decks were locked. Swaying from side to side with the movement of the ship, Jan clambered down to the lower decks. In front of him men clung to rope banisters to save them from keeling over. A man sat with his head between his knees. Jan steadied himself and breathed in deeply, but the air was fetid and sickly sweet. He watched as men keeled over and others were sick into thick brown-paper bags. There weren't enough bags to go round, so they used anything they could get their hands on that might hold the vomit, even their caps. Jan went along the deck just as a man projected spew in front of him, missing him by inches. Sick-bags broke as they became soggy and spilled on the already wet boards. Some men had sick down the front of their uniforms and the stench made Jan's stomach churn. His feet slipped on the deck and he leant against the wall clinging to the rope to stop from falling. His head spun. He could hear the desperate noises of the horses and dogs panicking in the hold below. The undigested remains of Lucy's cheese and chutney sandwich that he ate on the train started to rise up from his stomach. Opening a sick-bag just in time, he spewed into it. His head went dizzy and he felt like death. His legs buckled underneath him and he sat on the deck. Wetness soaked through the seat of his trousers and he rose a little on his haunches. A man saluted him with a smirk.

'Are you owlrite, Sir?'

'I'll b.. be fine.'

Jan pushed his way along the swaying deck searching for fresh air. He reached a port hole and opened it. Water from a wave rushed in followed by fresh sea air infused with salt spray. It covered his face. He breathed deeply then grabbed his sick-bag and dropped it through the port hole and into the sea before the paper split open. Another wave whooshed in through the porthole and Jan stepped aside as it hit the deck. He pushed it closed and made his way back to the cabin where, hardly able to stand and without speaking, he stumbled to the basin and splashed his face with cold water. He perched on the edge of the chair by his bunk, took off his puttees, boots and tunic and tucked them under the chair. He pulled down his serge wool trousers and rinsed the seat in the sink then hung them over the back of the chair.

'You look like death warmed up, Strang,' Second Lieutenant Jack Bell said as Jan lay down on his horsehair mattress.

'I know. I hope I can sleep it off.'

When the others settled down to sleep he sat up then gradually moved his hand to the chair and pulled out his tunic from under it. Feeling for the breast pocket he found the little tin Lucy had given him back at Victoria. He kept it tight in his hand and opened it under the blanket. He touched the tablets. Holding one between his index finger and thumb he put it under his tongue and let it melt. The ship rose and fell and Jan floated away in his mind to the days before the war. His head slumped forward. He dribbled down his chin and breathed noisily through his mouth. Within a few minutes the drug deadened the sickness in his stomach and washed into his system. His brain swam and then eased as he floated down a meandering river into sleep. But it was a restless sleep. His body burned and he twitched, turned and sweated. He called out 'Lucy' so loudly it woke the three other officers. He was hardly aware of them trying to shake him out of it.

'How are you Strang?' Jack Bell asked in the morning as Jan stretched his arms out and rubbed his eyes. 'You had us worried for a while there last night. You'll have to hurry, we're docking now.'

Jan felt panic as he realised he'd have to address his platoon before the train to Zillebeke and the Salient. His mouth felt like a rat had spent the night there and defecated on his tongue. He washed his face and hands in the sink and cursed as he cut himself on the neck with his safety razor.

'When do we get to meet our batmen?' he asked when he'd dried his face, wishing that someone could pack his stuff up for him.

'After we've landed and before we set off for the front, I should think,' Jack Bell said.

'Don't worry; no one will notice how ill you look. I was sick myself in the sink.' Charlie Baker said whilst packing up his things.

Jack Bell pulled a face. 'Most of the boat's been sick, or wished they had been. They'll all be too off-colour to care what you say. That's if they're listening. Once we get on shore they'll be serving up breakfast. You'll feel better after that.'

Jan looked at him shocked. Breakfast was the last thing on his mind. He felt nauseous. He dry-retched and managed to hide it from the others by turning the other way. He breathed in and turned back round to face them.

'Thanks Charlie,' he said with a smile. 'I'm sure I'll come round, in a bit.'

Jan sat on the upper deck looking out to Le Havre. Gulls of different sizes swooped around the ship filling the air with a kwaa kwaa sound. The sky had cleared, the sun shone and the morning breeze was blowing away the sickly smell of last night's vomit from the ship. Men washed the lower decks with mops and buckets but a nauseous smell still rose up from the hold where the horses were stowed. Some of the poor creatures, he heard, had been so terrorised during the crossing that they had died or were deliberately bled to death on the voyage.

The *Invicta* would have to stay anchored for at least two hours. It had to make way for the hospital ship HMHS *Salta* to leave the Quai d'Escale on its way home to Blighty. It felt like a stay of execution for Jan; a couple of hours to collect himself. Gossip was spreading that heavy casualties were being felt on the salient near Ypres. Nothing new, he thought, and reflected on what might happen to the spirits of the war-dead. He wondered if they returned home *en masse* to be with their families, like the wounded coming back in the hospital ships. More probable, he thought, that they roamed around the battle fields, lost and confused. Jan felt a bit better each time he breathed in the morning air. As he expanded his lungs he visualised taking control of the platoon with authority, just like he had been trained to. He swigged water from his regulation bottle and splashed some on his forehead. 'It's the boredom that can be the biggest enemy. It's all about patience and waiting,' Jan remembered Sergeant Major Walters saying to him back at the Officer's Training Camp.

He needed to stiffen his resolve and pass the time. The only thing that could possibly get him through the war in one piece was his training. With a pencil in his right hand, and a cigarette in the left, he wrote a list in a note pad on his knee: *1)Duty to the men 2)Behave like a leader 3) Appear to be infallible and never let it slip no matter what…* . The pencil tip snapped as he underlined the last words. Oh what's the bloody point, he thought. I'll probably be dead by Christmas. His cigarette burnt his fingers. He flicked the stub away and leant back against a cabin wall. He closed his eyes and drifted off.

In his mind's eye he could see Colonel Errington barking advice from the saddle of his grey stallion in his final address to the newly commissioned officers. 'Never swear in front of the men and never let them see you drunk or show the slightest sign of weakness or lack of resolve. You're all representatives of the Inns of Court Training Corps …' The image went away and then returned. 'When you're in a tight spot,' the Colonel whacked his palm with his baton as he dismounted and strode down the line of lieutenants, 'remember: self-control, self-reliance and action. Always maintain strict discipline, it encourages keenness, saves lives and bonds the men. Mark my words; they could very well save you and your platoon. Now go out and win the war! We are the Devil's own.'

A shadow blocked out the sun's rays that were warming Jan's face. He came round suddenly with 'Devil's Own', 'Devil's Own', ringing in his head. He opened his eyes. A major stood in front of him,

'Oh, sorry Sir.' Jan moved to stand up. 'I must have drifted off.' He spoke so softly that the major didn't hear him.

'Attention, officer!' the major said.

Jan quickly rose to his feet and saluted. 'Sir!'

'Look lively lieutenant, we'll be embarking soon.'

'Yes Sir. Of course, Sir.'

A ship's horn sounded from the harbour. The major turned round and they both watched the HMHS *Salta* steam out into the Channel. A loud cheering noise rose up from both ships. The major left him. Men on their respective decks waved to each other.

'Good luck Tommy,' they called from the *Salta*. Jan undid a button on the top of his tunic and held the touchwood around his neck with his fingers and thought of Lucy.

The slow methodical grind of the anchor being pulled up grated on Jan's ears. The ship shuddered as the engines fired and propellers slowly turned. The *Invicta* inched its way into the harbour, sidled up to the quay and banged against the boards that lined the stone walls. Men from the ship threw ropes over the side and men on the quay wrapped them round capstans, pulling the ship snug to the quayside. Hundreds of soldiers that had been penned into the lower decks raised a cheer as the gangplank lowered and fell with a bang and a crash on the stone.

Jan caught sight of his cabin mates and joined them and a group of about twenty officers. They walked down along the gangplank onto the dockside. The troops followed, marched by their sergeants.

'They look like shite,' Charlie Baker said, turning to Jan.

'Like I feel,' Jan said. He held his head up and took a deep breath.

The horses followed the men off the ship, staggering and neighing down the gangplank with their handlers in front and behind. The more distressed horses were lifted off with slings but most appeared relieved to be out of the ship's hold. Mules followed the horses with assorted small dogs behind them, barking and whining in wooden crates on trolleys. One of the crates slipped from the men's hands and the catches on the door broke open. Four frightened terriers scampered off into the crowd and out of sight. Wicker boxes of carrier pigeons cooing to be released were carried off after the dogs.

Hearing Sergeant Crawford's voice bellowing out orders to his men Jan thought he'd better walk over to join them when he felt a warm rubbing on the back of his legs. Looking down he saw a bedraggled terrier looking back up at him with wide brown eyes. He felt warm in his heart. It could only have been two or three years old: it was predominantly dirty-white and brown with a black and tan patch over its right eye. Its left ear was bent. It sat on its hind legs, raised its forelegs and pawed the air then scratched Jan's boots.

Jan crouched down to stroke it as it wagged its tail relentlessly. It squatted and a trickle of yellow liquid flowed from its behind onto the cobbles. It was a bitch. Jan picked her up and she licked his chin and the cut on his neck. A Private came up to him.

'Lieutenant Strang, Sir,' he said, saluting.

'Yes?' Jan put the terrier down. It didn't move from his side.

'I'm Jimmy Rutter; your servant, Sir.'

'Well I'm very pleased to meet you Rutter.' Jan looked him up and down. He was small, only about five foot four, with cheery smile and a bent nose.

'Fank you, Sir.'

'I think we have a difficult day ahead of us, Rutter.'

'Yes Sir,' he said, saluting again.

'We'll be at Zillebeke by the end of the day.'

'Yes, Sir. They need our support, Sir.'

'That's right.' Jan felt his heart palpitate. 'At ease, Rutter; no need to salute all the time.'

Rutter moved his legs apart and held his hands behind his back.

'Fank you, Sir. Is there anyfing I can do for you now', Sir?'

'Well yes Rutter, you can find my kit when it comes off the boat. It's all labelled.' Rutter looked at Jan, alert and attentive.

'I'll track down Sergeant Crawford. I heard him a moment ago. He'll get the men together,' he said.

Jan pointed to an old four-storey wool warehouse across the road. 'We need to wait in the building over there until we get notice of which train we're on. There'll be food and tea; coffee if we're lucky.'

The dog whined and nibbled at Jan's trouser leg. They both looked down at her.

'I think we need a mascot for the platoon, don't you, Rutter?'

'Yes Sir.'

'Any ideas for a name?'

'Well Sir, if you don't mind me saying Sir?'

'Yes Rutter?'

'Well she does niff a bit.'

'Yes, she does, doesn't she?'

'We could call her Stinker".,' Rutter smiled.

'Good name, Rutter.'

'Fank you, Sir.'

'Can you find some string for a lead and some water to give her a bit of a wash?'

'I'll do my best, Sir.' Rutter picked Stinker up and carried her off.

'She's one of the Devil's Own now.' Jan walked off, baton in hand, to find Sergeant Crawford and his men. 'We've a long day ahead of us,' he called back to Rutter but he was gone.

PART II

Chapter 8

18 December 1916

Stretcher Bearers roamed no-man's-land to reach the wounded before they bled to death. In the aftermath of battle, Jan lay in the swampy mud, his life seeping out of him, his shivering terrier nestling between his right arm and chest.

Cordite from the high-explosive shells infused the morning mist. Whatever horror they came upon, nothing was new or could surprise stretcher bearers Chas and Mark. They were long accustomed to the smell of rotting flesh, both human and animal, and the odour of quicklime used to hasten decomposition. But they never got used to the bitter taste of cordite that burned in their throats and noses. They wrapped whatever fabric they could lay their hands on around their faces and tied it up at the back of their heads and breathed through that. Their backs ached from the hundreds of times they had to bend down and pick up bodies in the freezing damp.

Jan heard them come close. Trapped in his wounded body he couldn't move or speak out but he could hear what they were saying.

'Sod all we can do for this one, best leave him,' Chas said looking down at Jan.

'Hang on Chas, it's Strang,' Mark said.

'Oh, God yes, I recognize him now.'

'Look, the shrapnel's gone straight through is helmet, poor bugger.

'Christ, it looks bad,' Chas said.

'Sorry Sir, you're gonna feel it when we move you,' Mark said, looking into Jan's eyes. Mark turned his head to Chas and snapped. 'Give us a hand quick, will you? They'll be firing shells again, soon as day breaks.'

'I always liked Strang, treated me like a human bein, not like some of them idiots, know what I mean?'

'Course I do but if you don't hurry up and get im on the stretcher he ain't gonna make it.' He bent down to move Jan onto the stretcher. 'God it's cold! I can ardly move me sodding fingers.'

Camouflaged with filth thrown up from yesterday's exploding shells, Stinker's head poked out from between Jan's right arm and his chest.

'Mark, hey, look here at this little dog.'

'Ahh. It's shivering with cold.

'With fright, more like.'

'I feel sorry for the dogs; they done nuffin do to deserve this.'

'What did any of us ever do?'

'I know.'

Jan tried to cry out as they moved him but couldn't. His facial muscles contorted and he screamed inside instead. Surely there could be no worse hell than this.

Chas knelt by Jan's head. 'It's awlright Sir, we'll get you safe but we have to move you and it's gonna hurt.'

As they lifted him onto the stretcher Jan, through the finest slit in his eyes, could just make out Stinker's brown eyes following his movements. He felt string tighten and dig into his ankles as they tied them together to contain the spasms as his legs and torso convulsed.

'Give him some morph for God's sake,' Chas said.

'There's not much left and I want some later,' Mark said, taking out his syringe from his shoulder bag. 'There's a bit left in the syringe.' He stuck the needle in through a vein on the back of Jan's hand. Jan hardly felt it. 'Sorry Sir, it won't be long now but we can't move fast; too many bleedin potholes and dead.'

Jan felt Chas' hand reach inside his trench coat and pull out his half-bottle of scotch. He heard the squeak of cork on glass as Chas pulled out the stopper to take a drink. Jan struggled to open his eyes enough to make out what was happening. He watched Mark wipe the top of his whiskey bottle with his hand and take a swig. They're robbing me, he thought, and they'll leave me for dead. Jan felt Mark lifting his back and pain shot through his arm. Supported by Mark he sat half upright resigned to whatever they were going to do to him.

'Here, get some of this down you,' Mark said.

He tilted Jan's head back, pulled his bottom jaw open and held his head between his fore and upper arm.

Chas rested the bottle on Jan's bottom lip and gently poured some whiskey out holding the bottle with two hands. Jan swallowed, spluttered, and then went rigid as an agonising pain shot down from his head. He felt some warmth from the liquor seeping into his stomach and became still. He closed his eyelids and felt Chas put the bottle back into his coat pocket where he had kept it safe since his father gave it to him on Victoria Station.

The sky became lighter as day broke and they carried him away. Jan flickered his eyelids open. He watched sleet fly straight into Chas' face as he stepped over what Jan presumed were shell holes, barbed wire, shell casings, dead bodies and God knows what else. Stinker ran by the side of the stretcher jumping and hopping over the obstacles, pulling her legs out of the mud when they sank in. As they put the stretcher down for a rest, Jan felt the splash of cold wet dirt on his face as Stinker shook the mud from her body. Jan's senses hadn't deadened much despite the shot of morphine in his vein and that glug of whiskey in his stomach. He felt frozen to the bone.

At the Dressing Station, they laid him down on the ground in the officer's portion of the tent. Lying motionless with eyes closed Jan drifted in and out of consciousness. He woke suddenly as an elbow from an officer next to him caught him in the face. Stretcher bearers were talking around him.

'I can't go on much longer, I'm serious. I'm not going out again. I'm completely knackered. Can't hardly move me legs and I'm piss wet through with … God knows what festering shite's in them shell holes. I'm covered in blood, lice and Christ knows what else. I need new boots. I'm sick to the back teeth. I've a good mind to shoot myself through the bloody foot, then I'll be out this friggin place,' one of them said.

'Shuddup will you, you bleedin' idiot. The tent's full of officers, they'll have you on a charge. You know what some of them bastards are like,' said another.

'Don't be daft, they're all half dead. I don't give a dam anyway.'

MO Garnett came in the tent, rain dripping from his hair.

'Here's another one for you. I don't s'pose he'll hang on for much longer,' Mark said.

'And look after the dog, will you?' Chas said.

'What's its name? It doesn't alf stink,' MO Garnett said.

'The whole place stinks,' Chas said. 'What's the difference?'

MO Garnett looked Jan up and down.

'He's out cold.' His fingers pressed in on Jan's jugular vein. 'He's alive, just. I can't work miracles you know. Miss Granger, can you dress this one? Just clean and staunch the wounds if they open up. We'll get his helmet off and the shrapnel out when I come back. If he wakes, give him morphine.'

'Yes Sir,' she said.

Jan twitched and half opened his left eye. He heard a whimper and watched the VAD stroke Stinker on the head. '

You naughty girl, you've made my hand all dirty.'

He half opened the other eye to see her wiping her hand six inches above the hem of her grey gown that had soaked up wet mud from the ground.

'What's your name tiny girl? Now just wait there and I'll bring you something nice.'

When she left, Stinker snuggled up to Jan's side. Jan now felt far away from the war and warmer than he had done in a long time.

He woke later with two figures peering down at him. The MO and the VAD propped Jan up against the side of the tent. Stinker licked Jan's fingers and looked up at the proceedings. The VAD tried to move her away; Stinker struggled and curled her upper lip. Two pairs of shadowy hands moved toward his helmet and gripped its steel edge on the sides by his ears. In a series of short back-and-forward, side-by-side and upward movements the helmet began to ease off his head. Jan breathed unsteadily. Fear and panic made his heart pound. They must have thought that he was, near as damn it, dead to the world around him, but he could see what was going on. He heard little sucking and slurping sounds as they wiggled the piece of metal out of his skull.

His arm hurt like hell and he thought it strange that he felt less pain from his head than from his arm. It throbbed in time to his pounding heart. Half of him wanted to die now and get it over with and the other half wanted to live and spend his life happily with Lucy, if that could ever be possible after this. He might end up a cripple or an imbecile.

They lifted his helmet off with the main piece of shrapnel attached to it. They said it had penetrated his head by over an inch. Jan felt himself drifting out of consciousness but could just hear as they used tweezers to pick small pieces of metal out of his head, which made a clink that echoed as they dropped them into the enamelled kidney dish. They washed the wound and staunched the blood and he felt them wrapping the bandages over and round his head and under his chin. His eyes flickered as the VAD cleaned his arm and dabbed it with iodine solution. He closed his eyelids as she injected the morphine and knew that he would never be able to describe the pain he felt that day.

Jan was awake when they came to look at him on their final round of the night. He tried to open his eyes but his lids were closed, encrusted with dried tears. If only he could blank out the cries and groans of the other casualties; then he could hear better what was being said. By the yellow light of a hurricane lamp the VAD dabbed his eyes with warm water that ran down his cheeks. He could glimpse her through flickering eyelids.

'You see the colour on his face; all yellow and pallid?' the MO said.

'Yes.'

'Well, I've seen it a hundred times before. And the lines on his face?'

'Yes.'

'They're signs that tell us the life won't be coming back. Look at him, it's not the same man that went into battle, the spirit's just about left him. Death's in his face; he won't make it. I'll tell Captain Grimshaw when he comes round later with new supplies. God knows we need them.'

Jan's heart beat faster, a feeling of panic reached his solar plexus and gas in his stomach bubbled up through his digestive system and belched out through his mouth.

'But there must be a chance,' she said.

'Not a hope in hell. He'll not last the night.'

'I see.'

'We should get a bit of peace now the casualties have stopped coming in. Go and get some shut eye, I'll finish off here.'

'Good night.'

The VAD turned and walked away down the rows of wounded with the sound of the rain pounding down on the canvas, blocking out their groans.

Later, minutes or hours, he didn't know, he heard the swish, swish of the VAD's gown. He listened to the hurried slurping of Stinker scoffing scraps; she was in good hands. He heard the gentle clinking on metal, splashing and dripping as the nurse washed Stinker from a bucket. Jan's nose twitched with the smell of disinfected water that splashed in his face as his little dog shook the water off, from head to tail. The thought that Stinker was happy and recovering gave him comfort. Stinker would get through this even if he didn't. He felt the lucky touchwood indenting his sternum and thought of Lucy, perhaps for the last time. If the MO's opinion could be trusted, he wouldn't be here tomorrow.

Captain Grimshaw arrived with the supply convoy that evening.

'Shell holes, pot holes, piss holes and rain,' he belted out.

'Hello Sir,' MO Garnett said from behind his table, rubbing his eyes. 'Nothing new there then Sir?'

'No nothing new.' The Captain stood with his hands on his hips. 'Held back by enemy fire. Thought we'd never get out of that hell hole. We had to leave two vans on the way.' He took his cigarette case out of his tunic pocket and opened it towards the MO. 'Gasper, Garnett?'

'Thank you, Sir.'

'Quite alright,' he said, rubbing the wheel of his lighter several times before offering the flame. 'Have to fix the suspension when the rain stops. Still only room to take about fifty back to Remy, though.'

'Better than nothing, Sir,' Garnett said, standing up and brushing himself down.

'Stand easy man, you must be exhausted. Any chance of a cup of tea?'

'Yes, of course, Sir.'

'Also, can you make me a list of the dead? I'll write to their wives and parents tonight and catch tomorrow's post.'

'Give me ten-fifteen minutes, Sir. Only two hands you know.'

A flash of anger came over Captain Grimshaw's face. 'Don't push it Garnett.'

'No, Sir. Sorry, Sir, I'm the only one up. We've had a busy day.'

Grimshaw's anger left as quickly as it had appeared. 'That's alright Garnett, the war's making us all a bit short tempered.'

Garnett, still standing with his hands behind his back, shuffled his feet. 'There is one other thing you should know about.'

'Yes?'

You remember Lieutenant Strang?

'Yes?'

'Came in this morning. He's barely alive, Sir, only just breathing. He won't make it through the night.'

'Never!' The colour left Grimshaw's face. 'That's terrible. Where's his batman, Baker I think he's called?'

'Couldn't say Sir, they suffered heavy losses. It'll be a miracle if anyone's left alive.'

Captain Grimshaw put his head in his hands and took some deep breaths. 'I know his family. They're Swedish, you know, lovely people. His mother will be devastated and he's not long been married.' He pulled on his cigarette.

Garnett looked to the ground and moved his weight from one leg to the other as his Captain continued.

'He wrote sometimes, you know. Don't know quite what, but can you try and find his note books and keep them safe?'

'Yes, Sir.'

'I want to see them. I'll get them to his family.'

'Will do, Sir.'

'And all his men dead, you say?'

'Probably, Sir.'

'Okay, Garnett. Get his bits and pieces for me, will you?'

'Yes, Sir. And the tea.'

'Yes, make the tea the priority and,' he paused, 'if there are any biscuits?'

'Yes, Sir.'

Garnett left and came back fifteen minutes later carrying a tin tray with two mugs of weak black tea and four plain biscuits. He put his hand in his trouser pocket and brought out Jan's watch, notebook and pencil stub, then placed them on the table in front of the Captain.

'That's all there is, Sir, except for a touchwood and a bit of whiskey left in a bottle in his trench coat. I thought it best to leave them.'

'Yes, of course. You did right Garnett, thank you. Drink your tea and get some rest now. I'll hold the fort. They're getting closer, you know. We'll be busy again tomorrow.'

'Yes, Sir.'

Garnett dunked a biscuit in his tea and half of it fell into the cup and sank to the bottom.

'They're too stale to dunk, Sir.'

'So I see.'

Garnett got up holding his cup. 'I'll drink this in bed if you don't mind, Sir.'

'Not at all Garnett; you need the sleep.'

'Thank you, Sir. Goodnight, Sir.'

'Goodnight, Garnett.'

Captain Grimshaw finished his tea and thought he'd better see the state Jan was in for himself. He walked carefully along the planks, trying not to wake anyone. Looking down at Jan he saw his head in bandages encrusted with dried blood. Jan was all but lifeless. A little dog nestled up against him and Grimshaw's eyes welled up. Garnett was right; he wouldn't last till the morning. He knelt on the floor next to him, held Jan's cold hand between both of his and prayed for Jan's soul and for his own forgiveness. Taking a syringe and two morphine phials out of his medical pack, he drew up the liquid from one phial into the syringe and then the other. He pierced Jan's skin and pushed the needle into the inside of his forearm. Pressing down the plunger he emptied the syringe. With his right hand, he made the mark of the cross on Jan's forehead then leaned down and kissed the top of his head through the bandages. Tears dripped from his eyes onto Jan's bandaged head.

At his make-shift desk Grimshaw sat down to write his death letters and was quite relieved that no one was awake to see his red eyes. He dropped an ink tablet into a brass tumbler, added water and stirred it with a pencil. Taking the top off his Onoto pen and dipping it into the blue-black ink was his horrible nightly routine. Before the war, he taught history in a public school and was often up late marking. Now he was part of the history that would be taught to boys of the future. He opened a wooden box under the desk, pulled out a half-empty bottle of brandy and poured out an inch into a glass. On most nights the letters followed a formula with most of the words pre-printed on a standard sheet, but tonight was different. Jan's parents were his friends. Because he had known Eva before she was married and Jan as a small boy he would write it all from the heart. He paused to think before he wrote and fancied that all this might be a dream and he might wake up back home safely in his bed.

December 17th 1916
Dear Eva and Peter,

I hardly know how to say this but I have to tell you that Jan passed away last night having died of wounds received in battle defending our lines near Hill 60, Ypres. He is a great loss to us all. He was a courageous officer and always highly regarded by his men, all of whom fell at the same time. Jan was hit by shrapnel from a high-explosive German shell and we can be confident that he would not have felt any pain. Our hospital staff attended him quickly but there was nothing they could do to save him.

I have also written to Lucy and intend, God willing, to deliver Jan's possessions and notebooks to her personally, when time allows. It is the official procedure that Lucy, as his wife, receives them rather that yourselves.

This has been a very difficult time for us all and we have suffered heavy casualties. You have my heart-felt condolences. Jan was a gallant soldier and died serving his country. He will be greatly missed.

None of us can know God's will.

Please let me know if there is anything I can do. I shall try to call in and see you when next in London.
Yours in deepest sympathy,
Robbie Grimshaw (Cpt.)

From daybreak the next morning for a full twenty-four hours MO Garnett and his team, busy with incoming casualties, hardly had time to eat, let alone sleep. On the morning of the eighteenth of December, the guns, except for the sound of the occasional sniper bullet echoing in the distance, stayed silent. The rain eased and then stopped and the sun appeared, casting its light over devastation. The tents warmed with the sun so that steam rose in the air around the camp. MO Garnett and two helpers were clearing out the dead to make room for the inevitable new influx of wounded soldiers. Jan twitched, his brain was working, just, but his body wasn't.

'This one's still breathing,' one of the men said as he came upon Jan's body, noticing him twitch. Stinker looked up at the man from the ground next to Jan; he patted her. 'You're a cutie. Give us a kiss,' he said putting his face next to hers. Stinker licked his face.

'It's a bloody miracle! He's breathing and look, there's some colour in his cheeks,' MO Garnett said. 'We need to shift all these other bodies now. Miss Granger, can you stay with him and try to get some water in his mouth? Give him food if he wakes.'

'Yes, Sir.'

'Then anti-tetanus and morphine, but not too much. We might save him yet.'

VAD Granger put her hand gently behind Jan's head and poured water from a jam jar so that it trickled into his mouth. Jan's lips twitched as they felt the wetness. Water ran down his chin. She opened his lips slightly with her fingers and poured more in. Jan spluttered.

'Shhh. You're at the Dressing Station. You've had a shock but you're going to be alright now, we'll look after you. Your dog's here, she hasn't left your side.'

Jan spluttered again then coughed weakly.

'Shhhh. You need to drink some more and then I'll get you some food. You must eat it before I give you something to take away the pain.'

Jan's head was empty of thoughts but he understood enough to nod, slightly.

VAD Granger came back with some cold porridge in a bowl and fed him with a teaspoon. He ate some, but more slipped down his chin onto his stubble than went into his mouth. When he'd eaten a few spoonfuls she wiped his chin and put the bowl by his side for Stinker to finish off.

'Are you in pain?' she asked, clearly pronouncing the syllables with exaggerated lip movements.

Jan nodded weakly and watched as she half-filled a syringe with morphine from a glass phial. As the amber liquid rose up the tube, tension began to fall from his face. She pulled up his sleeve, wiped his arm with iodine solution and found a place free of bruising. She pierced the skin, pushed the needle further in and slowly depressed the plunger. When it was empty, she pulled it out, wiped the needle with cotton wool and dropped the syringe into a kidney dish with a clunk.

Craaack

The noise from shelling broke the morning's peace. It thundered from the distance and the ground rumbled. VAD Granger showed no reaction just shivered a little as the beat of cold rain began to fall down again on the tarpaulin roof. She held Jan's hand and he squeezed hers with fingers that would hardly move. His grip loosened and he drifted away from the war.

As the ground shuddered beneath him and the battle moved closer to the hospital tents, Jan woke. Despite the noise and commotion, he felt rested and better than he had for a long time. He didn't know how long he'd been 'out' but he was alive which he didn't expect before he drifted off. Still, if someone was going to get through, even if he was unworthy, it might as well be him. He reached his hand down his leg to touch Stinker and check she was still alive. Her shivering, hairy back told him she was. Looking up he saw a woman ambulance driver looking down at him with arms crossed underneath her bosom.

'We're going to move you now,' she said firmly, presumably to ward off any arguments. She unfolded her arms; her bosom dropped an inch. 'The vans are ready and you're all going to Remy, a long way from the front line. There're doctors and surgeons there too.'

'You'll get better treatment there,' MO Garnett said. 'We just patch you up from the battle then move you on.'

The ambulance driver stood back to let a pair of men shift Jan.

'Altogether, one, two and li-ift.'

Like dead meat they moved him onto the stretcher.

'I wish they were all as light as you,' one of them said to Jan directly, as they took him out through the rain and over mud to an ambulance. The man holding the stretcher behind his head rested the wooden poles on the back of the ambulance then joined his mate in sliding it along the wooden floor. The operation paused as the stretcher canvas got caught on a protruding screw. They pushed him in harder and Jan clenched his buttocks and winced as it tore into his backside. Stinker jumped in the back.

'You'll have to take her with him, she won't leave his side,' VAD Granger said.

'Better behaved than the officers,' a wounded lieutenant in the van said.

They lifted him off the stretcher onto to a bunk and strapped him in. Pain shot down his left side. He didn't pull a face. Pain could be a good thing, it told him he was alive, but he could only take so much of it. Settling down with a blanket and Stinker by his side he wondered if he would ever feel warm again. The back doors closed with a squeak and a clunk. From their port-hole window, he and Stinker watched VAD Granger waving them off with a smile. They might never see her again but Jan would remember her parting smile. It stuck in his head as if it were etched there.

The ambulance lurched forward through sludge that had been mixed with rubble to make the road usable. Jan imagined passers-by being pebble-dashed with mud and gravel as the wheels spun. Moans and groans inside the van combined with the sound of the chugging diesel engine. At each bump in the road Jan's head pounded. He smoked and tried to think but needed something to slake a raging thirst. He would have drunk just about anything.

The van stopped not ten minutes into their journey. Inside they heard the engine rev and the wheels spin. The two ambulance men at the back opened the doors and got out.

A cheer rang out when they jumped back in to the moving van. They'd been sprayed with filth from head to foot. They cursed and wiped their faces with dirty rags.

The van picked up speed and from a bunk opposite Jan, a tenor voice sang out, 'Oh Danny Boy, the pipes the pipes are calling…'

Christ, Jan thought, that's all we need. But no one joined in the singing and his voice faltered and faded out almost as soon as it had started. Except for the tenor, they were all sick of songs.

'Give me a drink for Pete's sake,' one of the patients who had had his ear blown off, called out to the ambulance men with mud-smeared faces.

'There isn't any,' one of them snapped.

'What, not even a drop of rum?'

'If you don't shut it I'll put you to sleep with a bleeding mallet,' one of the officers called out.

'Hear, hear,' said another and another.

'Piss off,' the one-eared man said, moving off his bunk and wrapping his long bony fingers around the officer's

scrawny neck. The ambulance men, in one mind, pulled him off and tied him to his bunk with canvas straps and buckles.
'Bastards. I'll fucking kill you.'

'Shut up you block head' the first ambulance man said, and jumped up, took some rags out of his pocket and stuffed them into the man's mouth. The man 'grrred' and writhed as if an electric current had been shot through his body. Some of the men laughed, and everybody who was able cheered and clapped the ambulance man. Jan raised his good arm in solidarity and patted his thigh. Apart from the one-eared officer with his mouth stuffed full of dirty rags, the men's mood lifted. They were driving away from the front line and a humour that was darker than the mud on the ambulance men's faces was building up.

'We'll be there soon, it's only eight miles now, we're doing our best,' one of the ambulance men said and lit a cigarette, visibly relieved.

Parking up at Remy Field Hospital, a group of VADs and MOs came to meet them. The ambulance men held open the back doors of the van to save the wind slamming them shut. In the sleet the MOs assessed the wounded as they were unloaded. One officer walked, a couple staggered with help and some, like Jan, were carried on stretchers. Jan saw the bright Red Cross against a dirty-white background on the sloping roof of the main tent. He felt reassured, it gave him hope. The MOs put him in a corner at the end of the tent and went back for more as other ambulances parked up. He closed his eyes and, on the inside of his forehead, saw the Red Cross.

Re-opening his eyes he blinked and watched bleeding men being carried past him to the surgery table at the other end of the tent. Jan could only just make out outlines of the surgeons and their staff, as if they were in the far distance. The screams told him that they were closer than that and were amputating limbs and pulling out bullets and shrapnel. His nostrils twitched from the Lysol sprayed by the VADs to ward off gas gangrene and to mask the smell of gore. The sickly-sweet smell of blood filled the tent and turned his stomach. Stinker nestled under the blanket keeping warm. As Jan lay on his damp canvas bed, he slid his hand down to feel the scab made from the cut in his backside then closed his eyes.

They shook him awake and took him to a dressing tent. A VAD cut then peeled and pulled back his clothes, stiff with dried blood. She and an MO pulled off his boots, cut off the bandages from the dressing station and washed his wounds with pungent milky-looking disinfectant. At last they were cleaning him up. Looking down he saw his skin red raw with lice bites. His head and chin bled from nicks as they shaved him. Patting them dry they lifted him onto a stretcher.

On the operating table he wanted to but couldn't scream, he groaned instead as the doctor picked at his wounds with pliers and tweezers and cleaned out the dirt from the bullet hole in his arm. The doctor nodded to a nurse. She soaked a rag in chloroform and passed it to him. With both hands, he held it over Jan's nose and mouth. Too tired to struggle now and with eyes stinging from the vapour, Jan passed out feeling he might never breathe again.

Still on the operating table he opened his eyes before he should have. He heard screams from the table next to him, felt panic but was unable to move. Stinker yapped at the surgeon then whimpered and ran around the table legs.

'Keep that dog away from me, for Chrissakes,' the Canadian surgeon snapped at the nurse. 'Tie it to the table leg damn it. It's in the bloody way.'

Jan sensed the surgeon's hands picking at bits of metal inside his skull. 'This one's a lucky one,' the surgeon said to the nurse. 'If it had gone in any further he'd be dead for sure.' He picked up a dressing and pressed it to Jan's head. 'The next twenty-four hours'll be crucial.'

The nurse walked behind him. Jan felt her hands wrapping bandages around his head. It comforted him in a way a man's hands could never have.

'Over here boys,' the surgeon said. 'Take him to his bed and get some water down him when he wakes. Next one please! Is there any coffee for Chrissakes? I'm bloody frozen.' A VAD handed him a chipped enamel mug half full with coffee. He slurped a mouthful and wiped his mouth and chin with his sleeve whilst they lifted Jan down onto a stretcher and took him away. 'Next one, please,' he repeated with exaggerated politeness.

They jerked and jolted Jan back along planks that covered the sodden ground. The mud squelched under the weight. They laid him down unceremoniously on his canvas bed. A VAD tucked him in. Stinker lay by his side and Jan went to sleep thinking that he was in a lesser purgatory to the battlefield and dressing station.

On waking, he felt a fierce hunger. He forced his encrusted eyes open with his fingers and looked around. As his senses came back to him so did his pain. A deep groan emerged from his throat. Cries from the surgeon's tables echoed around the tent. A nurse heard him stir and came to his side with a water bottle. She took out an orange from the pouch in the front of her apron and half knelt beside him.

'It's a lovely little dog,' she said, stroking Stinker's head on the bed. 'She reminds me of home. We had one just like it. They're incredibly loyal, you know, little terriers.'

Jan looked down at Stinker. Moans from the beds around him blended into the background and combined with the pit-pattering of the rain that sounded like a thousand tiny drum beats. Rain water dripped through the oiled canvas roof and drops landed on their heads. He forced himself to stay awake and to savour the moment of this good-looking nurse by his side with a smile and an orange. Thank God for small mercies, his mother would have said.

The nurse hitched up her ankle-length gown to rest on her knee then crouched by his bedside and peeled the orange in front of him. The zest reached his nose; fresh and exotic. He turned his head towards her and pain seared from the hole in his skull down through his neck to the base of his spine. He gritted his teeth and made it look like a grin.

'You'll like this, they're really sweet,' she said, as she moved an orange segment dripping from her fingers towards his lips. He opened his mouth just enough for her to push in the sharp-sweet flesh. The juice burst into flavour in his mouth bringing his tongue and throat, which had seemed dead for so long, perhaps days or even weeks, back to life with a judder. Juice seeped through the cracks in his lips, stung them and then trickled down his chin.

She smiled, 'I'm not a real nurse. Just a VAD, but all the patients call me nurse except for the MOs who like to lord it over us. But we know as much as any nurse, the experiences we've had.'

Jan's brain was more alive now. He nodded. He wanted to say thank you and to tell her how much he appreciated her kindness; that the orange was a gift from heaven and that she looked wonderful, but, though he tried, no word would emerge, not a single syllable. Panic struck him as it crossed his mind that he might never speak again. She touched his cheek with the inside of her hand.

'Don't exert yourself; we want to get you well again, don't we? You can rest here and get your strength back. Then they'll send you home and you can take your little dog with you. I'll leave this water by you and come and see you a bit later with some tea and bread and jam.'

Her voice reminded him of Lucy; soft and comforting yet bright. It triggered a rush of memories of home. How would he tell them he had survived? He had to get a message out to them. The VAD pulled out a cloth from up her sleeve and wiped the juice from his chin. His freshly shaved skin came to life and stung. The blood returned to his lips and around his mouth. He felt alive. He watched intently as she rose from her crouching position. Her hem fell to just above her boots and brushed Stinker's head. Her breasts moved as she got up and brushed him accidentally. Through her grey gown he watched her young hips and buttocks as she moved with a sway along the line of canvas beds to her next patient, six beds along. The officer in the bed to his right leaned over on his elbow and faced him.

'That's Mandy Parkinson. She's a sight for sore eyes,' he said. Jan met his gaze. 'They're all after her you know. Like bees round a honey pot.' He grinned. 'I'm Jimmy by the way, Jimmy Hawtins, Lancashire Fusiliers.'

Jan nodded and raised his right hand in polite recognition. He smiled and nodded again before closing his eyes.

The voice of the Canadian doctor woke him. He could just make it out.

'Listen... important... not much morph left... only... quarter gram each.'

Jan opened his eyes just enough to see the doctor putting his hand on Mandy's shoulder. 'Dozen cases of brandy just come in... give 'em a glass of that... save the morph for surgery. Champagne as well... some for ourselves.'

Jan's eyes flickered then closed; concentrating on the words was exhausting him and he fell back into a doze.

When he woke, Mandy Parkinson was helping an orderly hand out tea, bread and jam in turn to all the patients in his row. Some took a little rousing with a gentle shake. Jan felt a pang of impatience; he wanted Mandy's attention sooner and for longer than she could possibly give it. She got to him eventually, though, and propped up a pillow behind his head. Her hand moved to pat Stinker before she put a bowl of water down for her.

'I'll bring some scraps for you later.' She looked lovingly at the dog then turned to Jan. 'When you've eaten some of this I'll come back and give you something for the pain.' She smiled at him with a smile that shone more from her eyes than her lips. Jan smiled back as best he could. Holding up his upper body with his right elbow and arm he leaned forward. Pain shot through him. She noticed, went straight to the tea trolley, came back with brandy and poured a couple of mouthfuls into a dented tin mug. Jan grasped it with both hands and felt the cold move through the metal to his finger-bones.

'Just sip it,' she said before going on to her next patient.

His lips were still sticky with orange juice as he raised the mug and swallowed. It seared his throat then burned its way down through his oesophagus to his stomach where it forced him to belch up foul gas. He coughed and spat phlegm out into a rag he was using to wipe his nose and eyes. More settled, he struggled but succeeded with some pain, in lighting a cigarette from the packet of Woodbines she left at his bedside. He tried to relax.

Wednesday 20 December 1916
Jan awoke slowly on what he presumed was the following morning. He was well-rested and feeling stronger but groggy and had a splitting headache. His stomach groaned. It was late December, he was sure of that, but he had no idea of what day it was or the date. Having cheated death, he was beginning to imagine that recovery might just be possible. Men with worse wounds had been patched up, sent back to Blighty and got on with daily life, so why shouldn't he? Then the thought crossed him that they might send *him* back to the front and fear gripped him.

With cracked and sore lips, he opened his mouth to speak to Jimmy in the next bed. No sound emerged from his throat and his anxiety increased. He could just make out Mandy down the row of beds and signalled to her with his good arm. She acknowledged him with a nod, like a waitress in the Lyons Tea Room on The Strand where he used to meet Lucy, then she turned her back on him. Ten minutes later she appeared at his bedside; his anxiety subsided a little.

Stinker wagged her tail and brushed against her muddied hem and stockinged ankles.

'Well, you seem a lot better,' Mandy said, helping him sit up. Jan clasped her hand in his. She let her hand rest in his for a moment. His frightened eyes stared at her. He released her hand and pointed towards his mouth.

'You must be ravenous. They're making up some bacon and eggs in the kitchen tent just now. Can you smell it? I can.'

Jan nodded.

'I'll let them know you're awake, you shouldn't have too long to wait and they'll bring you a nice cup of tea as well.'

'Mmmm,' was the only noise he could manage. Although he'd almost forgotten what the heaven of bacon and eggs tasted like, he needed a notebook and pencil more than breakfast. With his right hand, he made a writing gesture. Her face expressed recognition.

'I'm so sorry, I didn't think.' Sliding her hand into her hip pocket she handed him a little notepad of poor-quality paper and a pencil stub and smiled.

He tried to write straight away, but his hand shook and what came out was an incomprehensible scrawl. He felt useless when she leaned over and held the pad steady on his thigh, but the smell of Cologne on her neck made him want to live. With his second attempt, he wrote in capitals. It was just readable: *Writing paper, stamps – clean teeth*. He handed her back the pad feeling satisfied.

Her face expressed concern. 'Yes, but do you feel strong enough?'

Jan nodded once and then, though it sent a pain down his neck, twice more.

'I'll get them for you after breakfast and then we can clean your teeth. Have one of these,' she said handing him a cigarette from a packet she pulled out from her apron. Jan wandered what else she kept in there; hair pins and a hankie maybe? He took the cigarette, making sure he touched her ringless fingers, then put the cigarette to his lips whilst attempting a cheeky expression. She lit a match. Leaning forward he sucked in the flame, inhaled deeply, tilted his head back then let the smoke slowly out into the air above his head. A rattle emerged from his chest and Mandy left him.

When he saw the orderly bringing the breakfast, he stubbed the smouldering cigarette end out with his thumb and forefinger and left it on top of the box of matches by his side. The orderly put the plate on a board on his lap and cut up the bacon. He ate with the fork in his right hand in the American style. Sadness washed over him as the smell of cooking rose from the plate triggering memories of home. He lifted his head and breathed in lungfuls of the cold damp air to subdue his feelings then bent his head back down over his plate and resumed his eating. The food looked and, despite the state of his mouth, tasted wonderful. Stinker looked up at him, saliva dripping out of the corners of her whiskered mouth. Jan thought better of mopping up the egg yolk and bacon grease with the last corner of his bread and butter. Instead he put the plate down on the ground for her to lick clean. Jimmy Hawtins smiled and laughed and put his plate down for her to clean as well.

Outside, the sound of a motorbike backfiring startled just about everybody. A man, short but sturdy and wearing motorbike boots, entered the tent. He took off his leather headgear, goggles and gloves and pushed them into his shoulder bag. Jan thought he must be quite important as he kept shaking hands and talking to just about everybody he came across, including Mandy and the MOs. He had a nervous laugh and appeared to be listening to those he talked to, so he couldn't have been top brass. Too busy to listen, the top brass only gave orders. The man smiled at all he met. He tilted his head back, laughing nervously, his big ivory teeth flashing from under a thick-black English moustache. Moving among the patients bit by bit along the canvas beds he came closer and Jan noticed a dog collar, half-hidden by his tunic lapel. Their eyes connected. Jan looked down. A bloody chaplain, that's all I flaming well need, he thought.

The grinning Chaplain approached Jan's bedside, lowered himself down to his haunches and handed him writing paper, envelopes and pencil from his canvas shoulder bag.

'The nurse said you might need these.'

Jan smiled as a thank you then nodded once making sure he caught the Chaplain's eye. He had brought him exactly what he had wanted.

'I'm Briggs, Harry Briggs, very pleased to meet you,' he said, shaking Jan's right hand with a firm grip. Stinker put her front paws on his leg. Briggs stroked her head. Jan met his eye and gave a half smile. 'You've been through the mill by all accounts; they didn't think you'd make it. We all thank God that you did, though. By the way, I've heard there's been a terrible mix up; hence the envelopes.'

He paused to find the right words.

'Well, apparently, back at the Dressing Station, Freddie Garnett said you were dead meat and Captain Grimshaw wrote to your wife and parents that you'd died of wounds.'

Jan's eyes widened. His heart palpitated.

'So your family will be in some distress when the letter arrives. That was three days ago, so the letters will probably be there by now. We can't send a telegram but, as you know, it's a cracking postal service. If we send a letter in the morning it can be in London in two or, at the most, three days, certainly before Christmas Day.'

Jan sucked in air and stared wide eyed. Briggs opened a folding stool with a stretched grey-green canvas seat and sat down. Jan waved his hand with his first and index finger together and handed Briggs his packet of Woodbines. Briggs lit one and handed it to Jan then lit one for himself.

'The damp in the air gets to them, mine are soaked. I've driven through some terrible rain to get here. It makes you question the ways of God sometimes. We all have our doubts you know, even us "holy" men.'

Briggs let out a nervous laugh. Jan moved his head from side to side and looked down to show that he knew what he meant.

'Anyway, back to today's business. I'm most terribly sorry but these mix ups do happen from time to time and we have to sort them out as best we can.' Briggs looked serious and Jan felt sick breathing in the damp smoke. 'We can limit the damage if we get this letter written. I don't really think you're up to writing that much just yet, are you? So, may I suggest we compose it together? I can write it and then you can sign it. If we do it now we can catch today's post.' He blew his nose into a dirty-white handkerchief and put it quickly back in his pocket. 'The good news is that you're alive and comparatively *compos mentis*.'

Jan nodded his assent.

'Good, so. "If it were done . ... then 'twere well it were done quickly." The tea's coming, I'll let you drink that and come back prepared in a quarter hour or so.'

'Here you are sir, nice mugga tea.' The orderly was on his best behaviour in front of the chaplain as he picked up the breakfast plates from the ground by Stinker and placed the tea in Jan's hand. 'Best drink of the day, eh?'

Jan felt tired just from listening to Briggs. He dropped his cigarette end on the ground by his bed. He nodded and smiled without conviction to the orderly. Thanking everyone endlessly by nodding and smiling wasn't remotely achievable yet; it made his neck hurt and his cracked lips needed to heal. Although not feeling particularly worthy of life, considering all the better men who had fallen, he nevertheless took strength from everyone's kindness. The orderly left and Mandy sidled up to his bed, bringing with her a toothbrush, tin of toothpaste, mug of water and a small bowl to spit into which she put on the tray.

'Drink your tea first,' she said, perching herself on Briggs' stool by the side of the bed. Her hand moved to stroke Stinker who wagged her whole body as well as her tail as if she was shaking off water. 'It's not a bad morning you know, the sun's coming out at last and might dry the ground up a bit and warm things up a little. That'll make it easier for everyone, the damp gets everywhere you know.'

His eyes widened. He warmed to her as the hundreds that had preceded him must have done. But he still wanted to know everything about her: her family, where she came from and how she came to be here. If he could get her to tell him, her voice would be sweetness to his ears: lilting and seductive, cultured and feminine, it was a voice with no harshness in it despite the circumstances; an aural contrast to the war's guns and shells. He imagined falling asleep to it dreaming of gentler times.

'Let's do your teeth then. Soon you'll be able to do it for yourself.'

She wetted the brush, dabbed it on the block of Eucryl toothpowder and handed it to him. Jan scrubbed weakly. The brush dropped from his hand onto the blanket. He picked it up straight away and tried again. He felt her compassion shine as she watched him struggle. The toothpowder frothed on his tongue and stung ulcerations that he hadn't realised were there. Tiny pieces of old fetid food fell from his teeth as he slowly moved the bristles up and down. She took the brush back from him and watched with encouragement as he rinsed his stinging, but now very much alive, mouth and dribbled it out into the little bowl. With a clean mouth like this he could kiss someone. He smiled from his cracked lips and touched her hand.

'Well, I must be doing my rounds,' she said, standing up and brushing down the front of her gown as if to emphasise the point. 'Look the Chaplain's here,' she said, turning towards him. 'Have you met Stinker?' she asked Briggs.

Briggs was armed with pen and writing board and seated himself on the fold-up stool. 'Hello Nurse, yes I have, she's great isn't she?' His teeth grinned at Mandy. 'No time to put up any Christmas decorations then?'

'Not yet.' She emptied the water basin on the ground, picked up the rest of her tooth-cleaning bits and pieces and put them in a bag. 'If there's any decency left in the world there should be fewer casualties in the run up, so we may get time to find some sprigs of holly. The MOs have been talking about digging up a tree.'

'Splendid.'

'Some of the patients are getting parcels and cards from home.'

'That's good. I suppose most of their families don't know they're here yet and by the time they do they'll have moved up to a Stationary Hospital. I was up in Le Treport a few days ago and morale's good; I would say *very* good.' He turned to Jan with a smile: 'Well Jan, how are you feeling now after the hearty breakfast? Much better I'm sure.'

Jan touched his head and grimaced.

'I know, but it will get better in time. Time's a great healer. Nature's way is best. Ha ha.'

Jan looked at him askance.

'Just something to think about; now let's get down to the important business of writing.'

He sat down on his stool, put a board on his crossed knee and readied himself with pen in hand.

'Shall we start with me asking you some questions and you write your answers down as best you can, or indicate them through nods, headshakes and arm movements?'

Jan nodded.

'Then I'll suggest how I think the letter might go and you signal to me yes or no?'

Jan nodded. Briggs clearly knew what he was doing. Jan had warmed to him and instinctively trusted him. Perhaps it was intuition. In his thirty years, he had met enough swine and had accumulated enough understanding of his fellow man to see straight through the shallow and pretentious. Briggs was a good man; irritating but well intentioned and his efficiency and attention to detail were worthy of respect.

'I'll just put down the formalities at the top of the page. Now what's your wife's name and where is she staying?'

With shaky hand Jan slowly spelt out *LUCY* in capitals then his parent's London address.

'Good. Shall we start with, *My dearest Lucy*?'

Jan nodded.

'Fine, then how about,' he paused to blow his nose, '*The first thing I need to tell you is that although I've been badly wounded, I am alive and recovering well at Remy (Sidings) Field Hospital. My wounds appeared to be so severe that they took me for dead at the dressing station before I reached here. Captain Grimshaw was misinformed about my condition and naturally wrote to you with his condolences.*'

Jan stared at him, it sounded like Briggs had prepared it earlier.

'No point in beating about the bush, eh?' he said by way of explanation. He looked straight at Jan. 'Do you feel anyone was to blame for your misdiagnosis?'

Jan shook his head from left to right. To say no was the decent thing to do.

'No? Right ho, I'll put that in. How about, *No one can really be blamed as I have had a miraculous recovery*. That sounds nicely optimistic, don't you think?'

Jan nodded but didn't look convinced. Briggs struck through *miraculous* with his pen and showed it to Jan.

'I'll replace it with *good recovery* instead.'

Briggs smiled and Jan nodded.

'Then, how about, *I have asked our Chaplain, Lieutenant Briggs, to write to you as I am still a bit shaky from my ordeal. Although I am getting better I am unlikely to be sent back to the front so, all being well, I would hope to be back in London in the next week or two. Everyone involved is terribly sorry for the distress that you have been caused by the mix up. I do hope that this letter reaches you quickly to limit your distress.*' He paused for thought. 'Is that enough do you think?'

Jan nodded.

'So, shall we sign off with, *With deepest affection?* And you can write your name as best you can at the bottom. I think that should do it for now, don't you?'

Jan pointed to Stinker.

'Of course, I'll just quickly tell them about the terrier in a PS, shall I?'

Jan smiled and nodded.

'Alright, well, I'll write it up neatly and a similar one for your parents and bring them for you to sign. If we catch the post then, with God's speed, they should get them soon.'

Jan wrote *hurry* on his pad and pleaded with his eyes. He noticed Jimmy Hawtins in the next bed watching them. There are no secrets here, he reflected. Then he looked back at Briggs, pulled an agonised face and touched his head.

'I'll see if I can get something for the pain,' Briggs said.

A half an hour later he came back with the letters written in ink and a bottle of brandy with a couple of inches left in the bottom and the cork already loosened.

'No morphine pills, I'm afraid.' Jan looked disappointed. Briggs looked earnestly back. 'I wouldn't go on about this but I've seen great men reduced to ruins from morphine. Get off it as soon as you can. It's like the drink, you know, a great servant but a poor master, ha ha.'

Jan wondered why the hell he was he telling him this now when they'd only just finished picking bits of metal out of his head. What was he supposed to do, refuse it? He took the pen from Briggs and signed the letters with a scribbled *Jan* and an *x*, pressed them to his cracked lips and handed them back. As Briggs looked away at a minor disturbance down the ward Jan took a swig from the bottle and slid it back under his blanket. Setting off to catch the post Briggs called back. 'I'll be back for a chat in a bit,' he said. 'You've had a lucky escape, you know?'

Before he was out of earshot Hawtins called out from the next bed.

'Can you get *me* a bottle Rev?'

Briggs stopped in his stride, came back and talked directly to Hawtins.

'I'm not a barman you know. Ha ha.'

Hawtins looked uneasy. 'I'm sorry, it's just...'

'I'll see what I can do but I can't promise anything, the MOs are against giving amputees drink on the operating tables. I don't want to get into their black books.'

Hawtins lowered his voice to a whisper. 'I won't tell them where I got it.'

'Have some of Strang's, he won't need it all.'

Jan shook his head and looked heavenwards before bringing out the bottle from under his blanket and handing it to Hawtins.

'Thanks Strang, you don't mind do you?'

Jan did mind. Watching Hawtins' wet slobbery lips cover the end of the bottle made him want to puke. Hawtins wasn't someone he could ever warm to.

Briggs looked animated and talked to Jan. 'Now I'm only going to say this once because I think it might help you in the state you're in.' He raised his voice in exaggeration. 'And I don't mind Hawtins listening in. Ha ha.'

Hawtins laughed, turned his head away and closed his eyes.

Briggs settled down on his stool and whispered in Jan's ear. 'If you can't change something there's no point in letting it get to you. It's always a question of adapting to the circumstances.'

A philosopher with a sense of humour in a hospital tent: Jan liked him more and more. Briggs obviously believed in his work and calling and Jan needed a friend. Briggs explained what Jan had already worked out. In London, Lucy and his parents would probably think he was dead; there was nothing anybody could do to explain the situation till the new letters got to them. It was only then that *their* wounds would be healed. But anything could happen to a batch of letters in this war, so there were no guarantees. He took a slug of brandy from the bottle, spluttered and handed over to Hawtins who did the same without spluttering and handed it back.

Briggs coughed and blew his nose. He wrapped one hand around the other and looked with concern at Jan.

'You know, I'm certain that the only way to get through this hell is by having faith; to believe that there is a higher meaning to your life. I know, given the circumstances, what I'm saying must appear quite mad but I've seen it so many times.'

Jan shook his head as if to say, 'Oh no, not at all'. Hawtins stretched his head to listen in.

'The ones who have faith are the ones who survive mentally and heal more quickly physically. Not in all cases, of course, but without faith there's much less chance. You see the spirit dwindles and men lose their will to go on. I believe we're all here for a purpose and the fact that you've survived so far tells me that God has a purpose for you. It may not be apparent now and, by the look in your face I can see you're not convinced, but one day you will look back and realise that you were saved for a reason.'

Jan most certainly wasn't convinced but could see that Briggs was. He nodded to signal he was still listening.

'You know it doesn't really matter what you believe in either, as long as you believe there's a reason for your life. The Indian men: Muslims, Hindus, Sikhs, I've seen them pull through because of their faith. They could teach us a thing or two; they're stronger mentally than us lot.' Jan eyes flickered then closed. 'I'll come back later and talk if you like; it doesn't have to be about religion or faith. I'm rather fond of soccer; do you have a special team?

Jan wrote on his note pad *QPR*. Briggs gave a broad grin.

'I'm a Fulham man myself so we have quite a lot in common. I'll leave you now and I'll pop back mid-dayish.'

Jan wrote, *I think I've gone mad*, and passed the pad to Briggs.

'It seems unlikely. You appear sane to me.'

Will I talk again?
'I should say so.'
Jan nodded without conviction.
'Yes, most probably. Muteness is very common, you know. It's a nervous response to the shock you see. Most speak again from what I've seen and heard. Patience is the thing my friend; patience and faith.' He rested his hand on Jan's shoulder. 'When get you back to Blighty you'll be able to see some specialists who can help you.'

So, he *would* be leaving this god-forsaken hell hole, Jan thought.

Home? Are you sure? He wrote
'No doubt about it old chap. None at all. Ha ha.'
How long?
'A week, two at the most.'

Jan wiped the back of his hand over his brow and shaped his lips into a whistling shape.

'I've got a friend from Cambridge who works at the Royal London in Whitechapel and he's a specialist in psychiatry. Charlie Walton. He's been studying Freud. I don't know if you've heard of him? Walton that is, not Freud. Ha ha. I assume we all know about Freud.'

Jan shook his head and wrote just legibly: *Sister works at the London.*

'Well that's splendid. He may well know her.'
Jan smiled.

'Well, the last time I saw him he told me that there have been great advancements in curing neurasthenia and I think, apart from your physical wounds, this is what you have. It's bound to be psychological. Apparently, as I've said, it's common to be struck dumb from battle and quite usual to recover your voice sooner rather than later.'

Jan widened his eyes.

'And I'm not just saying that to make you feel better.' Briggs grinned and blew his nose.

Jan thanked him by taking his hand and smiling. Briggs had made him hopeful. Perhaps he could be cured. He might even heal naturally given enough time. He would hold onto that hope. He had to, or what was the point in going on? Briggs folded up his stool and left for other patients.

'Pillock,' Hawtins said from his bed. 'Faith won't bring my leg back.'

No, but it might stop you grumbling, Jan would have said if he could.

Chapter 9

21 December 1916

Eva heard the post fall on the door mat a little after ten. Alone in the house she walked to the front door and picked up the pile of letters. Ever since they waved Jan off from Victoria Station, apprehension filled her each time the post arrived. Today was no exception. Though sometimes her sister wrote from Sundsvall, there was rarely anything in the post for her. She could tell by the shape of the envelopes that there were a couple of Christmas cards and the usual boring business stuff for Peter that should have gone to his office. She browsed through them one by one looking at the handwriting and stamps and feeling the paper with her hands. Her eyes fell on one addressed to Mrs Jan Strang and another in an identical brown-paper envelope to Mr and Mrs Peter Strang, both in the same neat copper-plate handwriting. Her stomach tightened. She couldn't make out the franking without her reading glasses but could see that the blue-black ink had run in places where God's tears had splashed on the ink. She made her way into the front room, put the pile of letters on the sideboard, opened the envelope with her little fingers and picked up her reading glasses from the side table:

Dear Eva and Peter,
I hardly know how to say this ….

Still holding the letter, Eva's legs started to buckle under her and the blood rushed from her head. She just got to the armchair nearest the window in time to break her fall. Staring out into the dim daylight, tears flowed down her cheeks dripping onto her cardigan and blouse. Her only son was dead and there was nothing she could do to change it.

An hour probably passed before she could bring herself to properly re-read her old friend Robbie Grimshaw's letter. She always knew that this could happen. Dazed she rose and took tiny faltering steps to the kitchen, picked up the tea and hand-towels hanging by the range and brought them back to her chair by the window where she blew her nose into the tea-towel and sobbed until her eyes and cheeks stung with the tears. When the force of the tears subsided, she rang Peter who said he would get home as quickly as he could in a taxi. At around one o'clock she heard him come in and his rushed step down the hall.

Seeing Eva distraught in the armchair Peter dropped his coat on the floor and knelt by her legs. He held her hands and kissed her head. She tried to speak:

'Ahh, ahh, I cc, I, i, it...'

Sliding one arm around her waist and the other under her legs he carried her to the settee where he put his arm around her shoulders and let her head rest on his chest. Her tears wetted his shirt front.

'Can I see the letter?'

She saw the sadness in his eyes and from her cardigan pocket she pulled out Robbie Grimshaw's now crumpled letter. Peter took out his handkerchief from his trouser pocket and pressed it over his eyes and nose then unfolded the letter and flattened it on his thigh. Even though he knew what it would say, he shuddered with grief.

Lucy nodded to regular travellers on the train north to Kilburn. It was standing room only. One or two men would always stand up and offer her their seat. Usually she refused but today a middle-aged man with a pained expression said he was getting off at the next stop anyway, so she smiled, thanked him and sat down. She opened her *Daily Chronicle* to avoid catching anyone's eye.

Today had been one of those days she could have done without. They heard on Monday that one of the girls at work was pregnant and they all congratulated her and took her to the Buckingham Arms at lunchtime to celebrate. For Lucy, a trip to the pub would have been a welcome change to her weekly routine but something Beatty said earlier affected her deeply. Beatty, who was the most tactless woman she had ever known, said to the happy expectant young woman that she was lucky she had fallen pregnant because then, if her husband didn't come back from France, she would still have a part of him with her. Hearing this, Lucy felt anxious and couldn't get the thought out of her mind. If Jan died there would be nothing left of him but his belongings. She looked at Beatty over the pub table and tut-tutted under her breath then felt her fingers burn as her cigarette smouldered close her fingers. Dropping it in the ashtray she then downed her glass of light ale in one and went up to the bar to order a round of drinks, insisting that no one helped her to pay for them.

On the train, she brooded on Beatty's words and there was nothing in the *Chronicle* to lift her mood. Jan had written that he hoped to be home for Christmas but that was well over a week ago now and he had promised to write to her every week at least. But men were like that, forgetful, or just plain lazy. She thought about it and accepted that she really couldn't expect anything more in the middle of a war. Behind her paper she let her eyes close attempting to find some peace from her thoughts, but the peace wouldn't come. She smoked a cigarette and looked at the adverts on the walls to pass the time and to avoid unwanted eye contact from men on the train. She wondered if she should start wearing less attractive clothes. The screech of carriage wheels on rails as they approached Queen's Park roused her from her thoughts. On the platform, she pulled on her beige woollen gloves, tucked her matching scarf into her coat front and set off for home in the dark. The smoke from a thousand chimneys hung in the night air. Walking back to Chichester Road her empty stomach rumbled and she warmed at the thought of Eva's cooking. It was quite amazing what her mother-in-law could do with saltfish, potatoes, carrots and cabbage. Eva could add flavour to anything with her little pots of herbs and spices. Quite a change to the bland food her mother served at home in Uxbridge. Tonight, after dinner, she would put her feet up and have a nice warm night in front of the fire then hear from Peter about all the ships that got through to London bringing in timber from far-away places.

As she fetched her house keys out of her bag, Lucy reflected on how Eva and Peter couldn't have been more welcoming to her. Standing in the hall something was strange, the usual smell of cooking was missing and an unexpected silence made her feel uneasy. She closed the door behind her, took off her gloves and put them in her coat pocket, then removed her hat and coat and hung them on the stand by the door. In front of the full-length mirror in the hall, she ran her fingers through her hair and wiped a speck of dirt from under her eye.

'I'm home,' she called as she walked into the front room smiling.

Lucy didn't need to be told what had happened. On the settee, Peter held Eva in his arms. Eva was gripping a hand towel and her face was red. She knelt on the floor in front of them and held Eva's hands in hers. Eva pulled a hand out from under Lucy's and stroked Lucy's hair.

'It's Jan, he's dead,' Peter said.

On hearing the word 'dead', Lucy gasped for breath and sat down. A full five minutes passed before she managed to breathe properly and ask how. Her eyes followed Peter as he rose and handed Lucy her unopened letter from the side table.

'This is all we know'. His big right hand stroked her head as he went to put the kettle on. Lucy looked at the words in front of her. With her mind resting on the words, *None of us can know God's will,* she stood up.

'God's will?' she called out and beat her thigh with a clenched fist. Rage grew within her and then possessed her. 'It's all complete bloody nonsense. There's no purpose to any of it, any fool can see that. It's hell, that's what it is. God's purpose my eye.'

Peter had come back from the kitchen.

'I don't think he actually meant that there actually was a purpose, just that…'

'How can you be so calm?'

Lucy spoke out furiously in a voice unrecognisable as her own. Then, walking about the room touching first the curtains then some chairs and the table she started to cry. Slow aching sobs moved through her body. Her brain now numb was only able to cope with the one thought, that Jan was dead. She addressed him in an unconscious denial, lifting her head up and talking into the air. 'You should never have died. You bloody fool. You should never have gone in the first place. We told you not to. We all told you not to. Why were you so damned stupid? I never loved anyone else and now you're dead.' She screwed up her face and her tears mixed with saliva as they reached her protruding bottom lip. She felt Eva and Peter's staring at her. She pressed both palms to her eyes, grabbed the handkerchief that Peter offered her and wiped her face and blew her nose noisily on it then tried to collect herself by taking long deep breaths. 'I won't believe it. Why, why?' she asked the God in which she didn't believe but whom she needed to curse. Eyes bulging with more yet-to-be shed tears, she read the letter through twice and her anger surged once more. She paced the room shaking the letter. 'I don't believe it. It's not a credible story.'

'I'm sure you've got a point there, Lucy,' Peter said.

'It's lies, damned lies; how the hell could he not feel pain if he was hit by shrapnel, for God's sake?'

'Grimshaw must be trying to soften the blow,' Peter said.

Eva pressed the hand towel to her face as if it could shut out the sound of Lucy's anger.

'It's drivel, absolute drivel,' Lucy continued. 'He wasn't a "courageous officer". I doubt if he even shot a man.'

'I know, but it doesn't change the facts,' Peter said. 'It's standard practice to…'

'Bloody hell,' Lucy screamed, still pacing round the room. 'I'd rather die myself.'

She lit up a cigarette from the box on the side table and sucked in the Virginia smoke; it soothed her a little. 'I'll make the tea,' she said.

In the kitchen, she stemmed her anger long enough to lay a tray with cups, milk jug and sugar, no saucers, and to pour the boiling water from the kettle on to the leaves in the pot. The tray rattled as she brought it in. Unable to speak, she put the tray on the floor by her parent's-in-law's feet and sat on the floor beside them with her legs tucked under her.

Peter leaned forward, poured a cup of tea, added milk and stirred in two sugars. Passing it to Lucy, he said, 'Drink this.'

Holding the cup in two hands she drank it down, rested her head on Eva's legs and gently sobbed.

Chapter 10

21 December 1916

Stinker jumped up quivering onto Jan's bed. She woke him up by licking his nose and lips. Waking, Jan heard machine-gun fire not too far away. Then *Crash*, a shell exploded outside the tent and then another and another. Jan's legs started to twitch. Hawtins passed him a lighted cigarette. Jan sucked hard on it. He put Stinker on the ground. He would have screamed if he could.

Motorbikes roared, staff-car doors slammed and orders were barked over the commotion. The staff, used to the sound of shelling, went about the evacuation with little outward sign of panic. Jan saw Mandy Parkinson and an MO rush in through the tent flaps. She noticed his leg spasms, dashed over to him and jabbed him in the thigh with a syringe. His spasms subsided. Still conscious he watched her move on to calm a man down along the row who called out for 'sweet Jesus' to help him. Above the commotion, Jan made out some of the orders being called out:

'Evacuate the hospital ... battle's moving toward us ... sitting ducks ... train ... Le Treport ... belongings ... ambulances and trucks ... moving further back from the line ... two to three hours ... rain and sleet ... belongings by mule. God's speed to all of you.'

Mandy came back to Jan and Hawtins. Stinker looked up, whimpered and wet herself on the blanket as she approached. Mandy crouched between the two beds and spoke calmly.

'We're going to put you and the other men who can't walk on the train to the Stationary Hospital at le Treport. They'll look after you much better there. You'd have gone there in a few days anyway.'

'The further away the better,' Hawtins said.

She stood up and stepped back from them and addressed the row of beds. 'Now I need all of those who can, to tidy up your things.' She folded her arms in front of her. 'You'll be moving very shortly. Those who can walk, get out of bed, get dressed and gather your belongings. Doctor Harding and I will help the rest of you to get your clothes on and into to the trucks for the station. We need you out as quickly as we can.' She paused and raised her voice over the men chattering. 'More wounded from the German surge will be coming in all the time. We'll have to rush off and deal with them as soon as they arrive, so we need you out now.'

The Hospital train left at six pm on a much-interrupted journey that took twelve hours. Under better circumstances it would have taken two. Jan woke up to the deafening and unmistakable sound of carriage wheels on uneven track and he wondered how he had managed to sleep through the din for so long. He had a vague recollection of being carried onto the train but must have passed out in the midst of the commotion. He looked around for water but the only water he could see was in a little bowl left on the floor by his bed for Stinker who, noticing that Jan had woken up, snorted, rearranged her position on his bed and went back to sleep. As far as something for him to drink was concerned he could only make out a case of wine and a few bottles of spirits at the far end; it wasn't safe to drink the water anyway.

By the look of it, the carriage was a cattle wagon which had been converted with timber frames and metal brackets to make eight sets of bunk beds. The smell of pine from the freshly sawn wood hit his nose. Icy cold air blew in through the cracks from the boards and around the edges of a central sliding door. He was in a lower bunk which meant that, although he heard the noise acutely and felt a jolt every time the carriage went over a crack or join in the rail, he wasn't swayed to and fro at every curve in the line and was, therefore, less likely to throw up. Canvas straps fastened with sturdy British buckles made sure that those on the top were not thrown from their beds. An empty carafe stood upright by his bed for him to piss in. It was clearly the wrong shape, he thought, and was bound to get knocked over but the carriage stank anyway and he couldn't see how the smell could possibly get any worse, unless they were carrying a decomposing corpse. Anyway, they were all used to it. With no MOs, nurses or VADs in the carriage, the wounded were left to their own devices. Most had already started on the red wine and brandy and Jan saw no reason not to join them when a bottle was passed to him.

Spirits seemed high which, Jan surmised, was almost inevitable as they were moving further away from the fighting. There was also much talk of Christmas and of home. Jan lit a candle stub, dripped some of the molten wax on the floor by his bed and pressed it down. He lay on his side, propping his head up with his hand at the end of his bent elbow. The men drank, smoked and laughed at that particular form of black humour that is bred only in times of war. Though unable to verbalise any questions, by paying close attention, Jan caught up on all the news of those who had died and how pitifully the war was going. The alcohol lent warmth to his stomach and a smile to his face. Without really being aware of having done so, he noticed that he had polished off the best part of a bottle of wine and a good quarter of a bottle of brandy.

The carriage wheels screeched. As the train slowed down to a stop Stinker settled herself in a new hollow in the blanket, made possible through his bent legs. The heavy wide sliding door opened with the sound of rusty metal scraping against more rusty metal. A shortish man stood in the doorway, lit up with the glare of a storm lantern that momentarily startled Jan's eyes, obscuring the face of the man.

'We're stopping to take on water,' the MO said. 'If you can walk then jump off and stretch your legs,' he added with the air of a man who had no intention of helping anyone on or off the train.

When most of the men had clambered off, Stinker jumped out to join them. Jan pulled back his blanket, dropped his penis into the empty carafe and let out the urine that had been building up for hours. As the men came back from 'stretching their legs', Stinker whined, asking to be lifted back in. Jan motioned to the officer who brought her back to his bed to empty his carafe on to the tracks outside the door. The officer glared at him and didn't speak. He picked it up nevertheless and, when he came back from the errand, accepted the cigarette that Jan offered him with a smile.

'I'll be glad to have someone wait on *me* again,' he said, engaging Jan with his eyes. 'It could be hours yet,' he added, stroking Stinker as she settled back down.

A large, broad-shouldered man jumped up into the wagon then stood up with his hands on his hips. He carried a hurricane lamp that gave his face, that had a thick black moustache and grinning teeth, a strange otherworldly look. Harry Briggs coughed to clear his throat and to gain their attention. The sight of Briggs gave Jan a sense of security in this world, grotesque and full of men with whom, even if washed and sober, he could never feel comfortable.

'Okay everyone, listen closely.' His high-pitched, clear voice carried like a man who had addressed an audience before. 'I have important news for you all.' He paused and sniffed. 'Good grief it smells like a Yates' Wine Lodge in here.'

The men laughed. One man held out a bottle to him and Briggs held his hand up to ward it away. 'A bit early for me,' he said.

'Get on with it,' one of them called out, receiving the laugh he was hoping for.

'It is good news, you will be pleased to hear,' said Briggs.

'Hoo bleedin ray,'

'It may take some time but all you officers are being moved to Lady Murray's Hospital at Le Treport.'

'We know that,' one of the men called out.

'Just shut up and listen will you,' another said.

'Yes, shut up,' said a few more.

'If I may continue, this is great news for you. It's a long way from any fighting and you will be looked after very well. I've been there many times and the treatment and recreational facilities are second to none. They have books, papers and a gramophone and in the town, you should be able to see a film. The hospital can provide transport to and from the town.'

'What about some skirt?' one of the officers called out to a round of laughter.

'We want nurses, we want nurses,' others chorused.

'Really gentlemen, I've a good mind to have you sent somewhere else.' He paused to put his lamp on the deck. 'Now, there are two MOs working their way up the train as I speak and they have been given orders to disregard your rank and to treat you with contempt if you are too drunk because that's what you would deserve. They can restrain you if needs be and there are definitely no nurses or VADs on this train.'

'Boo,' someone said.

Briggs' words were clear enough but Jan couldn't see him properly in the flickering light and shadows. Raising a hand over his eye to help him see didn't work as well as he thought, but he could just make Briggs out in duplicate.

'Now, as I say, it may take some hours before we get there, so please be patient. After I've had a chat with some of you, I'm going to walk down the next carriage and have a chat with them.'

When Briggs had finished, Jan rested in that gentle place between being awake and being asleep where nothing can ruffle a man. Clouds came down behind his forehead to dampen his remaining thoughts and his eyelids closed. He felt a hand shaking his shoulder and heard a far-away voice:

'Jan, listen. This is important…. I'm taking Stinker. Don't worry, I'll look after her. You're not well… I'll bring her back when I can,' Briggs said.

Chapter 11

22 December 1916

The Strangs were more composed on the morning after Captain Grimshaw's letter. Peter made a pot of tea at around eleven, brought it into the sitting room and poured Eva and Lucy large cups with milk.

'I'm going to make a list of who we need to write to and who we should tell,' he said, stepping over to the roll-top desk, picking up paper and pencil and then sitting back in the olive-green armchair, poised to write on his knee. 'We should wait till after Christmas to tell the Swedish relatives, though; there's no point in ruining their Christmas. What do you think?'

He looked at Eva. Eva pursed her lips.

'No, not just yet,' she said, putting her tea cup and saucer down to avoid spilling it. Lucy lit her umpteenth cigarette of the morning.

'I'll ring Mummy and Daddy tonight. I don't want to go over there today. But I s'pose I should for Christmas.' She cleared her throat and coughed behind her hand. 'Sorry to ask but could I have a drop of brandy Peter; otherwise I just don't know how I'll get through the day?'

Peter paused and looked at Eva who looked straight back at him.

'By all means,' he said, ignoring Eva's gaze. He moved over to the drinks cabinet returning with brandy bottle in hand, poured enough into her tea for her to taste but not to affect her too much then placed the bottle back in the cabinet.

'Oh, do settle down dear, you're driving us all mad with your getting up and down all the time,' Eva said. She turned towards Lucy and said that they never drank at home before six in the evening; a fact that Lucy already knew.

'Jan does,' Lucy said.

Eva made a pained expression.

'Oh, I'm sorry Eva, it's like I can't believe he's gone. Look at me. I'm talking as though he's still here.' Eva was poised to speak as Lucy moved close up to her on the settee but Lucy spoke first. 'I'm so sorry, I didn't mean to upset you,' she said.

'I'm sorry too,' Eva replied, looking into Lucy's eyes. Eva held out both of her hands and Lucy took them in hers.

'It's as if he's still here. Half of me doesn't believe he's dead at all,' Lucy said.

Eva took her hands back, pulled her hankie out from her cardigan sleeve and sneezed. 'Oh, excuse me,' she said.

All colour had left Peter's face, 'It's going to take us all a long time to accept it,' he said. 'I don't think any of us slept last night.'

The thought of being with her in-laws all day filled Lucy with even more despair.

'I'll tell Eric,' she said decisively, sensing a means of escape. 'I'll tell him tonight. He's home on leave for Christmas. He only lives by the park.'

'Are you sure Lucy, dear? You don't want to upset yourself any more just yet, do you?' Eva said, lifting her head to see her daughter-in-law better.

Lucy said that she'd be fine whilst knowing that she wasn't fine and wasn't 'right' at all. She had stopped raging against the God she said she didn't believe in but her eyes flashed round the room looking up and down, this way and that. She felt a nagging sense of guilt at wanting to get out and see Eric. But then, after all, Eric was Jan's best friend and she should be the one to tell him and anyway she was desperate to get out of the house. The thoughts went round and round in her head.

'I just want to talk about Jan, how he was at school with Eric and his friends and all those kind of things. And he should be told by us rather than a third party. It's only right.'

'More tea?' Peter asked, as Lucy blew her nose into a monogrammed hankie that Jan had had embroidered for her before he went off to the training camp. Everything she saw and touched reminded her of him. She stared at the letters L.S. and reflected on how attentive to detail he could be.

'Yes, I'll have another,' she said and Peter poured the tea.

Time passed and morning moved into lunchtime and then into afternoon. Eva tried forlornly to entice Lucy to eat something and Lucy thought that if she didn't get out of the house and into some fresh air soon she would suffocate. Work had been her usual avenue of escape; a way to block out the ever-present fear that Jan might be blown to pieces at any minute. Dealing with a never-ending pile of paperwork at the Home Office was her anaesthetic but today she chose to top her teas and coffees with brandy from the cabinet. This time she didn't even ask. She just went up to the drinks cabinet, took out the brandy bottle, poured some in her cup and replaced it without saying a word.

Shortly after three o'clock, when there was still some light left in the sky, she set off for Queens Park and Eric. Eva insisted she wrapped up in her long beige woollen-coat and wore her warm grey cotton stockings. She felt dizzy and a little sick. Setting out through the front gate and down the road she was desperate for some space around her. She had repeatedly told Eva that she would be alright and there was no need to worry. Although wobbly at first, her stride got steadier as the cold air filled her lungs. But as the fog grew thicker, her thoughts raced faster. Trying to light a cigarette she fumbled with a box of matches and gave it up as the match heads broke off in the damp air. Nearing the park on Kingswood Avenue she tried again.

'Arrghh,' she cried out, as she slipped on a slimy-wet kerbstone and pain shot up her leg. Bending down she grabbed her shin and felt where the stone had torn into her bone and blood was seeping into her stocking. Her cigarettes and matches fell around her. She fumbled on her hands and knees picking them up. On the other side of the road an old woman moved towards her and insisted on helping her pick up the cigarettes before taking Lucy's arm and getting her to her feet.

'I'm sorry,' Lucy said, then bit her lip as she felt the pain shooting up from her shin. 'It's the fog. I just slipped. I didn't see the blasted kerb.' Hairs curled from moles on the old woman's weathered face and the smell of her coat hit Lucy's nostrils. It was as if her clothes hadn't ever been washed and Lucy had never been so physically close with someone as dirty and bedraggled as the old woman. A feeling of revulsion overwhelmed her then subsided.

'I know dear, the fog's dreadful, my chest is terrible with it. Will you be alright dear?'

'Oh, it does sting so, but yes, thank you, I will be alright. I do feel a bit woozy though. Thank you so much.'

''Ave a drop of this dear.' The old woman handed her a half-full, quarter-bottle of cheap gin from her ancient worn-out coat pocket. 'It'll do you good.'

Lucy shuddered a little before wiping the top of the bottle with her coat sleeve and taking a swig.

'Oh, thank you, I'm so grateful,' she said, handing it back.

The woman stared directly at Lucy's eyes. Her lips were parted showing brown decayed front teeth. Her eyes were glazed and full of red veins.

'They're never really gone you know. The loved ones, they've never really gone,' the old woman said before putting the bottle in her pocket and waddling off down the road.

'What do you mean?' Lucy called after her. 'What do you mean by that?' But the woman was gone and there was only fog left in her place. 'Oh, damn and blast!' Lucy cursed in the park before finding a bench to sit on. Her stockings had torn exposing the wound. Steadying her nerves with deep breaths she bent down and wiped more of the blood from her shin with Jan's handkerchief that was so wet with tears the salt stung her flesh. The peace of the park gave her a welcome feeling of loneliness, then tiredness hit her like a lead cosh on the back of her head. She lay on her side and dosed off with her head resting on her closed hands, palms together as if in prayer.

A firm hand on her shoulder woke her suddenly. She opened her eyes to see a thin policeman with wrinkled face and heavy bags under his eyes looking down at her.

'Are you alright, madam?' Lucy felt a sudden fear followed by a pressing need to pee. 'Oh, you startled me. Yes, yes, thank you officer, I'm fine.' She sat up straight and crossed her legs.

'Well you can't stay here. It's not safe after dark. Where do you live?' Lucy told him and made what she thought was a convincing attempt at appearing sane and collected.

'I can escort you home if you like, madam.'

'No, honestly. I'll be fine. Thank you so much.'

'Well, make sure you go straight home. It isn't safe for a lady to be here after dark.' The policeman set off walking steadily northwards up the side of the park to patrol his patch. Lucy rose, shaking a little, and walked along the side of the park in the opposite direction until the policeman was out of sight. She looked furtively around her and, after she was quite satisfied that there was no one around, returned to the park and squatted among some shrubs away from the sight of the road. Much relieved, she set off again for Eric's house.

'Lucy, what a surprise! Come in. You look like you've seen a ghost, are you alright? What is it? What's happened?' Eric said, as she stood on the doorstep of his mother's house. Lucy saw and sensed his shock. He held her tightly by the arm, pulling her in away from the sight of the neighbours. He quickly closed the door behind them then hurried her through into the hall. 'Come in, come in, we've got a lovely fire going.'

'Don't worry about me. It's not about me. It's Jan, he's dead,' Lucy said. 'I just had to get out of the house and come round here to tell you.'

Eric, who had already guessed and didn't know what to do, awkwardly put his hand on her shoulder.

'It's just been terrible, terrible.'

Eric helped her off with her coat and scarf and hung them in the hall then sat her down in the living room in a blue-frayed armchair in front of the fire. The smell of coal smoke and pine needles hit her and she sneezed. She looked around the room; an ad hoc Christmas tree made from two pine branches pressed into a bucket of earth and decorated with coloured paper stood a few feet away in the corner. Eric prodded the fire with a poker before putting on more coal slack from the blackened scuttle on the hearth stone. The fire sputtered and sparked and belched thick sulphurous smoke.

A series of tiny involuntary shudders came over her as she thawed out by the fire. She felt Eric's eyes penetrating hers and judging her mental state. He looked at her as if she were a wounded dog and told her how sorry he was. As he spoke she couldn't remember having ever seen him look so worried. Then, in mid-sentence, he left the room.

She was left with her thoughts. This was all new to her: she had never told anyone that their friend had died before. This kind of experience must be taking place all around the country and in Europe and Canada and Germany and... Oh, the whole thing was just too terrible. Listening to the sound of his footsteps pacing up and down the hall she sniffled into her wet, blood-stained handkerchief, took out her compact from her bag and looked in the small round mirror before dabbing her red, sore nose with powder. She snapped her compact shut and looked up as the door opened. Eric's eyes were redder than before he left the room. He sat down across from her in the other armchair, leaned forward and lit two cigarettes with a spill from a jar by the fire. She gazed at the swollen veins on the back of her hand as she raised the cigarette to her lips and wondered if he had anything to drink in the house.

Without explanation he stood up, took her handkerchief from her lap and left the room. The noise of a running tap sounded out from the kitchen. When he came back he laid the wet hankie on top of the fire guard to dry and she was reminded what a kind and gentle soul Eric was. She felt a connection with him and was glad that she came to see him as soon as she had been able. He sat back in his chair and looked down at the fire, unable to speak or even look at her. Steam started rising from the wet hankie. She looked at the monogram L.S. in red embroidered stitching and felt strange and ill and a pang of fear grabbed her insides. Eric started fidgeting. Almost in a shout he broke the silence:

'He signed up after me and now he's gone and I'm still here.' He paused. 'It's my fault. I got him to do it.'

Lucy leaned over and laid her hand on top of his. Eric's mother's voice bellowed from the upstairs landing.

'Who is it Eric? Tell them I'll be down in a minute,' Eric jumped up and called from the bottom of the stairs.

'It's Lucy Strang. There's terrible news.'

Mrs Hardcastle thudded down the stairs, appearing at the doorway with her arms open and hands held out. Lucy stood up and Eric's mum pulled her close drawing her to her bosom.

'Oh, my poor dear, you're perished.'

'I'm fine, honestly.'

Mrs Hardcastle turned her head away as Lucy's breath hit her. Lucy felt uneasy in the embrace and wanted her to let go.

'I'll go and make some tea and bread and butter,' Mrs Hardcastle said, letting Lucy go. 'You need food inside you my dear. We've already had our dinner.'

'Honestly. I'm fine Mrs Hardcastle. I really don't want anything.'

'Nonsense; there's some cold ham.'

'No, honestly.'

'You need to eat something my girl, just for me.'

Lucy's stomach tightened. 'Well just a little.'

Mrs Hardcastle looked Lucy up and down and spotted the blood on her stocking and the mud on her shoes. Lucy couldn't have felt more uncomfortable if it had been the policeman she had met in the park. Eric's mother looked searchingly into her eyes.

'I remember how lovely you looked at your wedding,' she said, which felt to Lucy like a reproach. 'It looks like *you've* been in the wars.' She turned her head to Eric and stared. 'Just go into the kitchen for a moment, will you Eric please?'

'But why?'

'Please don't argue, Eric.'

Eric left the room with his mother calling out after him, 'Bring in a bowl of warm water, soap and a clean tea towel.'

'Yes, mum.'

With Eric safely in the kitchen, Mrs Hardcastle pulled up her sleeves to her elbow.

'Come on girl, we'd best get these stockings off and clean that wound or it could turn nasty.'

'Well, alright but it's not the reason why I came. I wanted to tell you-'.

'It's alright, I know what you're going to say. You can tell me in a minute.' She smiled kindly. 'We can't change what's happened.'

Lucy raised her skirt so they could unhook the stockings from her suspender clips and Mrs Hardcastle rolled down the stocking on Lucy's wounded right leg and Lucy took the other one off herself. The blood hadn't had time to completely harden into a scab so it came off easily enough without hurting too much. 'You need a good long soak in the bath.'

'I know.' Lucy glanced toward the door and saw Eric looking in through the crack. She looked him in the eye and pulled her skirt back down to just below her knees.

'Eric, you can come back in now,' his mother called.

Eric put the things he'd fetched from the kitchen down beside her slowly, one by one. Mrs Hardcastle dabbed Lucy's shin with a cloth soaked in warm water and then rubbed soap into the cloth. She washed it gently in easy downward strokes, releasing the hair and dirt from the forming scab.

Lucy was thinking of Jan and not her own sorry state. She was oblivious to the pain from her shin. Eric's mum got up from her haunches, left the room and brought back an old piece of linen sheet. It made a tearing sound as she ripped it into a bandage, before wrapping it around Lucy's leg and pinning it behind her calf with a safety pin. Eric sat back down and stared into the fire whilst Mrs Hardcastle sat on the arm of Lucy's chair. Lucy was desperate to explain herself.

'Thank you so much. You see we got this letter telling us Jan died and I had to come and tell you. A part of me doesn't believe it. I could tell half of it was lies but Peter said that they always try to soften the blow, as if that were possible. My leg means nothing really.' She looked over at Eric. 'You've been such a good friend to us Eric. It's not your fault you know, you're a good man. You weren't to know what would happen. He'd have had to enlist anyway. Everybody has.' She leant over, picked up her now dry and hot handkerchief from the fire guard and blew her nose noisily. 'We all knew this could happen. He should have gone to Sweden like his mother wanted.'

'Make him proud of you,' Eric's mum said, holding her hand. 'I'll leave you two to talk for a while,' she added, before leaving for the kitchen.

A gust of thick smoke blew back into the room from the fire. Lucy coughed into her hankie and Eric flicked his tab end into the fire just before it burnt his fingers. They stared into the smouldering slack, saying nothing. They heard the sound of the kettle rising to the boil in the kitchen and the noise of Eric's mum preparing the tea tray. She returned from the kitchen and, faced with a plate of brown bread smeared with margarine and Marmite, Lucy felt her appetite returning. Without pausing, she ate three slices, washing them down with black unsweetened tea. It was only then that she became aware of the sadness in Mrs Hardcastle's eyes. Lucy looked at her and collected herself.

Mrs Hardcastle took in a deep breath and calmly told Lucy that Jan had been such a nice child, full of life and always getting into scrapes with Eric. Just little boys playing in the garden and the park.

'I remember once when they'd both been catching newts in the lake at the park and Jan fell in and they came back and ...' She paused to blow her nose and wipe her eyes. 'You see his mother was so particular that we had to dry him off and make it look as if nothing had happened. She must have known but never said anything, not to me or Jan anyway.'

Eric's ashen face seemed to be hardly listening to the stories that at any other time would have embarrassed him. But Lucy *did* want to hear the stories, even though they made her cry. She wanted to cry and cry and to hear everything and anything about Jan.

'That's enough for now,' Mrs Hardcastle said. 'Come round soon, Lucy dear, and we'll have a proper chin wag.'

'Thank you, I'd like that.' Lucy attempted a smile.

'There's so many gone the same way,' Mrs Hardcastle said, closing the conversation as she clacked the tea cups and plates together before taking them back to the kitchen. Lucy heard her filling the sink to wash up and whispered to Eric.

'Can we go to the pub? I need a drink.'

He gave her a look that she couldn't make out: his eyes were far away, somewhere else completely.

'If you're sure you want to?' He looked her in the eyes.

'Yes, of course,' she said.

He leant over and touched her hair. 'I feel numb myself. It's still sinking in.' He uncrossed his legs and stood up. 'Okay then.' He raised his voice just loud enough to be heard in the kitchen. 'Mum, I'm taking Lucy home now.

We'll call in at The Game Cock on the way. Don't wait up for me; I'll make sure she gets home safely.'

Mrs Hardcastle returned from the kitchen, drying her hands on a tea towel.

'You'll need these,' she said, rolling up Lucy's stockings and putting them into a brown paper bag she pulled out from her apron pocket. She pushed the bag into Lucy's coat pocket then pulled Eric hurriedly into the hall. Lucy listened. '...she's in no fit state ... not the pub ... for heaven's sake ..... You've had a shock ... You know how you get sometimes.'

Lucy was in no mood for taking advice, even if Eric had been bold enough to offer it. She felt her anxiety rise and a sudden, greater urgency, to leave. She got up and moved to the hall.

'Bye, bye Lucy, anything we can do, anytime, just call round,' Mrs Hardcastle smiled. Lucy and Eric put their coats on and wrapped scarves around their mouths and noses.

'Thank you, Mrs Hardcastle,' Lucy said, stepping carefully down the front door step into the enveloping smog.

Tobacco smoke drifted out into the street as they pushed open the swing doors of The Game Cock. The atmosphere was even thicker in the pub than in the cold night outside where coal smoke was settling down from the chimneys of numberless domestic hearths onto a head-high mist. Heaving with men on leave there was nowhere to sit so they found a window ledge, sticky with beer, to lean against. The walk to the pub had cleared Lucy's head some more and the bread and margarine and cups of tea had, to some extent, settled the gripping in her stomach. She thought of the times the three of them used to meet up in the evenings before Jan went off for his training.

'I want to drink barley wine in Jan's memory.'

'Are you sure?' Eric looked at her as if she was deranged but there was no point in questioning her sanity.

'Yes, of course, I'll be fine, honestly.' She paused and smiled like an angel. 'This is for Jan; he'd have wanted us to have one in his honour.'

Eric looked at his shoes then lifted his head. 'If you say so,' he said and smiled back. 'I'll join you and pour it into my pint; just like Jan and me used to.'

He left for the bar and, with him gone for what seemed an age, watching all the drinkers downing pints made her throat feel parched. She felt vulnerable to advances from groping drunks. Eric weaved his way back saying 'excuse me' to people who pushed into him and blocked his way. At last he handed her the glass of barley wine. She swallowed it down in one, letting out a short burp in punctuation.

'That's better,' she said and sent Eric back to the bar for another glass, pressing money into his hand in a way that nobody saw her do it. 'Can I have one of your ciggies Eric?' she asked when he got back. 'Mine got all damp earlier.' She extended her hand to brush off some cigarette ash from his shoulder. Eric glanced into her eyes then, blushing, fumbled with his cigarette packet and lit up two Woodbines with a match from his box. Lucy took the cigarette and lifted her glass.

'To Jan!'

'To Jan!' Eric said then sucked the froth off his pint and wiped his moustache with the back of his hand. 'The best friend I ever had.'

Blood rushed from Lucy's head. She was awash with sadness. 'I never really saw enough of him, what with all the training and going off to the front.' She sipped from her glass. 'But he did love me? He did love me, didn't he Eric?'

Eric looked as if he didn't know how to answer. 'Yes, of course he did. He was head over heels for you. He always was. You must know that.'

'But what about the others?' She gave him a pleading look.

'What others?'

'There were others weren't there? Jan told me there were.'

Eric hesitated and took a long draw from his cigarette. 'But they were years ago and they didn't mean anything to him. You were his only real love.'

'But not the first?'

'Well no, obviously.' He looked at her as if she were stupid. 'It's different for blokes.'

'Why?' she asked softly. Perhaps she shouldn't have put him on the spot like that, but neither of them were any good at small talk. Eric, clearly used to the depth of her thoughts, waited for a moment before answering.

'It's sort of expected. We don't always want to.' He paused and looked at the floor not really wanting to say anymore. 'It can be terrifying and, because it's frightening, it doesn't always work out as it's supposed to.'

'What do you mean?'

'I'm sure you know what I mean.' He stared at her. 'Please don't tease me. I feel bad enough as it is.'

'I'm sorry. You look so sad.' She touched his shoulder. Their eyes met, and if they were somewhere quieter both would have cried. Lucy breathed in more of the bar's dirty air. 'Let's have another. Here's some money, you get them, and twenty Player's, and matches,' she said.

'Well, alright, but do be careful Lucy. I'm not sure you should drink anymore; you've had a terrible day.'

'I'll be fine. I'll be fine. Don't worry about me.'

Eric looked past her shoulder. 'But I do Lucy, I do care for you and with Jan gone…'

'I know you do Eric,' she said, putting her hand on his shoulder again. 'But it's all just so beastly. I want to block it out.'

'Yes, but I don't want to have to carry you home.'

'I'll be fine.' She put her hand inside her coat pocket and felt for the little tin of morphia tablets she had bought three weeks ago. She had always been curious as to their effect; they were supposed to make you feel better and if she ever needed to feel better it was now. She showed him the patterned tin. 'Do you want one of these Eric? I don't want to take one by myself; I was going to send them to Jan but they won't be any use to him now will they?'

'No, not now. I feel so bloody about the whole thing. They might help, they can sometimes. It will slow your drinking down. The men take them after a battle. When they can get hold of any, that is.'

Lucy placed the little white tablet into Eric's palm. Not wishing to be alone in her experience, she watched him swallow his before she put one under her tongue and felt it melt. It left a bitter aftertaste on the back of her tongue that made her reach for her drink.

'Have you had one before?' she asked Eric.

'Yes, of course.' Eric looked smug. He liked to think of himself as a man of the world.

'Well it's my first time. They taste disgusting,' she said, pulling a face before washing it down with barley wine.

'You're supposed to swallow, not suck,' Eric said.

The pub was filling up and the fug of tobacco smoke thickened. Eric turned round and pulled up the sash window a couple of inches and he and Lucy moved to stand against an elbow-high partition. They were pushed, jostled and accidentally elbowed as people squeezed past them on the way to the toilets. Lucy's head spun and her stomach heaved. She swayed then steadied herself with a hand on Eric's shoulder. Feeling vomit rumble up inside her she forced her way past the Friday-night queue of women outside the 'ladies'. Both cubicles were occupied. A middle-aged woman blocked the way, her weighty body guarding the cracked and yellowed sink. Just before Lucy's sick erupted she pushed the woman aside, threw up in the basin, let out an *urggh* then ran the tap. She turned and straightened up holding on to the basin with her hands and glimpsed the woman's shocked face. Lucy felt her legs wobble then give way. As she fell to the ground, she cracked the back of her head on the basin and blacked out.

Slowly returning to consciousness she became aware of three women kneeled around her splashing cold water on her face. Her head reeled and her stomach churned as the yellow blotchy faces stared down and fussed around her.

'Are you alright dear?'

Her face tingled as they rubbed it with a cold wet towel. She felt them moving her and sitting her up against a wall then shoving her head down between her knees. Realising where she was and ignoring her pain, she pulled herself up by gripping onto the pipes to the side of the wash basin. Holding on to the edge of the sink with one hand she splashed her face with water then turned her numb lips to the tap. She sucked in and rinsed her mouth before spitting out the water and returning her mouth to the stream to suck in and swallow. Wiping her face with the towel she mumbled a 'thank you'.

'You should go 'ome,' one of them said.

'Where do you live? We'll 'elp you get back,' said another.

'I'm so, so sorry,' Lucy said. She stood up, just managing to focus on her surroundings. She ran her fingers through her hair, untangling some of the matted strands. She was struck dumb by the violence of her nausea attack and blackout. She couldn't reply to their questions and offers of help. Avoiding their eyes, she stumbled back to the saloon bar and Eric.

'Christ, you look dreadful. Thank God, you're back. I nearly went in there myself to drag you out,' he said.

She struggled to find words through the haze in her mind and the feeling of sickness in her stomach.

'I'm sorry. I feel awful. Can we get some air?'

Easing their way through the throng of drinkers, Eric pushed open the swing doors into the street letting out a billow of smoke and a babble of noise from the saloon bar. They leaned against the pub wall, looked at the street in front of them and stayed still for a while watching the reflection of the light from the windows on the wet cobbles. A sense of peace swept over her.

'We should get you out of sight,' Eric said.

But at that moment Lucy didn't care a jot who saw her. Nothing about her was important. She breathed in great lungfuls of the dank, smoggy air as people went past, uninterested in a couple of drunks. Eric giggled.

'What is it?' Lucy asked.

Three uniformed men had come out and were urinating together into a drain hole in the gutter. Lucy's eyes met Eric's and they laughed and laughed and couldn't stop laughing. She wrapped her arms around her waist as if to stop her sides bursting. Then the pub started to empty and groups of men sang *Keep the Home Fires Burning* slurring the words as they poured out into Kilburn Lane. Fear suddenly gripped Lucy and their laughing ground to a halt. She looked down, felt sick and grabbed onto Eric's arm.

'Are you alright now darlin?' one of the women who had helped her in the toilet asked. Eric grinned inanely at her. Lucy flicked her hair out of her eyes and managed a smile.

'I'll be fine,' she said.

Eric looked at Lucy. 'How are you now?' he asked.

'I can't go home like this. I feel like death.'

'We'll go back to mine,' Eric said.

Lucy steadied herself against him and they weaved and stumbled their way back to his mum's house.

Chapter 12

23 December 1916

She woke up at about one in the morning, lying next to Eric on the rug in front of the Christmas tree by the last embers of the fire. With eyes hardly open she gazed around the scene, terrified of what might have happened. Her stomach tightened; she didn't remember getting there and didn't remember anything since leaving The Game Cock. The memory of being sick in the pub came back to her and she blushed, though there was no one to see her embarrassment. Hardly believing her predicament she eased herself up and, careful not to make a noise, made her way to the kitchen. Bertie the cat rubbed himself against her leg.

'Jesus Christ,' she let out and immediately put her hand over her mouth. She turned on the tap, felt it splash back up from the sink, turned it back a notch, bent her head down and sucked water in. Her stomach burned and her head banged louder than she imagined the guns would on the front line. She put her hand to the back of her head and felt a lump, a scab and matted hair. Foul-tasting fur covered her tongue which she began to scrape off with a finger nail then retched and had to stop. The noise might wake up Eric, or worse, his mother. Her heart pounded. She had to get out quickly. With one hand on the side of the sink and breathing in to steady herself, she stood up straight and adjusted her skirt. In the front room, she stepped over Eric to find her shoes then tip-toed into the hall, got her coat, took one terrified look at her face in the hall mirror, then left by the front door and was out into the street with collar turned up. A chill rain had sprung up and blew straight at her, stinging her face. She wanted to pee so quickened her step. She lit up a cigarette as she walked. It tasted disgusting. She coughed and made her way back to Chichester Road. Against the night air, intermittent shivers ran through her body.

'Where in God's name have you been?' Peter got up and looked down on her as she stood in front of them in the living room. 'Can you imagine how worried we've been?'

Unable to meet his gaze, Lucy felt like she wanted to die. Cramps stabbed her intestines. Her in-laws were sitting in the lounge in their winter dressing gowns with the fire glowing nicely. Apart from straightening her skirt with her hands, Lucy made no attempt to disguise the way she looked. She was a complete mess and that was that. What could she do? She had never been in a situation like this. They were grief-stricken and might never forgive her. If they ever found out about what had happened in the pub… and if they told Mummy and Daddy? It didn't bear thinking about. It was all totally horrid, just ghastly. They talked to her and she didn't hear what they were saying. She bowed her head so that they didn't catch the smell of her breath. Her mind was scrambled eggs.

'I'm so sorry,' she said. 'You shouldn't have waited up. We just got talking about Jan and the time went by so fast. I didn't realise it was this late.'

'Well, I er …,' Peter said.

'Mrs Hardcastle sends her sympathy. Please forgive me, I feel terrible. I just want to go to bed now.'

'I hope you sleep well,' Eva said, meaning it, and her kindness stung Lucy as she didn't deserve sympathy at all.

'I'm sorry, I'm just so upset, I don't know what to do now Jan's gone.' Lucy flashed a glance at Eva but couldn't hold the gaze. It would have been so much easier if they had been angry like her parents would have been. 'Night, night,' Lucy said as she left them and mounted the stairs to the toilet and then to her and Jan's bedroom.

Lucy woke in the night with a lucid mind. A feeling of nausea lingered in her stomach. She had a fierce thirst. She sat up to take a drink from the glass of water that Eva so thoughtfully placed on the bedside-table every night. Looking to the foot of the bed she saw, quite clearly,

Beatrice, her great aunt, looking very much like she did when she played with Lucy and her sisters as children. Lucy closed and opened her eyes and her Aunty was still there, looking back at her smiling. Lucy wasn't frightened and didn't know why.

Auntie Bea's brown, silky hair was in a bun and she wore the same bright flower-patterned summer dress that Lucy remembered her wearing in their back garden in Uxbridge. Her body shimmered with a hazy light and she smelt of rose petals. Aunty B looked at Lucy with eyes that shone with love. An overwhelming sense of peace and tranquillity passed through Lucy's body; a kind of euphoria cleaning away her feelings of fear and guilt from the day before. She closed her eyes, rubbed them and took another look, half expecting Aunty B's image to have disappeared.

There was no question that Aunty B had died, Lucy had seen the body. It was in October, just over two years ago and all the family went to the funeral. She remembered vividly, on the day before, standing next to her emaciated corpse in the front parlour of her terraced house in Willesden. Lucy had forced back her tears. Doctor Kingsley said that cancer had spread from her breast, through her blood to the rest of her body. And they all understood that she would have died in the most dreadful pain if he hadn't come over and injected her with morphine in those last days. And now, here she was at the foot of her bed looking happy, healthy and radiant. It felt completely natural to Lucy and very comforting. Aunty B didn't speak the words 'Jan is alive'; she didn't need to, because in a single clear thought they came, as if spoken, into Lucy's mind assuring her of his survival and return. And then Aunty B just disintegrated like particles of sunlit dust into the atmosphere of the room.

In the few minutes of Aunty B's appearance something had changed in the deepest part of Lucy's being. She felt a transformation so profound that she knew that she would never feel so desperately miserable again. She had Aunty B's reassurance that she could cope with whatever came her way and that Jan was alive.

A spasm gripped her stomach, bringing back the reality of her immediate predicament. Still in yesterday's clothes she felt dirty but no longer degraded and certainly not hopeless. She drank some water, threw the bedcovers off, got out of bed and rushed to the bathroom across the landing before she could be seen. She slid the bolt on the door behind her then kneeled over the toilet bowl, chucked up water and bile and wiped her mouth with toilet paper. The brass taps squeaked a little as she turned them. She allowed the sound of running water to soothe her mind by thinking of a bubbling brook in Iver Heath where Aunty B used to take her and her sisters blackberrying in their summer holidays. She sprinkled lavender salts under the taps, watched the mauve colour swirl and breathed in the fragrance rising in the steam. Scattered memories of last night started to come back and her guilt made her retch. She moved her hand and felt her sex through her knickers, took them off, stared at the gusset. There was no sign of Eric's seed.

Avoiding her own gaze in the mirror, she scrubbed her teeth, only stopping when blood appeared on her toothbrush. She spat out the white and pink foam into the sink, watching it disappear down the plug hole then filled her toothbrush glass with cold water, drank it in one go and made a burp letting out stale air. She took the rest of her clothes off, folded them and laid them on the floor next to the wicker-washing basket. She would wash them herself.

She felt cold sitting naked on the edge of the bath and stroked her arms where goose bumps had sprung up. She inspected the gash on her shin and the unexplained bruises on her arms, hips and legs. Turning round to test the water, lavender-infused steam filled her lungs triggering a bout of coughs that brought up thick, grey phlegm. Leaning forward she spat into the sink, rinsed it away then stepped into the bath, sank down and let the warm water cover her up to her neck. With just her head and knees exposed she sighed as the warmth of the water eased her muscles and bones and the fragrant steam eased her mind. She closed her eyes and, without thoughts, drifted off.

Alone in the bath she felt safe. She sank her head beneath the water and blew bubbles. Then rising, rubbed shampoo into her scalp from a bottle that Jan had bought her on her last birthday. With a willow-patterned jug she poured clean warm water from the tap over her head, rinsing away the suds. She attacked the hard skin on her feet with pumice stone, picked up the nail brush, scraped it over the soap and, working her way up in tiny movements, scrubbed all but the tenderest parts of her body which she rubbed scrupulously with the sponge. Her skin shone red and tingled in a satisfyingly painful way. For the best part of an hour, whilst other thoughts came and went, she laid back, soaking and wondering how she was going to face Eva and Peter. The longer she laid there a clearer picture of the night before took shape, stinging her conscience. She pressed her hands together to her chest, composed her thoughts and with her eyes closed whispered, 'Dear Father God, I have behaved so badly but I really didn't mean to. I promise by all that I hold dear never to do anything like that again. Please bring Jan back safely to me and let all the men who have fallen and gone back to you find peace in their new world. I promise you that I will never knowingly commit a selfish act again. Thank you for sending Aunty B back to me, it was wonderful to see her again. Please give me the strength to cope with the days to come and to be a better person. Thank you, God, Amen.'

As the bath water turned tepid and the skin on her fingertips wrinkled she went over and over in her mind what she would say to Eva and Peter. She would do all she could to find ways to return some of the kindness they had shown to her. She had been selfish and hurtful but now she had changed.

Still feeling distinctly shaky and unwell she got out of the bath, dried herself then pulled the bath plug out with a sense of determination for the task in front of her. After washing the bath out with Vim and an old cloth, she went back into the bedroom and put on a royal-blue woollen skirt, white blouse and matching blue cardigan. She looked in the mirror and decided not to pat her cheeks and nose with powder like she usually did. With bloodshot eyes, her face feeling and looking sore and with a shiny red nose she slowly descended the stairs to face her in-laws.

She knocked on the living-room door and made her rehearsed entrance. Awake, composed and drinking tea they stared and smiled at her with concern. Before they even had a chance to say 'good morning' she opened her mouth and let the words pour out:

'I'm so sorry. I can't make any excuses but I can tell you that I will never behave like that again.' There, she had said it. It was the first step along the way to her retribution. Never again would she go into The Game Cock, but then she would never want to even walk past it. Eva and Peter's eyes looked at her, telling her that they had hardly slept and that they had no inkling of last night's events.

'Would you like a cup Lucy dear?' Eva asked.

'Yes, please, don't get up I'll pour it.'

'Would you like some aspirin?' Peter asked.

'Thanks but no. I'll feel better soon, I'm sure. The pain's my punishment for drinking. I just feel terrible for behaving that way and making you worry and…'

'Don't be too hard on yourself, after all, you've had a terrible shock,' Peter said.

'Yes, we all have,' Eva said.

Lucy had half expected them to be at least a little bit angry.

'But I was the one who behaved badly. I deserve to feel ill.' She would have continued had she not been interrupted by the familiar 'clack' of the shutter from the letter box on the front door as it snapped closed. Peter got up, looking as if every bone in his body ached.

'It'll be something and nothing,' he said, returning with a brown envelope. He turned it around in his hands. 'It's come by the Army Post from France. It's addressed to us all: Mrs Jan Strang and Mr and Mrs Peter Strang.'

'Well, open it,' Eva said.

'Just a minute,' he said, looking at the back of the envelope. 'It's from a Chaplain Harry Briggs from a place called Remy Sidings in France.'

He put his hand in his pocket for his pen knife and sliced it open. Lucy knew it would be good news. She perched on the edge of the armchair, hands together in her lap.

'What does it say?'

'Don't tell me any details if it's too awful. I just couldn't bear it,' Eva said.

Peter pulled out the letter and quickly looked up and down at it.

'Good God, I can hardly believe this.'

'Well?' they both asked.

'Jan's alive!'

'I knew it,' Lucy said, jumping up and making a clap.

'For God's sake Peter, read it out,' Eva said.

'He says, Harry Briggs that is…'

'Yes?'

'He says, err, Jan's been in a bad way but he should improve. He's at a field hospital at Remy Sidings, or was when this was written, and should be at Lady Murray's Hospital in the coastal town of Le Treport by the time we get the letter. There he'll be treated well and have the good medical help he needs.'

Lucy shivered and her skin came up in goose bumps. Aunty B was right. She sat back down in the arm chair and, with a satisfied smile on her face, let her body sink into its contours. Eva wept and Peter held her head to his chest.

'I'll look after him, whatever state he's in.' Lucy said.

Chapter 13

22 December 1916

The engine hit the buffers at Le Treport station with a slow thud that reverberated down the train. It was around 5.30 in the morning and still dark. The women ambulance drivers and VADs from Lady Murray's Hospital started loading the officers for the short drive along the coast to the No 10 Hospital.

'My God,' one of the VADs said, after she struggled to slide open the heavy door and venture into Jan's carriage. She put her hand over her face. 'They're absolutely filthy.'

'They'll've been drinking all night, and they're the officers,' a more experienced VAD, who was showing her the job, said. Together they lifted the semi-conscious Jan onto a stretcher. 'This one's pissed himself and probably worse,' the experienced VAD said.

'It's just horrible,' the new VAD said.

'You'll get used to it.'

The new VAD put her hands on her hips and looked her mentor in the eyes. 'But they stink! Someone'll have to hose these carriages out before they move on. I can hardly breathe in the air.'

They rested Jan's stretcher by the door for the MOs to lift off. The more experienced VAD wiped her forehead under the band of her cotton hat with the back of her hand.

'They were better behaved at the beginning,' she said, by way of explanation, 'but, as the war went on, the hope left the men, you see, and then the dignity left; with most of them anyway.'

'It's the drink that's lost them their dignity, surely, not the war,' the new VAD said, as her mentor shook her head and they moved away from Jan to their next patient.

Jan's mind and limbs were numb. It felt like an age getting him and the rest of the wounded up to the hospital in all the commandeered trucks and horses and carts manoeuvring round the front of the station. He had heard of the grand half-timbered building from an officer who had been there before, but Jan could see nothing in this dark and freezing fog that was making the weak-lunged around him cough and splutter. He was helped into the building from the back of a converted butcher's van by an MO who let Jan's good right arm hang over his neck and shoulders as he moved him. The MO dropped him down on a chair like a side of meat and followed it with such a look of disgust that, despite Jan's inebriation, the look stayed in his mind.

Before they were assigned to their beds, the casualties formed a ragged but calm queue waiting for their clothes to be removed. When Jan's turn came the VADs cut his trousers off with large dress-makers scissors. His cuts and lice bites stung as they washed him with sponges soaked in milky-looking disinfectant. They wrapped a towel around his waist to protect his dignity then dried him and helped him into white and blue-striped cotton pyjamas. His skin tingled. A nurse led him to his clean bed, where the smell of lavender hit his nostrils as he lay his head down on the pillow. Staying here would be sheer bliss. As he drifted in and out of sleep he heard the voice of an officer, full of self-important bluster, attempting to complain and Jan smiled to himself as no one took any notice. There was no doubt who was in charge here and it wasn't the Army officers.

Through his sleep, Jan heard the soft refined voice of a VAD waking him.

'... and if Lady Murray was running the war it would have been won by now. She'll come down and see you all later,' she said, smiling into Jan's eyes as he opened them. 'Now, let's get these off.' She moved her hands to his head and started to gently ease off the blood-encrusted dressings.

Jan signalled to her by pretending to write.

'We're really quite busy now, but if you're quick you can write on this,' she said, handing him a notepad and pencil from her breast pocket by the red cross on her apron.

Concentrating as best he could and, struggling with fingers that couldn't get a proper grip on the pencil, he wrote, *MY DOG?* in the best capitals he could manage.

'Oh dear, you are shaken up aren't you? I can hardly read this. Oh, I see, you've lost your dog, well, what does it look like?'

Little terrier.

'What's its name?'

Stinker.

Jan's mouth stretched into a big smile and the VAD let out a short laugh. He felt a warm pang of happiness rising from his solar plexus. Feeling comfortable he settled down to listen to her soft, feminine west-country accent and to feel her little fingers moving around on his head.

'I'm VAD Hare. It stands for Voluntary Aid Detachment,' she said, then sat on the side of his bed and explained, hardly pausing, and as if she was gossiping to a friend from her home town, that the hospital had two resident dogs who had been rescued from the job of message-carrying between the trenches: Hamish, who was a dirty-white West-Highland terrier, and Rosie, a tan-and-white terrier with a patch over her left eye. Rosie was a little bigger than Hamish and of undetermined parentage. They followed the nurses and VADs around the hospital and, although they got under everyone's feet, Lady Murray liked them, so they were there to stay. 'You'll see them before long,' she said, avoiding eye contact. 'Hamish and little Rosie always go around together. I don't remember seeing another scruffy terrier. Was it a pure bred?' she asked, and then continued without giving him the chance to answer. 'There is a hairy little mongrel that wanders into the grounds sometimes.'

Jan shook his head.

'Well I'm sure he'll turn up,' she said.

Jan wrote, *SHE*, on the notepad and showed it to her.

'Oh, that's nice. Well I'm sure she'll turn up, they're very good at finding the people they love. I was brought up on a farm and our dogs always found their way back.'

Jan let her words dissolve into his mind as she told him how she loved animals, especially dogs, and that just talking about it made her heart ache for home. He was thinking how he could have listened to her for eternity when she got up, disturbing his gentle reverie.

'I wish I could help the horses,' she said, picking up her pail where she put her dirty bandages. Tears appeared at the edge of Jan's eyes. His childhood had been nothing like hers and he wished it had been.

By mid-morning, the forty or so officers who had come up with him on the train had been cleaned, fed and watered with dressings replaced. Most were sitting up in bed with their heads resting back on soft, feather pillows, all of which had little cotton parcels of lavender pinned to them that gave them a sweet alternative odour to the foul air they had become accustomed to. Sparkling-coloured Christmas decorations, clean cream-white walls and the nurses and VADs briskly going about their business settled Jan's mind. Everything was ordered and in its place. Such close attention to detail at Lady Murray's led to many and repeated thank yous from men relishing the oasis of tidiness and order after the panic and gore of the trenches. A doctor, ward sister and an MO who had all been at the Field Hospital when it was evacuated, were working their way up and down the rows of beds, getting details of the officer's, their wounds and treatments as well as surgery already carried out.

'Good morning Lieutenant,' the Ward Sister said, looking down at Jan.

Jan smiled and nodded and wandered if he could wangle a shot of morphine out of them. He pulled a face and touched his head.

'What do you know about this gentleman?' she said, turning to the efficient-looking MO standing by her side with pencil and clipboard at the ready. Jan thought he could have been a solicitor's clerk in Civvy Street. The MO tapped the clipboard with his pencil.

'Oh, quite a bit Sister, the paperwork's all here. His name's Strang, Jan Strang. Lucky to be alive by all accounts: Gunshot wound to left arm; shrapnel pierced his helmet and penetrated his skull on that left side; definite neurasthenia and muteness - probably temporary - severe headaches, nightmares and convulsions. In pain most of the time. He's had enough morphine to kill a horse so he'll need regular shots: half a grain three or four times a day, I'd suggest, though that may not be enough.'

The doctor looked at the MO and thanked him for his diagnosis before explaining to him, as he moved his weight from foot to foot, that it would be he who would decide on the correct dosage and that he would reduce it by degrees over the next few days.

All the officers said that Lady Murray's was the best of the base hospitals in Le Treport and probably in France. It was one worry off Jan's mind. There were several hospitals in Le Treport dealing with hundreds of casualties each day from all ranks and nationalities, including Germans, but at Lady Murray's they just attended to wounded British officers. After the makeshift hospitals he'd been through and evacuated from, he now knew he was going to a good place where they weren't going to leave him for dead.

From her reputation, Lady Murray was the sort of woman that Jan admired but wouldn't dare cross and when he saw her he liked and trusted her straight away. Although clearly of the upper class, she had no obviously objectionable airs and graces. She chose to wear a simple grey and white uniform and her personal touch made him feel half human. She was strangely fascinating and he couldn't work out why. She was middle aged, physically unimposing and wasn't remotely attractive in a feminine way, to him anyway. Nonetheless, overwhelming feelings of gratitude and respect towards her rose in him and he was worried that a tear might run down his cheek. His eyes followed her movements as her thin fingers held his wrist, felt for his pulse and looked at the watch on her apron. She put his hand down gently on the bed then felt his brow. Two young VAD assistants stood to the back and slightly to the side of her, ready to take notes. Her voice was clear and refined.

'I do hope we can make you very comfortable here and that you may get better soon.' She gave him a kind smile. 'Your blood is flowing normally you'll be pleased to hear,' she said, with no hint of pity.

The next day his skin itched so badly they put woollen mittens on him to stop him scratching himself sore. He would have to wait for the mid-morning injection before he could get any relief and his head still hurt like hell. Patience was what war was about, patience and recuperation.

An officer using crutches made his way from down the ward and sat on Jan's bed. He told how he'd been back and forth to the front three times and still lived to tell the tale. He chatted away, teaching him the 'ropes'. He must have realised that Jan couldn't speak as he seemed unperturbed that he didn't reply.

'They don't keep anybody here any longer than they have to but, if you lay it on thick, you can get another day or two out of the place,' he said.

The upset that news of his death must be causing back home preyed on Jan's mind. And then there was Stinker. His mind was clearing and he remembered that Briggs had taken her away. Guilt gnawed at his brain; he'd been too drunk to care for the little dog that adored him. He fantasised that she might just come in, run up to him and lick his nose. Most of all he wanted to be back home with Lucy, far away from all this hell. From what the officer said, they could ship him back off to Blighty within days because they needed the beds. Nagging thoughts rushed round and round his head:

could he make love again? Would the war ever end? Would the headaches ever leave him? Would he be a dumb fool forever? Where was Stinker? How were Lucy and his parents? And when would they come round with the morphine to deaden his pain?

Chapter 14

23 December 1916

Luckily for Lucy, as it was so close to Christmas, she didn't have to go into work this Saturday. So, as Christmas Eve fell on the Sunday, she had four clear days off. Jan was alive and she would make sure that a good life and comfortable home would be there waiting for him when he came back. In the morning they all wrote letters to Jan. Peter, who needed to go into the office to check the mail, dropped them off at the post office on his way in. Lucy rang her mother to let her know that Jan was alive and they would be celebrating Christmas here after all and that she could hardly wait to see them. After the call, she set about cleaning the kitchen and was just sprinkling caustic soda into a bowl under a running tap when Eva came in and insisted she stop and spend the day with her, saying that the housework could wait. Alone together they talked, almost losing track of the time. Eva told her about her family and the cold, white Christmases they had growing up and how everything changed when she met Peter and they married, moved to London and he became successful.

'You must be starving.' Eva got up to make sardines on toast whilst Lucy made the tea.

Lucy wanted to get started organising the front room in readiness for Christmas. Dusting the ornaments and bric-a-brac on the shelves and surfaces, she hummed the tunes of popular songs that she had heard but didn't quite know the words to. Eva suggested that they went out to see what food, presents and decorations they might pick up at the market before the stalls packed up and darkness fell. Outside, the December air refreshed them. Lucy made a quick detour to tell Eric and his mother the good news and to thank Mrs Hardcastle for being so kind the night before. There was little left on the market stalls but they did manage to come back with some rather grubby looking potatoes, sausages, a cabbage as well as some beetroot and Eva said she would make thick gravy with onions for Christmas Day to go with the ham she had already ordered.

'Life has a way of picking you up just when you thought it couldn't get any worse,' Eva said as they unpacked their bags in the kitchen, and Lucy was beginning to understand what she meant.

Peter came in at about five and, with a big smile, placed two bottles of Italian red wine on the kitchen top.

'That's wonderful, darling. I think you must have had some already.'

'Just a drop at the office. Mrs Agnoli came in to type up some invoices to get them out before Christmas and left us these.' Peter spoke whilst looking through the shopping baskets.

'How thoughtful,' Eva said.

'I know; the Italians do take their celebrations very seriously.'

'I met her once when Jan showed me his office before we got married. She seemed such a nice woman, so welcoming,' Lucy said.

'So I hear,' Eva said.

'Do thank her and send my best next time you see her,' Lucy said.

'I will,' Peter said. 'She was overjoyed about Jan, of course. She was, I mean is very fond of him.'

'I'll finish off in here and bring out tea and toast in a minute,' Lucy said, as she put the kettle on and hurried them out of the kitchen into the warm living room. 'We've got sausages for dinner and plenty left for Christmas Day.

A letter fell through the front door; Eva opened it.

'It's a card from your parents, Lucy. Look it's got an angel on it and it and says underneath, "There's always hope", how lovely.' She passed the card to Lucy.

'Mummy says, if it's not inconvenient, they can come over tomorrow afternoon.'

'Well, that should be fine,' Eva said. 'It'll give me enough time to make some scones in the morning.'

The front door opened followed by the unmistakable sound of Gladys hanging up her coat in the hall. She stood in front of them in a stained uniform with her hair tied up away from her neck. Peter got up and poured her a cup of tea.

'Well? don't just stare at me. What's the news on Jan?' Gladys asked them.

'I had a chat with one of my contacts at the war office and he says that they never keep anyone very long at the coastal hospitals, as there are always more coming through to make room for. They'll probably keep him there over Christmas then ship him back as soon as they can after that,' Peter said.

'I hope he's in a better state than some of the poor buggers I have to see to,' Gladys said.

'Really Gladys, your language. And we don't need any more upsets, thank you. You should think of people's feelings.' Eva gave Gladys a penetrating look which Gladys ignored. 'We've got Lucy's family coming over tomorrow, I hope you don't intend to show us up,' Eva said.

'Jesus, Mother, don't you know there's a war on? Everybody swears nowadays.'

'Well, you're not everyone. What you do at work is your business but when you're at home….' Gladys sat down and lit a cigarette. 'You can help Lucy with some decorations after dinner,' Eva said.

'Pull the other one,' Gladys said. 'I'm knackered.'

Eva turned to Lucy. 'I don't know what half the words mean,' she said.

'Anyway, I've volunteered to go and nurse in France,' Gladys said.

'But you can't,' her mother said. 'Look what happened to Jan.' She paused to think. 'And we need you here.'

'Don't worry, I'll be nowhere near the front. Anyway, sorry, but I've already signed up.'

Peter looked angry and paced around the room avoiding looking at Gladys. 'But what if the Germans start winning

168

and they get to the ports? The danger you could be in, it doesn't bear thinking about. Have you thought this through? Why didn't you discuss it with us?'

'I have thought it through. That's exactly why I have to go and do my bit,' Gladys said. 'We can't all leave it to other people.'

Chapter 15

23 December 1916

After his morning shot and an hour's rest, Jan walked about a bit moving up and down the ward holding on to the iron bed frames, his legs striding between beds. To test his strength, he decided to go further and made gradual progress along corridors of the building, nodding with a smile to the staff who passed him, too busy to do anything more than smile back. With stick in one hand and with the other holding onto unvarnished pine rails that had been screwed in with iron brackets onto the oak-panelled walls, he remembered the delicious smell of raw pine with sticky sap as it was unloaded from the docks. A cold morning air blew in from the sea through ajar windows, sending a surge of energy from his lungs through to his veins. Going down the stairs he grabbed onto polished banisters and descended one step at a time. On reaching the ground floor, he rested his weight on his stick and muffled a cry of pain as he felt the gunshot wound in his arm split open. Damn, damn, damn.

Nearly recovered from the hurt in his arm and standing tall, he made his way to the Day Room. His head bandage absorbed cold sweat from his brow and the bandage on his arm soaked up the blood seeping from his wound. He smiled to the other men and sat in an arm chair that had floral patterns like the wallpaper at Lucy's parents' house. His mother-in-law might have designed the day room. He smiled to himself and, probably for the first time since he had met them, thought fondly of his in-laws. Her father seemed a lot less of an ogre now than he had done then. If only Francis T. knew how mistaken he had been about the war.

He sat down by a low table in front of a semi-circle of arm chairs. An old copy of the *Times* caught his eye. He lay his stick down by the side of his chair, leant forward and, showing no pain, picked up the paper and started reading. In the causality lists, he hardly knew any of the fallen. He only had a vague memory of two men from training in Saffron Waldon; men he'd heard of but couldn't actually remember meeting. He didn't recognise any of the officers either, and turned the page. A picture of General Haig stared straight at him with his open letter printed underneath:

The lessons which the people of England have to learn are patience, self-sacrifice and confidence in our ability to win in the long run.

That was fair enough, he supposed.

The aim for which the war is being waged is the destruction of German militarism.

Yes, well, he supposed so, he could go along with that.

Three years of war and the loss of one-tenth of the manhood of the nation is not too great a price to pay in so great a cause.

He threw the paper to the floor and closed his eyes to control the anger rising inside him. Jesus Christ, the man was a complete idiot. One of the officers got up and walked through a side door. Jan lit a cigarette, took in a lungful and coughed. Haig knew nothing, absolutely sod all about the real war. Anyone off the street could run the war better than that monkey. They could call for peace talks for a start and have a cease fire. He took a long drag from his cigarette. One day he would tell the true story, even if they said he'd lost his mind, which they probably would.

He heard a noise behind him and felt the hands of MOs holding his arms, lifting him off the seat. One of them took the cigarette out of his fingers and stubbed it out in the ashtray.

'Sorry, Sir. Come on now, Sir. We need to get you back to your bed.'

He struggled from the shock of being manhandled and it opened his wound further and his head started banging. They slung his right arm over a shoulder. Bloody hell, couldn't they be more gentle? Then they half carried him back up to the ward in just the same way, as if he had had too much in the pub and was being taken home. They dropped him onto his bed, springs creaking. Would his torment ever end?

'We'll leave him with you,' they said to the VAD, who was walking briskly towards them with determined look and syringe in hand. Holding on to Jan's wrist she rolled up his sleeve.

At about midday on Christmas Eve, at what was generally considered to be the best time of day for excursions around the house, Jan decided to take his first walk outside. His arm wound had been stitched up, breakfast had long settled and the ten o' clock cup of sweet tea with two Garibaldi biscuits had allowed enough sugar into his system to attempt an unaccompanied journey around the building. From the window, through the sleet on the glass pane he could see trees swaying in what must have been a fierce wind blowing in from the Channel. It was a bitter winter, the worst he'd known.

After manoeuvring down the stairs and borrowing a greatcoat from the peg by the main door which, with some difficulty, he rested over his shoulders, Jan left the building determined to catch what daylight he could. Outside, he walked along the gravel path and around a corner of the house flanked by rose beds with flowerless leafless thorny plants. The chill wet air rasped his lungs and hail stones blew in his face hitting him like so many bee stings. He took shelter in a side entrance. With numb fingers, he lit up and felt his skin prickle with the cold. His body was coming alive. His walk was successful.

'We nearly sent out a search party for you,' a VAD said to him, smiling, as Jan came back into the warm ward. A small plate of cold meat and a few potatoes lay waiting for him on his bed. He kept forgetting about his meals and knew that he must eat more. The VAD caught his eye. 'Have you forgotten?'

Jan looked at her quizzically.

'It's Christmas day tomorrow. Chop chop, we need all the help we can get.'

Jan, and anyone else who could move an arm, was roped into making decorations. So, following precise instructions from the VADs, he and the other officers stuck pieces of brightly coloured paper together to make chains to hang around the walls. Others twisted strips of crepe paper and pinned them to the ceiling cornices, stretching them to the central lights. A cheer rose up from the men as a seven-foot Christmas tree arrived wet, dripping and cut down from God knows where, which they dragged to the far end of the ward. They planted it in a giant terracotta pot weighed down with stones, covered it with silver and gold-painted baubles and showered it with tinsel. Unaccustomed cheerfulness reigned as the officers watched the nurses and VADs getting excited by it all. All the men agreed that without the women and their enthusiasm, Christmas would be just too sad to contemplate. And Jan saw himself in future years telling Lucy and their children of his wonderful rest at Le Treport when all the army officers sat down on the floor around a giant Christmas tree and made paper chains.

On Christmas morning 1916, every sick or wounded soldier in every Stationary Hospital, Casualty Clearing Station, Hospital Ship or train received a card from King George V and Queen Mary. Jan was lying on the top of his bed in his army trousers, newly-donated slippers and socks, all of which he had put on by himself. Lady Murray made it her business to hand the royal message out personally to Jan and the other officers. In gold lettering and on white card embossed with the Royal Insignia, the King expressed his

grateful thanks for hardships endured and unfailing cheeriness. The Queen and I are thinking more than ever of the sick and wounded among my sailors and soldiers. From our hearts we wish them strength to bear their sufferings and a speedy restoration to health.

Unfailing cheeriness, indeed. Inside Jan laughed a bitter laugh as he watched the pleased expressions on the gassed, wounded, shell-shocked and amputee officers along the ward. One of the men was so overwhelmed by the card that he started to tell everyone about how thoughtful the King and Queen had been and how, if he got back, he'd keep the card as an heirloom. Whenever the man came close, Jan feigned sleep.

Following breakfast, for which everyone had a boiled egg with white buttered toast, the VADs and nurses handed out small presents: sweets, packets of cigarettes, small cigars, note books, pencils and writing paper. Jan raised a smile as he lit one of his packet-of-five cheroots. Lady Murray announced that wine and brandy, which they had in reserve, would be available at six o'clock in the evening. Jan sighed, and the handful of hardened drinkers who felt they couldn't wait for six o'clock to come around tried, with all their well-bred charm, to persuade the VADs to sneak them a bottle. The VADs, though, knew better than to disregard Lady Murray's orders despite the silver tongues, offers of marriage and signed IOUs.

Jan heard footsteps, chatter and mild commotion outside the ward. The door swung open and Harry Briggs entered with a wiry-haired, waggy-tailed, terrier on a lead. Stinker, with Briggs behind her, went up to the beds and sniffed the cast iron legs. Jan became filled with irrepressible happiness. He watched his dog's progress along the beds and waved at Briggs. Stinker caught Jan's scent and pulled the lead hard. Briggs let go his grip, and Stinker jumped up onto Jan's bed making squeaky whimpering noises as she licked him under his chin and on his face. Jan stroked her wet fur and half lifted her up into the air, ignoring the pain that shot up through his left arm. He shuffled round and placed Stinker on the ground. Briggs extended his hand; Jan grabbed it with both of his and shook hard.

'Happy Christmas, Jan,' Briggs said, patting Jan's shoulder with his free hand. 'It's the little things in life that give us the greatest happiness don't you think?' Stinker settled down by Jan's legs resting her head on his foot. 'You appear much improved. It's good to see you, old chap, and under considerably better circumstances this time.'

Jan's face twitched as what felt like a shot of electricity ran up his neck through to his head but he had rarely felt happier. His face twinged twice more. Briggs, noticing Jan's pain, put his hand into his tunic pocket and brought out a little tin of pills. He moved his head to whisper in Jan's ear.

'Would you like one of these?'

Jan nodded twice.

'I always try to keep some for emergencies; there's been so much pain about. Haven't many left now and they're getting harder to come by.'

Jan picked two out, put one on his tongue and dropped the other in his pyjama top pocket hoping Briggs wouldn't notice. He sneered as the bitter taste filled his mouth. Briggs passed him a glass of water and winked.

'Don't mention it old chap but keep it under your hat, eh.'

Jan nodded and gave him a 'you can trust me' look.

'Now, I've got a service to conduct: third today and another two after this one. Should have done them last night really but it's all been such a bloomin' rush.'

Jan nodded.

'I've been made a permanent chaplain for all the Le Treport hospitals and they've given me a Vickers Clyno to run about in, minus the machine gun. But they have kept the sidecar, which is a blessing really, otherwise I'd be off it more than on. Takes a bit of getting used to I can tell you. It's seen action and it's probably on its last legs; that's why they've given it to me. Ha ha. They must think I get some help from upstairs.'

Jan nodded and wrote, *Letters home?* on his note pad.

'They would have got them yesterday or the day before, so don't worry old man. Their wounds will soon be healed.'

Jan exhaled and weakly patted Briggs' hand.

'What lovely Christmas decorations,' Briggs said. 'It's a fantastic hospital, definitely the best place for you at present. I hear they had the gramophone out last night. That must have bucked you up a bit.'

Jan nodded.

'Well there's a few more people to see and then I'll be back to take the service at ten. I've already conducted one at the Canadian Hospital and at the General and after here I've another two. Oh, I told you that already, didn't I? So, I daren't even have a drink or I'll be flat on my face by the end of the day, ha ha. Bye for now old chap. I can see you're getting that far-away look in your eyes.'

The next time Jan opened his eyes, he saw Lady Murray standing at the far end of the ward with her nurses, VADs and MOs on both sides of a table with a tall brass cross on a green, red and gold-coloured tablecloth. Smoke from the Christmas-tree candles curled up to the ceiling.

'Good day gentleman. On behalf of myself and my staff I'd like to wish you all a very,' she raised her voice, 'Merry Christmas.'

'Merry Christmas, Lady Murray,' they called with varying enthusiasm and strength of voice.

'Many of you will already know our new chaplain Lieutenant Briggs. He's been a reliable source of inspiration around Flanders these past two years and now they've taken him away from the front line to work in Le Treport's hospitals. We're all very happy to have him here. He will be conducting our service today.' She paused and smiled at Briggs. 'Lieutenant Briggs,' she said extending her arm, 'I'll let you take over from here.'

Those who had two hands to clap with clapped them. Others slapped one hand on their thigh or bed, some stamped and one whistled.

'Thank you, Lady Murray, for that wonderful introduction and a big thank you to all of you who have helped to make this such a very special day in which to honour the birth of our Lord Jesus Christ. This is undoubtedly the most splendidly decorated hospital in Le Treport, probably in the whole of France. I must extend my thanks to all those involved,' Briggs said.

'Hear hear!' someone called.

'Could you firmly extinguish all cigarettes and cigars please?'

'What about pipes?' someone else called out.

'Just leave them to go out by themselves. Now, please would you all join me in our first carol and, would those who can, rise please? Once in Royal David's City.'

'Once in royal David's city
Stood a lowly cattle shed,
Where a mother ….'

Those who could sing sang their best and Jan was almost glad to be mute. When the carol had finished, Briggs continued,

'Let us bow our heads and pray for the help and guidance of God in this time of war.'

The room fell silent except for a deep sigh from Stinker.

'God is our hope and strength.'

'A very present help in trouble,' some of them responded.

'Oh Almighty Lord, who art a most strong tower to all them that put their trust in thee: Be now and evermore our defence; grant us victory if it be thy will; look in pity upon the wounded and the prisoners; comfort the bereaved; succour the dying; have mercy on the fallen; and hasten the time when war shall cease in all the world.' He paused for a few seconds. Jan's eyelids drooped. 'Through Jesus Christ our Lord. Amen.'

'Amen,' they replied and Jan nodded off.

On Boxing Day morning, Jan felt better than he thought he ever would or could. The reduced morphine dosage over the last five days at Lady Murray's, combined with a healthy diet, allowed him to have his first normal bowel movement in weeks. He walked to the WC aided by his stick, holding his sponge bag and with Stinker scampering at his heel. He went into the cubicle and closed the door leaving Stinker to wait outside. He undid the cord on his pyjama bottoms, let them fall to the floor and sat on the toilet seat in the nick of time. As the great load left him he uttered a long sigh of relief. 'Thank heaven for small mercies,' Harry Briggs would have said. At the row of basins, he washed his hands and face, brushed his teeth, shaved and, with his fingers, flicked the hair that was not covered with bandages to the right. He stood tall and smiled into the mirror.

After a breakfast of porridge, buttered brown toast and marmalade and white coffee, which he consumed on a tray sitting on the side of his bed, he got dressed unaided. A Lady Chauffeur, apparently young and beautiful, was to take him and three of his fellow officers for a trip into Le Treport. The officers waited outside by the house steps surrounded by morning mist that had blown over from the Channel. It had a clean, fresh smell; no hint of smoke, explosives or disinfectants. Charlie Lewis, who'd an arm amputated from the elbow, turned to Jan.

'We'll have a good day today, Jan, don't you worry about that. When they went into town last week they ended up watching a film at the Canadian Hospital. It was about a tramp and they laughed all the way through. Then they listened to a French band in the town square and got hopelessly drunk.' Stinker pulled at her lead sniffing towards the rose beds. 'There's a lady driver apparently and it's a great motorcar as well: Sunbeam 16/20.'

Jan feigned interest, smiled and looked up towards the sky. He felt a gust of bitter sea wind dispersing the mist. He buttoned up his trench coat at the collar, opened a new packet of Woodbines and handed them round. Crunching tyres on the gravelled drive alerted them to their motor vehicle which was to take them to town. It stopped in front of them and the throaty engine-noise stilled. A handsome, slender woman in her mid-twenties, around five-foot-six, in smart grey coat and leather gloves stepped out. Her hair was shiny black and curled out from under her chauffeur's cap. She smiled with red lips and white teeth that could brighten the dullest of days.

'Good morning, gentleman, I hope you all had a damn good Christmas. For those of you who don't know me, I'm Edythe Lowe your volunteer chauffeur, all the way from British Columbia. No formal names or pack drill with me; just call me Edythe.' She shook all their hands in turn and they introduced themselves. She stood on the step leading down from the house. 'Gentlemen, before we start we need to get a few things clear. I'm told you can all walk about unaided so I'll drop you off in town and pick you up at the Hotel Le Richelieu on the quay side, just down from the casino, at 3 o'clock this afternoon, before it gets dark. You can't miss it, it stands out a mile and it's heaving with patients and hospital staff. Now, I haven't time to go looking for you so, if you're not there on time, I'll drive off without you and you can make your own way back. Do try not to get too hoofed. I really don't have the time to be a nursemaid.'

Stinker rubbed herself against the hem of the driver's navy-blue woollen skirt exposing her black leather shoes with half-inch heel.

'Now, Lieutenant Strang and the little dog can sit in the front with me and the rest of you guys can pile in the back.'

She bent down and patted Stinker whose little body wriggled with excitement then she gently took Jan's arm at the elbow and helped him on to the running board and into the front seat. Stinker jumped up after him and onto his lap. Jan watched as Edythe walked around the front of the car, stopped at the bonnet, bent down, inserted a crank handle into the grille, grabbed it with two hands and pulled upwards starting the engine first time.

'One of us could have done that,' Charlie Lewis said.

'Don't worry about me, Lieutenant Lewis, I'm quite capable and anyway there's a knack to it.' She released the handbrake and moved effortlessly off along the drive. 'Alright chaps, hold on to your hats,' she said, turning into the main road. As the Sunbeam sped along the road, a company of head-scarved fisherwomen turned their heads and waved. They waved back.

'Joyeux Noël,' they shouted.

Edythe gripped the steering wheel and swerved around the bumps and potholes. The officers were unafraid and it only heightened Jan's excitement and expectation of a day out in the town. She took them along the coast road, slowing down from time to time to point out the views and landmarks. Pulling up outside the hotel in such a motorcar, drew a small crowd of admirers pointing to and touching its body as if it contained some hidden magic. Jan stepped down from the running board feeling important. Stinker shivered as she looked around and smelt the commotion of soldiers, trucks, carts and horses.

'I'll look after her for you if you like,' Edythe said. Jan handed her the lead and smiled.

'Don't mention it. We'll have a lovely day together. We might even have a paddle on the beach.' She tickled Stinker behind her ears. 'You'd like that, wouldn't you, my little sweetie? You'll be safe with me.'

As Jan moved away, Stinker let out a bark and then an agitated yap. Jan turned, smiled, and took Stinker's lead back off Edythe holding her gloved hand as he did so.

'I can see who she loves the most,' she said, returning his gaze and leaving her hand in his for a moment as she did so. Jan gently squeezed her fingers and knew for certain that he was coming back to life.

Except for Christmas, Boxing Day was the quietest day of the year for the Le Treport residents but in these war years it was still busy. The bars and the cafés opened up to cater for the wounded soldiers and hospital staff, and to relieve them of their money.

Jan intended to explore the town by himself so left his pals at the Richelieu Hotel. Striding down the quayside with Stinker scampering by his heels, he swung his swagger stick with his good right arm and experienced a sense of freedom, unimaginable just a few days before. He was grateful to be alive.

Jan never felt comfortable in uniform. If he had the money on him and enough time for the fitting, he fancied he would have bought himself a fashionable French outfit and new walking cane. He still felt dapper though, making his way along the esplanade and passing the casino that had become just another teeming hospital. Brighton was just across the sea where as a boy with his mother, Aunty Elin and Gladys they would take trips to the pier to watch the Punch and Judy shows and to eat ice cream. The memory stirred his emotion. His step faltered and his legs started to give way; dizziness came over him. He leant against a wall and slowly took in deep breaths of sea air.

He entered a small café where a brass bell rang above the door. Faces at the bar turned towards him; taking no notice he sat at a small table, lit up a cigarette and wiped the cold sweat from his brow. His stomach tightened whilst he waited for his head to clear. The smell of coffee, red wine and French tobacco made him imagine himself as a travel reporter, or war correspondent, for one of the big papers. He looked at the bar and three old fishermen with blurred leathered faces looked back at him concerned, he presumed, that he might drop dead. An ageing serveuse walked up to his table.

'Bonjour Monsieur; joyeux Noël.'

Jan smiled then made a frown, touched his lips, and shook his head. He put his cigarette down on the ash tray, got out his notepad and pencil from his tunic pocket and wrote: *café crème grande* + *calvados* + *Caporal Bleu*.

'Oui, oui monsieur, je comprends.' She smiled and peered straight into his eyes as if to check his sanity. Stinker let out a little yap. 'Ahh, beau chien, beau chien,' she said, bending down to pat her head. Back at the bar she whispered with the men as she made up his order and Jan looked at the scrappy posters, postcards and notes pinned on the wall.

'Et voila,' she said, as she placed the drinks and cigarettes on the table before him. She then left the café through the front door. A gust of cold air blew in as the bell rang behind her.

Jan poured the calvados into his coffee, drank some and felt relief as the spirit warmed his throat and his insides. The serveuse returned from the street.

'Ah! tres froid aujourd'hui, n'est pas, monsieur?' she said, speaking her words slowly whilst rubbing her arms.

Jan smiled and nodded. The doorbell rang as a woman came in; her eyes settled on Jan. She pulled up a chair and sat down in front of him then took off a blue and red-lace shawl and laid it over the back of her chair. She was thirty-five, perhaps, with long hair; black like a horse's mane and plaited from behind her ear down her back exposing a long smooth neck of olive skin. Her dark eyebrows almost met above her nose. Little gold rings hung from her earlobes and a simple necklace of green and turquoise beads completed a décolletage of rustic beauty. Her perfume reached over from her neck almost cutting out the smells of tobacco, wine and fishermen. Her lips were red with bright lipstick and shaped like a kiss.

'Hallo,' she said, exaggerating the 'h' and staring at his head. 'My name is Marie.' She slowly pronounced each word in a thick accent. 'What is your name?'

Jan, he wrote on his pad as she gazed at him open-eyed through long black lashes and sienna eyes.

'Je comprend,' she said and moved her hand to touch his knee beneath the table then moved it up to his thigh. 'Jan is a nice name.' His hand shook as he offered her one of the Woodbines from his silver cigarette case.

'Thank you.'

She reached over to hold his trembling hand. It warmed and calmed him. She put the cigarette onto her lips and moved her head close to him over the table. He stroked his lighter with his thumb and together they sucked in the flame, inhaled smoke and blew it out above each other's heads. She leant back in the chair, kicked off a shoe, and, smiling, extended her foot to rub Stinker's tummy as the little dog rolled over on her back. Stinker nibbled her toes and Marie winked at Jan then laughed.

Jan smiled and wrote: *Veux tu bois, Marie?*

'Yes, sank you, Vermouth Cassis.' She called out to the serveuse. 'Madame, un cassis, sil vous plait.'

'Oui Madame.'

Jan looked over to the bar where the serveuse stirred blackcurrant liqueur into pale vermouth. He watched the colours swirl. She lifted the hinged bar-top and brought the drink over.

'Et voila,' she said, placing it before Marie.

Jan looked at Marie's eyes and then at her necklace. She smiled and stroked his calf with her foot. He felt the start of an erection, unstoppable and stronger than any he'd had in a long time. She picked up Stinker from the floor boards, put her on her lap, played with the dog's ears and made kissing noises as if Stinker were a baby, then let her settle down and stroked her back. She drank her violet-coloured drink, leaving red lipstick on the glass. Jan finished his coffee and calvados. He could have done with another one.

'Come with me?' she said, gently pulling at his jacket sleeve and smiling into his eyes.

He felt a surge of courage in his heart and got up, hoping his erection wouldn't be too obvious so that the men at the bar would laugh. He put his hand in his pocket to reposition himself then turned and looked at the serveuse quizzically.

'Deux francs,' she said.

As he pulled his hand out of his pocket, coins fell, scattering over the floor. Bending down to pick them up he lost balance and fell on his backside. Flushed and red he broke out into a sweat. Marie gave him an indulgent smile then hitched up her skirt. She reached down and helped him back to the chair then squatted to pick the coins up. She left two Francs on the counter and put the rest in Jan's hand. The men and serveuse looked but didn't move.

'Ca va?' she asked Jan, touching his face.

He nodded.

'Come,' she said, threading her arm through his.

'Merci, Monsieur,' the serveuse said.

'Merci, Madame,' Marie said.

The bell rang as they left through the front door onto the esplanade and he heard laughter back in the café. Wind blew sea spray into their faces. Jan shivered and wondered what he had let himself in for, but he had faced greater dangers. They turned up a side street and went up a few steps to a tatty front door with green paint peeling from years of wet salt air. Inside, Marie held Jan's arm as they climbed a flight of stone stairs. Stinker skipped up in front of them. Marie opened the door and they were greeted by two girls of, perhaps, four and five and a boy of about seven. The children gathered round Stinker.

'Petit chien, beau chien,' they said as they stroked and tickled Stinker.

'On y va! vite, vite,' Marie said, shooing them out of the front door and bolting it behind them. 'Ten franc for me,' she said to Jan and he handed her a pale-blue bank note from his wallet. She tied Stinker's lead to the table leg and put down a rug for her to settle on. Marie sat down with a little bounce on a stained beige two-seat settee holding Jan's hand and bringing him down with her. She let him rest for a couple of minutes before smiling into his eyes, playfully pouting her lips and kissing him on the cheek. Keeping eye contact she leant back and opened her red-knitted cardigan then unbuttoned her blue-cotton blouse. Jan stared at her skin. It was more exotic than any he had seen. She held his hand and placed it on her warm, yielding breast. Stinker settled down on her mat, groaned and turned the other way.

Gently, she held his head with both hands and guided his lips down to her dark erect nipple. She let out a slow murmur as Jan licked and kissed. She eased him off her breast, reached down for his groin and squeezed. She undid his braces, unbuttoned his flies, slid her hand down his underpants and held his stiff sex. She let go and reached out to a little table, picked up a jar of face cream then pulled down a small towel from the back of the settee. With heart palpitating Jan watched her long fingers as they unscrewed the lid, dipped into the cream, and slowly began to stroke him up and down. She whispered French words into his ear.

Jan moaned.

Maintaining a light and steady grip she speeded up her motion. He gasped and opened his mouth.

'Ahhh,' he cried, as she caught his semen in the towel. He shuddered and laid his head on her breasts. Instantly he felt an overwhelming sadness then guilt and wished he was with Lucy back in their own bed. A tear rolled down his cheek. He wiped it away with his hand but then another tear came, then another and another. He could hold on no longer. He cried and sobbed in an uncontrolled outpouring of pent-up grief and sorrow, unstoppable and suffocating. He gasped for breath through the tears. And it seemed at that moment that Marie understood, probably more than anyone could, about war and the struggle of life and of men's heartaches.

'Mauvais guerre,' she said, softly stroking his head where it was free of bandages. He wept, his tears rolling down onto her breasts. 'Mauvais guerre, pouvre homme, pouvre homme.'

Jan cried and, when he had no more tears left, she pulled a blanket over them and let him sleep in her arms.

PART III

Chapter 16

28 December 1916

Two days later they cleared out around half the wounded officers from Lady Murray's. Jan was deemed fit enough to travel and was sent out on the journey back to London, via hospital train to Le Havre. Here, along with men discharged from stationary hospitals from across Northern France, they set off for Southampton crammed on the hospital ship *The Western Australia*. After a typically chaotic disembarkation, they were walked and stretchered to a train that would take them to Waterloo station. Here, it was only a short trip in a converted Lyons' grocery van to London's Whitechapel hospital, known locally as the 'London', where Jan arrived on the evening of Saturday 30th.

Back at lady Murray's, the consensus was that Stinker was better off returning to Jan at a later date. Harry Briggs offered to look after her in the meantime.

'If I can't do it myself, I'll make absolutely sure that I'll find someone appropriate to take her to London,' Briggs told Lady Murray. 'Lieutenant Strang assures me that Stinker will have a secure home with his wife and family in Kilburn. It's just by Queen's Park, you know.'

'If you can't take him back yourself, Lieutenant Briggs, then I must ask you to bring her to me and I'll make sure that one of my nurses returns her safely,' Lady Murray said, picking Stinker up and tickling her behind the ears before handing her over to the Chaplain's care.

Once settled in his shared cabin on the *Western Australia*, Jan reread the letter he received from Lucy the day before:

Darling Jan,

I hope this reaches you in good spirits. I'm so sorry to hear that you've had such a terrible time. It was just dreadful to get that letter from Capt. Grimshaw telling us you had been killed. How they made such a mistake I really can't imagine. I was so upset that I lost my usual cool head for a while, I'm afraid. And, of course Eva and Peter and Gladys were absolutely devastated and so was Eric and his mother and my parents and sisters (You are so well loved my darling). And then we got another letter this morning from you saying that you were alive! It was such a relief, a miracle in the family. I know it seems silly but deep down I didn't believe you were dead.

Your chaplain Harry Briggs sounds like such a nice man. We might even meet him one day, you never know, I do hope so. And you have a little dog, how wonderful! I've always wanted one. We can walk her in the park together and have such fun again.

I don't want to tire you out darling; you must be in such awful pain. I just can't imagine how dreadful it must be for you and for all those other poor men; we hear such terrible things about the casualties from the men coming back and about the hospitals in France. And, of course, there are walking wounded wherever you go. It's too awful. I just wish there was some way we could help to stop the war once and for all.

I'm desperate to see you again. We would have all come over to visit you in your French hospital but we hear that, all being well, you should be back in England soon. Gladys thinks that she may be able to pull a few strings and get you to a hospital near home, hopefully the 'London' where she works and Eva Lükes is matron. Then we'll be able to see you every day until you're well enough to come home.

It must be just ghastly for you not being able to speak but we talked to Dr Cassidy and he said that it's not uncommon and that most men get their voice back after a few months or even sooner. He says that you can even see a hypnotist as they are getting good results.

I do know that you will get better and we can be happy again. Have a safe journey home.

All my love,

Lucy xxx

P.S. Sorry my writing's all scribbly but my hand's really shaky from all the emotion and excitement of seeing you soon. X

On this homeward journey being surrounded by blood and vomit no longer turned his stomach but the constant jogs and jolts brought the return of pains that he hoped had finished. His headache wouldn't go away and sharp pains shot down from his head via his buttocks to his right foot. It made him wince and want to shout out. The best way of getting attention and a welcome morphine shot was to make his pain clear to the MOs. So, when he saw an MO he beat his left hand on his blankets and twisted his face which had the required effect. Morphine appeared to be in good supply on the ship and he supposed that, although the crossing was unseasonably calm, without it the MOs would struggle to keep any kind of order. It was everyone's duty to get drinking, as they needed the empties to piss in. Bottles of whiskey and brandy were passed around and, after making his way through the top half of a bottle of some gut-rotting Armagnac, despite feeling quite sick, Jan melted into a satisfactory, half-conscious euphoria.

By the time he reached the Whitechapel the effects of his last morphine dose on the train hadn't quite worn off and he was still a little drunk. He refused a stretcher to take him into the hospital from the Lyons van and made his way with the other walking wounded. They shuffled through the reception area to an assessment room where they were strip-washed, checked for lice and given clean pyjamas before being ferried to their ward. He was so used to feeling ill that he didn't think much about it unless it was the shooting pains from his head. If that didn't get any better he might as well put a bullet through his brains, no one could spend a lifetime like that. Sinking into his new bed he felt the crispness of clean sheets infused with the smell of bleach. All the windows were open and it was bitter cold. He wondered why on earth hospitals thought that cold air was more healthy than warm. In his mind it would have been the other way around.

He woke up in the early hours of Sunday morning, lit a cigarette and waited till things got going in the ward so he could get the attention of a nurse when they changed the shifts. He knew that, as soon as the word got out that he had arrived back, Lucy and his parents would be by his side and he wanted to look his best. He signalled a nurse for a paper and pencil and wrote: *How do I look?*

'Just fine, but you need to sleep now,' she said. 'We'll look at you properly when you've had more of a rest.'

Lucy reread the letter from Harry Briggs letting them know how Jan was, folded it and put it in her handbag as they set off for the hospital. Before the war, she would have thought it outrageous that the usually strictly enforced visiting times had been relaxed because Peter's timber company had made a donation to hospital funds. It was strange how personal tragedy could change a moral principle so quickly. The fact that Gladys worked there and that they knew the matron must have helped; if *they* couldn't get in to see a patient out of visiting times then, she supposed, probably nobody, except for royalty, could.

Lucy, Eva and Peter were led into the ward. Lucy spotted Jan immediately six beds down, propped up with pillows. She rushed up to him and was glad his eyes were closed because she needed a moment or two to collect herself from the shock of seeing him like this. She thought she had been prepared, she had been told what to expect, but when she saw his face pallid with pale greyish-white skin, like a corpse, she felt the blood drain away from her face and a sense of panic. His face was thin and gaunt and he had a four-inch gash in his head that stood out all the more as his hair had been shaved away around it.

The noise of their family group around his bed must have woken Jan. He opened his eyelids and greeted them all with a smile from cracked lips. Lucy returned his gaze and smiled back but instead of his once keen azure eyes she felt she was looking into the eyes of a different man: bloodshot eyes with dirty-yellow edges that told her he was 'far away' and would need bringing home in more senses than one.

She sat on the edge of the bed looking at him and resisted the temptation to hold him tightly so, instead, she kissed him on the cheek and held his hand.

'Thank God you're safe; you must have been through hell. I'm so glad you're back.'

He smiled and nodded.

'Don't worry; we know you can't talk yet. Harry Briggs wrote to us and told us all about it.' She brought the letter and placed it on the bed. 'There's no need to explain. You will talk again, there's no rush.' She pulled her hankie out from up her cardigan sleeve and quickly wiped away a tear before any more could come. He squeezed her hand.

While Eva and Peter were talking, Jan's eyes moved to each person as they spoke. Lucy didn't hear their conversation as, in her racing mind, she went over the plans she had been making for their future. There were so many imponderable 'what ifs' and she couldn't possibly know if it would turn out well at all. She was stirred from her thoughts as a matron with a white lace cap appeared by the bedside, diminutive, thin and looking quite arthritic. Lucy remembered Eva Lückes from her and Jan's wedding. Her bony hand held Lucy's.

'So nice to meet you again, my dear,' she said, before turning to greet Peter and Eva. The matron put her hand on Jan's arm and smiled at him. Lucy paid attention.

'Gladys and I have been looking in on him. I don't think there's any doubt that he'll have a good recovery. We didn't wake him in the night because he needs rest more than anything else. He's had a very hard time and the journey from France will have sapped his strength but he'll get his colour back very soon. We know that he started to walk about at Lady Murray's and even had a day out in the town by himself.' She smiled at Lucy and talked directly to her. 'He'll get better, you'll see.'

The ward door opened and Gladys moved quickly up to them as Eva Lückes was speaking.

'His medical reports came with him and they do suggest that he'll need careful handling, for a while at least. You know most of the men do recover, I've seen it hundreds of times, but you will need to be patient. An ordeal like Jan's could well change his temperament until he's settled back into life at home.'

'If they don't send him back that is,' Gladys said under her breath. Peter coughed loudly.

Eva Lückes continued, 'From Jan's notes and from our observations, it seems that at present he can't speak at all.' She paused and looked around as if to check they were all listening. 'Now, this isn't unusual; over the next weeks and months he should begin to use a few words and make himself understood. He should improve quite soon as he becomes less anxious. He has a form of what they call "neurasthenia".'

'That's "shell shock",' Gladys said.

Lucy sensed that Jan was taking it all in and made a conscious effort not to let him see her concern and vowed not to let them take him away again. She thought that she knew what she was letting herself in for when they married and Jan went off to fight but it was much harder to bear than she could ever have imagined. Nothing could have prepared her for her suffering of the last two months. And she didn't know how she would cope in the months to come, what with working at the Home Office as well caring for Jan, but she knew that she would find the strength when she had to. She believed that more strongly than she had believed anything in her life before.

'I'm going to have to ask you to leave now,' Eva Lückes said. 'I've stretched the rules too far already. Jan will be much better tomorrow morning after some food and another good rest. I'm quite sure about that. I expect you'll be able to take him home in a few days. You can visit between eleven and twelve tomorrow.'

'Thank you,' Peter said, shaking the matron's hand warmly. Lucy kissed Jan and a tear rolled down his mother's cheek as she watched them. Peter rested his hand on Jan's shoulder. 'It's New Year's Eve and we'll all raise a glass to you tonight.' His father took a quarter-bottle of scotch from his pocket, slid it under Jan's pillow and winked. Lucy thought she had never seen Peter look so happy. 'It's good to have you back son, you'll be alright now. We'll look after you,' Peter said.

'What you mean is that Mother and Lucy will look after you,' Gladys said.

Lucy leant over and whispered in Jan's ear, 'You'll be fine soon. Don't worry. We'll get you home and well again my darling.'

Wednesday was cold and clear and Lucy got the morning off work. Full of hope and anticipation for Jan's homecoming Lucy, Eva and Peter set off in a motor Hackney Carriage to collect Jan from the Whitechapel Hospital. Lucy thanked providence that, even in the present climate where obvious expressions of wealth were seen as disgraceful, Peter decided to damn appearances and hire a cab. She didn't want a long journey and understood that Jan would struggle getting to and from the tube. She had seen his eyes well up the night before when she told him that they'd come and get him in the morning.

Neighbours watched as Peter paid the cabbie and helped Jan out the cab. Jan waved Lucy and his parents away, confident that he could walk unaided, but Lucy made sure to keep close by his side: over the kerb, up the steps, through the hall, into the lounge and onto the settee that she had made ready for him with extra cushions. Once settled down comfortably Jan wouldn't want any fuss.

Peter put sawn timber from packing cases that he got from the docks on the embers in the grate. The fire sparked and flared up. Jan sat up startled. He sat forward with his back straight and his body tense. Lucy, suddenly absorbing his fear, rubbed his shoulders then eased him back into the settee and leant forward to put his feet on a stool. She moved up close to him so their bodies were touching and he could feel her warmth and smell her cologne. She wasn't in the least surprised or hurt that his only response was to look straight ahead whilst giving her a tap on her thigh. In front of his parents he could never express his feelings and she would never expect him to. To feel the stress and tightness in his body subside was thanks enough.

'You must be sick and tired of sitting around doing nothing. Gladys says you'll have sores on your bottom from being in bed for so long,' Eva said.

Jan nodded knowingly to her and lit a cigarette. Eva poured them all a cup of tea. Jan left his to cool, finished his cigarette, and then picked the cup up with two hands. The brown liquid dribbled down the side of his mouth and on to his khaki shirt. He looked annoyed, took out his pad and pencil and wrote, *Stop watching me!*

'Don't worry darling. It's just we haven't seen you for so long,' Lucy said.

Jan stood up and moved to leave the room.

'What is it, Jan?' his mother asked.

Hate uniform, he wrote, then held the lapels on his jacket, shook his head and pulled a face. Lucy followed him up the stairs to their bedroom. She took off his coarse wool army jacket, undid his shirt, slipped it off and kissed the edge of the wound on his arm.

'You will be well again, darling,' she said, taking out clean clothes from the chest of drawers. He lay back on the bed. She nestled into him and he held her close. Ten minutes must have passed before she broke the embrace.

'We'd better go back down or it will look rude,' she said.

In the living room, slices of seed cake were arranged next to a fresh pot of tea. This time Eva only half-filled his cup and he managed to drink it without mishap.

'You must have a slice of cake,' his mother said.

Jan shook his head.

'You'll like it. We had such trouble getting the ingredients.'

He shook his head.

'But…'

'He doesn't want any, Eva. Let him be,' Peter said.

'I'm sorry, it's just…' Eva closed her eyes and breathed in. 'Oh, it doesn't matter.'

'Well, that's your war over with,' Peter said. 'I suppose we should thank God that you weren't hurt even more than you were.'

'It's a very strange God if we have to thank him for that,' Eva said, and no one answered.

Peter broke the silence. 'Eva Lückes says you should have a very good recovery.'

'Yes, we'll put the colour back into your cheeks,' Lucy said, trying to raise the mood. The carriage clock chimed twelve.

'I need to get back to work now, Son. We've got orders from the BEF coming out of our ears. It's a pity you can't be back helping me but all in good time; all in good time. I should be home by six and we'll all have a celebratory dinner. This is our Christmas and New Year rolled into one. Are you coming, Lucy, we don't want to miss the tube?'

'Yes, Peter, I'm ready.' She knelt by Jan's head and kissed it. 'I do so wish I didn't have to go back to work but I promised. Bye bye for now darling, I'll be back tonight, probably before Peter, but I must go now. I don't want to leave you. I was lucky to get the morning off, you know. They're a bit like slave drivers but we can't complain. We have a better lot than most.'

Jan touched her cheek with his open hand.

'Don't worry Lucy, he'll be alright with me,' Eva said.

'I know he will, Eva,' Lucy said as she left.

Lucy's anxiety about Jan filled her thoughts and the afternoon dragged. She had wanted to make his homecoming really special and it hadn't turned out like that. They'd hardly been alone together since he got back to London. She wanted them to just lie together and let the warmth of her body give life back to his. She would make it up to him tonight. The girls in the office, tactless as ever, told her, as if she hadn't thought about it by herself, how difficult it would be and how she would have to be patient and not expect things to get back to normal right away.

'Some can't do "it" again. Not like they used to,' Beatty said.

'You see, at the back of their minds they know that if they get better, they'll get sent back,' Vera said. 'They'd rather be crazy here than well and back there.'

'He's not crazy,' Lucy snapped.

'Yes, I know dear. I didn't mean to say he was but you know what I mean. Of course, your Jan won't go that way,' Vera said.

'The worry stops them getting better,' Beatty said.

Lucy put her hands on her face and sighed.

'But your Jan's made of stronger stuff,' Vera said.

That evening, Peter came in before Lucy and earlier than expected. He greeted Jan with smiles and general bon ami. It was a good feeling that his father was being so nice to him; it didn't happen under normal circumstances. Delicious smells of cooking seeped from Eva's kitchen which always put his father in a good mood.

'I'll just go and see what your mother's up to,' Peter said, heading for the kitchen.

Assuming he would be in there for a while, Jan got up to listen at the door. His hearing was good, maybe even sharper than before his accident, and he could hear Peter's voice quite clearly.

'I called in at Jack Cassidy's surgery on the way home. He said they're sending men back before they're ready. He said we may have to pull some strings to keep Jan at home. But he'll be alright for the next month or two.'

Jan's heart pounded and his legs felt weak. This certainly wasn't news. Everyone in the army knew it was happening but just hearing Peter say it made it seem more real.

'But he can't even speak, for God's sake,' Eva said in a low voice.

'I know but he could be better soon, now he's at home and can rest properly.'

'He's fighting to get better, for Lucy and us if not for himself,' Eva said.

'Don't worry, I'll make damn sure he'll stay put with us. They'll have another war on their hands if they try to take him back.'

'Going back there after all he's been through would send anyone mad,' Eva said.

'Haig's a damned imbecile. It'd be over by now if there were someone else at the top. Why they put him in charge I'll never know. I ask you. He won't negotiate, you know, and he could. He's too well connected. Even Lloyd George can't get rid of him; more's the pity.'

'Yes, yes, I know all that dear, but what are we going to do? Please don't worry him any more than you have to. He needs rest.'

Jan had heard enough. He stepped quietly back to the living room with his hand touching the wall. *I need a drink*, he wrote on the back of an envelope ready to give to his father.

The front door opened. Lucy hung up her coat. Jan's anxiety eased just from hearing her familiar footsteps coming down the hall, but he still felt edgy. He'd been almost counting the minutes till she came home and she was at least a half an hour late. He stepped into the hall and kissed her on the cheek. She looked at his face and eyes with concern then kissed him. It made him feel better but her kiss seemed more like a peck and he wanted more. They went into the living room and Lucy closed the curtains and started plumping up cushions. While she was looking the other way, Jan handed Peter the slip of paper.

'We decided to have a drink. Will you join us Lucy?' Peter said.

'No thanks,' Lucy said

'One or two won't harm. I've got some Canadian Club whiskey the Canadians sent me with their last shipment. I've been keeping it for a special occasion. We must toast our boy's homecoming after all.'

'No, honestly, not for me.'

Still in his business suit, Peter opened the walnut-inlaid drinks cabinet and poured whiskey for him and Jan. Lucy broke off from her tidying and sat down next to Jan.

'I should have told you earlier, Darling. I stopped drinking just before Christmas. I over did it terribly, I'm afraid, and don't intend to start again. Peter thinks I'll change my mind, but I won't.' Jan stared at her amazed. He lit a Player's and offered her one. 'I stopped smoking as well. I'll tell you about it later.'

They sat down to a dinner of sausages, mashed potatoes, carrots and gravy. With his shaky coordination it was easier for him to eat with his fork upside down in his right hand in the American fashion. With his left hand free he stroked Lucy's thigh under the table. He smiled to himself at the way she pretended not to notice and carried on eating. He had become so used to small meals over the last few months that he hardly had room for his dessert of stewed apples and custard but he did his best. The acid tang of the bramleys on his tongue made him shudder in a way that showed him that life was coming back to his senses. He nodded to Eva in appreciation.

As the evening went on, Jan felt his arm and leg pains getting more intense and his head banged. He needed morphine but didn't want to disgrace himself by blanking out the evening after all they had done to make him happy. Following Doctor Cassidy's prescription, he'd had a low-dosage shot in the afternoon and Cassidy had given instructions not to let him have another till bed time. If he had another shot now it would just cause a fuss. He drank the whiskey slowly to be polite but he really wanted to just grab the bottle and have a bloody good drink. There was little else he could do to mask the pain. In a day or two he would get to the pub in the evenings and drink with all the other wounded men who were wondering if they would get any proper sex back into their life. He was sure he could do it, even if some of them couldn't, but the time would have to be right. It would be better after a rest, not last thing at night when his body needed sleep.

He looked pleadingly at Lucy and so much wanted to speak. He wanted to tell her all about what had happened to him and how, for all the time he was away, he had longed to be back at home with her. He would make a big effort to get some words out tomorrow. He felt sure he would talk again before long.

It was hardly surprising that at the dinner table they all avoided talk of war, death and politics. It was a relief as he'd heard about nothing else since he signed up. He doubted if they could keep it up all night though. It made for a difficult atmosphere and when they left the table for the settee and arm chairs he sank into the cushions where he could nod off when tiredness took over.

Lucy sat by his side. Each time he lifted the glass of Canadian Club to his lips, she turned her head towards him. It made him feel as if he was under surveillance and he became irritated, more than he had any reason to be. From the corner of his eye he glimpsed Eva looking at Lucy and raising her eyebrows and he would have stormed off to bed if his legs had been up to it. As it was he would probably have fallen flat on his face. It was the best whiskey he'd drunk in a long time and it did feel good. Lucy helped him up the stairs to the bathroom twice during the evening. Being powerless made him angry at the very people who loved and helped him the most and he hated himself for having those feelings.

After his third whiskey, Peter broke the tacit pact about not talking about sensitive subjects. He started talking about the war and was apparently oblivious to the looks Eva kept giving him. He explained how President Wilson would have organised a settlement if the French hadn't been so 'bloody belligerent' and how Haig was an incompetent fool. But Jan knew all of that and so did everyone else in the country as far as he could tell.

Why were people so repetitive after a drink? Lucy wondered as she listened to Peter talking about what had been happening in the office and how the ships were only just getting through from Sweden and Canada and how so many of them had been 'blown out of the water'. She was tired and too concerned about Jan and their future to pay much attention to Peter. She did turn her head and listen, however, when he said that there was so much demand for planks that, if the war ended tomorrow, they could retire to Hove by the sea and never worry about money again. If that were the case, and she had no reason to doubt him, even if Jan couldn't earn a proper living, there would be enough money to provide for them both and the children she wanted. It wasn't so long ago that she would have been disgusted with herself for not having qualms about making money from the war. She consoled herself by remembering that it was the war that had put Jan in such a desperate predicament in the first place.

'You'll get better. I'm sure of it,' she said to him in their bedroom as she helped him undress, making sure that she gently brushed against his body as she removed his clothes. He had been unstable on his feet so she stood outside of the bathroom and listened in case he fell as he cleaned his teeth. When she was satisfied that he could manage by himself she returned to their room, turned the electric table light off, and lit a nightlight before getting into bed. She lay on her side under the covers and held her arm out to him as he walked through the door. He sat in his woollen gown on the dressing-table chair and lit a cigarette.

'You need morphine, don't you?'

Jan nodded.

Lucy slipped out of bed and went over to the dressing table. She glimpsed their reflections in the oval mirror from the dim flickering light and thought how tired she looked and how much Jan had aged. She had tried so hard to look her best but doubted if Jan had even noticed. Jan pulled his chair back to let her open the top drawer and stroked the small of her back. Before he went off to war she would have sat on his lap.

'You get into bed and I'll inject you.'

In the drawer, by the side of his Webley 45 service revolver, lay the leather pouch Jack Cassidy had given them. She unrolled it on the bedside table and neatly placed out a syringe, needle, morphine ampoule and a leather strap. She moved the chair to his side and sat down, frightened she might hurt him.

'They taught me how to do this for you at the hospital. They've all been very kind. And Gladys wrote out instructions.'

She unfolded a sheet of paper and stood it up against the water jug. Struggling to see with only the yellow flame of the nightlight, she got up and lit a couple more candles. Jan stared at her and she felt tense and uneasy. By the brighter light, she screwed the needle into the syringe, broke off the end of the ampoule and drew the amber liquid up into the glass tube. She pointed it heavenwards and squirted the air bubbles out of the needle's point. Some of the morphine fell on her nightdress and sudden panic hit her solar plexus. What if she did it all wrong?

'We'll have to ease you off it,' she said, before she could stop herself. She wondered how she could have been so stupid. It was bound to upset him. Jan knew this, of course he did. She didn't need to say it, not tonight anyway. She saw the eager gaze of his eyes, fixed on the syringe. Suddenly, he leant forward, grabbed the leather strap, wrapped it around his bicep and began moving his fingers until the veins on his forearm rose to the surface. She breathed in and looked at her instructions.

'I've never actually done this before, not to a real person.'

Before she could say anything else, Jan took the syringe out of her hand and held his other hand up, palm flat towards her telling her to stay away. A fierce look in his face told her he meant it. She felt like crying and wanted to look the other way but couldn't. Without hesitating he pushed it into his vein. She would have been much gentler if he had only let her do it. He slowly pushed down the plunger, waited a moment, then pulled it up a quarter inch and watched his blood washing around in the syringe. He depressed the plunger again and pulled out the needle. His expression changed from irritation to ease. Lucy felt his relief. The job was done. She dampened a swab of cotton wool with surgical spirit and wiped the puncture then calmly put the swab, the empty ampoule and hypodermic syringe into a kidney-shaped enamel dish. Jan lay back, loose and limp.

'I'll put it in water for now and sterilise it in the morning before your next dose.' She smiled and stroked his hair then cleared up the paraphernalia and hid it out of sight back in the drawer. She went to the bathroom locking the door behind her, sat on the toilet and cried as quietly as she could, raising her hands to her face to hide the sound of her sobbing. Before going back, she splashed her face with cold water and dabbed her eyes dry with a towel. She cleaned her teeth, watching herself in the mirror, feeling guilty for leaving him for so long. When she got back, he was asleep, or seemed to be, but it wasn't a proper, restful sleep. His breathing wheezed and rasped and he twitched at intervals like a dog asleep in a basket. His cigarette smouldered in the ashtray. She stubbed it out and settled him down in the bed. The smell of tobacco turned her stomach. She kissed the side of his head.

'Night night, darling.'

Though quite exhausted, she lay awake as Jan turned his head from one side to the other, sweated and called out. Each time he woke not knowing where he was, she would say to him, 'It's alright darling. You're safe at home with me.' Then she would cuddle him until he fell asleep again. Lying awake and desperate for sleep, she wondered why fate had dictated that their love would change so quickly. When Jan got better would their love return to what it had been in the days before they were married? For the time being, like everyone else, she could blame the Germans but how could she ever hate a whole nation? It just wasn't in her nature to hate. She didn't hate anyone.

Chapter 17

Jan made his first attempt at speaking when alone in bed with Lucy on the second night after his return. He knew he had been particularly irritable that night and didn't understand why. He had rejected little kindnesses from his mother, like when she tried to make him more comfortable by rearranging his cushions on the settee. He stood up, sucked in air, and wrote, *STOP FUSSING*. Later on, when Eva asked if she could get anything for him, he wrote, *I'm not a cripple!!* before crunching up the little notes he had written throughout the day and throwing them on the fire. He was aware of Lucy silently observing how edgy and hurtful he was being but he couldn't help himself. At no point did she give him a disapproving look, let alone a gentle reprimand. He was sure that he would never have been so calm and patient if their roles had been reversed.

Sitting up in bed he desperately wanted to thank her and, if he apologised in his own words, it would mean so much more than just writing another note. He had tried speaking single words during the day when nobody was around and what came out did approximate to what he wanted to say. He knew it would be harder in front of a person, even if it was with his ever-patient wife. There had to be a first time and it may as well be now.

'Th.., thth.., thth...' As he stammered and spluttered she looked at him, nodded in encouragement, and smiled. He thought she might tell him not to distress himself and to just write down what he wanted to say and to wait until he felt more able to speak but she didn't. She just watched and nodded. He felt foolish and embarrassed and mentally deficient and thought he was getting nowhere.

'That's wonderful, Darling.'

Her soft voice calmed him.

'B.., bbbbbu.. bbbbu...'

'I know you were trying to say thank you but I didn't want to interrupt you. It won't be easy but you will speak again soon,' she said.

'S.., ssss.., so.., so.., sor...'

'It's fine, darling, I'll get your syringe.'

In the days and weeks that followed, progressing a little more each day, Jan started to speak. To begin with it was nigh on impossible to get out his b's, f's, s's, p's, t's and th's and the whole excruciating process clearly distressed those who listened. But progress came; at first with just a painfully stuttered 'thank you' and 'please' and then small sentences. His mother smiled and encouraged him and, afterwards, would go into another room only to appear again after ten minutes with eyes puffy and red. Jan wondered how, without intending, one man could cause so much hurt in others. But the 'others' were clearly pleased and said that his recovery was good and, according to Doctor Cassidy, much better than could have been expected. Everyone in the household was satisfied by his progress except himself.

Gladys left for France in early January and within a week of her departure a letter arrived:

Dear All,

Well, we've all settled in now; totally thrown in at the deep end. We're so lucky, if that's the right word and I know that it isn't, to have had plenty of experience working with war-wounded men. It's a lot more gory nursing closer to the front. God knows what it must be like in the field hospitals. For one thing, a lot more die on us and it's a lot less comfortable and that's an understatement. You wouldn't believe the cold here. Apart from it being the worst winter anyone can remember, coal ships have been sunk in the Channel and this leaves us without any heat. It's so blasted cold that my hands have turned purple from washing countless wounded men in freezing water; hence the shaky writing. Trench feet are terribly common here as the winter drags on and the trenches are flooded. In London, *we saw their feet at a later stage and it wasn't nearly so bad as it had started to heal. Here the smell of the old flesh is absolutely foul and the feet are swollen with dreadful black bumps. Lots of the men have lost toes and will never dance again.*

Actually, there's no time to think about how badly we're being treated. Our Ward Sister looks like a rat in spectacles and yells out orders in a squeaky rodent-like voice that I swear would turn the milk sour if we had any. She hasn't got the time to censor our letters or this would never have got through to you.

The Canadian men and doctors are charming in a rugged sort of way and pushy at the same time. I know of two girls who have already succumbed to their attentions but don't worry about me, I know how to look after myself and will hit them off with a stick if needs be.

Jan, you have remarkable powers of recovery. So many of the men and boys (I swear some of them are only fifteen) just give up but you and I are made of Swedish steel from the frozen swamps of God knows where.

A chaplain called Briggs turned up and said hello. He has your dog and says he'll bring her over to you as soon as he can break away from his duties.

Send socks and fingerless gloves.
My love to everyone,
Gladys xxx

His Aunts Karolina and Elina, all of Lucy's family and Mrs Agnoli from the office came to see Jan. Letters from his mother's family in Sweden arrived, wishing him good health and recovery and offering him and Lucy asylum and a warm welcome any time. Eric's mother called in and Eric, when he was home on leave, would take him down to The Game Cock and get him drunk.

At night when he was relaxed after a good meal and a few drinks, he was able, at first with great difficulty and a fearful stammer but, as the days went on, with an erratic fluency, to tell her about the dreadful things he had seen: how men screamed when they were shot and how others were blown apart in front of his eyes and how dying men called out for their mothers. He told her of the responsibility he felt for his platoon which, as far as he knew, all fell at Hill 60. He explained to her that, even though there was nothing he could have done to change things, he still felt ashamed that they had died and how it hurt him that he had been too damaged to write to their loved ones; even now he couldn't bear the thought of writing to them. He told her how he had lain, left for dead, with corpses, breathing in the gore for what seemed like eternity. More memories dripped into his conscious mind each day as if his subconscious would only release enough horror for him to cope with at one time. And each memory tore at his heart and a fear came to him that could make him shudder and shake. But, when he talked to Lucy of the little dog who stayed by his side and gave him hope and made him smile, his mood would calm and his face would light up. He said he would look after that little dog for all its days if Harry Briggs, his Chaplain friend, managed to bring her back in one piece.

When he told Lucy of the horrors he saw and felt, it came out in a staggered, confused and unordered stammering splutter that could only have been vaguely comprehensible to her. At times, it made him wish he could die. When he had finished talking of his pain she would calm him down and inject him with morphine and lie with him until he drifted away. He was amazed that, even though he had lost the charm and tenderness that had so attracted her to him in their early days, she still listened and nodded, smiled with encouragement and held him close.

Lucy's suggestion that he should go down to one dose of morphine a day and take it around lunchtime made him grit his teeth and bite his knuckles. She could be so understanding at times but at others she had absolutely no idea about what he was going through. He thought about agreeing, just to make her feel better, but it would never work. He would have to secretly inject it and that wasn't something he could disguise; she would see it in his eyes, even if he used a low enough dose to stay awake. In the evenings, he could hear her upstairs checking the phials in the dressing-table drawer to see if any had gone missing. It was like living in a zoo with everyone watching and commenting on his movements. The world outside frightened him. He hardly got out except for a walk in Queen's Park when his mother went with him. When he felt a bit stronger, if he was desperate, he could get out by himself and seek out the secret places in Piccadilly where opium and morphine were sold to anyone who could pay. Eric had gone back to the front but he probably wouldn't have helped him; his self-righteousness would have got in the way.

Lucy wanted Jan's children and, although she struggled to understand her overwhelming wish to bring a child into a world full of war, fear and chaos, she was determined to get pregnant. Her desire for a baby was stronger than any rational thought. Their sexual union which, before Jan left for the war, had been a passionate and tender consummation of their love, had now become tricky for Lucy to negotiate. She found it difficult not to recoil at his breath. Whiskey and tobacco fumes were combined with a fetid and sickly-sweet smell that, Dr Cassidy had told her, was to be expected as a common side-effect from taking morphine.

The mechanics of their physical intimacy left Lucy feeling empty and failed to rebuild the spiritual love and closeness that she really needed. Neither of them found it easy to speak of their needs, desires and disappointments in the bedroom. Jan clearly wanted and needed her body and the comfort that sex would bring him but in the first few weeks of being home, due to his trauma, alcohol and morphine intake, he rarely had the ability to fulfil his pleasure. Lucy tried to help as much as she knew how. At first, she lay on her back submissively so that Jan could enjoy her body but repeated failed attempts meant that Jan became disaffected with himself. She would console him and tell him it didn't matter but the effect of his impotence caused him deep distress. Presuming that he wouldn't be offended she decided to take the leading role by getting him to lie on his back and stimulating him with her hand while letting him look at and touch her body. Then, when he was at his most excited, she would sit on him and he would thrust into her.

After they had sex, Jan could become annoyed and angry at himself. When he thought Lucy had gone to sleep he would often go down stairs and drink into the early hours of the morning. Lucy, on hearing him leave the bed, allowed herself to sleep for an hour or so then go downstairs to find him sitting up in an armchair having nodded off with glass in hand, or on the floor. Cigarette butts would have smouldered to ash in the ashtray. She would take his arm and silently lead him back to bed.

Jan's moods could rise to the height of optimism and then fall just as quickly to total despair. It could be frightening after he ejaculated his semen as he might shake and judder so that Lucy would pray that he wouldn't have a heart attack. She had heard stories at work of men coming home only to 'die on the job.' She had never imagined that sex would turn out to be such a responsibility when once it was fun. After Jan had a spasm, he could be quite settled and laugh and be cheerful then sit up in bed and smoke and want to talk for hours. At other times, he would want to cry without being able to do so. And then he would hold her tight as if he were frightened that he might lose her. She told him, as gently as she knew how, that he would have to learn to cope with life and pain without morphine if they were ever going to live a normal life.

Lucy had become masterful at hiding her feelings. Jan, through no fault of his own, had become a difficult man to be in love with. Their loving, tender moments became increasingly short lived. Jan's mood could quickly change from a period of gentle consideration to one of gloom and anger - emotions he never displayed before going to France.

Suddenly, without warning, he could pace up and down smoking and complaining in his agonised stammer about subjects that were unimportant. It was beyond her ken that such a sensitive and enlightened spirit with a quick intelligence that had so endeared her, could be so niggly and irritable. They used to talk about style and fashion and literature and how the Suffragette movement needed to succeed if there was to be any fairness in the country, but these things meant little to him now. Drink would put him in a better mood but only for an hour or so, after which it could turn on him and make him as tetchy as ever. Jan was going through what Dr Cassidy called a 'healing process' that could be painful for all those around him. Lucy was playing a role in his recovery that no one else could fulfil. Jan and Lucy both agreed that, given time and patience, this was a battle that they could win.

Lucy kept her eyes peeled for any reading material she could pick up in her lunch break or to-and-from the office. Sometimes people left newspapers in the train which she would fold up and put into her handbag and hand over to Jan on her return. In the evening, he would read these in conjunction with Peter's *Times* and inevitably ask the question of why, given the continued casualties and stalemate in the war, there was no dissenting voice from the press? But eventually this made the evenings boring for everyone. Both she and Eva would try to steer the conversation away from the war and put on a gramophone record. Jan would stand up and hold Lucy in his arms and they would hold each other close and move in small circles in the centre of the room:

'And when I told them how beautiful you are,
They didn't believe me. They didn't believe me!
Your lips, your eyes, your cheeks, your hair,
Are in a class beyond compare'

When one lunchtime on a street near Buckingham Palace, she saw a one-armed veteran with books laid out on a trestle table, she decided to get some. The man of about five-foot five, wore a great coat, cloth cap and a muffler around his neck with medals pinned across his chest. He said it broke his heart but his books were the only non-essential things that he could sell for money.

Overlooking the non-fiction, she skimmed through the novels, putting to one side what she thought were the better novelists like Dickens, Elliot, Kipling and Thackeray and leaving writers such as Charles Garvice and Zane Grey.

'I'll take what I can carry now and come back for the rest,' she said. 'They've all been cared for so well. I'll make sure they'll get a good home where they'll be appreciated.'

'Books find their way to those that need them most.' His voice was rough and sounded like his lungs were about to give way.

'My husband was wounded and has to fill up the day.'

'I wish him well, madam.'

'It can't be easy for you?'

'No, but I got out alive. I fought the Boers as well.'

'It makes you wonder when it will all end.'

'I know, madam. We've all had enough of it now.'

In the three trips it took her to get the books back to the office, she chatted with the philosophical veteran and learnt about his wife and that his war pension didn't really pay for their living costs.

'We've had to move somewhere smaller. We've no room for all these books now,' he said.

She kept the novels in several piles under her desk and took a few home every night until they were gone. They worked like a magic spell on the atmosphere at home by changing the topic of conversation in the evenings. Everyone dipped into them and Jan said she couldn't have given him a better present. The small print brought on his headaches but Jan read them, if necessary with a magnifying glass, and added them to his small library that was filling up the bookshelves at the back of the living room.

'You should be tested for reading spectacles,' Eva said. 'There's an optician just along from the office on Bishopsgate.'

'I kn.. know,' Jan said.

'I'll arrange an appointment,' Peter said. 'You know,' he turned to Jan and smiled, 'after the war, if you wanted, we could pay for you to read History and Politics at Cambridge.'

Jan's skin turned whiteish and he looked thoughtful. He told Lucy later that his father's offer was so unexpected he didn't know what to think. At first, he thought he might be joking.

'Of c.. c.. course, I'd l.. love to.' He shook his father's hand with both of his.

By mid-February, Lucy could see that Jan was strong enough and more than ready for a day out in town. Her plan was to spend the time walking around their old haunts and maybe reignite some of their love. On the Saturday morning, they walked down to the station with their collars turned up and the sun broke through the clouds to shine on them. Lucy greeted the man in the ticket office with a cheerful 'Good morning' and a smile. Jan asked how she knew all the people she nodded to on the way. *You said good morning to seven people,* he wrote on his pad.

'I walk down this way every day, silly.' She linked her arm in his. 'I'm proud to have you with me; I want to show you off. I must know just about everyone on the way; I only smile and say good morning.'

As they emerged from St James' Park station, a cold wind blew from the sea and up the Thames. Lucy's hat was safe; she had fixed it with an enamelled pin before she left but Jan had to keep a hand on his bowler. In the park their eyes engaged and they laughed out loud remembering the day when his hat blew off and he ran off to catch it. When they held hands, Lucy felt a happiness that was deep and warm.

'I still come here for my lunch break; when it's not chucking it down of course. They're talking about filling in the lake. Look at the tatty wooden offices they've put up. I bet your father supplied them with the timber.'

'I b.. b.. bet he d.. did.'

'It's still a romantic place even though it's packed out with dreary civil servants. Just another month and the spring birds will be singing again. Do you remember why you wanted to marry me?'

'Of c.. course.'

'Good. And I remember why I said yes.'

'Why?'

She stretched up to his ear and whispered, 'Well I think you're tall and handsome and quite a catch.'

They joined a queue outside a kiosk where men in khaki uniforms talked to their girlfriends and wives about the most mundane things. No one spoke of the war. Lucy paid for tea and iced buns which they ate standing up whilst pigeons rushed to their feet to pick up the crumbs that Lucy dropped, just for them. She put the cups back on the counter. People smiled and pulled strange faces at the babies who passed with their mothers in prams. Dogs barked and chased each other around the trees.

She whispered again, 'You're home for good now. I want your baby. Will you give me a baby darling?'

'Yes, b.. b.. b.. but it's a b.. b.. bit b.. b.. busy here.' They both laughed and Jan lit a cigarette.

'We'll just have to wait till we get home then, won't we?' She looked up into his eyes.

'Y.. yes, tonight?'

'Yes, darling, tonight. Mmmm, I feel lovely and warm now. Let's go this way; I want to show you something.'

She pulled on his arm and took him to the spot where he had proposed nearly two years ago. They embraced on the bench by the edge of the lake.

'S.. s.. sso m.. much ch.. change.'

'I know, the whole world went mad and doesn't know how to get better again.'

Jan got out his notepad: *It's the same for people.*

They looked at the shops around Piccadilly and the windows of the big stores in Regent Street but it was too cold to stay outside for long. Jan took her into Sotheran's to warm up and to look at the rows of books on shelves that lined the walls crammed with covers of every kind. He bought a second-hand copy of *The Way of All Flesh* and sat down on a hard-back chair.

'Are you tired now darling?'

Head spinning a bit, he wrote.

The proprietor brought Jan a glass of water, briefly resting his hand on Jan's shoulder. After a few minutes, Jan recovered from his dizzy spell and said he felt fine. Lucy took him to the Carlton on Haymarket for tea and sandwiches then, just for fun, they rode on the top of the horsebus to Hyde Park. The plane trees were bare of leaves, exposing their khaki camouflage-pattern bark. There were few people on the streets and they had the top of the bus to themselves. As she watched the colour rise in his face and the winter sun lighting up his cheek bones, Lucy thanked her providence. She nestled into his arms to feel the warmth of his love that had been buried at Hill 60 and worn down in the hospitals of Northern France.

They returned to Chichester Road where Eva had left a note on the hall table saying that they were playing bridge with friends in Kensal Green and wouldn't be back till after ten. It felt like a rare gift that they could be completely alone in the house. Jan said that he didn't want any morphine just then but maybe later and instead he lay down on the settee and closed his eyes. The worry left his face as he slumbered. It reminded her of what a gentle, loving soul he could be. Lucy checked in the kitchen to see what she could make them to eat later. She prodded the fire with the poker and banked it up with coal from the scuttle. It was only late afternoon but still she thought that she needed to rest and reflect on their day. It had been a success, achieving exactly what she wanted. They were still good together, happy just being in each other's company and enjoying the little things that London still had to offer. She climbed the stairs to their bedroom, sat on the bed with a pillow propping up her back. She pulled the eiderdown over her, closed her eyes and went into the calm and silent place in her mind where Aunty B had told her to go and find her peace. She wandered in a summer meadow full of flowers where the sun warmed her body with a golden glow.

The toilet cistern flushed. She opened her eyes, it was dark. Jan opened the bedroom door and the electric light from the landing shone on the bed. He lay down next to her and, with soft lips that tasted of tooth powder, kissed hers. He stroked her face with gentle hands that smelt of lavender soap. She slid down the bed happy and yielding. And, in the calm that followed their lovemaking, she understood how love and patience will always win over hate and war.

To satisfy their building hunger she made an omelette and served it with fried potatoes and cabbage with caraway seeds. She brought it in on a tray to the living room with bread and butter and a bottle of HP Sauce. He told her that it was the love that she put in her cooking that made it taste so good. Afterwards, Jan smoked and drank some light ale and Lucy drank tea. They held each other and lay silent, dozing together on the settee in front of the fire until Eva and Peter returned shortly after ten. Lucy sat next to Eva to talk to her about children and how Jan used to be as a boy. Peter talked to Jan about work, politics and the war and they stayed up till almost midnight.

'Your face is so radiant,' Eva told Lucy. 'I can see your day out has done you the world of good. And Jan looks happy. Without you I'm not sure he wouldn't have wanted to go on.'

'I'm not sure, I think he has his own strength and we just need to encourage him,' Lucy said, looking at Jan with a loving smile.

Upstairs, when everyone had finished in the bathroom, Jan injected himself sitting on the side of the bed. He let the syringe and phial fall on the floor as he fell back against the pillow. Lucy undid his tourniquet, wiped the puncture on his bruised, pinpricked inner arm with cotton wool and surgical spirit, undressed him to his vest and underpants then covered him with sheet and blankets. She nestled into bed beside him, kissed him goodnight and, before she slept, returned to her summer meadow and her spirit friends among the buttercups.

Lucy hadn't seen Eric since their night out before Christmas. This was partly due to circumstance, as he had returned to his regiment on the day after Boxing Day, but there was also a degree of reluctance on her part fed by lingering embarrassment and shame. It was Eva who took it upon herself to walk over and see Eric and his mum on Christmas Eve. Mrs Hardcastle, so Eva said, cried with joy at the news of Jan's survival just as she had cried when she thought he had died only a few days earlier and Eric, apparently, made tea and sandwiches for the three of them.

Lucy wrote to Eric via his battalion to let him know about how Jan's recovery was going but wasn't surprised when she didn't receive a direct reply. It would have been inappropriate for him to write to her. When a letter did arrive, it was for Jan and they both enjoyed the relief of knowing Eric was alive with no serious injury:

29 January 1917

My dear Jan,

I'm sorry it has taken me so long to write but, as I know you appreciate, conditions here aren't always easy or conducive. I do hope that you are recovering from what must have been a most horrific experience and that Lucy and your dear parents are well. I heard news of Gladys nursing in Le Havre from a friend who was patched-up by the nurses and sent back to our platoon. They truly are angels.

It was such a relief to hear that you had survived the attack on Hill 60 after we had the shocking news that you had died. We are nowhere near Ypres but, as you know, I can't tell you where we are stationed at the moment. Winter seems never ending and we live in cold wet mud. I don't expect it's any different from when you were at the front. Mum sends me most welcome parcels of socks, biscuits and old magazines.

I've been dodging bullets quite successfully but when cold hit the platoon it can be doubly miserable. The wet soaks through our lousy clothes and it's a devil of a job to stop our toes rotting. But that's enough said about that.

I don't get the feeling that anyone expects the war to be over in the near future. Most of the men still think that we will win it or that Germany can no longer win. We hear of mutinies among the French but I can't see that happening with us. The Boche may never give up and we'll have to grind them down till they can't fight anymore. I just hope I'm still alive to see it.

I must say my views on the war have changed. I was naive and I now agree with how you saw it back in the good old days before we enlisted but I don't honestly think hindsight could have changed anything. I do so wish we could get back to those times but I know that nothing can ever be the same again. We are victims entangled in forces far beyond our control and have our part to play. I hope I don't sound too morbid. Actually, we're quite a cheerful bunch considering and we've become very fond of the horses and the stray dogs that befriend us. I have taken up your habit of voracious reading and basically read whatever I can get my hands on.

Though none of us can look that far ahead, I should get some leave around Easter time and will call round when I do.

Your dear friend,
Eric

Chapter 18

3rd March 1917
> *Dear Jan,*
> *Thank you so much for your letter of the 27th. It was wonderful to hear your news and that you seem to be having a steady recovery and that your powers of speech have almost returned. My sources tell me that it's usual for a trauma-induced stammer to improve given time and a good supportive home life. If not, I've been told that hypnotism is successful in many cases.*
> *It was heart-warming for me out here in the midst of this cold and brutal war to hear of the care and encouragement you have received from Lucy and your loving family. War is the most terrible thing but it often does bring out the best in people. Very soon I hope to get the chance to meet them all as, if all goes to plan, I should be back in London on Tuesday the 6th. I will be staying with my parents in Fulham and, if convenient, will call on the Wednesday at around 11am as I have something very special of yours to return; happy and in one piece. I must admit that I have grown particularly fond of her and will find it difficult to hand her back.*
> *I recently met your sister Gladys when I was visiting No 2 General Hospital in Le Havre. We had an evening meal and a good chat in the town. I must say that I was decidedly taken by her lively and energetic conversation. She is certainly doing a great job over there and, like the rest of the hospital staff, working her fingers to the bone in the most testing of conditions. She tells me that she should be home for a week at about the same time as my visit so, hopefully, we can all meet up.*
> *Your friend,*
> *Harry Briggs*

'Well, this is wonderful,' Eva said to Jan after reading Briggs' letter. 'And Gladys coming home too. I'm just off to rummage through my oddments cupboard; I think I've got just the thing. Back in a minute.'

She came back with an old sun-faded, dark green velvet curtain. Jan pulled a quizzical face and held his hands open before her.

'It's for a dog bed. I think we'll need two. One for in here and we can put another in the kitchen for her to stay in at night. Now how big is she?'

Jan held his hands apart by about two foot.

'Ahh, she's not *so* tiny then. She must have had a terrible time over there. She'll need a long rest; just like you.'

Jan smiled and nodded.

'Is she British or, Belgian or French?'

'D.. d.. d.. don't know.'

'Well, you're a lot of use today, aren't you?'

Jan did feel excited about Stinker's arrival but couldn't show it. He always felt he had missed out by not having pets when he was growing up. But those things didn't seem so important now. Eva made a list of all the things that Stinker would need.

'There's some old bowls in the kitchen for her food and water. We can wait till she comes but I should think we'll need a new lead and collar.' She passed him an old sheet. 'Now you can tear this up into pieces for the stuffing.'

Jan took the sheet and Eva passed him scissors to start the tear.

They can use these for bandages, he wrote on his pad.

'I know dear but we do need to keep some things for reserve. Gladys says she should be here on Friday and she's bringing a friend.'

'I n.. n.. know.'

'And I'm very much looking forward to meeting this Harry Briggs at last. He sounds like such a nice man.'

On Wednesday at eleven o'clock, Jan and Eva heard hard knocking on the front door. Jan jumped up to let Harry Briggs in. As he opened the door, Stinker jumped up on his legs then rubbed her body against him barking and letting out little yelps.

'Well, aren't you going to invite me in?' Harry said.

'Yes c.. c.. c.. course. C.. c.. come in.'

Eva was standing in the hallway and held out her hand.

'Mrs Strang, how wonderful to meet you,' Briggs said with a grin.

'We're so glad you could come. We've heard so much about you.' Eva lifted Stinker up in her arms. 'She smells lovely and clean. We heard she was bit whiffy. I expected to be washing her in the sink.'

'Hopefully she won't get covered in that kind of mud again. Ha ha.' He looked at Jan and smiled. 'Or Jan for that matter.'

'And you're both wearing a collar,' Eva said with a smile.

'Yes indeed, two of a kind.' Briggs let out a laugh.

'Do you know, I think we should change her name. I wouldn't like to be calling "Stinker, Stinker, Stinker" in the park. It was very good name when she was stinky and covered in mud but now she's here…'

Jan let out a long disapproving moan.

'Wh.. w.. what th.. then?' Jan opened out his arms in front of him.

'I thought "Tinker",' Eva said. 'As in "Tinker Bell".'

'What a brilliant idea. Much more in keeping with her new setting, ha ha,' Briggs said.

'Well?' Eva asked, looking at Jan with her head tilted in a friendly way. 'You can call her "Tinker" and I can call her "Tinker Bell".'

'I su.. su.. pp.. ose so,' Jan said with a little laugh and a smile.

'Oh, thank you, Jan, I was so worried you might want to keep the name.'

Jan smiled and shrugged. Sometimes he thought that his mother didn't understand him at all. Of course, he didn't mind. *Don't dress her up in ribbons and bows*, Jan wrote and passed the paper to Eva and Eva then to Briggs. They laughed. Jan felt in such good spirits. Briggs was the only person in the world who had any real idea of what he had been through and he had brought back, no doubt with great difficulty, the dog who stayed by his side when he was all but dead.

'Has Tinker Bell eaten?' Eva asked Briggs.

'Yes, Mrs Strang. She won't need anything now till about five or six. You can give them too much you know. After all, she's only little.'

'I know. She's a lovely little thing. Look she's sniffing around the room now. I hope she's not going to…'

'I doubt it but sometimes, when they're excited…'

Eva gave Tinker a biscuit. 'She'll brighten things up for us all. It's been a long time since we had any fun in this house.'

'Really?'

'No, not since Jan and Gladys were children when they used to bring their friends around to play. We still see Jan's friend Eric from down the road but they lost their youth very quickly as soon as they started work. Lucy can be like a breath of fresh air but Jan's experience was a terrible shock.' She picked up Tinker, rubbed her tummy and looked at Briggs. 'Now, I insist you call me Eva.'

'That would be nice and you must call me Briggs, I prefer it to Harry. My job can be terribly dehumanising with all the military formalities and all the funeral services, so it's a joy to be with a happy family.'

Jan snorted, lit a cigarette and went into the kitchen.

'Don't make tea for my benefit,' Briggs called out. 'I can't stay. I've so much to do and so many people to meet. I'll miss her terribly, of course, but I'm so pleased that Stinker, sorry, "Tinker", found the way to her rightful home and a well-earned retirement. Grace and providence work for little dogs as well, you know.'

'No more roaming for Tinker Bell,' Eva said.

'No, she's seen enough trouble for one lifetime.'

'N.. n.. not th.. the only one.'

Briggs looked at Jan on the settee. 'Are you still on the morphine, Jan?'

'Cu.. cutting d.. d.. d.. down.'

'You're an inspiration to us all.'

Jan let out a hollow laugh.

'No, I mean that. You have come a long way.' Briggs turned to Eva. 'Many give up morphine altogether after a few month's rest, you know.'

'That's what our doctor says. He's a family friend.'

'And Jan was in such a bad way. But he had a loving family and wife to get well for,' Briggs said.

Jan nodded and flicked ash into the fire.

Eva stood up. 'Gladys and her friend Mel will be here on Friday and we're having a big dinner. We expect you to come.'

'Well, it's very kind of you but are you sure?'

'Absolutely and we won't take no for an answer.'

'Food *is* quite scarce.'

'We can always pick things up, what with Peter's contacts at the docks.'

Jan smiled at Briggs and nodded.

'In that case, I'd be delighted.' Briggs got up and handed Eva the piece of frayed rope he used for a lead.

'Six thirty for seven.' She held his outstretched hand. 'It will be wonderful to have all you young people around. I can hardly wait.'

'I'll open a couple of bottles of rosé, after all, we should celebrate everyone being together again.' Peter smiled and held up two clear bottles showing the pretty pink wine in them.

'These came from friends in Portugal before the German blockade.'

Lucy glanced over to Eva and saw her staring at Peter with a look that he pretended not to see.

'Thanks Daddy, we're all just about ready to let our hair down, I think. Do you know they give wine and brandy to the patients to knock them out?' Gladys said.

'Yes, we had heard,' Eva said. 'It must be so difficult to deaden their senses.'

'You're telling me. But it's not wine like this; this is too weak. They won't let us touch a drop ourselves, you know.' Gladys gave her mother a 'you-wouldn't-believe-it' look. 'Some of the girls sneak a crafty drink, though. They'd be sent straight home if any of them were drunk, I've seen it happen. I haven't done it because the men need it more but, you know, after a hectic shift I could do with blocking everything out; just to stop my head spinning with all the day's events. Honestly, we never stop. I'm absolutely drooping.'

'You're the only one of us who actually saw battle,' Gladys' friend Mel said, looking admiringly across the table towards Jan. 'You must have been very brave.'

Lucy averted her eyes from Mel and the string of pearls that hung down onto her red blouse.

'N.. n.. not really,' Jan said.

'Tinker saw battle,' Briggs said with a grin that exposed his teeth. 'Rather too much of it. But then any amount of battle is too much. Every time she hears a bang she shakes like a weeping willow in the wind.'

'It's all the fault of men you know. As far as I can see, not a single woman had anything to do with making this war, we're just there to clear up the mess they leave,' Gladys said. 'The suffragettes had it right.'

'She certainly has a point, I can't think of any women involved,' Briggs said. 'Maybe if we had some women politicians, the war wouldn't have happened.'

Lucy rubbed Tinker's back under the table with her stockinged foot. 'Yes, we should be heard more. And then little dogs like Tinker Bell wouldn't need rescuing,' she said, smiling around the table. 'But we're very glad to have her.'

Jan looked at Lucy and smiled with such warmth that it made her feel less out of place.

'Quite right,' Briggs said. 'She's been lucky to get through it all and now she can recover, put it all behind her and live to a ripe old age. And Jan can take her to Queens Park for a walk and a run with the other dogs.'

'They could both do with the exercise; two war veterans together,' Peter said.

'The way they treat the horses, you just wouldn't believe it,' Gladys said.

'Yes, it's not a place for animals. It breaks your heart each and every day,' Briggs said.

Lucy lifted Tinker onto her lap and rubbed her neck through strings of fur. She would brush her thoroughly tomorrow and give her a good wash in the sink. Lucy took a drink from her glass of water. Gladys finished her rosé, flicked the hair from her face, lit a cigarette and continued.

'Some of the poor buggers who get brought into the hospital, we can't do much for them at all except patch them up and hope for the best. One young sap, he could only have been about seventeen…'

'Not now dear and please don't use that language when we've company,' Eva said.

'Don't worry on my account,' Briggs said. 'I hear much worse and that's just from the nurses and VADs. Ha ha.'

'Sorry, Mother, but you can't hide from the truth,' Gladys said.

'No dear, I'm not hiding from the truth. We've all heard what it's like there but we don't need to hear army language and all the gory details at the dinner table.'

'We've all made such great friends,' Mel said. 'I met Gladys for instance and lots of soldiers from all over the world and we met Briggs in Le Havre. I've had several offers of marriage and I've only been there since the beginning of the year.' Mel's lips were rouged red. Her neck was white and her face freckled. Her red blouse and cultured pearls were half covered by wavy ginger hair. She stood up and they all watched as she stepped back from the table and lifted her black skirt up to her knee on one side to reveal silk stockings of the most beautiful violet. 'A young French soldier gave me these before he died. He had kept them for his girlfriend but knew he wouldn't see her again, so he gave them to me. He would have wanted me to enjoy myself. I kept them for special occasions like this.'

'It's all so sad,' Lucy said. 'In a way, you must feel privileged that you can give some comfort as they pass over.'

'Yes, in a mixed-up way but, as you say, it's all very sad,' Mel said.

'It's the same for all of us,' Gladys said. 'Offers of marriage are just part of a day's work.'

'It's a pity we weren't there at Remy when Jan was wounded. We would have patched him up and brought him round. Wouldn't we Gladys?' Mel said.

'We certainly would. There's so much incompetence, it's just unbelievable. Men die through stupidity and disease as much as anything else,' Gladys said.

'And we never hear of it in the press.' Peter stood up to pour out another glass of wine.

'Not for me,' Briggs said putting a hand over his glass.

'Nor me,' Eva said.

Mel swallowed her remaining wine and placed her glass in front of her. She dabbed the corners of her lips with her napkin. 'Talking about men; they're much less modest than us girls. Last summer I was visiting my friend who lives near a training camp in Essex.' They all turned their heads to her. 'Well, one day we were walking along the cliffs and we looked over onto the salt grass on the water's edge only to see hundreds of white bodies bathing. Honestly, naked soldiers jumping and leaping and splashing each other with sea water in the sunshine.'

'That's how men should be living, not blowing each other up into hundreds of pieces,' Gladys said.

'My father says that the U-boats had sunk so many merchant ships coming from America, that the Americans will join the war within weeks and that would be the end for Germany,' Lucy said.

'I think he's right on that one,' Peter said, filling up Mel's and Gladys' glasses.

Lucy felt a sudden cramp in her stomach. She was dying for the evening to finish so that she could lie down in bed and unwind. Her day at the office had been long and boring as usual and it was looking like they might all stay up talking and drinking for hours which wouldn't help Jan. He needed rest rather than stimulation. She was grateful, of course, for all the nursing Mel and Gladys gave to the wounded troops but tonight her gratitude almost left her.

Everyone laughed at Mel's stories. She was one of life's entertainers. Lucy knew enough women like Mel to know that she wasn't one of them. She had little in common with Gladys or Mel but she liked Gladys. The smell of Mel's perfume reached her over the table and she felt slightly nauseous. Mel was now in the middle of a tale about a nurse and her ambulance-driver lover escaping detection from the ward sister by spending the night in the back of an ambulance. The rest of the table seemed spellbound but, although it was hard to turn off Mel's husky-Scottish voice, Lucy was hardly listening. She wasn't quite sure why she found Mel so irritating. It wasn't envy; no part of Lucy envied Mel. It might, she wondered, have been Lucy's mother's influence, who never held back in telling her daughters when she thought that a woman dressed like a tart. Or maybe she could see into her soul?

At one time, she would have wished she could have been Mel, but not now. In the time since she married Jan, she had become comfortable just being herself. In much the same way as flamboyance empowered Mel, Lucy felt stronger because she wasn't flamboyant. She shut Mel's voice out of her mind and thought instead about a saying that was going round in her head: *This above all: to thine own self be true.*

Peter, Jan, Gladys and Mel were finishing a glass of Johnny Walker whilst Eva started to tidy up the glasses from the table and empty the ashtrays into the embers of the fire. Lucy watched Tinker saunter over to her new bed by the fireplace and chew on a small clump of rags Eva had made. The voices had grown louder and louder over the course of the evening and just as she wished they would all quieten down, she saw Gladys and Mel whispering like conspirators. Gladys stood up as if making a declaration of independence.

'Let's go up the West End,' she said.

Lucy's legs went weak. She sat down next to Jan and held his hand.

'Oh yes, let's go out and have some fun,' Mel said. 'I've never had a night out in London.'

'I'm sure it's too late. They must be closing by now,' Eva said.

'I know somewhere that will serve us,' Gladys said. 'And Jan definitely will.'

Lucy turned to Jan, gently squeezed his hands in hers.

'Please don't go,' she said softly.

'I'll b.. b.. be f.. fine.'

'You know you could be very ill if you drink much more.' Jan looked away. 'But you still intend to go on drinking?'

You're embarrassing me, he wrote on his pad.

'You won't die from embarrassment. Don't you understand this is dangerous for you and humiliating for me?'

'Y.. you're in v.. v..vited,' he screwed his hands up into tight fists and Lucy knew that nothing, including another war, would stop him.

'I'm not that stupid,' she said more loudly, then lowered her voice again. 'It's a pity you can't see yourself after you've been drinking.'

'I really don't think you should go,' Eva, who had been listening in, said to Jan.

'I agree with your mother. It's not a good idea,' Peter said. 'It can get pretty dodgy in those places and you're really in no position to defend yourself.'

Lucy stood in front of the door leading into the hall. Smiling as demurely as she could manage, she said, 'Sorry but I have to get up for work in the morning, so I won't be going. Please be careful. All of you.'

'We will,' Gladys said.

'What about Jan?' Peter said.

'Don't worry, I'll look after him,' Gladys said.

'Make sure you do,' Peter said.

Briggs took Lucy to one side. 'I'll go with them and make sure he keeps out of harm's way.'

'Thank you; you're a good friend to him. Heaven knows he needs one.'

'I'll stay by him all night and bring him back home by myself if needs be,' Briggs said.

Tinker milled around their feet as they were on their way out. She got up on her back feet and scratched Mel's stockings around her calf.

'Ow!' Mel said, and poked Tinker in the ribs with her pointed grey shoe.

From Oxford Circus along Regent Street, revellers and drunks congregated in small groups deciding what to do now that the pubs had closed. Mel and Gladys' heels clip-clopped on the granite pavement echoing into the night; Jan stumbled trying to keep up with them and cursed his dwindling strength on the war.

Briggs caught him before he fell. 'You can change your mind and go home if you like,' Briggs said holding Jan up by his arm.

'Th.. that h.. hurts.'

'Sorry old man.'

Two privates, still in uniform, hardly able to stand, wolf-whistled and jeered at Gladys and Mel from across the street.

'On yer bike,' Gladys called out and they all laughed.

'I must say the cool air is clearing my head a bit,' Briggs said.

Excitement gripped Jan's stomach as the doors opened on Murray's Club and the unmistakable sound of jazz clarinet penetrated the night air. The old doorman, who looked as if he couldn't stop a determined mouse from coming in, nodded and smiled at Jan. A large book lay open on the counter and Jan put his signature next to each of his party as they signed in as guests. Jan opened his wallet and paid the entrance fee before slipping the man sixpence.

The dance floor was packed. High-society ladies in long black sequined dresses and jewellery seemed out of place next to the more fashionable younger women with pastel-coloured dresses, sleeveless and with hems above-the-ankle. Gladys and Mel appeared a bit out of step with their black skirts, colourful blouses and necklaces. Army officers, some in uniform, some in lounge suits and some, like Jan, in fashionable flannels and blazers were helped in their steps by ladies of all ages who pretended not to notice the injuries and deformities of their dance partners. A sprinkling of hostesses mingled with the single men standing out to all but the most naive. Hugging the wall, a tall man in a dark double-breasted lounge suit and spats cast his eyes over the busy floor. Briggs, standing next to Jan tapped his foot almost in time as the Negro drummer effortlessly beat out a dance rhythm. Jan turned his head from right to left before loosening his tie. Tiny beads of sweat dripped from his forehead and temples.

Jan felt a bit guilty about Briggs's lack of ease but let the feeling pass. It was, after all, Briggs's decision to come and he wasn't in the mood to mother him. The irony of a man who seemed more comfortable among the dead and wounded than in a London night club made him chuckle. Drinks were clearly the best solution so Jan moved towards the bar. Since the war started, waiters were in short supply.

Briggs had seen Jan move and joined him. He would be difficult to shake off.

Jan ordered vermouth for the girls and whiskey for Briggs and himself. The barmaids' ears were attuned to hear customer orders above the noise of well-oiled carousers pushing and shoving at the bar, vying to be heard against the penetrating sound of syncopated Dixie jazz. Briggs asked, 'how much?' and stared vacantly at the barmaid in disbelief when she said four shillings. Jan stepped in and handed over a crown before Briggs had a chance to get his money out. They took the drinks to the girls who had sidled off to look at the dancers on the parquet dance floor and were chatting to a couple of young officers.

'It's not the sort of place I'd take my sister to,' Briggs shouted in Jan's ear with a laugh. You don't know Gladys, and Mel's worse from what I hear, Jan wanted to say but talking with his stutter over the noise was pointless and he had more pressing things on his mind. When Briggs was enjoying a banjo solo from the stage Jan took the opportunity to down his scotch and disappear into the crowd leaving Briggs with the girls and their officer friends. Looking back over his shoulder he saw Briggs holding his head back, laughing in that nervous way that he must have thought was sociable. Jan felt hot, really hot. A cold sweat erupted on his brow and his shirt felt sticky on his back. He took his jacket off, slung it over his shoulder, undid his tie and put it in his pocket. His braces made creases in his white shirt as he leaned against a wall near the entrance to the 'Gentleman's', lit a cigarette and looked out into the crowd. The man in the lounge suit came up to him.

'Awlright, Pal?'

Jan knew him by sight but not by name.

'W.. w.. what you g.. g.. got?'

'Dope.'

Jan looked quizzically.

'Snow!' the man said with emphasis and walked into the Gentleman's toilets. They stood at the urinals until an older man left. The floor was spattered with piss.

'I fucking hate these places,' the man said. 'They've seen better days.'

Jan knew exactly what he meant, they used to be spotless before the war, but he was in no mood to discuss it. The man had obviously never been near a trench.

'O k.. k.. kay,' Jan said.

The man pulled out a brown paper packet hardly bigger than a cigarette card. 'Two and six,' he said. Jan handed him the coins. 'Don't worry; its good stuff.' Jan, with pulse racing, looked unconvinced.

In the cubicle, he took a drag on his cigarette and dropped it into the toilet bowl. It hissed as it hit the water. He locked the door, leant his cane against it, sat on the seat and opened the package on his lap. He tapped half of the powder into the well between his wrist and thumb. His hand shook and some of the powder missed the spot. He raised his hand to his nose and sniffed it hard up his nostril then licked the residue off his hand. Instant relief overwhelmed him. His head cleared and he smiled, knowing now he could enjoy the night properly. He folded the remaining powder back up in its envelope, unscrewed the brass knob on the top of his cane, dropped it in the cavity and screwed it back up.

Back on the dance floor, Gladys and Mel were following some unfathomable steps to a rag-time tune that all the women seemed to know. Their young officers tried to follow but with little success. Jan saw the lights radiate a pink hue that shone back off the bare arms and made-up faces of the women. His height allowed him a view of the lights reflecting off the polished heads of men who were taking themselves too seriously. Jan laughed out loud; it was a long time since he saw such a ridiculous sight. In small groups, new arrivals whose night was just beginning came through the doors waving to friends then joining them at their tables. Murray's was a lot of fun. He should have come here weeks ago; it would have lifted his mood.

The Negro knocked out a beat and the rest of the band in their matching fawn suits, white shirts and shiny-black bow ties came in with two trumpets, clarinet and piano and an unrestrained freedom that made Jan's body tingle with sexual feeling. A hostess, painfully thin with a spangled cigarette holder and wearing a thin black evening dress was talking to Briggs who strained to hear her. She put her hand on his shoulder and whispered something in his ear. Jan went over to him in time to hear him say.

'I'm afraid I'm not interested.'

'Then what have you been talking to me for?' Droplets came out of her mouth as she spat out her words.

'I must have been under a misapprehension. I'm terribly sorry,' Briggs shouted back. Mel and Gladys came over. Mel squared up to the hostess and stared her in the eye.

'Keep away from him,' Mel said putting her arm through Briggs's. The hostess waved her sparkling cigarette holder as she was about to speak.

'You'll poke somebody's ruddy eye out with that,' Gladys said. 'Just get lost.'

'I wouldn't stay with that pillock anyway,' the hostess said, and walked away into the crowd.

'Sod off, you old crow,' Mel called after her.

Gladys' face furrowed with concern. 'Are you alright?' she asked Briggs when there was a lull in the music.

'I'm fine, but this really isn't my sort of place,' Briggs said. 'What a dreadful woman. Do you know her breath smelt awful - and I work with the dead and dying!'

Gladys and Mel, taking advantage of their sex and relative youth, had several drinks bought for them. They danced with officers of various ranks who waited their turn for the privilege. And, not too vigorously, they fended off roaming hands. Mel, when one of the better looking young men's arms was around her waist, pulled him against her thigh, let him rest there for a moment, then smiled in a wicked way and kissed him quickly on the lips. When Gladys' head was turned, she left the dance floor holding his hand, manoeuvring him into one of the alcoves lit with a single flickering nightlight. A lascivious excitement shot through Jan as he watched them kiss and canoodle. When they came back laughing together, Gladys stared at Mel with her hands on her hips.

'I had to rush to the ladie's room, there was a queue. Sorry.' Mel's face cracked into a laugh.

'Briggs has disappeared; I'm going to find him. It's time we left,' Gladys said.

Jan swayed to the rhythm of the music, smoking and viewing the scene with a benign smirk. He would have danced if he thought he could manage it without falling flat on his face. A crooner with an unconvincing American accent stood to the front of the stage and sang, 'If you were the only girl in the world and I were the only boy,' and the band played in a gentle lilt behind him. Dancing couples held each other closer.

'Come on, Jan, let's get Briggs, we're going,' Gladys said looking at Jan who felt like a boy being told what he could and couldn't do and where he could go. 'No buts Jan, and anyway, you'll be bankrupt if you don't stop buying drinks for people. You need a bloody nursemaid.'

Mel said *au revoir* to her young man, promising that they would meet in France.

'Unless the war's over by the time we go back,' he said, laughing.

'Fat chance,' Gladys and Mel said together exchanging looks.

They found Briggs with head slumped forward sitting with a group of Murray Club habitués at a round table on the edge of the dance floor.

'Bless him; he looks so peaceful,' Gladys said to Mel then woke him with a gentle rub on his shoulder.

He looked startled. 'I'm so sorry. I must have …'

'Don't worry, it's fine,' Gladys said. 'You must have been totally bored. Anyway, we're off now you'll be pleased to hear.'

'Oh ah, well yes. I'll be right with you. I just need to pay a visit first,' he said.

Jan looked at his watch. It was four am and there was only one place to go. Swaying a little down the street, Jan, feeling bright and cheerful, guided them to Luigi's Breakfast Club. He hadn't been there since before he got married. He felt pride in a London where, not even a war of this magnitude, could close its nightlife down. Luigi smiled when he saw Jan and greeted him with an open hand.

'Another one of my boys has come back safely,' he said, before shaking Jan's hand with both of his.

Gladys, Briggs and Mel sat down on the plain pine chairs at a table with pink-and-white-check table cloths while Jan poked his head round into the kitchen. The walls were yellow from years of cigarette smoke and ingrained grease. Pictures of Milan, Rome and Naples along with photographs of friends and family hung in a haphazard order around the walls. Condensation ran in rivulets down the inside of the windows.

'This is more like it,' Briggs said, with a broad grin.

Luigi shared a glass of Grappa with Jan then set about frying bacon and eggs.

'You're a genius Jan, knowing all these places,' Mel said. 'You do know how to have a good time, don't you?'

Jan smiled back at her.

'It's not like this in Kirkcudbright, that's for sure,' Mel said.

'The smell of that bacon is giving me quite an appetite. I could eat a horse,' Briggs said.

'You probably have,' Gladys said. 'The patients get served up with it regularly.' She pulled a face. 'But I think I've managed to avoid it so far.'

'I think we might allow ourselves to forget the war for a little while now, couldn't we?' Briggs said.

'I agree, sorry, but I can't seem to ever get the images out of my mind,' Gladys said.   They tucked in to their breakfast. Egg yolk dripped down from Briggs's lips onto his chin.

'How come you're still awake after all you've had to drink; and you don't seem to be hungry?' Mel asked Jan.

Jan smiled and winked, rested his cigarette in the ashtray and gingerly started to prod his food.

'I'll explain later,' Gladys said.

Chapter 19

Tuesday 13 March 1917. Medical Board at the Department of Army Personnel Services, War Office, Horse Guards Avenue, Whitehall, SW.

'You'll be alright son. They couldn't send you back after what you've been through,' Peter said, as he and Jan walked down from Charring Cross Station.

They were in good time for Jan's appointment with the Army Medical Board at the War Office, which wasn't until 2.30 pm. Jan wore his Officer's uniform, Burberry coat and cap, and Peter was in a navy and silver pin-stripe suit, dark-navy woollen coat and bowler. Two women smiled at them as they passed by but Jan hardly noticed. The sky was overcast and showers were threatening. They filled their lungs on Victoria Embankment with the cool air that blew up the Thames from across the North Sea and the Low Countries.

'Just don't start telling them that you've been feeling better,' Peter said, as if Jan hadn't thought of that. 'We've got time for a smoke before we go in.'

Jan took two from his cigarette case and turned away from the wind with his collar up to shield his lighter. He lit one and handed it to his father then lit his own. They walked past the make-shift wooden annexes, turned the corner into Horse Guards Avenue and the colossal building came into sight. Jan looked up at the Baroque domes and great arches looming over them. He was insignificant to the powers that be, everyone was. Except for his father, of course; it was different for him. There were seven floors and two and a half miles of corridors and his father didn't seem in the least intimidated by the building's immensity. Peter Strang had been to the War Office on several occasions since the war began, initially to negotiate a price for low-grade timber for duck boards and later for the better quality Norwegian pine for temporary buildings.

'There are hundreds of officers in the same position as you and the Board are far too busy to go into your case in any depth. Don't worry; they'll just try to get you in and out as quickly as possible. The medical reports speak for themselves. You're not fit to fight let alone command a platoon. As long as you don't dance a jig you'll get through alright.'

'I b.. bloody well h.. hope s.. so.'

Jan had heard that Major Holborn was heading the committee. The rumour was that he had been taken off the British Expeditionary Force as he couldn't control his temper.

'Arrogant b.. b…bastards,' Jan said, as he flicked his cigarette butt into the road.

'Look, its two fifteen. We'd better get a move on. Don't worry about Holborn, he's been reprimanded, that's why he's back here behind a desk; to keep him from making any more costly mistakes.'

The War Office smelt of floor polish and was awash with people bustling about their business. Women typists and secretaries populated the rooms on either side of the corridors and everywhere Boy Scouts in short trousers scuttled around delivering messages in sealed envelopes.

'Excuse me, young man. Can you give me directions to the Army Personnel Services?' Peter asked one of them. The boy's long green socks had fallen to his ankles and he bent down to pull them up.

'Yes Sir, go down the corridor, up the stairs, fourf floor.'

'Thank you so much,' Peter said and handed him a penny.

'Thank you, Sir,' the boy said, making a salute with two fingers to his forehead then going about his business.

The place was so big and cold it was exhausting. Going up all those stairs brought back memories of his first steps in Le Treport. Jan was hot with the effort but the sweat on his forehead was cold. His legs ached and a sharp pain shot through him, straight down from his buttock to his left foot.

By the time they got to the fourth floor and Room 14, Jan felt sick and his head swam. A queue of wounded officers waited outside. Some were standing but nearer to the door they sat on a bench.

'They put it on the fourth floor because they reckon, if you can walk up here, you're fit enough for the front,' one of the men said to Jan and Peter, loud enough for everyone to hear. Peter smiled at the man but no one laughed. Another officer arrived two minutes later and he said the same thing to him.

'By all accounts, Holborn used to be a right swine but then he lost his son on the Somme and ever since had been a bit of a lost soul. The Board's running about a half-hour late,' an officer in front of them said. Jan offered him a cigarette and they leaned back against the wall blowing their smoke into the air. The door opened at about twenty past three and a middle-aged officer with a swagger stick came out and looked up and down the queue. Jan's insides churned and he wanted to puke.

'Lieutenant Strong?' the man boomed.

Brushing off offers of help from the stenographer, Jan walked with his cane to the interview room.

'Thank you, Mrs Young,' Major Percival Holborn said to the stenographer at her desk to the side of the main table. 'Please do sit down Lieutenant Strang. I'm Major Holborn and these are Captain Negus and Lieutenant Hooper, who is a medical doctor. I will be presiding,' he said, with a broad welcoming smile and indicating the single chair three yards in front of them.

'Th.. thank y.. y.. y.. y..___'

'That's quite alright; please sit down.'

Jan saluted and sat in the chair.

'First of all, Lieutenant Strang, I would like to extend my and my colleague's thanks as well as those of His Majesty and His Government for the service, leadership and sacrifice that you have already given to the war effort.' Jan was about to rise to reply. Holborn raised his hand. 'Please Lieutenant

Strang, don't get up.' He turned to his right and waved his arm. 'May I hand the proceedings over to you now Captain Negus?' he said, not expecting an answer.

'Thank you Major,' Captain Negus said and fixed his eyes on Jan's. 'Now, Strang, we have your last medical report in front of us and the purpose of this interview is to make a judgement on your capabilities as a commissioned officer in the Post Office Rifles to serve His Majesty in the war effort.'

'Y.. y..yess, S.. s..sirr.'

Negus bowed his head and waited for Jan to finish.

'Now, I just want to go over some of your details as is required. I'm sure I can speak for the other members of the panel when I say that, considering your speech impediment, we would only ask you to nod or shake your head for "yes" and "no" in answer to these questions.'

Jan nodded.

'That's fine. Now am I correct in saying that you were wounded on December 20th 1916 by high-explosive shrapnel near Hill 60?'

Jan nodded.

'The shrapnel entered the upper part of your left arm?'

Jan nodded.

'And a large piece stuck in your helmet piercing the metal and causing you severe concussion of the brain?'

Jan nodded.

'The shell exploded close to you while you were on duty in a front-line trench and the shock of the explosion badly shook your nerves?'

Jan nodded.

'Thank you, Strang,' Captain Negus said. 'Can I hand it back to you now Major Holborn?'

'Yes, by all means. Thank you, Captain,' Major Holborn said with an exaggerated grin that exposed greying teeth below his propeller-like moustache. 'Now, Strang, I have the letter you submitted to us where you outlined your injuries, symptoms and how this has affected you. If nobody objects,

I would like to read from your letter which, I must say, is well-written and in a particularly steady hand.'

Jan's heart started to beat faster.

'You say, and I quote:

I have been suffering from continual headaches since the wounding. When out walking, I become dizzy and my eyes ache in spite of the fact that I am only able to walk slowly and for a short distance.'

Major Holborn had a rasping deep voice.

'I couldn't help but notice that you are walking uneasily and that you have a pronounced stammer,' Holborn said.

Jan nodded, barely able to concentrate on what the Major was saying. His eyesight blurred and he smiled to himself as he imagined the Major's moustache moving independently of his facial expressions.

'It is apparent that you suffer from neurasthenia,' he said, then paused and looked Jan straight in the eye. 'Are you paying attention Strang? Strang?'

Jan moved his head with a jerk and nodded.

'Would you put it on the record that his eyes seem glazed,' Lieutenant Hooper said to the stenographer. Major Holborn coughed and continued. 'Please forgive me Lieutenant if I say that symptoms of this kind are seen as subjective and are certainly difficult to quantify. Although they can be permanent, it is my belief that they need not necessarily be. Of course, your symptoms are by no means the most severe we have come across.'

Jan smiled and nodded. The sickly feeling in his stomach became pronounced and he wondered how much longer this was going to last. There was a chance he might throw up.

'We are acutely aware of current developments in psychology concerning victims of neurasthenia. These views are not of one accord and there is, indeed, much debate on the matter. Having had these views expertly explained to us by Dr Yelland, a leading psychologist working with neurasthenic casualties, this board does take a positive view about the potential for recovery. We have seen evidence of Dr Yelland's successes in helping victims to recover and return to their units to continue to serve their King and Country. God knows we need every man we can find at the moment.'

Jan shuffled in his chair. The blood was draining away from his head. He wiped the beads of perspiration from his brow. Lieutenant Hooper looked at Jan with concern.

'Would you like a glass of water?' he asked, then poured him one and brought it over to him before Jan had a chance to answer.

'Don't worry, Strang, we don't intend to send you back to the front or over to Dr Yelland,' Major Holborn said with a faint smile. He turned around and made some kind of facial gesture to Hooper and Negus who both nodded. 'I think that, at the moment, you have little capacity for concentrated thinking and that sending you to do war work would be counterproductive.'

Jan nodded trying not to show his relief.

'We see from your records that you have been receiving regular doses of morphia. Although initially it may be difficult, I am ordering that you receive no more morphia from Army sources or Army prescription. It is in short supply and the priority must be for the field of battle.'

Jan could comprehend enough of what the Major was saying to understand that his worst fears wouldn't be realised. His mind, though, turned straight away to how he could obtain a regular supply. Cassidy could prescribe him more but he, also, wanted Jan to cut down. He could always top it up from some of the sellers on Piccadilly but that would be unreliable as well as a bloody nuisance and some men had died on that stuff. He could do with a shot now.

'You see,' Major Holborn said, 'morphia is a necessary evil in times of war but there does come a point when an injured soldier must fight pain by himself and we believe that you have reached this point. Do you understand, Strang?'

Jan nodded.

'Jolly good. Now, we have already spent more time on your case than I had intended so I would just like to conclude by saying that we recommend that you have a further six week's leave after which your case will be reconsidered. If you show signs of a good recovery, we will consider letting you return to your battalion in Flanders. However, if you are still unable to fight, you will be found work with the War Department on the home front.'

'Thank you very much for attending, Lieutenant Strang. Mrs Young will send you an official record of the Board's recommendations which you should receive within the next few days.'

Jan stood to attention, saluted the Board, picked up his cane and left feeling as if he had just had just been saved from the scaffold.

'How did it go?' Peter asked, taking hold of Jan's arm.

'Pub,' Jan said.

'Well, alright but they won't be open yet. We can go the Charring Cross Hotel on the Strand. Only for a couple though; we don't want to upset your mother and come home tight.'

Chapter 20

As winter faded and spring approached with birdsong and lighter days, a warm feeling of optimism, like sunshine, invaded Lucy's body and her thoughts started to dwell on a happy future. She felt sure that she had conceived on that night in February when they made love following their day of being happy together after returning to St James' Park. It felt, on that day, that Jan was really close to her for the first time since he came back from France in such a dreadful state. It was as if his tenderness had been frozen and was now thawing out and coming back to give new life.

Although she didn't doubt her intuition, she decided, for the time being at least, to keep to herself the feeling that their baby was growing inside her womb. In March, when her period didn't come, she understood it as confirmation and when, later in the month, she started to get irregular but sharp stomach pains she felt so exuberant that she sung popular songs around the house: 'I would say such wonderful things to you. There would be such wonderful things to do. If you were the only girl in the world and I were the only boy.' And on her morning walk to the station she hummed nursery rhymes remembered from her Sunday School in Uxbridge.

She made an appointment with Dr Cassidy about her probable pregnancy. He said that it was still too early to be sure, but that it was more likely than not and there was no harm in being optimistic. So she decided to break the news to Jan that night. She wasn't sure how he would take it but his face beamed in a smile that was sunnier than any she had seen on him in a long time. Although she knew his moods could change quickly, she took it as a positive sign. She saw that deep down he hadn't lost the love in his soul that had so endeared him to her. She set her mind to Jan's recovery and the future of their child.

Jan said that back in Le Treport, Harry Briggs had planted a seed in his mind that psychoanalysis and hypnotism might cure him of his nervous symptoms. She didn't know why it had taken him so long to mention it. Admittedly his brain was still befuddled and, of course, with the war still raging, he had little incentive to get well soon. According to Briggs, however, the Freudian approach had helped others and was talked about with respect among military doctors and those specialising with trauma. She brought the subject up with Dr Cassidy when she saw him for a check-up about her pregnancy. He said that the conclusions that the Medical Board came up with had bought Jan some time to recover, and that he had heard encouraging reports of a psychoanalyst who used hypnotism on soldiers invalided with nervous and obsessive complaints. His surgery was just off The Strand in Burleigh Street.

'I don't see how anyone could have gone through what Jan has and come out mentally unscathed,' Peter said one evening. 'He's probably done better than most.' He turned to look at his son. 'You need rest and a lot of it.'

Peter's compliment would mean a lot to Jan, though Jan would never admit it. Jan lit a cigarette, got up, poured himself a whiskey and sat back on the settee next to Lucy. She rested her hand on his thigh and gave him a reassuring smile to settle the unease he often felt when they were all together as a family. She didn't expect him to say much, as he closed down more when his father talked, especially when the subject was Jan's mental state. His parents believed that Jan honestly did want to get back to the way he was before the explosion damaged his nerves, but they also knew that, as much as he tried, he didn't seem able to drink less or cut down on his morphine doses. At night, in bed next to Lucy, his nightmares still raged. The consensus was that hypnosis was worth a try; after all, there was potentially a lot to gain. No one said it but their real concern was that, if he became too well, and the war didn't end soon, then he might be sent back to fight.

'I'll d.. ddo it!' Jan said. He touched his head. 'I w.. want tt.. to stop th.. this m.. madness.'

Lucy kissed him on his cheek and held his hand.

'D.. d.. don't f.. fuss'.

Lucy felt a sting each time Jan snapped at her but would never let it show.

'I'm so pleased. I know you can get well again,' she said. 'I can kiss you if I want to, can't I?'

Jan smiled.

Lucy asked for time off work to take Jan to see Mr Bentley, the psychoanalyst. Her manager agreed as it was, after all, in aid of the war effort. On their initial visit to the psychoanalysist, Lucy developed a growing faith in Mr Bentley; she could tell he was a decent man and seemed genuinely concerned about Jan and getting him well again. He made a point of putting her and Jan at ease. She noticed in his body language those hard-to-describe but natural gentlemanly traits. His surgery was furnished with arm chairs, and a chaise longue was placed in front of a polished mahogany desk covered with note pads, books and pens. Mr Bentley didn't look anything like what she had imagined an eminent psychoanalyst to look like: there was no frock coat, top hat, beard or foreign accent. In fact, he sounded like a country gentleman from one of the Home Counties. He wore a tweed jacket, dark-green woollen tie and Saxony check trousers. He couldn't have been higher than five-foot four and was almost bald with a tiny pencil moustache. Lucy supposed he must have been about fifty but everything about his demeanour was that of a younger man. She could see that Jan liked him as he didn't look nervous at all. Mr Bentley put his fingers together and leant back on his leather chair behind the desk.

'It is very often the case that, on return from war, the unconscious self refuses to allow the victim of trauma to resume normal relations with his life and family. And so, the unresolved conflict may then send the victim towards addiction and obsessive behaviour, particularly when addictive habits have been fed…' He paused and pulled on his cigarette. 'Shall we say by the medical and army apparatus.' Jan's eyes didn't leave Bentley; his brows were furrowed in concentration. 'My job, through hypnosis, is to bring the man back from the outlying areas of his mind where the trauma has forced him to live, and then to return him to his normal self.'

'You make it sound so easy,' Lucy said, with a little laugh.

'It can take a while but we usually do get the mind back to something approaching normality,' Mr Bentley said. He looked at Jan with a friendly smile. 'I can see you later in the week if you like but it would be best if you brought Mrs Strang with you.' Bentley smiled at Lucy.

'I won't be able to get off work, I'm afraid,' Lucy said.

'Somebody else then, your Father perhaps.' He shook hands strongly with Jan then held Lucy's lightly. 'I can fit you in on Thursday, I should think. I believe we had a cancellation.'

On the Thursday afternoon, Jan and his father strolled from Charing Cross and along The Strand to Mr Bentley's surgery on Burleigh Street.

'We could call in here later,' Peter said, as they passed the Charing Cross Hotel.

'G... good, I.. I'll n n.. need a d.. dr.. drink b.. by then.'

'I was thinking of tea,' Peter said.

'Mr Bentley will be with you very soon. Please take a seat.' The receptionist showed them the row of upholstered straight-backed chairs against the wall.

Peter opened up his *Times* and started to read the financial pages. Jan looked over to the receptionist and the vase of daffodils on her desk. They made the room smell of spring. She smiled as she caught his gaze. Jan brushed some imaginary dust off his knee, looked into her eyes, and returned the smile, knowing full well that to be pleasant and welcoming was just part of her job and she would have no interest in a worn-out shell-shocked soldier like him. Jan thought for a moment, took out his notepad and pencil, wrote a couple of sentences and put it back in his breast pocket.

The door to Mr Bentley's office opened and a young man, looking fresh-faced and healthy came out after shaking Bentley's hand. Jan was feeling hopeful this morning; it was like the winter was over at last.

'Do come this way,' Bentley said, welcoming them into his office.

'I find the whole idea of hypnosis absolutely fascinating,' Peter said.

'It's not a new thing at all,' Bentley said.

'So I believe,' Peter said.

'It's been used for centuries. It's just that now, in this modern world, we're directing it towards new areas of healing.' Bentley waved his hand toward the armchairs. 'It's quite a natural process and can't possibly cause any harm. Do take a seat.'

Jan lit up without offering them round. He was glad that his father had come with him; he would never have got past the first pub otherwise. But he found his father's know-it-all attitude, that he inevitably displayed if any professional person was present, to be almost insufferable. He drew on his cigarette. A part of him did believe that hypnosis might work but, although optimistic, he was far from being convinced. He had heard of cases where men who were in a terrible state had apparently recovered. But Jan didn't feel he was like other men; he was complex and nothing like the normal Tommy who served on the front. He felt decidedly uneasy and fidgeted in his chair. God only knew what he might say under hypnosis. Briggs had told him that these hypnotists made you re-live the trauma, and even if it was now only a memory, it was an ever-present one. He didn't want to go back to Hill 60, no matter how much it might help him.

'Would you mind sitting in the reception room, Mr Strang?' Bentley said, looking directly at Peter.

'Not at all.' Peter smiled and moved toward the door.

'Miss Tulip will make you a cup of tea and there are some papers to read; but I see you have the *Times* in your pocket.'

'Indeed, I don't know why I read it; it is very depressing. I suppose one day it will say the war has been won and we can get back to some kind of normal life again.'

'Yes, yes, but I suspect things will never be the same.' Bentley paused and rubbed his chin. 'We should be about half an hour or so but don't be surprised if it lasts longer.'

Jan waited till the door had closed behind his father before tearing off the top sheet from his notepad and handing it to Bentley. It contained instructions to inject him with morphine if it all went belly up. A part of him was feeling quite relieved something was being done at last that might actually help him but another part was terrified of what it might bring up.

'Rest assured that there is no possibility of you having a convulsive fit under hypnotism. I know that you have some understanding of the process of hypnotism, I just want to reassure you that it is a wholly natural and relaxing experience.' Jan looked at him. 'You will be aware of everything I say and you will listen to my voice at all times.'

Jan nodded; Bentley's tone was reassuring.

'Now, please settle back in your chair and make yourself comfortable. By all means prop a cushion up behind your head.'

Jan let out an 'uh huh'. He looked at his hands and saw that his fingers were sore at the edges of his cuticles where he had been picking them. He stubbed his cigarette out in the ash tray, stretched out his legs on the upholstered footstool and rested his head on a soft embroidered cushion. It smelt of lavender like the pillows in Le Treport. He kicked off his shoes without untying the laces. They fell onto the Persian rug with a dull thud. Bentley closed the long deep-blue curtains that hung down to dark-wood floor boards and the room fell into twilight.

'Don't worry, we won't be in total darkness. I just don't want the sun shining in and causing a distraction.' Bentley moved up from his desk and stood in front of Jan. 'After I have taken you into a light trance state, I will ask you questions and listen to what your un-locked subconscious mind wants to say. The extent to which you respond, however, will depend on how susceptible you are to hypnosis. With some it comes very easily and with others we don't necessarily achieve as much as we would like at the first attempt. Now I want you to listen to my voice and to breathe slowly and deeply and, as you do so, feel your body relax.'

Jan obeyed and felt comfortable. The combination of Bentley's voice and slow deep breaths began to clear the pains, fuzz and insanely negative thoughts that recurred in his head.

'As I speak feel your eyelids getting heavy.'

Jan nodded involuntarily.

'Heavier and heavier. Now, close your eyes firmly shut and don't open them until I tell you.'

He tried to test Bentley and keep them open but they wouldn't respond.

'I want you to concentrate on your toes, wiggle them and feel them losing any tension.'

Jan did exactly as Bentley said.

'And now feel all the tension leaving your ankles …., calves …, thighs …, stomach …, back …, neck ………., eyes

'Now imagine you are walking through a meadow on a still summer's day. You feel happy and completely at ease. The warmth penetrates your bones …. beautiful smell of wild flowers …

'I'm going to count backwards from ten, and when I reach the number one you will be in a deep state of hypnosis – ten, feeling sleepy; nine, going deep; eight, deeper and deeper; seven…; six…

'Now, go back to the time just before your stammer started.'

'Yes.'

'Where are you?'

'In the trench with my men.'

'What's happening?'

'Noise, unbearable. Shells exploding around me; can hardly see for the smoke; Germans coming towards us; stupid bloody hats, they're throwing grenades, firing hand guns. ... "Wait men, WAIT don't fire until they're thirty feet away." Jesus Christ they're nearly on us. "FIRE, Fire." They're dropping like flies ... more coming ... I shoot but .....'

'Yes, what's happening now?'

'I can't do it.'

'Do what?'

'Can't do it. I shoot at their legs. I haven't killed anyone. I can't.'

'What, no one?'

'No one.'

'I see.'

'The men kill but I can't. Damn, they've got me. Men dead and injured all around me; Germans too, they're screaming with pain. I don't know what to do. I can't do anything anymore.'

'Are you badly hurt?'

'Shot in the arm. Arm's buggered. ... A big shell next to us ... Sweet Jesus.'

'Now what's happening?'

'Don't know, there's nothing. Can't see anything now.'

'Jan? ... Jan? ... JAN!'

'Yes.'

'Everything is fine now. I want you to leave where you are and slowly become aware of your surroundings and the room we are in.'

Jan touched his face; his cheeks were wet with tears and he felt a satisfying sense of relief. The tension that had been gnawing away in his solar plexus since he went out to fight was gone. He wasn't in the trench, he was in London. Thank God.

'Open your eyes and come completely back NOW.'

He opened his eyes and saw Bentley standing in from of him smiling gently and holding out a glass of water. Jan took it, drinking it straight off.

'I don't remember being asleep but I suppose I must have been.'

'With hypnosis, a part of you is always aware of what is happening.'

'I remember...' Jan felt scared.

'Yes?'

Jan covered his forehead and eyes with his hand.

'I remember what I said.'

'That's good. You are extremely susceptible to hypnosis. We have opened up a channel between your conscious and unconscious mind in order to release your repressed feelings and heal the rift that has been affecting your nerves.'

'You mustn't tell anyone.'

'Of course not; everything you tell me is entirely confidential.'

'I bloody well hope so. I could be shot for this.'

'My lips are sealed and you are able to speak normally.'

'I know; it's a flaming miracle.'

'I wouldn't go that far. It's psychology; we have released some of your suppressed fears. There will be others and of course there is still the issue of addiction.'

'Of course, yes. And I've behaved terribly at home.'

'With your permission, in our next session, I can, when you are under hypnosis, implant suggestions that may help with your erratic moods and reduce your drinking and need for morphine. We will have to see how you go on in the next few weeks. I think you should see me again in a week and then every few weeks after that for a while.'

'Yes, absolutely. Thank you, Mr Bentley.'

'You may feel a bit light-headed for a while so take it easy for a few hours. Your father will take you home, I assume?'

Jan nodded then stood up. His legs nearly buckled underneath him. He felt like a jelly but, by Christ, he could speak.

'You should feel better with a strong cup of coffee or tea inside you and, what's more, you will be able to order it yourself. Goodbye for now.'

'Well, it appears I can speak again,' Jan said to his father.

'That's marvellous.' Peter shook John's hand and patted him on the shoulder. Jan winced. 'I never imagined it would work so quickly. I'm absolutely lost for words,' Peter said.

'How unusual.' Jan's thoughts became more focused and, as they strolled down the Strand, his legs started to feel stronger. Men in uniform milled around the grand station entrance. Jan and his father walked over to the two pillars holding up the portico over the doors to the Charing Cross Hotel.

'Good afternoon, Sirs. Please follow me,' the doorman said.

The staff at the London hotels were all pretty much geriatric and this doorman was no exception. With a slight limp, he showed them through the foyer with its dracaenas and potted palms, past a pair of tall, polished-wood, etched-glass swing doors in the Art Nouveau style, to a comfortably decorated lounge. The air was thick with smoke from the cigarettes and cigars of the well-dressed and well-to-do avoiding the wartime licensing hours. Jan watched the smoke swirling in the light cast from grand-arched windows that faced onto the street. They sat down in leather arm chairs much like those in Bentley's surgery. A piano player with enlarged arthritic knuckles was plonking his way through a medley of Scott Joplin tunes. On the piano top rested four port-and-lemons that, Jan presumed, had been bought by customers grateful to him for playing their requests.

'Thank God he's not singing,' Jan said.

'Yes, we have much to be grateful for,' Peter said. A waiter with a grey upturned moustache hovered, ready to take their orders.

'Tea for two please and do you have any sandwiches?' Peter said.

'Thank you, Sir. I can offer you sardine sandwiches.'

'Lovely, thank you,' Peter said.

'And a pale ale.' Jan felt his father's stinging look. Peter offered Jan a cigarette.

'How do you think it went?'

'Well, I can talk properly for a start and, before you say anything about the drink, I can't think of a better cause for celebration.'

'I suppose you do have a point.'

'I'm still coming round. It's like waking up from a dream.'

'It sounds almost too good to be true. I couldn't feel happier for you. What did he do?' The people at the next table seemed to be listening in, so Jan and his father leaned in towards each other.

'I can't remember it all. He just talked to me to begin with. Then he started to count down from ten and the next thing I knew I was back in the trench with my men and re-living the experience.'

'It must have been dreadful.'

'You would think so but it wasn't that bad. I was there but it was like I was detached from it as well.' He pulled on his cigarette. 'Very strange really.'

'But it's such a sudden recovery.'

'I know, he said I was one of the most susceptible people to hypnotism he had ever come across.'

'Good lord. What else happened?'

'I don't really remember. The next thing I knew, I woke up and my face was wet with tears.'

'Is that it?'

'Yes, that's about all. And he wants me to go back next week.'

'That's good, isn't it?'

'Yes, he says he can work on my moods.' Jan blushed. The waiter brought a tray and laid out the tea, beer and sandwiches before them. They stubbed out their cigarettes and whilst Peter poured the tea Jan drank his beer down in one.

'Another of these,' he said clearly, holding his empty glass up to the waiter before he had a chance to leave the room with his book of orders. Heads turned from the adjoining table. A lady decked out in an outfit intended for a much younger woman and smelling of perfume which, mixed with tobacco smoke, created a vile odour, leaned over to Peter.

'I'm sure he deserves it. They're doing such a good job keeping the Germans away,' she said. Peter smiled but didn't reply.

'Nosy old bat,' Jan whispered in his father's ear. But nothing could take the shine off his happiness today. The sardine sandwiches came with thin slices of cucumber and were delicious; the beer gave him a warm glow in his stomach and this was the first day of the rest of his life.

Chapter 21

Jan hadn't heard from the Medical Board since they gave him six weeks leave back in March. His father had approached the War office at the beginning of April and managed to obtain special dispensation for Jan to work with him at his offices until the Board had the time to revise his case. His anxiety about returning to the front had eased somewhat as there seemed little chance of being called back to an over-stretched War Office for another interview. Peter had successfully argued that timber was essential war work, which, of course, it was. At times, Peter was a useful father to have. He didn't always show it but Jan was grateful, more than his words could express.

Jan's mental wellbeing was improving beyond everyone's expectations. Since he started visiting Bentley, he could talk properly, which was a miracle in itself and, following this, his panic attacks had become rarer and less intense. His headaches were still bad but, instead of using drink to block out the pain, he would now lie down in the bedroom with the curtains closed. He wanted to drink but understood that eventually his cravings would subside. Sometimes he would go for days without a drink and at the weekends he and Lucy would take Tinker for walks and go into town. He surprised everyone when he voluntarily reduced his morphine intake to one grain twice a day, thinking he might as well get all the hard work out of the way and have a fresh start.

Jan started doing small amounts of office work at his father's Bishopsgate premises; just simple jobs like checking invoices against the stock, authorising payments and composing letters and orders to their suppliers in Sweden, Norway, Canada and the US for Mrs Agnoli to type up. He enjoyed getting back into a routine. Just the same as before he signed up, he would take the bus down to the docks to see Harry and check that the timber was being offloaded properly from the ships into the ragged and deteriorating assortment of BEF transport, both horse-drawn and motorised. He would watch as the timber was then shipped out on different boats to Le Havre to be used to build temporary barracks and as a duck boards to cover the wide swamps made by the perpetual shelling of Flanders' fields.

Jan was the first to admit that he still had a long way to go before he would be back to his old self at the job. He found it difficult to write with the tremors in his hand and sometimes he could barely concentrate on the simplest things. When his headaches started, he would try to clear them by having a smoke in the street and, when it got too bad, he would go home. Some days he wouldn't go into work at all but mostly he stuck it out; he was better doing something at work than allowing his feelings of self-pity, misery and depression to descend on him at home. That attitude could only lead to a morning drink. In the office, led by Mrs Agnoli with her embarrassing familiarity, they encouraged him and didn't rib him for his absences as they would have done before he went to the war. When at home, Lucy and Eva told him how proud they were of him; he didn't say it, but it made him feel worthwhile for the first time in months. Jan now believed that he could live a normal life and become the husband that Lucy deserved.

Gladys wrote home and said the war was getting worse and there were worrying reports of disruptions in the French Army. In London, however, with spring in the air, there was a feeling of optimism that it would be won before long. America had now joined the allies and, when their troops eventually landed on the coasts of France and Belgium, the long battle would surely be over, by the end of the year, perhaps.

Today, June 13th, 1917 Jan had arranged to meet Lucy at St James' Park to eat their sandwiches on a bench by the lake, just like they used to before they were married. It was a place that they loved to return to. With clear skies and fair weather, he left the office at eleven thirty and made his way along Bishopsgate to catch the Circle Line train at Liverpool Street. He heard a mechanical groan in the air then:

Boom, crash, crack.

Sounds of exploding shells echoed out from the docks. He quickened his steps to get to the station when he heard bombs dropping closer. Gotha engines roared behind him. Looking up he felt a shiver as they blocked out the sun and the bombs fell from the sides of the planes.

Jesus Christ. He quickened his pace into a trot. He looked up just as two bombs crashed down through the station's arched-glass roof falling on two stationary trains. *Boom*, the trains rose into the air scattering twisted metal and glass across the platforms. People were thrown up and fell mangled on stone slabs. Coaches flew from the tracks and set ablaze; pieces of upholstery, haloed with flames, landed making the place thick with the black smoke. A clock still hanging on a wall said 11.40; *Thank God*, Lucy would still be in work.

He stopped hearing the screams around him and ran east along Eldon Street. The bombs followed him. To his side, a horse-drawn omnibus exploded with a direct hit. He kept on running. *Bang*: mutilated shop-window dummies blew out from a dressmaker's window and mixed with the real dead and wounded, among the bricks of collapsed walls and roofs. People were helpless; mothers screamed out their children's names over and over. Jan paused to get his breath. He had seen this kind of devastation in the trenches but this was different; women and children and old people weren't killed in the trenches, only soldiers. These poor sods had no idea it was coming. They thought they were safe and now they were sprawled around, injured and crying.

He thought his heart would burst.

At the office, Peter and his staff heard the noise of the bombs. They all rushed out into the street where they were joined by scores of others as the buildings along Bishopsgate emptied. They half-ran towards Liverpool Street as the wounded came towards them with blood running down faces from the shards of glass imbedded in their skin, hair and clothes. As Peter got closer to Liverpool Street a bomb landed in the road ahead of him. A horse reared up in fright and its cart overturned. The horse lay dead, bleeding in the road, its driver crying as he stroked the lifeless chestnut head. Office workers tore at the rubble to reach the injured. Peter, by now covered in dust from brick and plaster, prayed that Jan wasn't among them. *Bang*, another bomb fell. Mrs Agnoli screamed as she caught the force of the blast and fell in the middle of the road with the side of her face hitting the cobbles. Peter stopped and rushed to her side. He took his jacket off and placed it under her head. Her spectacles had broken and scratched her face and an earring had torn from her ear lobe. Blood dribbled from her ear and the silver and pearl ornament that hung from the clasp had pushed into the side of her cheek piercing the skin. Her blood soaked down onto his pin-stripe jacket. He took out his handkerchief and squeezed her ear lobe to staunch the bleeding.

Lucy and the girls in the office first heard the bombing when it started down at the docks. Instinctively she put her hands over the new life in her stomach. The drone of the engines travelled through their open windows as the planes moved north. An overwhelming sense of disbelief pervaded the office staff as bombs fell in the direction of Liverpool Street. She had been watching the clock, ready to leave at the stroke of twelve and meet Jan in the park. If Jan was on time he would be getting on the train about now to meet her just after twelve. He could be in the middle of it but he was often early. She felt the urge to run straight up to St James's Park station to see if he was waiting there for her. The office girls stood up from their desks and rushed to the windows. Lucy followed suit and stuck her head outside to better see the commotion. Dust rose and nearly blotted out the sun as bombs landed a mile or so to the east. The girls ran outside.

The office manager came with them and then urged them to return to the building and make their way to the basement floor where they should be safe. Vera and Beatty ran off to their respective homes whilst Lucy dashed behind the Home Office and half ran towards St James' Park Station. A woman in the street with two children clutching to her skirts asked Lucy what was happening. Lucy ran past ignoring her. A Railway Guard stood outside the station with a growing crowd around him all asking what had happened:

'I'm sorry,' he said. 'It's too soon to know any details.'

'You must know more than that,' a woman called out.

'All I can tell you is that there has been a bombing raid at Liverpool Street and all trains have stopped running until we can assess the situation and make things safe,' the Railway Guard said.

A quiet came quickly after the last bombs fell and the planes flew off. The sun shone through the settling clouds of dust. Lucy hailed a motor cab but the driver refused to go any nearer to Liverpool Street than Shoreditch. She paid him without comment and ran the extra quarter of a mile to the station. People were pulling away at the rubble to get to the wounded and Lucy instinctively followed suit. A police officer trying to organise the rescuers called out to her to leave the heavy lifting for the men. He said she could help, with the other women, by taking care of the children and wounded until the ambulances and nurses came. Wherever Jan was, her chances of finding him now were out of her hands so she stepped around the bricks and debris listening for cries of help from those trapped in the rubble.

She sat down on a block of stone to catch her breath; brick and mortar dust in the air had stuck to her forehead and, as she wiped perspiration from her brow with her forearm, it scratched her skin. The smell of roasted rabbit stuck in her nostrils and then she realised it was the smell of burnt human flesh and retched. Close by she heard a child crying from under a mangled sheet of corrugated iron. A girl of about five, covered in red-brick and yellow dust, looked in Lucy's eyes. The girl's legs were severed from just above the knee and the loose limbs were just attached to her legs on a flap of skin. Blood pulsed out of the stumps. Lucy crouched next to the girl, cradled her head in her arms and stroked her curled blonde locks. Her blood felt warm as it soaked onto Lucy's skirt.

'Where's mum,' she cried and looked at Lucy. 'The pain; the pain is terrible.' Then she stopped crying. Lucy felt the girl's body go limp in her arms. Her immediate thought was that she must find the girl's mother but then she turned her head and saw, forming from mist, six girls and boys in clothes from the middle of the previous century. They came close enough to touch her and imparted to Lucy an inner understanding that the girl would be cared for and would never be alone. They then rose up through the air and drifted away into the sky holding onto the hands of a double of the dead girl, ethereal and undamaged by the blast. Lucy stared after them as they faded away above the damaged buildings. Still holding the lifeless head Lucy closed the girl's eyes with her finger and thumb.

Stunned by what she saw, she didn't have time to let the vision sink in. She could think about it later. Now there were far more important things to concern her. She looked around and told some men moving bodies with a makeshift stretcher that the little girl had passed away. She coughed to clear the dust from her lungs. Her throat was parched and she felt hot and dizzy. She looked around and saw mannequins strewn outside a dress shop; unhesitating she rushed in and snatched a loose summer dress, about the right size, from a rail that was still standing. The sound of running water was coming from a pipe in the ground behind what was left of a wall in a dilapidated room. Here was some privacy. She unbuttoned her blood-stained skirt at the waist, let it fall to the ground and stepped to one side. She pulled her blouse off over the top of her head, soaked it in the escaping water from the burst pipe and wiped her legs clean of the little girl's blood. Turning her head, checking in case someone might be watching, she dropped the blouse on the ground, put her arms through the sleeves of her new floral-patterned dress and did the buttons up at the front. She knelt by the pipe, splashed her face as much to cool down as to wash away the grit and grime, then took a long satisfying drink.

As the afternoon went on, hardly believing what had happened, she did what she could. With other women and teenage girls, she comforted the bomb-damaged children as much as was possible and bandaged their wounds with torn-up cotton vests that she took from the wooden draws in the dress shop. When the roads had become clear enough to move down, Lucy helped the girls and boys onto horse-drawn carts bound for St Bart's Hospital. Some of the dead children were so mutilated that their mothers could no longer recognise them. The sound of sobbing droned in the air. By five o'clock there was no more for her to usefully do, so she walked down Bishopsgate to Peter's offices where only he and Mrs Agnoli remained.

'Oh, sweet Jesus, Lucy, are you alright?' Mrs Agnoli said. Lucy, for the first time, saw Mrs Agnoli's face free of earrings and make-up and realised she was older than she had thought.

'I'm fine. But, how are you? You're covered in bits of gauze and you've got a handkerchief stuck on your ear,' Lucy said.

'I am fine also, Missis Lucy. Mr Strang patched me up.' Mrs Agnoli looked over to Peter and smiled.

'I don't suppose there's much more we can do just now. It looks like my father-in-law's done a pretty good job,' Lucy said.

'But you looking tired: your arms is covered in blood. And the dust. Oh, my dear. And your clothes are all torn and youse scratched all over,' Mrs Agnoli said.

'Sit down, Lucy, for God's sake,' Peter said. 'Have my chair behind the desk, it's the most comfortable. Can you put the kettle on please Teresa, I mean, Mrs Agnoli?'

'I'm fine, honestly, please don't make a fuss. But I couldn't find Jan,' Lucy said, sitting down in Peter's chair.

'We don't know where he is either.'

'He may have been hurt by the bombs but I don't think so,' Lucy said.

'I doubt it; he's got nine lives that boy. It's his mind we have to worry about. He could be at home by now but the telephones don't work so we can't know till we go there. We stayed put here, just in case he came back.'

'Eva must be worried sick about all of us,' Lucy said.

'I know. I paid a boy to get over to Chichester Road and tell her we were alright but he isn't back yet. I don't think he will though; you know what these boys are like. We've spent the afternoon helping clear the road. Mrs Agnoli got a big crack on the head but she says she's alright. Only time will tell with an injury like that.'

Lucy lowered her voice to a whisper. 'Didn't one of her sons die on the Somme?'

'Yes, and her husband and her other two sons are in France.' Peter put his finger to his lips as Mrs Agnoli returned with a mug of tea for Lucy, sweetened with condensed milk.

'Do you know, I feel quite dreadful?' Lucy tasted the tea. 'But I've never known a better tasting mug of tea.' Lucy started to talk about what had happened since she left work. How ghastly it had all been, how a little girl died in her arms and how other children had been maimed and their lives ruined, almost before they had started. A school in Poplar took a direct hit and St Bart's didn't have the room to take all the children, what with all the war casualties arriving from France. She heard how old men who had come to buy a ticket or to meet friends at Liverpool Street station were taken away dead on barrows. The nurses were working in the street with anyone who could help. She put the empty mug on the table in front of her, settled down in the chair and closed her eyes.

When Lucy opened her eyes again, she was lying back on the settee at Chichester Road with her feet up on the arm rest and a cushion under her knees and, although it was a warm night, she was covered with a tartan blanket from the waist down. A sensation in her nasal passage irritated. She rubbed her nose and sneezed twice. A dishevelled Dr Cassidy stood in front of her holding a bottle of smelling salts. Tinker, who had until now been sleeping on the floor by her side, looked up at her looking worried.

'What? Where? How did I get here?'

'Don't worry, Mrs Strang. You've had a terrible ordeal and your body decided to take a long rest. I took the liberty of listening to your tummy with my stethoscope while you were asleep and your baby appears fine but you must take things easy and recover your strength. There is no question of you going into work for a while.' He looked distracted and ran his fingers through his hair. 'I won't be able to stay long, I'm afraid. All us doctors are working flat out. It's been a terrible day.'

'We got you home in a cab,' Peter said.

'But where's Jan?'

'We don't know,' Eva said with red, tired eyes then turned towards the window.

'I dreamt he was alright. I'm beginning to remember now,' Lucy said. Peter handed her a glass of water which she drank in three successive gulps. She spluttered. 'My throat, it feels so rough.'

'Please don't strain yourself, Mrs Strang,' Cassidy said.

'I dreamt he was lost but was coming back.'

'I'm sure he will but you must get some rest, drink plenty more water and tea and try to eat something.'

'He's right dear. You really must rest,' Eva said.

'I know, I know, but it's Jan; he must be wandering around lost. We have to look for him.' Lucy got up, felt her legs buckle and fell back onto the settee. She looked down at her torn dress and scratched legs. 'I'm in no fit state, am I?' she said with a half-smile.

'No. And, as your doctor, I must insist you stay where you are. You have the baby to consider and you've had a terrible shock.'

'I have the most terrible heartburn,' she said.

'All we can do is wait,' Peter said. 'There's no point in wandering around London on the off chance of spotting him.'

'He's right,' Cassidy said.

'God knows, anything could have happened to him,' Lucy said.

'Yes, but what can we do?' Eva said, gesturing with open arms.

'I know you're right but there must be *something* more we can do. Has Tinker Bell had her walk?'

'Oh yes, I just couldn't keep still with all my worries. I've been into the park with her today, three times already but she was terrified by the sound of the bombs and kept pulling to come back home. I think she must be quite exhausted with her memories,' Eva said, rubbing Tinker's tummy.

Dr Cassidy went into the kitchen and left the door open. Out of the corner of her eye Lucy watched as he half-filled her glass with water and poured in some tincture out of a bottle that he fished out of his leather bag.

'Please drink this, Mrs Strang,' he said, returning from the kitchen and holding the glass out to her.

'No!'

'I really must insist. You've had a terrible shock and you have your baby to consider.'

'Exactly!'

'It will make you relax,' Cassidy said.

'I'm quite relaxed as it is, thank you.'

'Lucy dear, you should listen to the doctor,' Peter said.

'Well I won't drink it so please don't ask me again.'

'I'm sorry Jack, her mind is made up,' Peter said.

'Well, whatever the outcome, she should have complete rest for the next seven days and spend as much time as possible in bed,' he said, looking at Eva as if she had control over what Lucy did. 'I'll call round tomorrow after morning surgery and see how she is.'

Lucy kept quiet this time; there was no more to be said. Assuming Jan came back relatively unscathed she could be back at work on Friday, then be able to rest with Jan over the weekend. Cassidy meant well but sometimes you had to stand up to doctors. Jan was never patronising to her. If he had been like that she would never have married him. She closed her eyes and said a little prayer, to whom she didn't know, to ask for Jan's protection.

'Bye bye and thanks for coming round,' Eva said, accepting Cassidy's outstretched hand from her chair.

'I'll see myself out. No need to get up. A busy night ahead, I'm afraid.'

As the door banged behind him Lucy let out a sigh of relief and moved to get up.

'Stay where you are,' Eva told her then went into the kitchen and returned with a plate containing some salad vegetables, pickles, cheese, cold potatoes, bread and margarine. Lucy realised that she hadn't eaten anything since breakfast and, despite her burning indigestion, ate the food quickly from a tray on her lap, with Tinker looking up at her with pleading eyes and saliva dripping from the corners of her mouth. Eva took Lucy's plate away as soon as she had consumed the last crust of bread. Tinker whimpered. Eva came back with a bowl of cold stewed plums and custard and Tinker watched Lucy's every move as she ate, more slowly this time, savouring the tang of the plums. She left a little custard in the bowl and took it to the kitchen for Tinker to lick clean.

'I've heated water if you want a bath,' Eva said.

'That's a very good idea,' said Lucy.

It was still light enough at ten-to-ten to see the street from the window. Lucy was sitting on the window ledge looking out when she saw a police constable walking towards the house with Jan. She got up, ignoring her aching limbs, and opened the front door. Peter and Eva stood behind her. Tinker saw Jan, wagged her tail, sniffed him and went back to her basket.

'Oh, thank you, Constable. Thank you, so much,' Lucy said, as she and Eva took Jan inside. Jan's body trembled, his clothes were torn and stained and his eyes were wide open with pupils dilated like a feral cat at night. He looked at them, vacantly. Peter stayed on the doorstep talking to the policeman.

'We found 'im wandering round Kilburn Park. He can't talk and doesn't appear to be clear in 'is head so it's just as well we know 'im and where 'e lives,' the constable said.

'Yes, thank you officer, it's so good of you,' Peter said. 'He was caught up in the bombing and we very much appreciate you bringing him back.'

'Well here 'e is, Sir, good luck with him; he's dead drunk.'

'Here's something for your trouble,' Peter said.

'Thank you, Sir.'

The smell of stale drink and tobacco on Jan's breath made Lucy move her head back as Jan moved to kiss her. Eva and Lucy sat him down on the settee.

'It must have been awful but you're safe at home now,' Lucy said, worried that he might have lost his mind for good this time. Jan's initial agitation after being brought in by the policeman eased visibly as he settled down.

'B...b...b.. I...I...I...'. Eva gave him a glass of water; he held it with two hands, placed it on the side table, leant back and stared into a distance that only he could see. Peter came back in from the doorstep.

'A hundred at least killed and hundreds more injured, the constable says. Apparently, children are still dying from the bomb at the school in Poplar.' Peter moved his head from side to side.

'I hope they burn in hell,' Eva said.

'The Germans you mean?' asked Peter.

'No, just the ones who did it,' Eva said.

'Can you help me get him upstairs?' Lucy asked whilst removing Jan's filthy shoes. She and Peter picked him up under his arms. His left foot kept getting caught on the steps as they half lifted and half dragged him. From the landing, it was easier and Jan, quite conscious, almost got to the bedroom on his own accord. The springs creaked as they let him flop on the bed. Lucy and Eva started to undress him and Peter left them to it.

'I'll throw these things away,' Eva said, picking up his trousers and underpants and leaving the room holding them at arm's length and pulling a face. She returned a few minutes later with a bowl of warm water, soap and a flannel and together they washed him clean in a well-rehearsed routine that both of them had thought they might never have to go through again.

'S... s.... sor..' Jan started to tremble.

'It's alright darling; we know you're sorry; you've been through an ordeal. It's just horrendous. We heard the bombs and saw the devastation. I tried to find you but ended up helping people out of the rubble and patching them up. We're just glad you're alive, that we're all alive. It's been a terrible day.' Jan made a sort of groaning but not quite crying noise. 'You'll be right as rain in a few days, you'll see,' Lucy said.

'B... b... bu....' Jan twisted and moved his legs as if to get up.

'Shhh, keep still, you need to sleep now,' Lucy said, stroking his hair. She looked over to Eva.

'I'll hold him still,' Eva said grabbing his wrists and holding them by his side. 'It breaks my heart. You didn't deserve this, Lucy dear.'

Lucy moved over to open the dressing-table drawer and came back with his morphine paraphernalia which she laid out on the bed beside him. She took some cotton wool and surgical spirit, cleaned a patch on the side of his knee, snapped the top off a phial of morphine, filled the syringe and injected him. Jan's expression changed and, as the stress left his face, his bladder emptied on his legs and the sheets underneath him whilst he stared again into that space where only he knew.

They all piss themselves, Gladys had told them in a letter back home when Jan was still in hospital. *But you soon get used to it. I've cleaned the poor buggers up hundreds of times. I would get a rubber blanket if I were you. You'll need it.* Lucy and Eva rolled him on his side to remove the wet sheets and wash the urine off the red-rubber under-sheet. They washed him again and covered him up with clean sheets. It had been six weeks since Jan's last bout and Lucy had begun to believe that it wouldn't happen again, despite Bentley's caveat that there was always the possibility of relapse. But now it looked like all the good work of the last six months had come to nought.

That night, next to her in bed, Jan tossed, turned, sweated and occasionally screamed out. But Lucy hardly noticed and slept through it with only faint recollections of being woken in the night. At ten the next morning Eva woke them with cups of tea.

'Thank you so much,' Lucy said gently, rubbing her eyes as Eva put the cups down on their bedside tables, drew the curtains and opened the window wide.

'It's fine. I thank God that you're both still alive,' Eva said, closing the door behind her as she left. Jan, stirring, grabbed hold of Lucy's hand and kissed her on the cheek. Lucy held her breath.

'D... d..don't l.. l.. leave mm m.. me,' he said, squeezing her hand tighter and staring with frightened eyes.

'I won't,' Lucy said with a big smile and kissed his head. 'We're lucky to be alive, both of us.'

Lucy sat up in bed with her pillow propped up behind her back. The hot tea slaked the thirst in her dry throat like nothing else could. Her arms and legs ached but she felt good after the night's rest. Her baby was safe and so was Jan. He had got better before and he could get better again. She flung the sheet and blanket over to Jan's side of the bed and inspected her legs, exploring them with her fingers. They were badly bruised in places and her leg hair had stuck to the scabs that had formed on some of the deeper cuts on her shin. Her forearms were scratched and grazed and her upper arms bruised so badly that it looked like she had been punched by a boxer. She placed her hand over the bulge of her tummy and felt a thrill run through her as the baby moved. The little miracle of life was safe, warm and protected. She moved her hand up to her breasts and gently squeezed. They were sore and tender. Looking to her right, Jan was curled up in a foetal position with his cup of tea going cold by his side. Apart for the gentle wheezing of his breath, he was calm and peaceful. She leant over, picked up his tea, sat back and drank it.

Lucy couldn't stop thinking about the little girl who had died in her arms. But she didn't really die at all, only sailed away to another place. In her mind, Lucy went over the moments when the Victorian spectres held the girl's hand and led her away from the pain, suffering and war that surrounded them. She thought it must be terribly difficult for the spirit people to carry off all those thousands of men whose lives had been cut short on the battlefield and she wondered if they had hospitals in the spirit world. A notion came into her head that they did. Her mood lifted further as she realised that the heartache and struggle of this life were only temporary and a better world was waiting. She had lost any fear of dying.

Doctor Cassidy came round late in the morning, red faced with his hair in a mess and thick dark bags under his eyes.

'I just need to examine you. Please sit down,' he said to Lucy. Lucy lifted her hand to him: he pressed two stubby fingers against the vein on her wrist whilst looking at his fob watch and let her arm fall by her side. He looked at the wall as he felt her tummy through her cotton skirt. Her baby moved. 'Well this one appears to be alive and kicking.' Cassidy smiled. He took a four-inch glass thermometer out of his bag, shook it, and placed it under Lucy's tongue. It tasted faintly of pine sap. Then he connected his stethoscope to his ears and listened to her chest through her blouse. He lifted his head and smiled encouragingly to both Lucy and Eva.

'You're a healthy woman and your baby seems unaffected by yesterday's goings on.'

'You'll have a cup of tea?' Eva said, handing him the cup before he had a chance to answer.

'Thank you, I will. You know, the longer I'm in this business, the more I'm amazed at the strength and capacity for recovery that the human body has. Sometimes it is simply miraculous. I'll just go up and see Jan. Please stay where you are,' he said, putting his cup down. Lucy got up and started to clean in the kitchen. Eva followed her.

'Please don't do any of the cleaning and tidying today,' Eva said.

'I just want to keep busy. I ache all over but I don't think I can relax. A little girl died in my arms you know and Jan's in a mess again. Sometimes, life is just so awful.'

'We're all safe and sound and you have done really good work, thank God,' Eva said.

'There's really no great cause for concern,' Cassidy said, returning after only about five minutes. 'He has suffered quite a setback but, as we know, he has recovered from worse.'

'Exactly,' Lucy said. 'He got better before and can get better again.'

'He should come around soon. I think, though, as he is prone to agitation, now isn't the right time to continue to reduce his morphine. On the contrary, I recommend that he should return to two injections of four grains morning and evening for the next week and then we can see how he is and review the situation. Don't offer him alcohol and make an appointment with Mr Bentley as soon as you can.'

'Do you know more about the bombings?' Eva asked. 'Peter's paper hasn't yet arrived.'

'That's understandable; there's been a lot of disruption around Fleet Street but I can't see the Germans halting the press for long. I heard this morning that one-hundred and forty have been killed and they're still counting as more die, but that will be slowing down now. Of course, there are many more casualties. They've been working through the night at the hospitals. I'd go down to Bart's to help out but I've got enough to do with my own patients. Quite a few of my clients are coming straight to the surgery with injuries; there was a queue outside the door this morning. My secretary's been bathing and dressing wounds. It'll be the same for every doctor in London, so, as much as I enjoy your company, I can't linger.'

The blood rushed from Lucy's head as it hit her that some of the children she had helped would have died through the night. She thought about going down to the hospital to see if she could help when she suddenly felt cold and dizzy. She held her head in her hands and, not being able to hold back any longer, started to cry. Dr Cassidy put his hand on her shoulder. 'It's been a terrible ordeal and we need you to be strong now. It's the women who hold everything together, you know.'

'We all know that. The men make the mess and the woman have to clear it up,' Eva said.

'I know, I have to be strong. I won't let anyone down, especially my baby.' Lucy smiled.

'And you must rest when you can,' Dr Cassidy said.

Fat chance, Lucy thought and dried her eyes.

Lucy felt involved with those people and their families who she helped on June 13th. In the two weeks after the bombing she passed funerals in church yards and saw the corteges moving down the streets with coffins on horse carts, followed by crowds wearing the best and darkest clothes they could find. She would, as everyone did, stop in respect until the procession passed, watching as men and boys took off their caps and hats. She asked for, and was granted, time off work to attend the communal funeral of the children killed at the Poplar school. Hundreds turned up from all over London. The poor and unknown as well as the rich and titled that had never set foot on these deprived streets with their dirty slums and fatherless children.

Little coffins were laid out in All Saints Church and hundreds of wreaths, made from sprigs and flowers taken from gardens and parks from across the capital, filled the Town Hall across the road. She followed the mourners as the coffins were moved to the East London Cemetery. Whilst they were being interred, the woman next to her, pale and thin, told her that the coffin that was unmarked contained the remains that could not be identified as belonging to any particular child. Grief suddenly hit Lucy and she cried as quietly as she could. When all this was over, she thought she would like to work for the poor in some way or another.

In London, the mood changed after the bombings. For those civilians who hadn't fought, it made them face their mortality. The raids continued throughout the summer and the indiscriminate way the bombs fell and killed the young, old and innocent made Lucy see that Londoners had a dogged determination to stick it out, no matter how much longer it took. Bombing civilians had to be a sign of German desperation but it did ignite a side of the Londoners' character that made the whole Strang family relieved that they lived out in the Kilburn suburb. The same people who so generously took in thousands of refugees from Belgium and Russia in 1915 began to turn on foreigners. Following the bombing raids, in the docklands areas and the East End in particular, anyone who had a foreign accent or foreign-sounding name could be set upon and kicked close to death. Shops with German-sounding names were smashed and looted. Peter, two summers before, had changed the name on the sign outside his office from Strang's Timber Agents to Strong's Timber Agents but he and Eva still had noticeable Scandinavian accents and had to be careful where they went.

As the summer passed and the day of her giving birth drew closer, Lucy's friends at the Home Office would knit and sew baby clothes and leave them on her desk with notes sending their blessings. People on the train, to and from work, who saw her every day, rarely saying a word, started to ask her how she was and when she was due. They wished her well.

Jan, however, wasn't getting any better. London was slowly killing him; he needed a new start away from the temptations of the capital. He didn't go back to work with his father after the ordeal of June 13, and a subsequent medical examination certified him as unfit for duty as an officer. He would make improvements but they were cancelled out by setbacks as any excuse would take him back to heavy drinking. From what Eva said, while Lucy was at work, he would find reasons to argue with her so that he could leave the house and go to places to drink during the day. Lucy shuddered to think of the company he was keeping. Sometimes he wouldn't come home until the early hours and sometimes he would stay out all night, returning after Lucy and Peter had left for work thereby avoiding a confrontation with his father. Lucy could see by the appearance of new puncture holes on his arms and legs that he was injecting more than his prescribed dose. Dr Cassidy had warned him strongly against using any equipment for injecting himself unless it had been boiled for at least five minutes beforehand as there was a high risk of infection. But Jan didn't seem to care. When Lucy was in the position where she would need to inject Jan with morphine, she would struggle to find a space to put the needle and more than once used his ankle and the spaces on the side and behind his knee. At night in bed, he would say he was sorry and ask for her forgiveness. And he could be kind to her, stroking her hand and encouraging her to eat more to keep her strength up and feed their baby. Lucy felt the size of a whale but, even if her body could have been available to him, he wouldn't have been interested and neither would she.

Chapter 22

Over the summer, a sense of excitement was building within Lucy, so much so that she sometimes let out a laugh of joy at the most unexpected times and in unexpected places. When she smiled to herself on the train to work, her happiness would become infectious so that other passengers would smile back at her. Her mood could change quickly into anxiety though, as she also had a nagging fear that something could go terribly wrong. Visions of children dead and maimed from the bombings stayed in her mind making her determined to leave London as soon as circumstances would allow. She wanted to move to the south coast where her baby could grow up happy, safe and close to the sea and countryside. Jan agreed but couldn't make too many plans whilst technically still a commissioned officer. After the war, they could live in Brighton or Hove, he said, and he could get the train into London for work. At night, before she fell asleep, she would close her eyes and inhabit the space between wakefulness and sleep where she would sit on a lawn in a sweet-scented rose garden and listen to a slow-running stream with willow branches bending over and touching the water. Here she would meet her Aunty B and her spirit friends who told her that she would have a strong and healthy baby girl on a day when the saints would be watching over her.

By October her back ached so much that she could no longer disguise her pain and discomfort getting in and out of her chair at work. She hoped that no one would see the faces she pulled as she winced when sharp pains stabbed her abdomen or shot up her back. The other women in the office, of course, couldn't help but notice the tell-tale signs that her time was drawing closer. Lucy, when she said that she wanted to work right until the last minute, neglected to tell them that the main reason was that it was almost unbearable to share the house with Jan when he was drinking and smoking like a chimney. It made her feel sick.

At the end of the first week in October, Vera and Beatty went to the office manager to let him know that, although Lucy was prepared to carry on, it was definitely time for her to leave and have her baby. So, on the following Monday, the Office Manager told Lucy that her last day would be Friday 12 October.

Lucy struggled to keep up with them when they headed for The Buckingham Arms at twelve thirty, which they inevitably did when there was any excuse for a celebration. She sat with her work mates in the public bar by an open window so the smoke didn't turn her stomach. They brought her a pickled egg and a couple of pickled onions back from the bar which she ate with her sandwiches as the girls around her drank and told tales of pregnancy and childbirth and how the first child was always the most difficult. Lucy, suddenly overwhelmed, used her handkerchief to wipe the drops that trickled from her eye.

'I'm sorry; I was just thinking how much I'll miss you. I know the war is terrible but working here with you all has been so good for me. I never wanted to be stuck at home knitting socks like my mother. I don't expect they'll let me back after the baby,' she said.

Wednesday 31 October 1917
Lucy thought she was coming into labour at about 11 pm so Eva rang Dr Cassidy at his home. He arrived twenty minutes later.

'This is Miss O'Connor,' he said introducing a rather time-wearied nurse who looked as if she needed a good meal. 'She allowed me to persuade her to come out of retirement to help me with my rounds when it became clear that war could last quite a bit longer than we first thought.'

'And I've been working harder now than ever before I retired,' Miss O'Connor said with a smile and a little laugh to Lucy and Eva. 'And you must call me Mary; there's no point in being formal when someone's having a baby.'

Lucy, reclining on the settee, put her hand on her stomach.

'The contractions are speeding up,' she said, feeling pleased and apprehensive at the same time. The nurse smiled and held her hand.

'How long do they last and how often do they come?' Dr Cassidy asked.

'Ohh, they last as long as a minute sometimes and come about every ten minutes; quicker, if I move.'

'I see, well we can be pretty sure it's on its way,' he said. They heard a groaning hum in the distance and turned to the window.

'It's the Gotha engines again. Will the buggers never give up?' Peter said, pursing his lips and clenching a fist. 'Damn them.'

Bang, bang, bang! The boom of bombs exploding carried through the night air.

'They're coming over the docks,' Dr Cassidy said. Eva opened the curtains. All of them except for Jan jostled for the best position to look out of the window. The moon was full and the sky had turned red south of the river as flames lit up patches of cloud above the Thames. The deathly planes made black silhouettes against red clouds.

Crack! *Crack!* *Crack!* Shots rang out from anti anti-aircraft batteries but none of the planes fell. Jan started to tremble in his chair and fear lit up in his eyes.

'B... b... blloddy hell,' he said and lit a cigarette.

Dr Cassidy took his bag into the kitchen and returned with a small glass containing the reddish-brown liquid of diluted morphine sulphate.

'Drink this,' he said to Jan, who nodded and drank it in one go.

'It's not the best night to have a baby, is it?' Lucy said.

'Shh, listen. The bombing's stopped and the planes have gone. We can have a quiet night now,' Mary O'Connor said.

'God help the poor souls round the docks,' Eva said.

'The firemen and the police will be in real danger now,' Lucy said. 'If I was fit I'd go down there and help them.' Jan appeared more relaxed. Expression had left his face and the light had left his eyes.

'I'll stay with you but the men may as well go to bed; they'll just be in the way,' Mary O'Connor said, looking at Peter and Jan with her hands on her hips.

'I think you and me should follow orders and hit the sack,' Peter said to Jan.

'Jan must sleep in Gladys' room. Lucy will need the double bed,' Eva said. 'I've made it up.'

'Come on, matey,' Peter said, offering his hand to Jan who had slipped a few inches down his chair. Jan grabbed his father's hand and let him pull him up. He moved over to Lucy, put his arm around her waist and kissed her on the cheek.

'G.. good luck.'

'Thank you darling. We'll wake you as soon as the baby's born,' Lucy said. He smiled and waved his hand to Lucy as he left the room and followed Peter up the stairs.

'I'll be off too. I'll be busy all night. God only knows when it will all end. For now, you couldn't be in better hands than with Miss O'Connor,' Dr Cassidy said, making a move to leave. 'And I'd better go to where I'm most needed.'

'Thank you so much for coming round so quickly,' Lucy said.

'I'll see myself out.'

'Godspeed,' Eva said.

Mary O'Connor put her hands on her hips.

'Now the men are out of the way I need to take a look at you. I'll just go and wash my hands.'

Eva showed her the kitchen. Lucy's her heart dropped. She hated the examinations and being touched by strangers but at least this time it was by a woman. If only her mother was with her. She should have asked her to come over during the day. She had felt a fierce tightening and a painful discomfort all day but it was too late to use the telephone now, even if they might still be working. And anyway, there was no way for her mother to get over until the trains started.

Mary returned from the kitchen. 'Now lie back on the sofa, put your heels together and let your knees fall to the side,' she said to Lucy.

'I'll put the kettle on,' Eva said.

'Don't you worry now darlin', I won't hurt you.' Lucy felt the nurse's fingers move inside her. She wanted to say something to lighten the mood but couldn't think of anything. 'You're dilated alright but it could take a while yet,' Mary said. 'It's your first time and you don't have big hips. You and me and your mother-in-law, we'll be awake for most of the night now. We'll take you up to the bedroom in an hour or so. For the time bein' let's just have a nice cup of tea and a chat.'

The three women talked through to the early hours and Eva told them all about how Jan had come out backwards and how it took ages and that Gladys was easy and almost fought her way into the world. Mary O'Connor could lighten the mood in a morgue, Lucy thought, grateful that it could momentarily take her mind off the pain. The nurse chatted away keeping them awake and making them laugh with stories of childbirth and things that they didn't know about Dr Cassidy. She told them that he only wore the morning suit because when he first came to London, back in '08, his starched-shirted senior partner in the practice insisted or, the partner had said, 'they wouldn't think he was a proper doctor at all'. So, he wore the jacket and stripped trousers but flatly refused to wear a top hat. He said that top hats were stupid and a thing of the past and the world was changing and we wouldn't recognise it in ten years.

'How right he was,' Eva said. 'It's the next generation that's our hope.' Lucy tried to hide her torment but couldn't help screwing her face up every few minutes as the pains came and then subsided.

'This lot have made a proper mess of things, that's for sure,' Mary O'Connor said. 'Did you know that Jack Cassidy sets off on foot to see all his patients and only uses his bicycle at night?'

'We didn't know that. He must be very tired by the night time,' Eva said. Lucy moved her position and a terrible pain shot from the base of her back and passed through her hips down her legs.

'He's married to his job and helping the poor,' Mary said. 'I joined him when he used to visit the slums on the West Hampstead side of the Kilburn High Street; I had to almost run to keep up with him. That's when there was the polio and the typhoid and all the consumption. And the tenements: four and five stories high and four or five families in each, would you believe. And they're big families, mind, with only one tap and basin on the landing and a privy for all of them in the yard. And at night, after surgery, he would work with these poor people and even help the working girls, may God forgive them.' Mary crossed herself.

'I had no idea,' Lucy said. 'But I always knew he was a good man. You can tell; he has that feeling about him.'

'Oh, and he's a modest man, that's for sure. He always has a surgery on the Saturdays and Sundays so the men that can't afford to leave their work can come and see him. And with the Jewish quarters, he respects their Sabbath and only visits after dark on the Saturday or leaves it to the Sunday.'

'I never would have thought.' Lucy was suffering; hardly concentrating on what the nurse was saying.

'Oh yes, he's a saint alright, is Jack Cassidy. And, did you know he's a Fabian?'

'No really?' Eva said.

'His wife will be lonely,' Lucy said.

'I know but she must have known what she'd be lettin' herself in for before she got married,' Mary said.

'None of us know that when we get married,' Eva said with a wry smile. The baby kicked hard inside Lucy. She looked at Eva and winced.

'You're probably right, my dear. We weren't born for pleasure alone, that's for sure,' Mary said. Lucy looked up at the wall clock. Five o'clock.

'Ohh, oooh.' Lucy contorted her face. 'The contractions, they're, oooh, coming quicker. Dear me it hurts.' Mary went to Lucy's side.

'It's time for the bedroom now darlin'. It's starting proper,' Mary said.

Climbing the stairs to the bedroom, Lucy grabbed the banister and gasped for breath as more contractions hit her. She stopped as wet ran down the inside of her thighs.

'I'm so sorry,' she said.

'Don't you worry,' Eva said. 'Let's get you up the stairs.' Lucy felt dreadful. With head spinning she sat on the edge of the bed. Eva helped her off with her loose clothes, pulled a nightdress over her head and let it drop to her waist. Every movement seemed to tire her as she moved round to try and find a comfortable position. She rested her back and head against pillows. Another stronger contraction hit her.

'Ohh, God save us.'

Tinker ran around the bed and stood on her hind legs to see what all the commotion was about. She nearly wriggled out of Eva's hands when she picked her up and put her out on the landing. Behind the closed door, she scratched and whimpered.

'Let her stay,' Lucy said.

'I don't mind the little thing,' Mary O'Connor said. 'Just don't tell Dr Cassidy; he says they're unhygienic. He'll give us a telling off if he finds out.' She opened her mouth in mock horror.

Eva opened the door and Tinker ran back in wagging her tail. She put her front paws on the bed frame and Lucy stroked her head. Tinker licked her fingers then ran under the bed scratching her body on the cast-iron legs making little grunts.

'Oooh, aach. There must be something wrong. I've never known pain like it.'

'It gets easier darlin' but might get a little bit worse first. We was born to suffer the pain. It's a good sign; it's telling me everything is workin' just as it should be.'

Eva held Lucy's hand. The contractions speeded up then slowed down again.

'The first one's always the most difficult,' Eva said, resting her cool fingers on Lucy's brow.

'I know it's a girl,' Lucy said. 'I'm going to call her Liza. Jan likes it.'

'She'll be a special girl, just like you,' Eva said.

'I can't get to the telephone. Let my mother and my sisters know in the morning first thing.' Lucy closed her eyes and said a little prayer for her baby about to be born. She was getting hotter and her skin felt blotchy and swollen. She wouldn't want Jan or any man to see her like this. Perspiration dripped from her brow and her head went dizzy. Mary took a piece of torn sheet from the pile Eva had put by the bedside. She twisted it tight into a rope.

'Bite on this if it gets any worse. And you might want to hold onto the bedstead when it puts its little head out,' Mary said.

'But this is nineteen seventeen not the dark ages. I'm not going to bite on a rag.' Lucy pushed hard as if to remove an obstruction in her bowel. Nothing moved so she pushed again; still nothing happened. She didn't know if she could push any harder. Lifting her arms above her head she grabbed the metal frame. It felt cold against her hot hands.

'Patience, my dear, patience,' Mary said and Lucy felt a rush of anger.

'Can't you do something?' Lucy said.

'Best do it natural. Give it a minute or two then start pushing again. I can use the forceps to widen your cervix but you don't want that darlin', not unless we have to.'

'Ohhh, my God. It's terrible.'

'I know darlin' but it's worth it when it's over.'

'I'll make some tea,' Eva said.

'For heaven's sake; do you ever think of anything else?' Lucy said. She didn't want tea, she wanted her mother.

'Patience is a virtue,' Mary said, holding Lucy's hand. Lucy wanted to scream.

'Back in five minutes,' Eva said with exaggerated cheerfulness as she left the room closing the door behind her. Tinker barked at the door. Mary picked her up, rocking her in her arms like the baby soon to be born.

'I think she needs to go out.' Mary pulled a face and turned her head away from Tinker. She called after Eva. 'Can you let the little one out when you're down there?' she said.

'Oh, dear yes, I'd forgotten all about that,' Eva said. Tinker ran down the stairs. A few minutes later Eva returned with the tea tray and Tinker at her heels. She poured milk into a saucer and put it on the floor for Tinker who lapped it up quickly; tiny droplets of splashed milk reflected on the floor boards.

'I think we're all ready for this cup of tea.' Mary said, wringing out a flannel in a bowl of cold water. She pressed it against Lucy's brow, rubbing her back at the same time.

'Thank you, thank you,' Lucy said. She thought she must have been making too much of a fuss and knew she was edgy. She was tired and excited at the same time with pain and expectation keeping her awake. If only her mother were here.

'What time is it?' she called out.

'It's nearly seven,' Eva said. Peter would be getting up for work soon and Jan would still be fast asleep.

'Oh, dear God, something's really happening now. I think my back's going to break. You must have something for the pain.'

'You're starting properly now darlin'. You must push as hard as you can and I'll get something to ease the suffering. Now, Push! Push! Push!'

Eva went over to the window and opened the curtains to a clear bright day that lit up the room and made Lucy squint. As she pulled up the window, clean air gushed into the room cooling Lucy down and helping her breathe. Mary talked to Eva in a voice too quiet for Lucy to hear then Mary nodded, walked over to the dressing table, opened her black leather nursing bag, took out a small brown bottle and poured a small amount of liquid onto a wad of white cloth. Lucy could smell it from her bed: sweet pungent fumes that reminded her of the wards at the Whitechapel Hospital. A knock sounded at the door.

'Are you alright in there? Can I do anything?' Peter said from the other side. Eva opened the door just a bit.

'No, we're fine in here,' she said and closed the door. Mary moved close to Lucy and put her hand behind her head. Eva came to her side.

'Just something to take away some of the pain, like you asked me. Dr Cassidy gave me instructions,' she said, and pressed the wad of damp lint over Lucy's nose and mouth before she had a chance to say anything. As soon as Lucy had breathed in Mary took it away and smiled. 'It won't knock you out darlin', I didn't give you enough for that. Now don't stop; keep pushing, hard as you can.'

Lucy pushed and pushed but the baby was in no hurry to leave the warmth of her womb to enter their world of woes. Lucy's pain was now muffled, less intense. She pushed hard then felt relief in her back and bones and pelvis. Lucy looked down to see Mary O'Connor holding little Liza's head as she left her body to be born into her new life. Liza Strang took her first breath at twenty-two minutes past eight on All Souls Day, then cried as Mary O'Connor tied the cord between mother and daughter and cut it with scissors. From the window, sunlight shone on the baby as Mary held her up to the new day. Lucy stretched her arms in front of her. Mary laid the baby in a towel and passed her over.

'My beautiful, beautiful girl,' Lucy whispered in her tiny ear.

'Praise God,' Eva said, and Mary made the sign of the cross over her chest.

The sight of baby Liza lying peacefully next to Lucy moved Jan. Still in his pyjamas, he stood in front of them not knowing what to say. He held his hand out to touch Liza's tiny fingers. The baby's eye caught his. He winked. She smiled, or so he thought. Lucy patted the space on the bed beside her and he settled down next to her. Lucy let out a little laugh, kissed him on his cheek and handed Liza over for him to hold. She was so light, delicate and vulnerable; an example of God's perfection. She was part of him; the result of his and Lucy's love. Working with his father, signing up for the Army, becoming an officer, nearly being blown to pieces; none of these things made him feel like a man but being the father of a beautiful baby girl did. He had never experienced such a sense of overwhelming responsibility. It was overwhelming, overpowering. His job in life from now on was to protect his baby, to protect them both. He looked down at baby Liza in his arms, watching her gentle, almost imperceptible breaths as she closed her eyes and slept.

'I'm g.. going to change,' he said. He didn't expect her to believe it but he meant it. Lucy smiled at him, warm and comforting. 'Honestly, I m.. mean it. I'm going to cut out the drink and I'll go back to B.. B.. Bentley and conquer my insanity and mmm.. my st.. stammer.' Looking at Lucy his eyes welled up. 'I've been such a d.. dreadful mess.' He lifted Liza and put her in Lucy's lap, put his arm around her shoulders and let her lean on him. No one would ever be able to understand the depth of his guilt and regret.

'We can be happy now,' Lucy said. He lowered his head. Tears rolled down his cheeks, cleansing his body and soul of a sickness that had attached itself to him without his say so.

'I'll make you both proud of me and never let you down again.' Jan wiped his tears away with his pyjama sleeve.

'I know darling, it's not your fault; you've been ill. I always believed you would get better.'

'I want to get a ph…, Ph.., photographer here in the next w… week to c… capture her beauty forever,' he said.

'We can get lots of post cards made and send them to the family. But let's wait for the Christening,' Lucy said. 'Then everyone should be happy.'

'Whaaa,' Liza started to cry. Lucy pulled down the front of her nightshirt, moved Liza's lips to her nipple and Liza became quiet.

'I'm very tired now,' Lucy said.

In the days and weeks that followed Liza's birth, 43 Chichester Road came to life in a way that had not been seen since the Strangs moved in ten years earlier. Despite the darkening days and winter cold, life and happiness filled its rooms. Eva came out of the gloom that had surrounded her since Jan was pronounced dead, then found alive and returned home with injuries that ran deep into his mind. She rushed around washing nappies, bibs and bedclothes and tempting Lucy with the most nutritious foods she could muster. She cleaned the house so that the constant visits of family and friends, who brought little gifts and doted over baby Liza, only thought the best of the Strang household. Tinker was in a constant state of excitement, running up to and greeting all who came to the door scampering round heels as acquaintances and relatives walked in the house.

Lucy's family were never far away. Her mother, Anne Green, came round later in the day after she heard of the birth on November 1st and sat with mother and baby, off and on, for the most of the rest of the day. Clair and Julia, Lucy's sisters, were now working as post women, delivering letters and parcels on bicycles, so couldn't get there until late afternoon when they had finished their shifts. Lucy hadn't realised it but since her marriage and especially since Jan's return, she had felt isolated from the stream of seemingly insignificant information that her sisters could bring. 'Do you remember Mrs so and so from number 10? Well …..' and Lucy would get the full story and they would laugh as if they were in their teens again. There were times when Lucy had looked down on gossip but now it felt like it connected her back to her old life before marriage; uncomplicated and innocent.

'You're so lucky. I should have been married by now,' Julia said, sitting next to Lucy on her bed with Liza in her new cot of pink-painted wood and white sheets with laced edges by her side.

'And so should I but there's no men left that aren't damaged.' Claire put her hand up to her mouth. 'Oh God, I'm so sorry. I didn't mean ...' Lucy stroked Claire's hair.

'Don't worry. I can't take offence at things like that. If you'd been through the troubles I have, you'd get a different perspective on life. Anyway, I know exactly what you mean. I still love Jan but if I were you I'd stay single for as long as I could.'

'Do you really think so?' Claire said.

'Yes, absolutely. If you can work and have your own money ...'

'But I want children,' Julia said.

'There's no way round that then,' Lucy said, and they all laughed. 'But seriously, don't rush into anything. Wait till after the war. So much will change.'

'I will, but just seeing little Liza there, it makes me go all soft inside,' Claire said.

Lucy recovered well from the child birth, her strength picking up and appetite returning straight away. After the birth, Dr Cassidy came around mid-morning pronouncing Lucy strong and well and on his several visits in the following weeks he said the same thing. Mary O'Connor called to see how they were and to hold Liza as many times as she could.

'Please don't walk out of our lives just as suddenly as you walked in,' Lucy said to Mary, holding her hand. 'I want you to see us and baby Liza whenever you like.' Lucy passed Liza over to Mary. 'She's already bonded with you.'

'Oh, thank you. You don't know how good that makes me feel. But how are *you*, my dear?'

'I've been so thirsty, drinking water all the time and it hurts me just to sit down and my stomach cramps.'

'You're better off just staying in the bed for a few days. Let them look after you for a change.'

Lucy took her advice. In the days since Jan came back from the war, Lucy never thought realistically that she could ever be really happy again. Happiness was a thing that young people experienced before they fully understood what a world of trouble and responsibility they lived in. But now, despite feeling totally drained and exhausted, she was happier than she could ever remember. She would look at Liza and feel a different kind of love than she had ever known.

Everyone, except for Dr Cassidy, wanted to have the christening as soon as it could be arranged.

'I don't agree,' he said. 'There really is no need to rush. She's a perfectly healthy baby and isn't going to pass away. I don't see the point in frightening the poor little thing. She's just adjusting to her environment here. Why give her a shock like that?'

Lucy thought he made a good point but all the women around her persuaded her that it was the thing to do.

'Oh, Dr Cassidy, he's an old misery,' her mother said. 'It never did any of you any harm and we could all do with a celebration. God knows we've had enough trials and tribulations over the last few years to last us all a lifetime.'

And Lucy had to agree. 'Well, that's fine but it must be at St Augustine's,' she said.

Lucy didn't see herself as a Christian with a big C but, since last Christmas, she had sought the peace of mind that just sitting peacefully in a quiet church could bring her. The atmosphere in the house had so often been fraught, with Jan being on edge most of the time and everybody worrying about her and the baby and, of course, Jan. He tried to hide it but Jan was obviously desperate to get out of the house and visit the pub in the evenings. Instead of complaining, which would have had no effect, Lucy had started visiting St Augustine's on Kilburn Park Road. The church had an atmosphere like no other she had ever known. It had a presence more like a cathedral than a parish church. It wasn't an old church but Lucy was awed by the design of the interior with its gothic pillars and arches and beautiful sculptures in medieval style.

As much as she loved her adopted family, in the evenings a sense of claustrophobia often hit her and she needed to get out of the house. Clearly, she thought, there were times when Eva and Peter needed to argue by themselves but their good manners forbade them to do so in front of her. It was only a ten-minute walk to St Augustine's; the fresh air did her good and she would take Tinker with her. If she went after their dinner, evensong would have finished and only a few people, if any, were left in the church. Sometimes she would see grieving widows and mothers and old men with their heads in their hands. She would pray for them and, if the opportunity arose, tell them that she didn't think that death was permanent and that those who had died just lived in another place where they could still watch and be close to the ones they had left behind. Lucy would sit silently with Tinker on her lap, breathe in the smell of incense that always lingered in the church, close her eyes and turn off the worries of Jan, two families and war. Sometimes it was so still that the slightest sound would echo through the nave and transept. She would look up at the tall, vaulted ceilings and understand that, in the whole scheme of things, her earthly concerns would soon be forgotten and mankind would continue in much the same way as it always had. She felt that this inner peace was permanent; a place where she could always return to and feel safe.

Chapter 23

Saturday, 10 November 1917
Jan opened a letter from the War Office in the front room with his mother-of-pearl inlaid pocket knife. Lucy had Liza in her arms and he could feel Lucy's and his parent's eyes watching him, waiting for him to finish reading and explain the contents. Only Liza and Tinker seemed uninterested.

'I.. I'll t.. take T.. Tinker to the p.. park. Have a look at it; see w.. what you th… think,' Jan said, handing the letter to Peter before leaving the room with Tinker on her lead.

As Peter started to read, Lucy was half annoyed and half perplexed. She wondered why he gave the letter to his father and not her. The thought of disturbing Liza by passing on her anxiety and irritation stopped her from interrupting.

'Well!' Eva asked. 'What does it say?'

'It says what we already know, that Jan's still debilitated, he's nervous and "his speech is hesitating". It recommends he does some outdoor work in a "suitable climate."'

Eva looked at him. 'Yes, and?' she said.

'It says his condition is the result of "shell explosion and not aggravated by negligence or misconduct". It says he's "very nervous and tremulous: tachycardia" and so on. "Takes his food well, has insomnia. Sixty percent disabled." But they don't see it as permanent. "Suitable for sedentary employment only." It says he's classified as "Cii", whatever that means, and that's err, well, nearly it.'

'It's good news then?' Eva asked.

'He's obviously not going back out to fight, so it *is* good news; incredibly good news,' Peter said.

Lucy fidgeted in her chair waiting to ask questions. 'We know Jan's always been worried they might send him back. It's added to his tension. What else do they say?'

Peter coughed and looked down at the letter. 'They've assigned him to a position of "Timber Clerk" at the Glanusk Saw Mill near Crickhowell in the Brecon Beacons.'

'Where's that?' Eva asked.

'It's in Wales, deep in the countryside, in the middle of forests, hills and streams.'

'It sounds like where I grew up,' Eva said, interrupting Peter, smiling and rubbing her hands together.

'Yes, it sounds good,' Peter said. 'He can recover there, away from all the distractions and the things that frighten and disturb him in London.'

Lucy folded her arms and looked straight at Peter.

'There won't be any bombings where he's going, no danger at all except …'

'Except what?' Lucy asked.

'Except that there's a POW camp there and he may be asked to help out guarding the prisoners and overseeing their work. They'll be the main supply of labour for bringing the logs in and moving the timber about.'

'It sounds like the best place for him,' Eva said.

'By all accounts the prisoners are happy there. They don't want to go back and fight, that's for sure. Nobody does,' Peter said.

'It sounds like you've known about this for a while,' Lucy said, catching Peter's gaze.

'Well, err, yes, but I didn't know if we could pull it off.'

Lucy picked Liza up from Eva and rocked her in her arms, hardly moving her eyes from Peter. 'I think you should explain,' she said.

'The first thing I wanted to do was make sure that Jan didn't go back to fight. All the forestry in the country is run by the Board of Trade, so I asked around to see if we could get Jan a job away from any more bombings. London isn't good for him. I would have told you but I wanted to see if it was possible first.'

'I really think you should have told me about it,' Lucy said. 'Did you know about it, Eva?'

'Only little bits Peter told me,' Eva said, looking towards the window.

'From what my contacts tell me, this saw mill is in the middle of nowhere. For Jan, it's perfect. There will be little opportunity for drinking and the only morphine he can get will be his prescription. It's a good place for him to recover: gentle work, close to nature.'

'And when did he go for this medical?' Lucy asked.

'A few days before you went into labour,' Peter said. 'That's why we didn't tell you then.' Peter held his hands out in front of him. 'Honestly, otherwise we would have done.'

'And how long could he be gone for?' Lucy asked.

'For as long as the war lasts. It might not be all that long now.'

'We've heard that one before,' Eva said.

'No one can say but we can be sure he'll be safer there than here,' Peter said.

'And what about visiting? He's the father of a gorgeous new baby girl.' She pulled smiling faces at Liza.

'Crickhowell is miles out of the way, Glanusk is a mile further. Visits to him will hardly be possible but he will be able to come home every few months using the military transport.'

'You have it all planned out, haven't you?' She passed Liza over to Eva to hold. 'I agree, it looks like the best answer for Jan, but you really should have told me. I *am* his wife. This has come as a shock. How do you think it makes me feel, hearing it this way?'

'We're sorry but you had so much to worry about. We wanted the best for you,' Eva said.

'And we didn't know if the plan had worked until the letter came,' Peter said.

'Your hearts were in the right place I suppose.' Lucy half smiled and shook her head. 'Is there anything else I should know?'

'Oh, only that he leaves Wednesday week,' Peter said, passing the letter over for Lucy to read.

That night, sitting up in bed together with Liza in her cot beside her, Lucy turned to Jan.

'For heaven's sake, when will you understand that I'm your wife? How could you keep quiet about such a thing? Not telling me you were going to a Medical Board wasn't protecting me. I'm so disappointed in Peter and Eva. We've been so close these last two years and now this. It's treating me like a child. It's insulting that you all seem to think I'm not capable of coping with the information. I'm quite strong enough to face up to life's surprises. God only knows what I've had to cope with since you went away. After all that's happened, do you really think that telling me you're going for a medical would tip me over the edge? It's not me who's the war casualty.'

'No, I.. I'm s.. sorry.' Jan took a cigarette from his case. Lucy snatched it out of his lips.

'Please Jan, no more smoking in bed. It can give babies bronchitis and I don't like it. Really, sometimes you have no idea.'

'Sorry.'

'Honestly Jan, we have to go through life together for better or worse; that's what we promised, in front of all our friends. That means not keeping stupid secrets.'

'I know, b.. but I w.. w.. wanted to protect you.'

'Well don't,' Lucy said. 'I'll have to arrange the Christening before you go.'

'W... won't th... that be difficult?'

'Your father isn't the only person who can pull strings,' Lucy said.

Lucy rubbed her eyes and focused on the new day. She had woken in the night with Liza crying. In half-sleep she picked her up, fed her and put her back in her cot beside the bed. In those moments of feeding and nurturing she understood that the period of peace and rest following Liza's birth, which she had been hoping for, would probably never be realised. In her mind she went over the consequences surrounding Jan's imminent departure.

Liza's birth had clearly changed him and his attitude to life but it was too early to tell if this was a permanent change; he had made promises before and, although he meant them when he said them, his illness was stronger than his will. For Jan, a long spell in the countryside could well be a good thing for his mental balance. It had come at the right time but left Lucy in a difficult situation. If Jan was away for months on end then she and Liza would be better off living back in Uxbridge with her parents, if for no other reason than it was further out of London, away from the possibility of more bombings. Although she had a deep affection for Eva and felt the warmth of her friendship and kindness every day, Lucy really wanted to be home with her mother and sisters. After the war, she and Jan could find a house by the coast and build a home of their own but, until then, Uxbridge would be best for her and Liza. She would have to wait for the right moment to tell Jan and her in-laws. There was no knowing how Jan would take it.

But today there were priorities. She went downstairs with Liza and, enjoying her first cup of tea of the day, she got out her hard-bound notepad, the cover watermarked in swirls of red and purple. She wrote in pencil *CHRISTENING*, at the top of a clean page then started a list of people to invite. She tapped the end of her pencil on her front teeth and realised that she wouldn't be able to do a thing without consulting both Eva and her mother. Letters would have to be written and invitation cards sent out; food and drink arranged, or rather, delegated. But first she would have to see Reverend Philip Leary, vicar of St Augustine's.

She set off for the 10.30 Sunday Service at St Augustine's with hat securely fixed and woollen coat buttoned up to the top. Ignoring Eva's advice, she took Liza with her for extra bargaining power with the vicar. She held Liza in her arms wrapped securely in a blanket, praying that, after her morning feed and nappy change, she would sleep through the service.

Lucy found a pew at the back of the nave, close to the door so she could sneak out if Liza started to cry. She felt a surge of energy run through her body as the organ blew out the opening bars of *Bread of Heaven*. She wasn't too flummoxed by the order of the service, remembering the times she attended Christmas Mass with her parents and sisters. She had forgotten some of the responses and when to stand up, kneel or sit down. Seeing and hearing everyone else replying to the Vicar's words, she followed suit and most of it came back to her. The service lasted for the best part of an hour and she thanked providence that Liza, for the present at least, was a baby that could gently sleep through commotion. In the congregation she recognised several of the faces from people she saw in the streets and shops around Kilburn, as well as from when she had sat in contemplation in the church in the evenings. Today, however, she would rather have not known anyone. So much had happened that really she would have liked just a few days of rest. If it had been possible she would have simply blended into the background. By holding Liza close to her breast, she was conspicuous and would have no alternative than to be sociable. She put on a brave face. As the congregation drifted out after the service, person after person said hello and wanted to fawn over Liza asleep in her arms but Lucy needed to corner the vicar before he left the church. As the well-wishers were talking to her, her eyes flicked from them to the group surrounding the Vicar vying for his attention. Practising formal Christianity, she decided, was an exhausting and competitive business and could never be her own spiritual path.

The Vicar greeted Lucy, recognising her from the times they had exchanged passing pleasantries in the quiet of midweek evenings. He was charming and, despite his imposing white cassock and golden stole, approachable and friendly; a shimmering light seemed to surround his head. He said that he understood perfectly that she and her family wanted to arrange a quick Christening and suggested that she should see his Rector to arrange a date. As far as he was aware, they could fit Liza in after Solemn Mass the following Sunday. That would be perfect, Lucy thought.

The group of assorted Strangs, Greens and their friends waited outside 'St Gussie's', as Jan called it, before the service started. It was a cold morning with the sun peeking from time to time through the clouds. The lady's [ladies'] hats were secured with pins and clips so the wind that blew along Kilburn Park Road caused them little concern apart from lifting an occasional hem above the ankle. The men smoked and were listening to Lucy's father talking about the dangers of a Bolshevik revolution starting here in London. Jan, with one hand in his pocket and the other holding a cigarette, leant against a lamppost blowing his smoke into the air. The women and children clustered around Lucy who was holding baby Liza, asleep and snuggled up in her white-laced Christening gown. Lucy, standing arm-in-arm with her mother and with her sisters by her side, felt that it was all a bit unreal, as if she didn't belong here with all the fuss and commotion.

It had been an impossible task to get together all the people they would have liked to in just a week: Gladys couldn't come and no one seemed to know where Eric was. His mother came and said she only knew that he was somewhere in France. Jan managed to get in touch with Harry Briggs who arrived just in time to agree to be a godparent along with Clare and Julia. Mrs Agnoli came from Peter's office and Vera and Beatty from work and, of course, Mary O' Conner. From the Strang side of the family Peter's sisters Karolina and Elina were there, standing tall and blonde, almost dwarfing their friend Eva Lükes from the hospital.

The service only lasted twenty minutes or so and went without a hitch. As Harry Briggs read from Matthew 18 in a slow clear voice that reached heavenwards up above the triforium and clerestory, Lucy looked up and saw amongst the angels and saints in the wall paintings and sculptures a family of people from young to old in clothes full of colour looking down on the proceedings. She felt their excitement and well wishes reaching through the air to Liza:

'... the disciples came to Jesus and asked, 'Who is the greatest in the kingdom of heaven?' He called a child, whom he put among them, and said, 'Truly I tell you, unless you change and become like children, you will never enter the kingdom of heaven. Whoever becomes humble like this child is the greatest in the kingdom of heaven.'

Multi-coloured light shone through the stained-glass windows on the font as the Vicar baptised Liza with Holy Water and made the mark of the cross on her forehead:

'... in the name of the Father, and the Son, and the Holy Spirit'.

Lucy handed Jan Liza's Christening candle to keep safe. Lucy whispered to him as he stood proudly by her side, 'We should make this happiness last as long as we can. We may never be all together like this again.'

Jan realised that going far away to the Brecon Beacons was indeed fortunate, even though it was such a distance. He didn't want to leave Lucy and Liza but had amassed enough self-awareness in the last three years to know that he could be, at times, angry, selfish, deluded and drunk. It never crossed his mind to tell Lucy, or anyone else for that matter, about the dark thoughts that ran around his mind. At some point on most days he honestly thought that they would all be better off without him and then the world would be a better place. He knew that he wasn't fit to be around mother and daughter with all the sickness in his head. In his mind he would go over various methods of managing his own death and then imagine his funeral and all the people who would grieve for him, or not. He didn't expect many to turn up; he didn't have many friends. There was little point in his existence, he was useless and his brain was damaged. The

Army had made it clear that they didn't want an invertebrate like him to fight for King and Country, even as cannon fodder. At least that was a blessed relief.

At other times, however, something inside him said that he could get better, if he were safely away from London with the fear of more bombs and the unremitting sight of maimed soldiers on the street with their brains turned to pulp from the hell of the war. Each time he went out and got blasted drunk he hated himself but still held on to the hope that, given time and the right place, he could get better. He had managed to book a session with Bentley on the Thursday before the Christening to try to get rid of his flaming stammer for good. The hypnosis had worked before but the bombing had brought it back. Jan's logic said to him, no bombs, no stammer.

'I feel obliged to remind you,' Bentley said, looking at Jan in a matter-of-fact sort of way, 'That your stammer reflects your internal conflict, whereby you need to hide your dilemma about being unable to kill another man, from an army that expects you to kill like a machine.'

'It's s... s... simple, isn't it?' Jan said.

'Yes, it is. I was surprised that you didn't come back to see me after the bombings in June. Your father came and said you had something of a breakdown but, of course, unless you ask me I cannot help.'

'I jj ju... I wanted to be l.. l.. left alone, to block everything out. I'm a f... father now and w... want t.. to get b.. better for her.' Jan dabbed his eyes with his handkerchief then lit a cigarette and looked down avoiding Bentley's eyes.

'Well, congratulations. I had heard and I'm very pleased for you. I have two girls myself, but if you want to overcome your addictive behaviour, you must want to do it for yourself, not for them.'

'I see.'

'A lot of men find religion helps. You could try that.'

'I see.' Jan wondered, and not for the first time, how you could believe in something so profound one day that you didn't believe in the day before. He supposed others had done it but he felt more intelligent than that.

'But we *can* cure the stammer again through hypnosis. Now, if you could put your cigarette out and lie back and relax ....'

When Lucy told Jan that, as he was going away, most probably for months at a time, she and Liza would be better off living back with her parents, he couldn't help but agree that it probably was the best plan. But, after he said it, without speaking or looking into Lucy's eyes, he walked away from her, went upstairs and injected himself in the bedroom. It was the middle of the day and he didn't want to do it and he knew he shouldn't, but he had no will when faced with the pain of hurt and rejection. He remembered Briggs saying back at Lady Murray's that morphine was a 'good servant but a poor master.' How right he was. Jan hated himself for being weak and selfish but when the drug rushed into his brain he no longer cared about himself or anyone else. He became a citizen in a world far away from responsibility. As the drug washed through his veins, he went on a journey that he couldn't remember. And when he came round and looked down at himself, lying fully clothed on the bed with sleeve rolled up and empty syringe on the floor, he felt sick and disgusted. Feelings of shame and remorse overwhelmed him. He went into the bathroom, scraped the foul-tasting fur from his tongue and cleaned his teeth avoiding his reflection in the mirror.

Chapter 24

Safely ensconced in the Baron of Glanusk's Estate in the county of Brecknock, Jan had his own room in a ground-floor wing looking out onto the courtyard of the great house. He had a chair, dressing table, bed-side cabinet and a small wardrobe. The food was the best he had been served at any time whilst on service: lamb or beef with potatoes, parsnips and tasty onion gravy all dished up by local women and girls who had managed to avoid labouring on the claggy land. Women always seemed to brighten Jan's mood. They liked him and found the time to exchange passing pleasantries. The only other time he had been around so many women was when he was half dead and tended by nurses. His duties as a Timber Clerk were simple enough. He checked the logs coming in from the forest and counted and recorded the planks as they came through the thundering giant saws at the other end of the mill. He wasn't expected to guard the German POWs except at weekends when he became a working Second Lieutenant again. With his team of war-damaged soldiers, he gently marched the POWs on excursions along the canal towpath into Crickhowell returning through the fields along the river and over the bridge with its mock-medieval tower back to the Estate.

On the evening of his second day, Jan's work friends borrowed a horse and cart from the Estate and rode the mile into Crickhowell to visit The Dragon and The Bear; two hotels with blazing fires and comfortable chairs. They drank the mild ale in preference to the local cider that was cloudy and, by all accounts, rotted your guts. It was the first drink Jan had had in weeks and hardly alcoholic at all, so he knew he wouldn't need to pick it up again when he went home. Visiting these two hotels became a regular evening pastime. On Fridays and Saturdays, the bars would fill up with women who had been working on the fields around the town and the atmosphere seemed so friendly and relaxed that Jan thought he could happily live somewhere in the country like this. In the spring of 1918, as the days got lighter and the weather was less bleak, they would walk to Crickhowell along the road and, on going back, chatter and joke under the moon and stars. Later, sitting up in bed in good spirits, he would write to Lucy. It was as if he was rebuilding his marriage by post. The letters weren't by any means as passionate as they were when he was training in Saffron Waldon but marriage moves along in stages and things are different after the first child, or so he had been told. He needed Lucy's love and forgiveness and believed he could prove to her that he was, despite his afflictions, a worthy husband. He kept her letters in the drawer of his bedside cabinet, underneath the books he was currently reading from the library that the men organised by pooling their reading matter. Re-reading Lucy's letters eased his sadness:

Barker House,
Grove Road,
Uxbridge

10th December 1917
My Darling Jan,

I was so pleased to hear that you had a safe journey to Glanusk. It's such a strange name but I suppose you're technically in another country, one without the troubles awaiting those poor souls in France. It does sound like such a nice place; we had a look at it on Daddy's Post-Office map and it took a while to find. I wish we had the chance to breathe in all that country air you've been enjoying, though the smogs don't reach out here as much as they did in Kilburn.

Mummy and Daddy have been so pleased to have me back but I do miss your parents, especially my chats with Eva. Mine are so starchy and Daddy can get ever so grumpy. But they all dote on Liza, and Claire and Julia are so very helpful and Mummy washes Liza's nappies for me. Peter and Eva have been over to see us. They brought Tinker with them and she's quite at home by our fire; it's always sad when she goes. Peter brought some bottles of wine that he got from the docks which cheered Daddy up no end and Eva made some little dolls for Liza from old scraps of material.

Even with all the help I get it still seems like being a new mother is more than a full-time job and I can get tired. We have a different doctor, of course, and he says I shouldn't put Liza on solid food for another five months. I'll be so glad when that day comes as the feeding can be awfully sore for me and she wakes me up several times in the night when she's hungry. She's a very lively and strong little girl.

Thank you so much for the little wooden figures you carved for her. They have a lovely smell of fresh wood. I put them in her cot to begin with but she kept sucking them (she sucks everything and we got her a dummy made from rubber but she spits it out) so I moved them to the shelf above so she could still see them.

If you can't get over for Christmas, then I hope it's very soon afterwards and Mummy and Daddy say you would be more than welcome to stay here with us. I do miss you.

All my love,
Lucy xxxxx

Jan smiled as a surge of pride ran through him. He had succeeded in something at least; fathering a healthy baby girl. How strange it was, how the very thought of staying with his in-laws could strike a fear in him almost as strong as the fear of going off to war. Her father was such a blasted bore, ignorant to boot, and always asking him difficult questions about his prospects, which was quite unnecessary considering he knew that Jan would inherit his father's business. And her mother never stopped fussing around; picking things up and putting them down again and always dusting. Once, some of his tea dripped from his cup onto the living-room rug and you would have thought another war had broken out; she rushed out, came back with a bucket and cloth and got down on her knees to mop and scrub what was hardly even noticeable. Jan would never be able to relax in that place. There must surely be a way out of it: he could stay at Chichester Road, buy a motorcycle and visit often enough to see Lucy and Liza in daylight hours and not appear rude.

In the months after Liza was born, Lucy didn't think it would ever be possible to love anyone as much as she loved her sweet baby girl. She was so relieved when they moved out from Kilburn to her family in Uxbridge. Here they were further away from the City's dangers. She had the support of her family and ate fresh eggs every day from the half-dozen chickens in the back garden. In Wales, Jan seemed safe; no longer a constant worry. Her father told her before Jan signed up that a war could make a man out of him but he forgot to say that it could break a lot more than it made. Jan's letters though, filled her with hope that he could recover well enough to live a good family life together in their own home.

16 December 1917

My dearest Lucy,

Life here is quite bearable and such a contrast to London. Everyone I work with seems grateful and relieved that we are so very far away from the war. My duties are light and mainly clerical. To be honest, I could do with more physical work because it would help to stretch my muscles and clear my head from the pain that still keeps banging away in my head. The noises of the giant saws don't help but there is no smell quite like that left by a freshly-sawn tree-trunk. I do get a fair amount of exercise though and you may not believe this but I have been going to church. On most Sunday mornings, along with the other Army men, we have been guarding the POWs who nearly all voluntarily attend the little Penmyarth Church on the estate. The German POWs have got together a splendid choir that almost raises the roof off the church and it can be quite moving. It doesn't hold enough for the other bigger services though, so for Christmas, if I can't get leave to come home, and for Palm Sunday and Easter Day, we will be marching them to St Edmund's in Crickhowell. I called in and had a look at the building when I had a spare half-hour coming back from picking up supplies from Gilwern Station (the nearest to Crickhowell) and it is a splendid and peaceful place. I said a prayer for you and baby Liza. I can't help thinking that life would be much simpler if I had the faith that some of the Christians I know do. With all the trouble in our world a God doesn't make any sense to me, except when I'm wandering around in the countryside with the sun shining.

The POWs keep themselves busy and play football on Saturday afternoons. It's almost like going back before the war and watching good old Queen's Park Rangers play Fulham at home.

Although I haven't caught anything yet, as we have to wait till March, I am being taught the theory of how to fly-fish for salmon and trout. I was sitting on a fallen branch by the river Usk (it runs north around Glan<u>usk</u>) on Saturday afternoon looking at the birds that nest along its banks (I can't distinguish them all yet but have borrowed a little bird-spotting book so I will soon know which are which – we have a small library and I always have a couple on the go). I was thinking of you both and how, given better times, I could bring you here and show you these places. Sometimes you can almost forget that there's a war on. With all this nature around I've become convinced, like you, that when all the troubles are over, we should move out of London to the coast where the air is clear and we can bring up Liza, and any more children that may come along, away from the big city with all its noise and smoke. And I always thought I was a committed Londoner.

I do hope you find my weekly £5 Postal Order useful. Hopefully, you will be able to contribute to your family's household budget whilst still being able to treat yourself and Liza.

I realise how busy you must be nowadays with Liza and with your mother and sisters around you all the time but I never tire from your letters and your news about our darling baby girl.

Please send my best regards to your family.
All of my love,
    Jan xxx

> *P.S. Oh yes, I also learnt to ride a motorcycle which is great fun when the road is dry.*

Jan came home on 14 January for two week's leave and looked for a motorcycle. He saw a second-hand, four-horsepower Douglas advertised in Finchley in the *Evening News* for twenty-five pounds. When he went to see it, he didn't have the heart to knock the war-widow down on the price, even though there seemed to be something wrong with the exhaust. She offered him her husband's leather jacket and boots. Jan accepted the poor man's goggles but wouldn't have felt comfortable in another man's clothes. It might bring him bad luck.

He rode up to the Green's house with his exhaust making such a racket that he didn't need to knock. Lucy and her mother came out to the drive and laughed at the sight of him with rain running down his trench coat. Claire and Julia said they had Douglases at work at the Post Office and they were hoping to get to ride them. They asked if they could have a go when it stopped raining but their father told them that they couldn't, as it was unseemly for young ladies. Jan was relieved that nobody seemed to mind him setting off back to his parents in the evening. Lucy always said she missed him but understood how hard it would have been for him to stay. Of course, it was nigh on impossible to be alone together for any length of time without Liza crying for food or a nappy change or Lucy's mother calling out, 'Would you like another cup of tea, Jan?'

After their evening meal, Jan kissed Liza and Lucy goodnight promising to be back in the morning. He kick-started his motorcycle and drove east, back to Kilburn, calling in at pubs on the way that either looked curious or had a good crowd milling around them. He would smoke and drink pale ale, deeply inhaling his cigarettes as if they were the perfect release for all anxiety. Before very long, when someone came and talked to him, he would get out the post-card photograph of Liza he kept on him from the

Christening and tell them about his little daughter and beautiful wife.

From the spring of 1918, Lucy and the Greens heard of more and more cases of a deadly influenza that, instead of picking on the weak, sick, old and very young, as diseases of that sort usually did, actually seemed to pick out the strong and healthy. As the year went on, the number of incidents rose. On one of Lucy's visits to her in-laws, Dr Cassidy called by and said he'd never seen anything so bad in all his time in practice and told them about one of his patients who seemed to get better and then suddenly died.

'It gave us hope then took it away,' he said. 'She left two baby boys to be brought up by her parents and they're almost too frail to cope.'

The papers warned that it could hit anyone at any time and that it had been festering on fetid battlefields and now, when the Tommies and Foreign and Colonial troops were coming to London, it was spreading the virus. In general people avoided public places and even abandoned the churches for fear of catching it there. Lucy did her best to protect Liza. Gladys had been writing to Lucy off and on since sending apologies for not attending the Christening. She stressed that none of them should leave the house without a linen mask and that they all wore them in the hospital. Lucy's mother made 'flu masks' from old pillow cases.

Gladys came back from France late in November and continued nursing but, instead of coming home to Chichester Road, she got digs with two of her friends in Whitechapel for fear of spreading the bug from the hospital. Eventually, Lucy stopped borrowing books from the library and everyone at the Greens' only opened letters with gloves on. Both Francis T. Green and Peter Strang even stopped shaking hands at work.

But Lucy and Liza were happy and no little girl could have been better cared for. When the sun shone, Lucy would take her for walks in her new Silver Cross perambulator by the river Colne or along the canal towpath where horses pulled barges full of wheat, potatoes and turnips along the dirty water to London. She pushed Liza to the common and would rock her gently whilst sitting on a bench contemplating the future. Together they watched and listened to nature as snowdrops were followed by crocuses and then daffodils pushing their way up through the grasses. Lucy enjoyed it when there was a chill in the air; it made her feel more alive. She would pull her mask down and lift Liza's pram cover, made from a cotton-lace curtain, then breathe in and let her mind feel settled. In April, when the birds started to sing at their loudest, Lucy watched Liza as sparrows and blue tits played in the bushes and the trees and came to feed on the bread crumbs and kitchen scraps they brought to feed them.

All the time she had been working at the Home Office she had put a half-crown each week into a special Post-Office savings account for a rainy day and, after Liza came along, she left it there and added to it whenever she could, as a nest egg for Liza's future in an uncertain world.

Mr Fitch of Fitch and Solomon, on Windsor Road, invited Lucy with Liza in her pram into his office. He quickly smiled at Liza through the net covering her face and asked Lucy how he could help. She sat down opposite him at his desk. He had a goatee beard and looked old and worried peering down his nose through wire spectacles. The sun shone through the window highlighting pinkish brown blotches on his almost bald head.

'Thank you, Mr Fitch,' Lucy said a little nervously but with quiet determination in her voice. 'I would like to make a will.'

Mr Fitch looked at her without expression. 'Yes certainly, Mrs Strang. If you so wish. But are you aware that your interests are usually combined with your husband's estate?'

'I do understand that but I wish to make sure that, if anything happens to me, some money that I have been saving will be spent on my daughter's education.'

'I see,' he said, with a kindly look. 'I think we have all been worried about this terrible flu, haven't we?'

'Yes, we have,' Lucy said.

'And it makes us question our mortality.'

'Just so.'

'And what does your husband think about this intended legacy?'

'He is serving away and I haven't told him.'

'I see. And why is that Mrs Strang?' Lucy felt irritated.

'I don't really see why that is relevant, Mr Fitch.'

'Please forgive me Mrs Strang but I do need to ask these questions or I wouldn't be doing my job properly.'

'I understand but why …'

'You see, in the unlikely event of you dying before your husband, if he didn't know about this will, he might possibly contest it. So, my Job is to make sure that we cover all eventualities.'

'I see. Actually, there's no reason why I shouldn't let him know. I will tell him next time I write.'

'And when might that be?'

'Probably tonight.'

'Splendid, so once we know that he has received the letter and has had the time to reply, I will be able to make a note on the will that Mr Strang is aware of your wishes and is in agreement. If I make you an appointment for the same time next week, we can draw up the will then.'

'Thank you, Mr Fitch.'

Mr Fitch got up from his chair and walked toward the door. 'You're very welcome Mrs Strang. Oh, and you will need two witnesses over the age of twenty-one.'

Walking back home she tried to think of who she could possibly ask to be witnesses considering she didn't really want her father to know. He would assume that it was because she didn't trust Jan to be an adequate provider but she couldn't help what he thought. She would ask her Mother and Father and suffer his difficult questions.

In the summer, the MOD put a stop to all but essential or compassionate leave. The Glanusk camp had stayed free of the flu virus and the Army wanted to keep it that way for as long as they could. Cases of flu, however, did inevitably break out in the region, starting in Abergavenny then spreading to the surrounding towns and villages. When the virus came to the Glanusk Estate in the autumn, just when they thought the war was all but over, about one third of them caught it and several died. Restrictions on leave and visiting were not rescinded as the authorities didn't want to spread it further. Jan would rub a bar of carbolic soap over letters he sent to ward off the infection.

After the success of the Allied offensive in Amiens in August, they had all known that the war was coming to its protracted end. A few of the POWs thought that the Germans could still win but they were solitary, deluded men. Jan's father had always said that the war would be over once the Americans had got their troops over to France and he was right. News of an armistice was long expected in Glanusk and the celebrations were short lived. Jan and his friends walked into town cheering and whooping when carts passed them. Crickhowell soon ran out of beer, so they came back and danced with the women on the estate and even had a sing-song of *Keep the Home Fires Burning* with the German prisoners who tried their hardest to pronounce the words properly. For Jan, though, it all felt hollow; after all those who had died and been wounded it didn't really seem like much of a celebration. It was more of a commiseration and there wasn't enough booze in the country to anaesthetise their wounds. The war had lasted so long and destroyed so much that few of the serving men could really conceive of what normality, if ever possible, would be like. The one thing that they all knew was that nothing could be the same again.

Barely two weeks had passed after the Armistice before Jan was transferred from Glanusk to 'light clerical duties' at the Board of Trade in Whitehall Gardens just at a time when many more prisoners were expected. The task of guarding them would go to returning, able-bodied men.

Lucy and Liza came back to Chichester Road in December to join Jan and he promised Lucy that he would be a new man.

Chapter 25

24 June 1919

Once the War Office had relinquished his commission on 1st March, Jan and Lucy made plans to move to the south coast. On Saturday, 24 June they left Liza with Eva and took the train to Hove where they saw three properties. The third house was a brick-built end-terrace house on Granville Road. Lucy looked at Jan, smiled and nodded to him out of sight of the agent. Jan wanted to be anywhere where they could be happy, put the past behind them and start again. He was determined to get the house for her; he felt he owed it to her after all he had put her through. Here was somewhere they could be a proper family, caring for and looking after each other. It was a short walk from the promenade and the shore where Liza and Tinker could play and Jan would be able to commute to London for work. Family and friends could come and see them and catch the last train back in the evening. It had a small front and back garden and, from the upper windows, they could see the Channel. On the way back to London, in a carriage empty but for themselves, Lucy rested her head on Jan's shoulder and they looked out on green fields with brown cows and piebald horses grazing in the hazy light of the long summer evening. Jan felt tired and satisfied after a successful day.

As his headaches had been getting too intense for him to concentrate at work, his father told him there was no point in him being there and that he should take the rest of the week off. Jan was running short of morphine so Lucy rang the surgery and arranged for him to see Dr Cassidy and to pick up his prescription the following day. It was a beautiful, delightfully warm morning. Eva and Lucy were watching Liza toddling around the sitting-room floor trying to grab hold of Tinker's tail, softly falling down on the deep-piled rug every time Tinker moved away.

Looking out onto the sunny street Jan thought he would go for a walk. Normally he would have taken Tinker but

Liza was so happy playing with her it would have been a shame to take the dog away from her. With clean white shirt, beige summer flannels and jacket, canvas braces and brown Irish brogues he stepped out, hatless, into the day with cane in hand.

'I might be a couple of hours,' he said closing the door behind him. He lit a Player's and smoked it walking down the street in the direction of Maida Vale; there might be some cricket on the Paddington ground. He always felt good in the summer when the days were at their longest. The cricket ground was empty so he headed for the canal taking a detour down Formosa Street. He looked at the open doors of the Prince Alfred and walked in. Seeing no harm in having a pint on a sunny day, he ordered a Young's Bitter and some cigarettes at the bar. In a corner by a dark-wood, ornately etched bay window he recognised two men; he didn't quite know from where but because they waved to him, he went over to see who they were. They smiled and shook his hand. Jan was only going to have one pint and head straight back home after that but, as it turned out, they were ex Post Office Rifles so they all had a lot to talk about. One of the men got up for the Gents and bought three pints at the bar on his way back. Jan could hardly refuse. The other man got a round in after that and then it was Jan's turn. It took a while to exhaust the inevitable conversation after meeting up with old Army friends:

'Do you remember old Jack? Well, he fell at the Somme in '16. And Jimmy? He married a French girl and brought her back to Shoreditch.' Feeling good and warm inside, Jan told them about Lucy and Liza and the arrangements for their new life in Hove that were all but completed.

The men left when the pub closed at two-thirty. Alone in the street, Jan's mood dropped to a low, dark level when he thought of Lucy and Eva's reproachful eyes as he walked through the door full of beer. He needed something to break his mood and cheer himself up; then he could go back and face them. Pain had been nagging in his head. He took an omnibus to Regent Street and smoked on the open-top deck looking down on the town he knew so well.

Alighting from the bus, Jan was dying for a piss. He was edgy and impatient. He stepped in to the Café Royal, strode past the tables of afternoon drinkers, entered the Gents, went into a cubicle, closed the door and sat on the toilet seat. Having emptied his bladder, he took out from his wallet a small envelope of cocaine he had been saving for emergencies. He rested it on his knee and scooped up some of the powder into the silver spoon he carried on his key ring. He could see there was something not quite right about it; it was too yellow and lumpy for cocaine but then, he had had it for a while. He sniffed a tiny spoonful up one nostril and again up the other then sneezed. He covered his nose with his handkerchief and sneezed again. A stinging sensation ran from his nasal passage and made his face feel numb. He felt dizzy and his stomach churned. He half stood and turned around just in time to bring up the beer in his belly into the toilet bowl. Sitting on the floor he stared around him, not really sure where he was; the walls spun then moved and distorted. He closed his eyes to fend off the feeling of sickness and had just enough sense left in his brain to know that he had taken something dodgy and, if he waited, the episode would pass.

He woke up to a loud crash as the lock on the cubicle door flew off and the door swung open. Looking up from his crouching position on the floor he saw two burly, bearded and smartly suited doormen staring down at him.

'Can you get up now please, Sir?' one of them said.

Jan looked at them. He felt so ill he couldn't think, let alone speak, as they gripped his biceps and lifted him up at arm's length. The sudden rush of cold of water over his head as they shoved him under a tap made him shudder. He retched but there was nothing left in his stomach to bring up. They stood him up and held him against the wall and pulled his trousers up. Water ran down from his hair wetting his clothes.

'Do you know who he is?'

'No idea.'

He felt their hands rummage through his pockets.

Another man came in.

'Get this idiot out and send him home in a cab. They'll be hell to pay if he croaks here.'

'Yes Sir,' the men said.

'I'll get a cabbie and have him waiting round the back. Don't let anyone see you,' the man said.

Parking up outside 43 Chichester Road, the cab driver got out, walked up to the house, and came back with Peter. It was seven pm. They brought him in, took him upstairs and left him on the bed. Lucy and Tinker ran up the stairs and into the bedroom. Jan saw both their looks of fright and concern. He stretched down to stroke Tinker. His head was pounding and it felt like he had been kicked in the chest by a horse.

'Will you never learn?' Lucy said, kneeling down by his side and holding his hand in both of hers.

'I'm sorry.'

'I know you are. You always are. What have you taken?'

'I don't know.'

'How can you not know?'

'I don't know.'

'You must sleep now; you look barely alive.'

'Might be a good thing.'

'Don't talk like that.'

'Sorry, but …'

'I mean it, Jan. It's self-indulgent. Think about your daughter.'

'I was.'

'You must eat something.'

'I couldn't.'

'I'll bring some soup up and you must try.'

'Please, I couldn't; not yet, just water.'

'We *will* get you better, you know.' Jan closed his eyes and leaned back on the pillow. 'If it's the last thing we do.' The smell of soup rising from downstairs made him want to throw up.

'I'll leave you to sleep and see how you are later,' Lucy said, leaving with Tinker.

'Will it never end?' Peter said from his chair, smoking with the evening paper on his lap.

'I just don't know what to do,' Eva said, dabbing her handkerchief on her sore and bloodshot eyes.

'You've done all you can,' Lucy said.

'I thought the responsibility of having a child would bring him to his senses,' Peter said.

'We're so, so sorry, for you, Lucy dear,' Eva said.

'I'm really worried about our plans,' Lucy said. 'I don't see how we can go ahead with them.'

'Really?' Peter said.

'Well, no. How can we live away in Hove? It's just not possible when Jan can fly off without warning and get into states like this. Just when he seems to be getting better then …'

'I know,' Peter said. 'It can happen at any time. He's become a Jekyll and Hyde.'

'Anything can trigger it.' Lucy held her hands out. 'Or nothing at all.'

'Sometimes it just looks hopeless,' Eva said. 'He was such a lovely boy.'

'We would understand if you wanted a divorce,' Peter said.

'We've talked about it and we would understand,' Eva said.

Lucy didn't want to think about it. 'I still have hope,' she said. 'It's just that when he gets like this …'

'Yes?' Peter said.

'Jan's in so much danger when he goes out and doesn't know what he's doing.'

'It's no life for you,' Eva said, then blew her nose. 'Jan's run out of morphine. He was supposed to get some more from Jack Cassidy in the morning.'

'I know. He'll need it when he comes around. He'll be very jittery,' Lucy said.

'Can you get it for him?' Peter asked Lucy. 'He'll be in no fit state himself.'

'Yes, of course, but I've got a terrible feeling.'

'How do you mean?' Eva asked.

'In the pit of my stomach; it's like impending doom. I haven't felt like this since Jan went off to the front.'

Peter stood up and paced. 'He can't even get his own prescription. Sometimes I wish he'd …'

'Don't ever say that Peter,' Eva said. 'He can't help it, he's ill.'

'I know. It's just that…'

'Yes?' Lucy asked.

'Oh, never mind. I didn't mean it,' Peter said.

'I'll go in the morning. I don't mind, honestly. I'll take Liza out in the pram and Jan can stay in bed,' Lucy said.

'Best place for him,' Peter said, stubbing a cigarette out in the ashtray.

That night Lucy and Liza slept together in Gladys' room. In the morning, she lay in bed, afraid of the day ahead. Thoughts ran through her mind. At some point, if Jan didn't get better, she might have to go back and live with her parents again, if only for Liza's benefit. She didn't want to divorce him, not until she'd given him more time to get better. She said that she would stand by him and she would keep her promise. She still loved him, no longer in passion but with a kind of maternal tugging. Eventually she rose at eight and, after putting her head round Jan's door to see if he was still alive, left him to sleep. Lucy lifted Liza up into her arms and took her down to her grandmother in the front room before quietly getting washed and dressed. She could hear the sound of Liza's laughing coming up the stairs, it was such a joy to hear. In the mornings, Liza loved playing with Tinker. Lucy came down and watched her crawling on the floor, toying with a rag doll and a pompom that Julia had made with the wool from an unravelled jersey. Tinker took the pompom and put it down in front of Liza and, when she went to grab it, Tinker took it away. Liza giggled and Tinker did it again.

'How are you this morning?' Eva asked.

'I didn't sleep well. Actually, I feel awful. I have such a bad feeling.'

'I'm sure Jan will be alright; he's been through much worse,' Eva said unconvincingly.

'Well, if our prayers could make him better he'd be well by now. Where's Peter?'

'He caught the early train.'

Lucy picked Liza up, held her close in her arms and kissed her.

'Were going for a nice walk soon, my little darling.' On hearing the word 'walk' Tinker pricked up her ears. She looked up at Lucy and wagged her tail. Lucy turned to Eva. 'I'll just make some tea and porridge. Would you like a cup?'

'Yes, but please but let me do it.'

Lucy put Liza back down on the rug with Tinker and her toys and went into the kitchen.

'I'll keep an eye on Liza then,' Eva called out from the living room. 'I could go to the surgery and get the prescription.'

'No, no. I'll do it. The air will do us good.'

'Well, okay but do be careful.'

'We will.'

Lucy came back with tea for Eva and sat with her bowl of porridge and milk on the arm of Eva's chair. She ate a few spoonfuls then filled a teaspoon with the cooler porridge from the side of the bowl, blew on it, and fed it to Liza. Half of it dribbled down her chin. Eva leant forward to wipe Liza's face. After three spoonfuls, Liza spat the fourth out onto her bib. Lucy finished off the porridge and put the bowl on the floor for Tinker to lick clean then got down on her hands and knees and tickled Liza's feet. Liza giggled and wiggled her toes. Chirruping sparrows in the crab-apple tree in front of the house rang through the open window.

'We must get off now,' Lucy said, as the carriage clock on the sideboard chimed ten. 'Expect us back by twelve. I'll take some bread with me. We can come back through Queens Park and feed the ducks.'

'Do take care,' Eva said.

You could always tell that Liza loved being pushed around in the outside world in the perambulator. She would sit up and, with eyes flickering, turn her head to take everything in. As Lucy put her into the pram that stayed parked by the front door, Liza let out a shrill noise of excitement. The sun shone on them through the leaded stained-glass panel above the door. Tinker looked up with warm adoring eyes as Lucy bent down to attach her lead. Lucy tucked Liza up in the pram then buckled the strap tightly across her waist and set off down the front steps holding tightly onto the pram handle so the whole caboodle didn't slip or bounce. The springs slightly squeaked and Tinker pulled on her lead. It was a beautiful sunny day. It would only take ten-minutes to walk to Dr Cassidy's surgery in Brondesbury Road.

Hattie Dixon turned to Freddie Timpson-Garner at their table inside the Café Royal.

'Don't be such a bore Freddie, I wouldn't be with you if I thought you'd be so jealous. It was nothing serious. Aubrey and I were only having a bit of fun and anyway you were flirting with Clarissa all night.'

'Hmmm. Only because you were too busy eyeing up every gadabout in the place.'

'Just because you didn't get your way with her doesn't mean you can take it out on me.'

'Well, I won't be with you much longer if you continue to behave like a tart.'

'Really, Freddie, now I know why Lottie passed you over for Dundas.'

'Dundas is an ass.'

'Well Lottie says he's better than you.'

'And what did she mean by that?'

'You know exactly what she meant.'

'No, I don't.'

'Don't make me spell it out for you.'

'Yes, damn it. What did she say?'

Hattie paused as a waiter with long white apron passed slowly by them. She whispered in Freddie's ear. 'She said Dundas was a fantastic lover and that you could never satisfy her.' Freddie's face reddened, he raised his voice. He thumped his fist on the table. Heads turned towards them.

'Well she's wrong. Dundas is an arse of the first calibre.'

'Sally Spalding said he was considerate.'

'She's married. She should be more discreet. I've a good mind to tell Lord Crawford.'

'Oh, he knows.'

'Does he? Well he's an idiot.'

'As well as everybody else?'

'Yes, they're all damned idiots.'

'Freddie I'm tired can we go to the country now. All these mirrors give me the spooks. I need a rest and so do you. You can drive. We could be in Leighton Buzzard by lunchtime.'

'Yes, alright, alright. I'll need a pick-me-up though. I'll be nodding off if I don't watch it.'

Hattie put her hand in her black-leather shoulder bag and handed Freddie a little blue and green enamelled box. Freddie snatched it from her hand and walked towards the gent's toilet, dark thoughts raging in his head.

'I'll swing for Dundas next time I see him,' he mumbled as he left.

Hattie hailed a passing waiter and ordered two café crèmes. 'Could you arrange for someone to bring Mr

Timpson-Garner's two-seater round to the front in about ten minutes?'

'Certainly Madam.'

Hattie watched Freddie as he came back looking even more agitated and, as they drank their coffees, she noticed that the skin on his face had turned from being red and angry to cold, grey and corpse-like.

'Thanks Hattie, but I'll need something stronger if I want to last out,' Freddie said, wiping beads of cold perspiration from his brow with his shirt sleeve. Hattie took her hankie out of her bag, leant over the table and wiped the white residue from his moustache.

'Just get wine, Freddie; you know how cross you get on scotch.'

'I'll be alright,' he said. He got up, strode off to the bar and ordered a bottle of Johnnie Walker. The bartender smirked at him. 'No need to look at me like that.' The bartender didn't reply. He put the bottle in a brown-paper bag and handed it to him slowly.

'Shall I put it on your account, Sir?' Freddie grabbed it from him.

'Yes,' he said, and went directly to the gent's where he pulled out the cork stopper and took a good swig. He put the bottle down under the sink and splashed his face with cold water then looked in the mirror and ran his fingers through his hair. He turned the tap to run slower, topped the bottle up with water and pushed the cork back on. Before leaving, he pulled a hand-towel from the rail, wiped his face, wrapped the towel round the bottle and put it in the bag.

Out in the street, the light and fresh air hit them with a sudden ferocity. Hattie's legs wobbled and began to give way. She held onto Freddie's sleeve to halt her fall. Freddie's two-seater Humber convertible was waiting outside the entrance with motor running. The doorman doffed his cap and held the nearside door open for Hattie. She sat down feeling queasy. Freddie tipped the doorman, sat in the driver's seat, slammed his door, let the handbrake off, loudly clashed the gears and drove off along Regent Street. He flared his nostrils and breathed in. A euphoric rush ran through his head as he turned left down Oxford Street heading for Edgware Road. Hattie lit two cigarettes and handed one to him. He put his foot down and tore up through Maida Vale into Kilburn High Street.

'Freddie, slow down for God's sake. You'll frighten the horses.'

'I'm only doing forty.'

'I feel sick. Turn off down here somewhere and find somewhere with a toilet.'

'Jesus Christ, Hattie, you've hardly eaten anything for two days. How can you have anything to throw up?' Freddie pulled the steering wheel to the left. The car swayed on its suspension as they turned into Brondesbury Road. A horse and cart carrying milk churns was coming the other way. The horse reared up, making a high-pitched whinny and bolted ahead dragging the overturned cart behind it. Milk churns spilled their contents onto the street. Freddie swerved to avoid them just as Lucy, Liza and Tinker were crossing the road to Jack Cassidy's surgery.

Startled, Lucy turned to see the motor car heading straight at her. In the split-second she had to think, she let go of Tinker's lead and pushed the pram away. She turned and started to run when *CRASH* the two-seater hit her straight in the back. Her head slammed forward and cracked open onto the cobbles.

Chapter 26

26 June 1919

When he heard that Lucy was dead, Jan disappeared somewhere in his mind and no one could bring him out. Eva left him alone and looked after Liza and Tinker. Gladys came home as soon as she heard the news and, before her parents had time to really know what to do, threw out every last bottle of alcohol that she could find in the house. She spent the afternoon opening cupboards, looking under beds and on top of wardrobes. She found a half-bottle of brandy underneath Jan's socks in his chest of drawers and looking in the back garden she returned with two bottles of wine from the coal bunker and a bottle of scotch from the tool shed.

It was hot and sunny the morning following Lucy's accident. Jan sat in an armchair in the parlour with the curtains drawn, smoking and gazing blankly into nothing and nowhere. Jack Cassidy called and told them that Jan was in a 'semi-catatonic state'. He'd seen it in returning soldiers and said that it would pass. When Cassidy had gone, Peter opened wide the parlour door then drew the curtains letting the light in. Jan shaded his eyes with his hand. As his father lifted up the window, a breeze fluttered the curtains. Peter stood in front of Jan looking down at him with arms crossed.

'I know you can hear me.'

Jan didn't look at him.

'For the time being I'll be keeping your morphine supplies on me and, on the doctor's orders, I can only allow you two quarter-grain phials a day, one at night and one in the morning.'

Jan heard him but didn't move. He really didn't care one way or the other.

For the next two days, he slept in the chair in the same clothes that he wore in the day. When Peter offered him morphine in the morning before he went off to work and in the evening when he came back, Jan moved his head from side to side in refusal. Eva brought him food and water on a tray and emptied his ash tray. Sometimes he ate a little but mostly he left his food untouched. Summer flies settled on the plate. He drank the water and, when he used the toilet, went straight up the stairs to the bathroom and straight back down not answering his mother as she tried to speak to him.

On the night of the third day after Lucy's death, Jan went upstairs, undressed and lay unsleeping on their bed. In the morning, he washed, shaved and changed. He came downstairs, brushed his mother's hand with his and sat down across from her at the breakfast table. He drank tea and ate some toast watching Liza try to pull Tinker's tail. He picked Liza up, sat her on his knee and whispered in her ear. She turned and looked at him, not understanding a word. Tinker came round him and rubbed her side against his calf then sat before him and barked. Jan put Liza down and stood up. Tinker shook herself; hair and dust from her body settling down through the sunbeams.

'I'll take the old girl to the park,' he said.

Oblivious to the nods and smiles of the people he passed, he paced down the terraced roads lined with cherry and plane trees in full leaf. In the park, he sat on a bench, lit up, and thought of the times Lucy could have sat on the very same spot. There were all sorts people about: couples promenading and children running around. Dogs came up to Tinker, barking at her, wanting her to play. He let her off her lead and watched as she ran, taking it in turns to chase and be chased by the other dogs. He turned his head to look at the war-wounded and war-weary sitting on chairs around the bandstand that would spring to life with a medley of popular songs later in the afternoon.

He felt better for the walk and back in the house made a pot of tea.

'Why are you here?' he asked his father.

'It's Sunday,' Peter said.

'Oh, I see.'

'Welcome back to the living,' Peter said.

'Thanks.'

'How are you?' Eva asked.

'Terrible, I just feel terrible but better than before.'

'Do you need morphine?' Peter asked.

'No, I don't want to take it anymore.'

Peter took a second look at him.

At eleven o'clock Eva and Peter, taking Liza and Tinker with them, set off to see Lucy's parents in Uxbridge. They would eat there and be late back. Eva said that the Greens had invited him but Jan knew that it would only have been for the sake of politeness. He couldn't bear going back to Barker House and didn't imagine he'd be welcome. The atmosphere would be excruciating. They would be making arrangements for the funeral and discussing whether they could make the police prosecute the man who drove the car that killed Lucy. It was all so predictable.

Sarah and Francis T. Green would agree to bring up Liza as their own as it would be the best for the child. Peter would make a financial arrangement with Lucy's father to pay for Liza's upkeep and her future education. Jan would be no use to anyone. His greatest fear was that he might lose Liza and that the Greens would ask him to stay away and he would become just a footnote in her life.

Jan's mind, freed of drink and drugs for three (or was it four?) days, was more lucid than it had been for a long time. He understood with absolute clarity the undeniable fact that he was just as responsible for Lucy's death as the idiot who drove the car that knocked her down.

During his days of torment, Lucy came to him in his dreams. She didn't recriminate him, instead she told him that she would always be there when he needed her. She would lend him strength. She said she would help him to leave his anguish behind and find a place where he could be happy and she could be proud of him. Jan, for his part, swore to her that he would never take morphine or drink again and that he would be a better man.

Jan woke with a plan emerging in his mind. He needed to talk to someone he could trust so he rang Harry Briggs in Fulham and arranged to meet him the following day at ten. He left the house with plenty of time and let the air of the summer morning revive the numbness in his head.

'My dear chap, I'm so glad you called me,' Briggs said, leading Jan into a small private study room in his parents' house. 'Sit down, sit down. You must be absolutely distraught.'

'I am. Believe me when I say that after all the dreadful things that have happened, I have never felt more of a wretch than I do now.'

'I can only imagine. I rang your house when I heard about Lucy's accident but your father said that you were "unreachable".'

Jan looked straight at Briggs.

'Here, have a smoke,' Briggs said.

Jan lit up, inhaled deeply, let out a cough and leant forward.

'I need you to listen. You see I'm responsible for Lucy's death and I need to make amends. I don't expect forgiveness from any god, I just have to put things right.' Jan words stopped in his throat.

'It's alright. Go on, it's important to get it out,' Briggs said.

'She deserved much better than me and always did. It looks certain that her parents and sisters will bring up Liza. It's undoubtedly the best for Liza but it's all too much to stomach.'

Briggs gave him a questioning look.

'Mother will cry and Peter will be strong as he always is.'

Briggs nodded and half-smiled in a consoling way.

'I failed everyone. I don't know what made me the person I became. I see now that I was always self-centred but I used to be so high-minded with so many dreams. Then the war knocked all of that out of me. I know I can't blame the war for my failings; thousands have suffered worse and turned out better than me.'

There was a knock at the door and Briggs' mother came in with tea on a tray and a plate of home-made biscuits. She smiled at Jan then left silently. Briggs poured the tea.

'You know this morning, even though she couldn't possibly understand what I said, I lied to Liza. I told her that her Mummy died from an accident and that it couldn't be avoided.'

'There's some truth in that,' Briggs said.

'Not really.' Jan shook his head. 'It's a lie that both of our families have convinced themselves of but they and I know, deep down, I'm really to blame. When Liza is older and asks them, the story will be that it was the driver and his stupid girlfriend's fault. Their anger will be directed against them, not me. And it *is* a lie. You see she went out on my business and died for it. I was selfish and I don't know how I can live with that.' Jan picked his cup up and drank the tea down in one and put it back down on the saucer.

'You may see things differently in the future; time is a great healer,' Briggs said, as he poured more tea.

'But time can't change the facts. You see, I was too hungover so Lucy went out to get my prescription. The car should have knocked me down and killed me, not her. I told Lucy that I was crippled with pains and my stomach burned with acid, just because I wasn't man enough to find the strength to walk down the road.'

'Sometimes …'

'I have to try and put things right as much as I can.'

'Address the balance?'

'Yes.'

'I see. And what do you propose?'

'I'm going to change.'

'I see.'

'But I'm not sure if I'm strong enough.' Jan leaned back in the chair collecting his thoughts.

'I doubt if any of us are,' Briggs said.

'Oh?' Jan looked at him strangely.

'Yes, you see, that's when the spiritual side comes in.'

'It's funny you should say that. You may not believe me but I could swear that Lucy came to see me in my dreams. She was as beautiful as always, radiant, and she said she loved me as much as ever and that she was still my wife.'

'That's wonderful.' Briggs beamed.

'Yes, I know.' Jan shook his head. 'I feel she's with me now, giving me support.'

'I understand, I really do. You see I have Jesus.'

'She had some kind of second sight. She said her Aunty, who had passed away quite a few years back, used to come and see her when I was in France and told her that I hadn't died when they all thought I had.'

'I've heard of other cases.'

'And she could see the spirit leaving the dead.' Jan looked straight into Briggs' eyes.

'Like some of the nurses in the hospitals and some men on the front line?' Briggs asked.

'Exactly. Those people with that kind of gift always seem better people. You know, more spiritual.'

Briggs nodded.

'I do know what you mean. I've known quite a few like that.'

'I won't touch a drop of drink again or take any more morphine, I swear by her and all that's holy.' Jan started to choke up. 'And I'll be a good man and work and ...'

'Yes?'

'Provide for my daughter.' Jan spluttered, took out his clean white handkerchief, held it over his eyes and nose and bent his head down. He tried but couldn't stop the tears and the sobbing almost stopped his breath. The war had taught him that there was no shame in tears. When Jan composed himself, he blurted out: 'I'm such a terrible, terrible man.'

'No, you're a man and human just like the rest of us.'

'I honestly believe I can get better and do the right thing for everyone but there's so much pain in London. I'm in such a mess, honestly I am. Everyday I'm faced with the same thing: memories and sadness wherever I look.'

'In its aftermath and in our reflection, the war goes on.'

'I'm lucky, though.'

'Oh?'

'Yes, my Mother's family in Sweden have offered to let me stay with them. They said that before I joined up.' Jan drank more tea and shook his head. 'They live in the country just outside Sundsvall. That's where they ship the timber to us. I'd be far away from wars and reminders.'

'Our memories are always with us. They follow us wherever we go and whatever we do.'

'I know but it could be easier. You see, I'm constantly fighting a need to block out the pain. I need to be far away from temptation until I'm strong enough to cope again.'

'You need a rest from the battle.'

'Yes, I do. That's exactly what I need.'

'It won't be easy and if you hardly know your relatives …'

'I know but it's my best chance. I'm no use to anyone as it is and to be honest, they'll all need a rest from me. After a while I should be able to work. I was pretty much okay in Crickhowell. The countryside can heal me.'

'And your guilty feelings?'

'I have to live with them; I've no choice.'

'And you say you feel Lucy is with you.'

'Yes, I'm certain but you're the only one I've told. Please do keep it to yourself.'

'That goes without saying.' Briggs changed his expression from that of concern to a bright smile. 'I have Jesus as my guide and you have Lucy. God works in mysterious ways.' Jan nodded and gave a knowing look. He got up and they shook hands.

'If I can follow my conscience as I intend to, some good may come out of the whole thing.'

'Absolutely, old man. See me again whenever you can.'

'I will. Now I've made my mind up, I should have things organised within a week or two. Au revoir.'

'Au revoir, old pal.'

'But there's one more favour.'

'Yes?'

'The funeral's the day after tomorrow at Saint John's in Uxbridge. Will you come along? I need all the support I can get.'

'Absolutely, old man,' Briggs said.

There must have been over fifty in the congregation. It was a wonderful service with an inspired summing up of Lucy's life by a Vicar who hardly knew her. Claire and Julia both spoke bravely about their sister from the lectern. For Jan, though, it was a blur. His father held him up as his legs gave way after he placed a red rose on the coffin and the vicar followed it with a handful of earth.

In the days after, Jan, taking Tinker with him, went around the old places where he and Lucy used to go: the tea rooms and book shops, parks and street markets. He went down to the docks to say goodbye to Harry and stood by the gates for ten minutes smoking and watching the commotion of horse and motor wagons before realising he couldn't bring himself to go past the gates. He turned back. Some things were better left, he decided.

He visited the Greens and was surprised that Lucy's father no longer seemed such an ogre; his daughter's passing had left him weak and wounded. The whole family were grieving and tried to let Liza take the place in their hearts that Lucy had always filled. They were kind to Jan. They fed him and watched him play on the floor with Liza, who was showing more interest in Tinker than her father who was trying to make the moment last. He might not see her again for a long time. It made him feel a little better knowing that they didn't hate him but their pity stung him. They wished him well on his journey and told him that he would be welcome to come and see them all when he came back to London sooner rather than later.

On the morning of his sailing, weighed down by two suitcases, Jan walked through the rain to the cargo steamer setting off from the Greenland docks and found some shelter on a deck beneath a higher walkway. The funnels hooted and the engines strained. He waved to his parents and Gladys, who was holding onto Tinker walking around her heels. He felt anxious but invigorated. His thoughts turned to Lucy and the tragedy of their love and he didn't suppose that would ever change. Sundsvall and a new life awaited him. Gulls squabbled and squawked on the water as the ship steamed out from the quay lapping the banks with its wash.

adrianhornwriter.com

Made in the USA
Middletown, DE
26 November 2017